OTHER BOOKS BY K.D. MASON

HARBOR ICE (2009)

It has been a brutally cold winter in the New Hampshire coastal town of Rye Harbor, leaving drifts of sea water frozen solid in the salt marsh. Finally, the weather warms enough for the ice to begin to break up and drift out to sea. That's when a woman's body is found under a slab of ice left by the outgoing tide. Max, the feisty redheaded bartender at Ben's Place, recognizes that the body in the ice is her aunt's partner. This triggers a series of events that will eventually threaten Max's life as well. It is up to her best friend, Jack Beale, to unravel the mystery.

CHANGING TIDES (2010)

Fate, Chance, Destiny… Call it what you will, but sometimes life-changing events begin in the most innocent and unexpected ways. For Jack Beale that moment came on a perfect summer morning as he stood overlooking Rye Harbor when something caught his eye. In that small space between the bow of his boat and the float to which it was tied, a lifeless body had become wedged as the tide tried to sweep it out to sea. That discovery, and the arrival of Daniel would begin a series of events that would eventually take Max from him. Who was the victim? Why was Daniel there and what was his interest in Max? Was there a connection? And so began a journey that would take Jack from Rye Harbor to Newport, RI and, eventually Belize, as he searched for answers.

DANGEROUS SHOALS (2011)

Spring has arrived in the small New Hampshire coastal town of Rye Harbor and all seemed right in the world. Jack Beale and Max, the feisty red haired bartender at Ben's Place, are back together after their split up the previous year and are looking forward to enjoying a carefree summer together. Then, someone who they thought was just a memory reappears, pursued by a psychotic killer. When he ends up dead, Jack and Max become the killer's new targets. What should have been an easy, relaxing summer for Jack, Max and his cat, Cat, becomes a battle of wits and a fight for survival.

KILLER RUN

KILLER RUN

K.D. MASON

The author may be reached through www.kdmason.com

This is a work of fiction. All of the characters, places, organizations,
and events portrayed in this novel are either products of the author's
imagination or are used fictitiously, and any resemblance to any actual
persons, living or dead, business establishments, events, or locales is
entirely coincidental.

ISBN-13 978-1480092457
ISBN-10 1480092452

Cover and book design by Claire MacMaster
    Barefoot Art Graphic Design | deepwater-creative.com
Copy Editor: Renée Nicholls | www.mywritingcoach.com
Cover photo: Lisa Dressel-Rohr
Back cover photographer: Richard G. Holt
Printed in the U.S.A.

Dedicated to all my running friends
for all the miles run together and experiences shared.

* * *

Writing a book is never a solitary endeavor. From the first germ of an idea until you hold the finished book in your hand, many people touch the project and leave their imprint.

Of all those people, I must first thank my wife, Nancy, without whose support and encouragement I could not have done this.

Others who deserve special mention are:
My good friends and early readers for their comments and observations
    Maj. Ken Goedecke, USMC
    Deb Merrill
    Marsha Filion
Patrolman Taryn Brotherton, Ipswich Police Dept.
Carrie Monahan, Essex County District Attorney's Office
Jim Gilford and the The G.A.C. for hosting one of the best trail races in New England
Lisa Dressel-Rohr for the great cover photo
Renee Nichols and Claire MacMaster, who transformed the manuscript into a finished book

If I missed anyone else, please accept my apologies and heartfelt thanks.

MALCOM INHALED DEEPLY, closed his eyes, and then exhaled slowly as he reopened his eyes and looked around in the pre-dawn darkness. He wasn't alone; there were over a hundred other runners gathered in the field on this crisp fall morning, ready for the Rockdog Run. He chuckled to himself thinking that to an unknowing observer, it must look like some kind of an alien gathering. Each shadowy shape wore a small bright headlamp that bobbed and weaved as they moved about, lighting up just enough so they could avoid tripping or bumping into each other. Occasionally, two lights came together and for a brief moment both faces were lit as they greeted each other. Then the lights shined back at the ground as they separated.

He was dressed for running, not standing around. His teeth began to chatter and his arms were covered with goose bumps. It was cold, and as the early morning breeze rustled the few remaining leaves in the surrounding forest, it sounded even colder. His whole body shivered. The only other sounds were the soft murmurings of quiet conversations as everyone prepared for the start of the day's ordeal. He would be running a full marathon, 26.2 miles, on difficult trails through the Willows State Park in Ipswich, Massachusetts. That would be daunting enough, but others would be running the companion event, fifty miles, hence the pre-dawn start. Glancing down at his watch he saw that it was nearly time to start, a fact confirmed when a voice came over a loudspeaker and broke the quiet. Everyone moved simultaneously toward the voice, and as all those bodies came together, he could feel their collective warmth.

"Good luck," an unseen voice whispered from behind.

"Thanks, you too," he replied, but as he uttered those words, a chill ran down his spine and fear filled his mind. He felt certain that he knew that voice. He started to turn his head, but the gun fired, and all the runners surged forward, forcing him to keep his eyes focused on what was in front of him. He had to run or risk tripping and falling. He moved forward with the mass of dark shapes following the trail of green glow sticks that led across the field and into the even darker woods beyond, all the while hoping he was wrong.

CHAPTER 1

THREE MONTHS EARLIER . . .

"HEY MAX," SAID JACK AS he walked into the bar at Ben's.

Max looked up from the book she was reading. It had been a quiet night in the bar. Rainy nights were like that. "Jack. I didn't hear you come in. Is it that time already?"

"The rain's stopped so I walked over. Parkin' lot's empty."

"I'm sorry, I haven't even begun to close down." Blushing in embarrassment, she said, "Some guy left this book here. I picked it up and made the mistake of starting to read it. It really sucked me in and I completely lost track of time."

"Give me the book. You have work to do."

Max handed him the book. "Want a beer while I finish up?"

"Sure."

Max drew him an ESB draft, returned, and placed the beer in front of him, then turned to go lock the door. Jack looked at the well-worn book. A sticker on the cover indicated that it came from the dollar bin at a used book store. The title was *The Captain's Quilt* and the author was Polly Christian. The cover showed a beautiful young woman with flowing dark hair standing on the deck of a ship. She looked fearful while a handsome (but obviously dangerous!) older man stood next to her. Jack chuckled just as Max returned to the bar. "You were reading this?" he asked, trying not to make fun of her and failing totally.

Max snatched it out of his hands and feigning indignation said, "It's not what you think." Turning it over she explained, "It's a story based on some actual letters written by a young woman in the late 1700s who came to New England from Antigua, in the Caribbean." She read the back cover copy aloud: "During the voyage she comes to know some information that will have a dramatic influence on several families' fortunes and maybe even influence the course of history. The dark underbelly of the rum, slave, and tea trades form the background for betrayal, murder, and love as she finds a new life in the colonies. Among her possessions is a quilt, which she uses to conceal those secrets." Max stopped and looked at Jack. "Come on. What's not to love? And so far it's pretty good."

Jack reached out his hand and motioned for her to give it to him.

"No!" She put the book down on the bar just out of his reach. "Come, help me get this place closed so we can go home."

Jack began to stretch for the book. He was curious, but she pushed it further away and gave him a look that stopped him cold. "Fine," he said shrugging, "What can I do?"

"The dining rooms are all set. Could you take the trash out while I finish here in the bar?" Max really hated to take the trash out. Even though it had been a couple of years since she was kidnapped off the loading dock, she was still nervous about going out there alone.

"No problem." Jack began to consolidate and then tie up the bags of garbage. As soon as five had become two, he headed out back. When he returned, he found Max standing at the bar reading.

"Max," he said, surprised to find her so engrossed again.

She looked up, slapped the book shut, and pulled her keys out of her pocket. "All set. Let's go."

CHAPTER 2

THE SUN HAD JUST RISEN. Jack slid out of the bed as quietly as possible so as not to disturb Max. Cat lifted her head and gave him a look that said, "What's the matter with you? It's too early!" Then she tucked her head back under her forearm, sighed once, and promptly fell back asleep. As he looked down at the two sleeping forms Jack paused, thinking about how lucky he was to be alive and how it was because of them.

He hadn't slept well since spring. He rarely did. Most nights, sleep came in small doses, the longest no more than four hours. After that, he would toss and turn. He wasn't really sound asleep, nor was he wide-awake. During these hours, dreams, ideas, memories, and solutions to problems mixed together and filled his head.

The one constant that remained and haunted him was the shadow of evil that had so affected all of their lives. It was fading, but some things can never be erased. Cat had fought that evil presence and, though wounded, survived. Max had saved his life and together they had watched his boat sink. She held him without question when the nightmares were the worst. He would do anything for her, but he still felt that he could never fully repay her. He marveled and wondered at the source of her strength.

Stepping out of this reverie, Jack grabbed his running stuff and then slipped out of the room. As he dressed, a welcome sense of anticipation crept in. For Jack, running in the early morning was different than running at other times of the day. Physically it was the same—the breathing, his stride, the stretching of muscles, the sweat. The difference was more spiritual. A new day was beginning, he had survived another night's demons, and now with a run to clear his head, he had a chance to start fresh. It was a time when emotions and feelings seemed much purer, before the cluttering influence of a busy day's activities.

As Jack slipped out of the apartment, he took a deep breath, exhaled, stretched his arms up, and then twisted from side to side. That was enough. He never felt the need for any great amount of pre-run stretching or warming up. That's what the first few miles were for. He glanced at his watch and then took the first steps of what would turn out to be five miles.

There was little traffic on the roads, and the air was still infused with the coolness of the night. Within a half mile, his body had begun to adjust to its new reality. His stride became smoother, his breathing deep and regular, and, as he had expected, he could feel the demons of the past night fading, replaced by the clarity and optimism of a new day.

As he ran, his ideas and thoughts morphed into one another, and within another mile or so he was thinking of the race that he and his best friend, Dave, had signed up to run. It was called the Rockdog Run. There were several distances to choose from, all on trails: a full marathon, a 50k, or a 50 miler. Dave and some of his other running friends had run the marathon before and had convinced him that it would be fun. He wasn't so sure, but he had still allowed them to talk him into it. The idea of a marathon in the woods was intriguing.

As he rounded the final turn that would bring him back home, Jack felt renewed. He slowed to a walk as he reached Ben's, and out of habit he walked through the parking lot and stood at the edge overlooking the harbor.

A faint breeze was blowing from the west. "*That will keep the ocean flat,*" Jack thought to himself. He watched as his friend Art skillfully guided the *Sea Witch* away from the commercial wharf and pointed her toward the mouth of the harbor. Art made his living lobstering, and Jack knew that there weren't too many days when the ocean was as flat as it was this morning. This would make Art's job much easier.

As he watched the *Sea Witch* glide through the stillness, he recalled similar conditions just months ago when Art rescued him and Max after *Irrepressible* sank. The morning's sense of perfection shattered, and a great sadness washed over him.

Now his eyes were drawn first to the empty pier in front of Ben's and then out to the mooring where *Irrepressible* should have been floating peacefully. She had been his pride and joy for nearly twenty-five years. Some of the happiest days in his life were spent on *Irrepressible*, as he sailed her all over the Caribbean during his youth. When the woman he loved was killed, *Irrepressible* carried him north to Rye Harbor in New England, and in the process helped heal his soul. Every great event in his life had included *Irrepressible*, and now, looking out over the harbor where she should have been, all he had were her memories. He turned and began walking home.

About halfway back, a radio show, that he had heard recently, suddenly flashed through his head. The topic was unique destinations for the fall foliage season. The woman being interviewed told how she and her husband came to run a bed and breakfast up north called The Quilt House, which was named for the quilts they had found in the house when they bought it back in the early seventies. As she recounted the story, she told how she had even written a book back then based on some letters they had found in with the quilts. Now Jack made the connection, she had written the book that Max was reading. As he recalled more of the interview, he remembered that her husband was a runner and he had cleared miles of trails for hiking, skiing, and running, which made their B&B a popular destination for sports-minded people.

An idea began to form in his mind, and the melancholy that he had felt as he looked over the harbor began to lift. What if he took Max up there for a few days? It would have to be after Columbus Day because of work, but by then the leaf-peeping crowds should have thinned. As an added bonus, he could get in some trail running as part of his preparation for the Rockdog.

The more he thought about it, the better the idea seemed. He would set it up so it would be a complete surprise for Max. By the time he reached home, he was all smiles as he thought about how she would react.

CHAPTER 3

"MAX," SAID JACK AS HE SAT at the bar at Ben's nursing a beer. Several days had passed since he had made his mind up to ask Max about going up north. The night was nearly over and Jack was the only customer left in the bar, although the dining room still had a few. He had done the research, made the reservations, and now it was time to surprise her. This was usually tough to do, considering all of these years they had been together, first as friends and then as a couple. Now he was sure he would succeed.

She turned toward him, but before she could say anything, he asked, "What would you say to getting away, maybe going up north for a weekend sometime this fall?"

She froze and silently stared at him, stunned, as his words echoed in her ears. *"A weekend up north?"*

"I've made reservations for us at a B&B just after Columbus Day. I thought it might be fun."

She still didn't move, and her expression remained frozen. As she continued to stare at him, her mind started racing. *"This is not like him. He's up to something—what?"* If she had thrown out the idea herself, he probably would have whined a bit and then agreed. But for it to be his idea—he had to be up to something.

"What do you mean?" she asked tentatively.

"Just what I said. I made reservations for us to spend a couple of days up north at a B&B." Her mouth opened to speak, but before she could say anything he cut her off. "I heard about this place on the radio, and like I said, I thought it would be fun."

"Wh-, when?" she stammered.

"After Columbus Day."

"Why?"

"Leaf peep, I don't know. It just strikes me as a fun thing to do."

Max stopped and stared at him again. "*A fun thing to do?*" she thought to herself. She didn't know what to say or how to react. This was not her Jack speaking.

Before she could find words, the register came to life, spitting out another drink order for someone in the dining room. Automatically, she turned and tore off the order slip and reached for a glass from the shelf, her thoughts still on his invitation. She turned back to him and said, somewhat warily, "Sounds like fun. Let's talk about this after I get off."

Jack swallowed the last of his beer. "Okay."

He slid off his chair and headed for the men's room, leaving Max standing there, glass in hand, completely confused.

Seconds later, Max's best friend, a waitress named Patti, came in from the dining room to pick up the drinks, which normally would have been waiting for her. Instead she found Max standing perfectly still with an empty glass in hand and a strange look on her face.

"Max," she said.

Max remained motionless.

Patti stared at her and then repeated her name. "Max."

Max slowly turned her head and looked at Patti.

"Max, are you all right?"

"Yes, yes, I'm fine." With that she began making Patti's drinks.

"No, you're not. I know you too well. Something's up. What's going on? Is it Jack? What happened? Where is he? Did he do something stupid?" All of this came out in one breath. When Patti got excited her tongue would often outpace her mind.

Max finished making the drinks and placed them on Patti's tray. "Patti, stop. Take a breath. He didn't do anything stupid, and he's in the men's room."

Patti's customer was probably checking his watch, but sorting this out seemed much more important. "So I was right. It was Jack. I knew it. What did he do?"

"He didn't do anything."

"Then what?"

"He asked me if I wanted to go up north after Columbus Day for a couple of days. He made reservations at a B&B." Max said this as matter-of-factly as she could, as if by doing so it wouldn't seem quite so unusual.

Patti stared in silence for a moment before blurting out, "Shut the front door! No way!"

Max could see that she was about to get wound up again, and Jack was due back any second. Before Patti could say anything else, Max urged, "Patti, go. Go serve your drinks. We'll talk later. Go."

CHAPTER 4

AS IT TURNED OUT, those were the last drinks of the night. Jack returned to his seat at the bar and waited for Max to close up. Max, still puzzled, said little while she began the end-of-night ritual. As she worked, she frequently glanced over at Jack, and once or twice she even turned toward him as if to say something, but didn't. All the while a full conversation continued in her head.

While Max finished in the bar, Patti followed a similar routine in the dining rooms, and she was equally curious. It didn't take long for them to finish. Finally, the doors were locked and all that remained was to leave. Only thing was, no one was leaving. Patti came in, took a seat at the bar, turned, and stared at Jack while Max poured him another beer.

Patti and Max had become friends shortly after Patti began working at Ben's. While she pursued her lifelong dream of being a professional photographer, waitressing at Ben's paid the bills. She had been introduced to Jack's best friend, Dave, when Max had been kidnapped several years ago. Now the four of them were best friends.

Before Max could even sit down, Patti started in. "So Jack, what's this about going up north after Columbus Day?"

Max flashed her a look that said, *"Stop. Leave Jack alone."* Aloud she said, "Patti, I can finish up here. Why don't you head home for an early night with Dave? Go get your things and then I'll walk you to your car."

Reluctantly, Patti headed back to the dining room to look for her pocketbook. With her best friend out of the picture, Max looked at Jack and said, "So tell me more about this idea of yours."

"What's to tell? I just thought it would be a nice thing to do." He knew that this answer would drive her crazy.

"Jack," she gave him a light punch in the shoulder. "You know that's not what I meant. Whenever we have gone away like that, it's always been my idea. You've never suggested doing something like this. Now tell me what's going on."

Jack looked at Max and took another sip of his beer. She was right, of course, and as he looked at her he was trying to find the right words to explain this sudden departure from character.

"A couple of days ago, after an early morning run, I was standing by the harbor." He paused, then started again. "Actually, I was in the truck a few days before that, and on the radio there was an interview with a woman who, with her husband, has a B&B up north. It was pretty interesting. It's called The Quilt House. Anyway, as I was running, it dawned on me that she wrote that book you're reading. Then, as I was standing by the harbor, the idea came to me. I know how wiped out you are after Columbus Day, so I thought a getaway would be nice and you'd have a chance to meet a real live author."

Max was still looking at him, and he wasn't sure how to read the expression on her face. Happy, shocked, puzzled, confused, he couldn't decide which.

Patti returned with her pocketbook, and Jack watched as the two women walked out of the bar and turned down the front hall. He heard the click of the lock being turned and the clingle of the bells that hung on the door as it was pushed open. Then it was quiet. Max didn't return immediately, and he found himself listening really hard for any sound that would announce her return. As the seconds became minutes, his anxiety began to increase. Bad things always seemed to happen late at night, and he and Max had experienced more than their fair share of them.

The minutes that Max and Patti had been gone suddenly seemed like hours. Leaving his half-finished beer on the bar, he headed for the door. His heart rate increased, as did his pace. When he reached the door, he saw that the keys were still in the lock, but there was no sign of Max or Patti. He opened the front door, stepped out onto the porch, and saw only an empty parking lot. Panic began to take over. He called out, "Max!" but there was no answer. Images of that winter night, not so long ago, when she had been kidnapped flashed through his head. His heart was pounding and his breathing became shorter as the panic grew. He leapt down the front stairs and began to run across the parking lot to the spot where Patti usually parked her car. It was gone and at that moment a dark sedan drove past Ben's toward the boulevard. His panic was now full on and he sprinted back to the front door. He needed his keys and he had to call the police. Just as he picked up the telephone, the bells on the front door clingled again, and when he turned his head toward the sound, he saw Max pulling the door shut and turning the key.

CHAPTER 5

"JACK, YOU ARE BEING SILLY."

"No, I'm not," he replied. "You know how I worry, and when I went out to see what was taking you so long, and you weren't there, and Patti's car was gone, well . . . ."

She started to say something, but he cut her off. "I panicked."

"Jack. There was nothing to worry about. I was only gone for a few minutes. All I did was walk Patti out to her car."

"But it wasn't there."

"She got in a few minutes late and had to park further out back."

"I didn't know."

"You wouldn't. We were just talking for a few minutes before she drove off. Nothing was going to happen."

"You don't know that."

"No. I do. Everything was fine."

Jack looked away from Max and remained silent. He knew that what she had said was true, that he didn't have anything to worry about, but he couldn't help himself. Now he was beginning to feel embarrassed for acting like a girl.

"Jack, look at me."

He turned and looked into her face. There was a softness, a vulnerability in the look on her face, and her green eyes had a sparkle to them that made him blush. She put her hands on his cheeks. Her hands were warm and she gently pulled his face toward hers and kissed him softly on the lips. Then she whispered, "I love you Jack Beale." Jack looked at her and saw the barest hint of a smile touch the corners of her mouth. In that moment, everything returned to normal. She giggled first. Then he cracked and began to chuckle too, and in a matter of seconds, they were both laughing uncontrollably.

As they began to catch their breaths and the laughter subsided, Jack said to Max, "Thank you."

She looked at him. "You're welcome."

* * *

Later, at home, they talked for what seemed like hours, until Max asked, "Could we ask Patti and Dave to join us in the mountains?"

Jack hadn't considered that possibility. "Sure. Why not, I'll ask him tomorrow."

With that settled, love and sleep overcame them.

CHAPTER 6

"SO DAVE, . . . HOW WOULD YOU . . . and Patti like. . to join Max and me . . . for a little trip to the mountains . . . after Columbus Day?" Jack squeezed the words out between breaths as they ran along.

They were running the trails in Maudslay State Park, alongside the Merrimack River, and the shade provided by the dense woods provided welcome relief from what had been a very warm, late summer day. But as warm as it had been, Jack could sense a difference in the quality of the heat, as the seasonal change from summer to fall had begun.

The trail had suddenly widened, and Jack knew that for the next mile or so they would be able to run side by side. There weren't quite as many roots and rocks here as on other parts of the trail. With better footing, the need to concentrate on each step lessened, and it was easier to talk.

He had promised Max that he would talk to Dave about going up north, and now, about three miles into what would turn out to be a seven-mile run, it seemed like as good a time as any.

Dave replied with a question of his own. "So that's what's going on? . . . She . . . has been . . . hinting at something for . . . the past few days."

"Sorry."

"Don't be . . . . So tell me what it's all about."

"You know . . . I don't have the boat this fall. . . . I just felt the need to get away. . . . Max is reading this book . . . on quilts, and I heard . . . about this B&B called . . . The Quilt House. . . . It's up in the mountains, and . . . with the Rockdog Run coming up later, I . . . thought that maybe I . . . could get in some training runs . . . and kill two birds with one stone."

"Sneaky. Does Max know about . . . this idea?"

"Only the B&B part. . . . If you and Patti come along, then . . . the running part will be easier to explain . . ."

"Sure. . . . Sounds like it could be fun."

With that settled, the remaining miles passed quickly and silently.

* * *

Max greeted Jack at the door, and it was obvious that she wanted to know what Dave had said. "So?"

"So, what?"

"You know what."

"We had a good run. Much cooler in the woods."

"Jack! Come on, what did Dave say?"

"Oh, that."

"Yeah, that."

"He said it sounded like a good idea. I'll call the place tomorrow and book another room."

Max's face lit up as she threw her arms around him and gave him a big hug and kiss. "It'll be so much fun; you'll see. Now, go take a shower. You stink." She pushed him away. "I've got to call Patti."

CHAPTER 7

The next morning, Christine could not bring herself to leave her cabin. She ignored the pleadings of the kindly old cook to eat something, as she would not open the door for him. She remained behind the closed door through the mid-day. As the hours passed, she noticed that the motion of the ship had changed. No longer did the ship cleave the water in a lazy, gentle manner, but rather with more force and urgency. She could hear commands being shouted, followed by other shouts, and the footsteps on the deck above her head seemed louder as the crew ran about. Sails started clapping and the ship moaned while chants accompanied the heaving of men as they pulled as one on some unseen rope or line. The ship heeled, forcing her deeper into her berth and fear began to creep into her soul.

* * *

Max shivered and put the book down. She knew that feeling. She had felt the same fear that Christine was feeling, except that for her, it had been real. Christine's experience was only on paper, the product of imagination.

Max had fallen so deeply into the story that as she looked around the room and saw the clock, she was surprised at how much time had passed. She took a deep breath. All was as it should be. Jack was out and Cat was curled up on the couch next to her. The cries of gulls fighting over some scrap blew in through the open window, carried by a freshening breeze. She stood, walked to the window, and pulled it shut. But as Max looked out over the marsh, Christine was still in her head. She stretched, returned to the couch, and stroked Cat. Then, without thinking, she picked up the book again.

* * *

There was a knock on the cabin door. She struggled to her feet and with great difficulty made her way to the door. It wasn't locked, but everyone on the ship respected its closure. As she grasped the handle, the ship lurched, throwing her back and pulling the door open at the same time. The force with which she fell back ripped her hand off the handle and she cried out as she fell. At first, the astonished old cook could only stand and gawk at her. Then, as he gathered his wits, he said, as if nothing had happened and she were not on the floor, "Beggin' your pardon Miss. The Captain asked me to see if you was all right since it looks like we are in for some weather this night and it would be best if you were to stay in your cabin."

"Yes. Yes, I'm fine. Could you please help me?"

"Oh, yes Miss." He crossed into her cabin, offered his hand, and helped her to her feet.

She was surprised at how strong he was. "Thank you."

"May I bring you something hot to eat? The cook fires soon will be out and all that will remain until the storm has passed will be some biscuits and perhaps a bite of cheese."

"How kind of you to ask."

"Miss." With that he turned away and left the cabin. He pulled the door shut, leaving her alone again.

* * *

"Hello. Max, you up there?" Jack's voice came from the bottom of the stairs.

"Up here," she shouted back.

Cat lifted her head to see what all the noise was about. When she saw it was Jack, she nonchalantly put her head back down and closed her eyes again.

"Hey. What're you up to?"

"Reading."

He glanced at the couch and saw that it was the book she had found in the bar. "How is it?"

"It's surprisingly good. I'm finding it hard to put down"

"Cool," said Jack, happy to end the literary discussion there. "I ran into Dave while I was out. He said that Patti is really excited about this trip and that you should call her."

"I just talked to her this morning."

"Call her anyway."

"As soon as I finish this chapter."

CHAPTER 8

THE QUILT HOUSE WAS DOWN a long gravel drive that was lined with stone walls. To reach this destination, guests first had to follow a winding narrow road that was both cracked and tortured. The house, well over 200 years old, was situated on sixty-five acres in Leavitt Town, New Hampshire. The property included pine and hardwood forest, fields, and even some low-lying marsh down by the creek that ran across it. According to the brochure, for guests seeking a quiet getaway from the rigors of everyday life, it offered the perfect mix of quiet seclusion and relaxation in a historical location. As an antidote to the scrumptious home-cooked meals, there were miles of trails that could be used for hiking, biking, running, and cross- country skiing or snowshoeing—depending on the time of the year.

The house itself, a huge, white, two-story colonial, had been built by Captain John Leavitt, who had fought at Lake George during the French and Indian War prior to the revolution. Leavitt Town, named after the Captain, was incorporated in 1778. According to census figures, by 1790 it had a population of 154. It took nearly 200 years for Leavitt Town to double in size. Then, in the last fifty years of the twentieth century, the town exploded to a population of almost 1500 residents.

To the present owners, Malcom and Polly Christian, who bought the property from the last descendent of the Leavitt family in the late seventies, it was a dream come true. Prior to the purchase, they had traveled Europe extensively, finding it much more rewarding to stay in private homes than in stuffy hotels. The dream was born when the young couple decided to return home, find the right house, and open it up to weary travelers.

Finding the house was the easy part. When they first saw the

Leavitt House, they knew it was the right place. The house was far enough from the main roads that led to the mountains and lakes of northern New Hampshire that it felt quite remote, giving the out-of-state tourists a sense of real adventure. The reality was that after a short thirty-minute ride back to the highway, the lakes and mountains were only a little bit further up the road.

Today, people around town call them visionaries, but when they bought the old run-down house, crazy was the more frequently used term. Together, they worked hard to make their dream come true. They did most of the work themselves, and as they learned new skills, they made and corrected mistakes. Perseverance was the key to their success.

CHAPTER 9

IN THE BEGINNING, back in the seventies, while they scraped and painted, pulled weeds, and planted gardens, Malcom and Polly debated names for their new home. The Rocking Chair, The Leavitt House, and Polly's Dream were all considered and eventually rejected. One day, Malcom was up in the attic repairing some cracked rafters. There was a lot of old furniture and boxes up in the attic that they had not yet had time to examine, and he was standing on what looked like an old, dust-covered chest when Polly appeared at the top of the stairs. "Hey Mal, lunch is ready."

"Great, I'll be right down,"

She glanced up at him. "Be careful."

He looked down and said, "I will." He began to turn to climb down from the chest. As he turned, the heavy pry-bar that he was holding hit another piece of furniture, knocking him off balance. As he tried to recover he slipped and made a much more rapid descent than he had intended. Polly opened her mouth to shout a warning, but it was too late. He hit the floor, and the cloud of dust that erupted nearly made him disappear.

Polly screamed. He was so covered with dust and the cobwebs that had moments before been lacy curtains hanging from the roof, were now so laden with dust that they were more like strings, making him look like a crumpled marionette.

He began coughing and Polly moved toward him. "Mal, are you okay?"

"I'm okay," he managed to croak as he coughed again.

Polly began to giggle. "You sure?"

"I'm sure."

"What were you thinking?"

"Seemed like a good idea at the time." Mal began laughing, which quickly turned into another coughing fit.

"What's this?" she asked, pointing to the chest.

"Don't know; I just found it up here. There's another one over there." He pointed to his left.

"What's in it? Did you look inside?"

"No, I didn't. First things first, and these rafters are more important." As he stood up, he brushed his hands over his arms and the front of his shirt. That stirred up more dust and more coughing.

Polly moved toward the trunk, gently brushed more dust away, and tried to lift the lid. It didn't move, so she paused, readjusted her grip, and pulled again. When it still wouldn't move, Malcom's voice broke the silence. "Wait."

She stopped and looked at him. He continued, "Go easy; don't force it." Then, pointing at its face, he said, "There's a keyhole on the front. Maybe it's locked."

Polly stared down at the chest. "Oh."

Malcom saw the disappointment on her face and heard it in her voice. "Tell you what. Let's get it downstairs, de-dusted, and then we'll try to get it open after lunch."

CHAPTER 10

THEY WRESTLED THE CHEST down the stairs. While Malcom went to clean up, Polly studied the chest. With a soft-bristled foxtail brush she began brushing the dust off. It was the kind of fine dust that only accumulates over many years of stillness in attics and other little-used places. With each gentle stroke another layer came off. Most of the dust landed on the floor, but she had to pause every now and then to let the inevitable cloud of dust settle.

Slowly, the chest began to reveal itself and even to her untrained eye, she could tell that this was no ordinary trunk. No doubt, it was old. It was a rectangular chest with a flat top, approximately 45 inches long, 20 inches deep, and 20 inches high. On the back there were two ornate brass hinges. The dings and dents of many years of use marred its surface, yet it still possessed the quiet dignity of finely designed and built furniture. She looked at the keyhole and then gave the lid another small tug. It didn't budge, and she couldn't tell if it was because it was locked, the hinges were frozen, or the lid was simply stuck.

After sweeping up the dust from the floor, she began to wipe it off the chest with a soft cloth dipped in a bucket of Murphy Oil Soap and wrung out until just damp. The wood had a fine grain and was a deep, brownish red. In a word, it was beautiful. She was so focused on her project that she didn't realize that she was being watched.

"Nice job. It looks like mahogany."

She jumped at the unexpected sound and turned quickly in its direction. Malcom was standing in the doorway, a half eaten sandwich in his hand, and they both began to laugh.

"That wasn't nice," she said, still trying to control her laughter. "You scared the shit out of me. How long were you standing there?"

"Long enough. I thought we were going to do this together?"

"I couldn't wait. Isn't it beautiful?"

He swallowed his last bite of sandwich. "Have you tried opening it?"

"I gave it a gentle tug, but it wouldn't move, so I decided to wait for you."

He knelt down next to the trunk while she looked on. He looked into the keyhole for the lock, bent close, and blew into it. A small poof of dust erupted, which made him sneeze and her laugh. He couldn't tell if it was locked or not so he tried to lift the lid. It moved. Not much, but enough to confirm that it wasn't locked. He tried again, and it opened a couple of inches, enough that with a flashlight they could peek in and could see that it was full of some kind of fabric.

After a few drops of oil on the hinges and some gentle coaxing, the lid finally opened.

"It's a quilt," said Polly.

"A quilt?" A hint of disappointment lingered in his voice.

"And it looks really old." Polly leaned over and began to lift it out of the chest. It was heavier than she had expected and it began to unfold. "Mal, help me. Grab that corner."

He followed her lead and together they lifted the quilt out of the chest. "There's another under this one," Polly said, nodding her head toward the chest.

Holding it high, they slowly unfolded it. A beautiful geometric pattern revealed itself. Reds, blues, and greens were the predominant colors, although the whole spectrum seemed to be represented. Some parts of the quilt were more faded than others and there were clear lines where it had been folded.

"It's beautiful," she said.

"I wonder how old it is?" Malcom added.

"Don't know. Maybe there's a historical society in town."

"Even if the quilt's not very old, I bet the chest is. Let's fold this one back up and look at the next."

They took each quilt out, unfolded it, admired it, refolded it, and moved on to the next. There were six quilts in that chest, each one different. Some appeared older than others, some were just patterns like the first one, and others were more like a picture. As soon as the last quilt was folded and put back into the chest, they returned to the attic for the other chest and began the process again.

The second trunk, while similar to the first, was a bit smaller. This one was the color of dark honey, and from the number of blemishes, it had obviously been well used.

It too was filled with quilts, and these seemed older than those in the first chest. Each was removed in turn, unfolded, looked at, refolded, and carefully placed on the floor next to the chest. The fifth quilt that they removed was stunning. The two center squares in the top row, along with the two bottom corners, were larger than the other squares that made up the quilt's perimeter. A total of fourteen perimeter squares surrounded a large center square. While the other quilts were all symmetrical, the arrangement of the four larger perimeter squares prevented that here.

At first glance the couple found the asymmetry a bit off-putting, but they soon realized that it was impossible to pull their eyes away from it, much the same way that Mona Lisa's smile captivates. In the central square was a large sailing ship and embroidered under it the date: 1773. The squares around the edge each had a different scene depicted. Some were bright and cheerful, others dark and foreboding. There was silence as the couple took it in.

"Have you ever seen anything like this before?" Polly eventually asked, her voice reflecting the same amazement that was in her eyes.

"Never."

"Look. Start at the top. If you follow the squares around, it's like they are telling a story." She pointed at the square to the right of the two larger ones in the top row and swept her arm around the quilt in a clockwise direction.

"So it is," said Malcom.

"Oh Mal. This is amazing."

He agreed. Then, having reached his quilt quota, he said, "I need another sandwich." He lowered the corner he was holding and draped it over a nearby chair.

Polly continued to stare at the quilt, ignoring Malcom's desertion.

Soon Polly could hear Malcom foraging in the fridge. She continued to stare at the quilt until her arm couldn't hold it up any longer. She put her corner down, folding it over the same chair Malcom had used to drape his corner. She'd need his help to better refold it. Turning toward the chest she glanced inside again.

"What have we here?" she said aloud. The bottom of the chest held one more carefully folded surprise: a faded and stained piece of cloth. She couldn't tell if this was another quilt or just some material not yet used. Whatever it was, it looked as if it could easily fall apart.

She was about to begin lifting it out herself when Malcom walked back into the room holding a plate with her lunch in one hand and a half-eaten sandwich in the other.

"Mal, there's one more. Will you help me? It looks pretty flimsy."

"I brought you your sandwich."

"Help me."

"Sure." He took another bite and then placed his sandwich beside hers. He set the plate down.

Still chewing, he examined her discovery. At one time, it might have been white or ivory, but now all he saw was an old, ratty, piece of material: stained and faded, with frays and tears that spoke of many years of use. Together they lifted it out of the chest and placed it on the floor.

Mal was eager to return to his sandwich, but Polly was fascinated. "I think it's a quilt of some sort. It looks really old." She never took her eyes off of the folded material. "Help me here . . . please?"

They each took a corner and, one fold at a time, slowly and carefully coaxed it open. Finally, they peeled back the last fold and afraid to hold it up, looked at it as it lay on the floor. A chill went down Polly's spine. Work done, Malcom turned for his sandwich just as something at the bottom of the chest caught his eye. Beneath the spot where the fabric had been placed so carefully, a stack of papers was tied together with a faded piece of ribbon.

CHAPTER 11

HE BENT DOWN AND PICKED up the bundle of papers. The sheets were old and brittle, some more faded than others. He let the faded ribbon that had tied them together dangle between the second and third finger on his left hand as he carefully held the loose pages with his fingertips. Realizing he'd found a new treasure, Polly abandoned her quilt. As Malcom moved toward the open door for better light, she came and read over his shoulder.

The script was tight and swirly. Each letter was precisely formed and flowed elegantly into the next. Something about it seemed familiar. Then it came to him. His grandmother wrote with that same careful, flowery, measured hand, not like the scribble that most people he knew tried to pass off as writing. His sandwich was forgotten.

June 4, 1773
My dearest sister,
We have been at sea now for two days and I wish that I had never begged father for the chance to visit aunt and uncle in Newport. While the weather has been good and the breeze fair and the sea calm, the motion of the boat does not agree with me. I have spent most of the time in my cabin. I cannot eat and if I try, the seasickness returns. The ship's cook, a kindly old gentleman, has brought me porridge and biscuits this morning, but I could not bear the smell of them, let alone taste them. I feel so bad for him. He tries so hard to cheer me up and give me encouragement and all I can do is glare at him and then bury my face in the bucket next to the bed. He says that this will pass, but I fear that I am dying. He has tried to coax me to come up on deck, assuring me that the fresh air will do me good, but I think I would just rather die than move

from my bed. If I do not die, I shall continue this letter on the morrow.

Your sister,

Christine

June 6, 1773

Dear sister,

I have not died, yet. Food is still abhorrent to me and sleep still provides the only respite from this malaise, but I did venture out of my cabin and saw the sky for the first time. The ocean is so vast and this ship, which seemed so large when I first saw it at home, is now so small. Perhaps it was the fresh air, but for a moment I felt better. The Captain was on deck and greeted me with a smile and commented that father would be pleased, were he here, before returning to his duties. Tonight, the cook again brought me some porridge. I managed to eat several spoonfuls. My eyes grow heavy and sleep calls. Goodnight dear sister, I miss you.

With love,

Christine

Next to him, Polly shuddered. "I'm getting seasick just thinking about it," she said. "You keep reading and let me know if anything exciting happens. I want to take another look at those quilts."

Malcom paused for a bite of his sandwich, wiped his hands, and then carried on alone.

June 8, 1773

My sister,

This morning I awoke for the first time desiring food. I left my cabin and went out onto the deck. The sun was just showing itself on the horizon and the few clouds that were in the sky were lit in shades of pink and orange. The breeze was just strong enough that the ship moved easily through the water and the sea was quite flat so the motion was not uncomfortable, or perhaps I am just getting accustomed. I was able to stand there alone for several moments, before the crew noticed me.

I watched as they went about their duties and could sense a real joy in what they were about, that is, until the Captain appeared. As soon as his foot hit the deck, the atmosphere changed. It was as if a shadow had descended over the ship. He barked several commands and seemed quite dissatisfied, until he saw me. A smile was forced onto his face and he greeted me, commenting on how much better I looked. After these few pleasantries, he suggested that I return to my cabin. It was said in such a way that I had little choice and he said he would have the cook bring me some breakfast.

Do you remember when we were little and we had hid papa's pipe and how angry he was, and we were so scared that we just hid, while he punished the staff and for days there was a gloom that filled the house and it wasn't lifted until we were able to replace his pipe without anyone knowing it was us. Even after he had his pipe back, that blackness persisted. That was the feeling I had.

Your sister
Christine

June 14, 1773
Dearest Sister,
We are now into the second week of this journey. I must be getting used to the motion of the ship since I am no longer sick. The Captain puzzles me more each day. Most of the time he seems kind and charming, like the man Papa knows and would have stay with us at the end of a voyage. Other times, for no reason that I can discern, a darkness comes over him, and he shows a temper

that is quite fearsome. Today, while I was on deck there was a commotion, what happened I don't know, but suddenly he was at my side and commanded me to my cabin. I began to protest when he grabbed my arm, and while squeezing it hard enough to bring me to tears and, in a low voice almost like the growl of a rabid dog, he repeated his order. In that moment I feared for my life and fled to my cabin.

Safe below, I could hear above me much shouting and thrashing about. Then, there was silence followed by the most horrible of screams. I remember, once when I was much younger, hearing those same sounds. I had wandered away from the main house and out by the cane fields I saw Mr. Roberts, the overseer, raising his whip against one of the field slaves. The sound of the cracking whip and the screams of that poor man were so terrible that I ran back to the house and hid in my room for the rest of the day. I could never look at Mr. Roberts again without hearing those screams.

As the screams faded, so did my memories and before long, the silence was soon followed by the sounds of water splashing and holystones rubbing the deck. I can only imagine that blood had been spilled.
Christine

June 15, 1773
Sister,
Yesterday, after the flogging, the captain came to my cabin. The blackness that I had seen in his eyes was gone, and his manner was no longer so fearsome, but rather kinder. His considerable charm held sway over me as he apologized for having been so rough with me. It was as if he were a different man. He spoke as if nothing had happened and even suggested that I join him on deck for some fresh air. His invitation, as kind as it seemed, was

*less a question than a command. Puzzled, I had no choice but to
agree.*

*On deck, standing at the rail, he tried to engage me in pleas-
ant conversation and my fears were forgotten for a moment. I
don't know what overcame me, and I asked him about what had
happened yesterday. He stiffened and turned away from me, and
as he turned, his whole demeanor changed. I watched as he took
a deep breath, and felt a chill course through my body. When he
turned to face me again, whatever kindness had prompted him
to invite me on deck was gone. He spoke slowly and calmly to me
saying that I was never to question him about the running of his
ship. Then he turned and strode away, leaving me alone with my
thoughts.*

*Later that evening, I went back up onto the deck. The moon
had not yet risen, and the stars were so bright that no other light
was necessary. It was beautiful. The breeze had freshened and it
seemed as if we were flying across the ocean, chased by a trail of
phosphorescence that followed in our wake. Before long the moon
appeared on the horizon, and as I stood watching it rise into the
heavens, I felt a presence by my side. I turned. It was the cook
who had been so kind to me when I was so sick. He asked how I
was getting along. I thanked him for his concern and then asked
if he knew where we were. He told me that we had passed by the
Bahamas Islands during the day and that soon we would be more
than halfway to our destination. Nothing else was said. Then,
as silently as he had arrived, he disappeared into the night. I
remained there, alone, for some time before returning to my cabin.
C.*

June 20, 1773
Sister dearest,
It is now clear that we have left the tropics. The ocean is different.

Its color is no longer the deep vibrant blue that we see at home, but rather it's less intense, darker and more cold looking. The breeze is cooler, especially at night. Today another sail was spotted on the horizon. That prompted a great deal of activity as everyone was on deck to see what ship it was. . . .

* * *

"Mal . . . Mal." He didn't hear her voice until she touched his arm, breaking the spell. "Mal. I know what we should name the house."

He looked up. "Huh?"

"I know what we should name the house."

"Oh, yes, the house. What?" It took a while for his brain to catch up to what she was saying.

"The Quilt House. We can hang a quilt in each room and name the room for the quilt."

"The Quilt House. I like it." Then he looked back down at the papers in his hand and continued reading. The final pages detailed that meeting at sea with another ship, Christine's introduction to its master, and her subsequent discovery of the purpose for the rendezvous until the letter stopped abruptly. Frustrated, he read the last lines again.

. . . There was a letter on the table. I couldn't help myself. I picked it up and began to read. The words tore at my heart and I gasped. I fled the room before finishing the letter, but I had read enough, and now every fear that I had ever felt in my entire life took form. . . .

CHAPTER 12

NAMING THE INN HAD BEEN EASY compared to the work needed to restore the old farmhouse into their dream bed and breakfast. Finally the task was done and The Quilt House sign was hung.

One day, shortly after they had started accepting reservations, Mal was busy stacking firewood when Polly joined him outside. The days were getting shorter and he wanted to finish the job before dark, so he was only half paying attention when Polly said, "Mal, I have a great idea."

His only response, other than a grunt, was to place another armful of cut and split wood onto the pile.

"Did you hear me? I have a great idea."

"I heard you. Can it keep for a few more minutes while I finish here?" He tried not to sound too disinterested, but from the look on her face, he knew that he wasn't successful.

"I suppose," she said as she walked back toward the house.

"Shit," he mumbled as he tossed another log onto the pile.

Thirty minutes later, Malcom walked into the kitchen. Polly was sitting at the table. To his surprise, in front of her, splayed out all over the table, were the letters they had found in the trunk. She was writing on one of those yellow pads of paper like lawyers would use—furiously writing.

"Hey, Pol. So what's this idea you have?"

"Shhh." She didn't look up, but kept on writing on the pad of paper.

Malcom shrugged and thought to himself, "I deserved that." He went over to the sink to wash his hands.

As he reached for a towel, Polly put down her pencil and looked over at him.

"So tell me. What's your idea?" he asked again.

"Those letters that you found in the bottom of the trunk gave me a great idea. I reread them and once you get past the seasickness, it's a great story. I'm going to write a book."

"You're what?" Malcom didn't know what else to say.

"I'm going to write a book. I was rereading these letters and they gave me the idea."

"A book?"

"Yes. Look, we found all these quilts and that gave us the idea for what to name this place. And these letters were probably written by whoever belonged to the quilts."

"You're going to write a book," he said, still grappling with her first statement.

"Mal, aren't you listening to me. These papers tell a great story, and if we had a book based on that story, it would be great publicity. People will flock here."

"I'm listening, I'm just having a hard time picturing you writing a book."

"I can do it. You'll see."

* * *

"I am so proud of you," said Malcom.

Those first two years of their dream were a blur of activity. The Inn was open and thriving and Polly's novel became a reality. She said nothing, but the smile on her face said it all. She gingerly reached into the box and took out a book. "Oh, Mal. Look," she said as she stared at the cover. "*The Captain's Quilt* by Polly Christian." She began to slowly turn it over and over in her hands, studying it from all angles.

Malcom took another copy from the box and did the same. Then he reached out and pulled her to him and wrapped her in a hug. "You did it," he whispered in her ear. Suddenly, she pulled away and let out a scream of joy and began jumping up and down like a five-year-old opening her first Christmas present. All he could do was stand there, grinning like an idiot as he shared her joy.

CHAPTER 13

MAX PICKED UP THE BOOK AGAIN. She'd call Patti shortly, but first, the ship was being battered by a storm and until all was safe, she couldn't put the book down.

* * *

The cook returned with some biscuits and cheese. "Beggin'
your pardon, Ma'am. The Captain had the cook fires put out so's
this is all I could bring you. The glass is still falling."
"What does that mean?"
". . . means that it looks to be a bad storm," he grunted as he
put the tray of food on the table and turned to leave. She thought
she detected something else in his voice and looked at him expecting
more, but he offered nothing. Her anxiety must have been obvious
because when he was in the doorway, he turned and looked at her
with something between pity and caring. Then he added, "She's a
stout ship. All will be fine."
She hadn't realized that she had been holding her breath
until she tried to speak and all that came out was a feeble "Oh."
Then he was gone before she could thank him for his kindness.
Christine was not reassured. The motion of the boat continued to
increase and she began to feel the effects. She opened the chest that
contained all the possessions for her new life and took out the quilt
that her mother had given her. It wasn't finished, and working
on it made her feel connected to her home and family. She closed
her eyes, pulled the quilt to her face, and inhaled deeply. If she
concentrated she could still smell home: the sweet fragrance of the
frangipani filling the air after an afternoon shower and the fresh
smell of the sea transported by the soft tropical breezes while coffee

brewed in the early morning. There would be no needlework on a night such as this, but just holding it still gave her comfort. For a moment she wished that she were still there, safe in the bosom of her family. Christine wedged herself into her berth and pulled the quilt tight around her.

The boat shuddered as a wall of water slammed against its side, and her dreams of home were gone in that instant, replaced by fear. A drop of water anointed her head. The shock of that small, cold drop ignited her imagination and she looked up, expecting to see a torrent of water about to flood her cabin. Instead of the expected torrent, another small drop landed on her face.

As the ship rose, fell, and twisted, each moment brought its own terror, but as those moments became minutes, and those minutes became hours, she began to notice subtle differences in how the ship reacted to Neptune's onslaught. At times the ship would attack. She would throw her bow and all her weight and strength into the oncoming waves as a woodcutter would drive his ax deep into a tree, the shock of the blow cleaving the wood and water. Other times, she was defensive as a wave hit from an unseen direction, and she would take the blow as would a fighter, outmatched by a superior foe, ducking and cowering, but still rising to continue the fight.

The small lantern in Christine's cabin swung violently back and forth. The shadows that it made danced on the walls like phantasms of another world, adding to her dread. But, as anxious and uncomfortable as the ever-increasing drips of water made her, as terrifying the motion as the ship slammed into the sea, and as disorienting the battle for light over darkness that was being waged by the swinging lantern, what scared her the most was the sound, or more precisely those random moments of silence that gave hope to a desperate situation.

The high-pitched whine of the wind in the rigging, the

moans and groans of the ship as it reeled from each blow that the sea hurled against it, and even the occasional faint and the desperate cries of men were nothing compared to the silence. Silence in the middle of the maelstrom. She didn't think it possible, but every now and then, she swore it was so. Sometimes it was only a pause and other times it lasted a moment, but it was enough to give her heart hope that the ordeal would end. Then, just as she would feel the light, darkness would return as the storm seemed to redouble its efforts to destroy the tiny ship, and her fears would return.

She prayed, she begged, she pleaded for the storm to end. Sleep was impossible. No sooner than she would close her eyes, the ship would lurch violently and her eyes would open wide. Demons, given shape and form by the flickering light of the swinging lantern, danced about her cabin, adding to her fear. And so it went through the night, with each hour feeling like a day.

CHAPTER 14

THE PHONE WOULD NOT stop ringing. Despite the storm, Max picked up the phone. Before she could even say "hello," Patti's voice grabbed her.

"I am so excited. Can you believe that Dave said yes to going up North with you and Jack?"

"Hey, Patti. Yes, I heard."

"We are going shopping." The excitement in Patti's voice was contagious. Next to photography, shopping was Patti's favorite pursuit.

"What about the guys?"

"They won't care. Dave told me that this place has miles and miles of running trails and since they are getting ready for that race, they'll want to go run in the woods. That means we'll be free to shop till we drop."

Patti had it all figured out. "And, as long as . . ."

Max cut her off. "Patti. Stop. There are running trails?"

"Yeah. Yeah. Didn't Jack tell you?"

"No. He seemed to have forgotten that part."

"Yeah. They can go run while we go shopping." Before Max could reply, she continued. "I'm so psyched."

"Patti, have you checked out this place?"

"Not really, I just know what Dave told me. Something about quilts."

"I did, but I must have missed the part about running trails. It's called The Quilt House and it goes back to the 1700s. Each room is named for a quilt."

"That's nice." Patti really didn't care; she was thinking only of shopping.

They talked for another five minutes before Max heard the sounds of two sets of feet on the stairs. Cat arrived first. She bounded up and jumped onto the arm of the couch, stopped, and stared at Max with a look that said, "I'm here." Then she began to purr. She climbed into Max's lap, head-butted, and then pushed her head into the phone as if to say, "Pay attention to me. Me. Me. Me."

"Cat. Stop it," Max said as she pushed the insistent cat away. "Patti, I've gotta' go. Jack just got back. Talk to you later . . . Bye."

She hung up the phone as Jack reached the top of the stairs. Cat, seeing his arrival, jumped down and began her "Feed me—I'm the center of the universe" dance.

"Hey, Max. What's up?"

"Not much. I've been chilling and reading and I just got off the phone with Patti. She's really excited."

"That's what Dave told me."

CHAPTER 15

"HELLO," MALCOM CALLED OUT as he pressed the door closed. The latch clicked and the small bell that was attached to the door jingled again. He looked around. As his eyes adjusted to the low light inside, he could see shelves and counters filled with the most eclectic assortment of stuff and it gave him hope.

He smiled. "*Timing is everything*," he thought to himself. It was the first week after Labor Day. Schools had started, so the summer crowds were absent. After nearly three decades of running the Inn, they had learned that this was the best time of year to go searching for new things with which to decorate the Inn, and this year it was his turn. The roads weren't so crowded and the tourists who remained seemed more relaxed.

The drive down to Essex, Massachusetts, had taken over two and a half hours. He had two reasons for choosing this destination. First, he had heard that there were many antiques shops in the Essex/Ipswich area, and second, Ipswich was where the Rockdog Run would be held in November. He was looking forward to running it for the first time. Today, if all went well, he would be able to get all of his treasure hunting done in time to go for a run on those trails before the long ride home.

He was studying a brass lantern when a voice close by startled him. "Oh, hello. I didn't hear the bell ring. I hope you haven't been here long."

Malcom jumped slightly and turned toward the voice as he put the lantern back down on a display case. "No. No. Not long at all," he stammered. In an effort to regain his composure, he reached out, offering his right hand in greeting to the man who had just appeared. "Hi, my name is Malcom Christian." The man just looked at him, making no effort to reach out to complete the handshake.

"My wife and I have a B&B up north in New Hampshire," Malcom continued in an attempt to engage the man.

Malcom withdrew his hand while the man continued to stare. "*Okaay,*" he thought to himself. As much as Malcom wanted to disengage, he could neither move to avoid the man's stare nor stop staring himself. What began as an awkward moment of silence between the two men was now becoming uncomfortable.

Malcom began to tick off in his mind the details of the man's appearance, hoping that the exercise would relieve his growing unease. His most distinctive feature was the extreme narrowness of his face. Second were his eyes. They were less like eyes than dark, black holes in the center of the large dark circles that surrounded them and were exaggerated by the exceptionally thick, round, seriously out of style, wire-rimmed glasses that were perched atop an equally narrow, hooked nose.

Of average size, he seemed smartly dressed, but on closer inspection, wasn't. His shirt, buttoned all the way up to his neck, had short sleeves, and the plaid fabric seemed to be something from a bygone time. Since the shop had no air conditioning and the day was quite warm, keeping it buttoned all the way up seemed like a curious choice to make. His slacks, though neatly pressed, also showed their age. His hair had clearly been brushed, giving the impression of fastidiousness, and yet there remained a touch of bed-headedness. A pair of well-worn running shoes completed the ensemble. Somehow, Malcom sensed that underneath his I-don't-get-out-much, nerdy appearance, he was actually quite fit.

"Can I help you find anything in particular?" The man's deep, but slightly nasal voice snapped Malcom out of his analysis.

"Oh, sorry. Like I said, my wife and I have a B&B up north and we are always looking for new things to change the look."

"Nautical? New England-countryside? Tools? Kitchen goods?" As he shot off questions, he continued to look straight into Malcom.

Malcom found this a bit unnerving, but he decided to chalk it up to eccentricity. He smiled and said, "I'm not sure." He hesitated then added, "I didn't catch your name."

"Alfred, Alfred Whitson."

"Nice to meet you Alfred." This time Malcom did not extend his hand. In an attempt to start a conversation, he began to tell Alfred about the Inn. "Our B&B is called The Quilt House, and each room is named for a particular quilt. When we bought it we found several old chests in the attic filled with different quilts. There's one we call The Captain's Quilt because it seems to tell a story of a sea voyage. Years ago, my wife wrote a novel and named it after that quilt. Maybe you've heard of it. *The Captain's Quilt* by Polly Christian?"

"I haven't."

"It was a long time ago. Well, anyway, I was looking for something nautical to play off that theme."

"*The Captain's Quilt.*" Alfred repeated the title. "Sounds interesting. That lantern, the one you were looking at, it came from a ship back in the late 1700s."

"No kidding. 1700s. How'd you come by it?" Alfred told him a story, but Malcom wasn't sure whether to believe him or not. Antiques dealers had a propensity to stretch the truth, although most were basically honest, and the value of what they were trying to sell was always so subjective and usually open to negotiation

Not yet ready to negotiate, Malcom continued his attempt to engage Alfred in conversation. He asked, "How'd you end up in this business?"

Reluctantly, Alfred answered the question. "My family originally came to this area in the early 1800s. My father came from a long line of merchant seamen, and my mom did sewing, mostly curtains. I had a twin brother, Thomas, but when we were twelve, he died."

"Twelve? That must have been tough. Did you have any other brothers or sisters?"

Alfred hesitated, then simply said, "No. Only the two of us."

Malcom could see how reluctant Alfred was in disclosing even this small tidbit of information so he didn't press him any further. He turned away and quietly continued his tour of the shop. Secretly he was glad Polly wasn't there because she would be interrogating Alfred mercilessly about whether or not he was married and anything else personal that she could tease out of him.

As silent as a shadow, Alfred followed Malcom around the shop. To Malcom's surprise, whenever Malcom stopped, Alfred would continue his story. "After my brother's death, my mother was never the same. She never really got over my brother's death. I ended up having to care for her. My father abandoned us and went back to sea. I heard he was washed overboard somewhere between here and England. After my mother died, I ended up being taken in by the couple who owned this place."

"You don't have to tell me all this," Malcom interjected. He hoped that if the story was cut short, Alfred would leave him alone.

"But you asked."

Before Malcom could reply, Alfred continued, "They never had any kids, and they kind of adopted me. It gave me an escape because they had so much cool stuff and everything had a story. I learned a lot. I could pretend to be anyone I wanted. It was how I dealt with things. As they got on in years, they promised me that I could have the place when they were gone. And that's how I ended up here."

Malcom didn't intend to encourage Alfred to keep talking, but without thinking, he asked, "What happened to your brother?" As soon as these words came out, he wished he could take them back.

Alfred stared at him for a long moment. Then he looked away and in a voice that was barely audible said, "He broke his neck."

An uncomfortable silence filled the store before Alfred abruptly turned back toward Malcom. He said, "Tell me more about your B&B."

This surprised Malcom, but as he shared more of the story, he relaxed. He was starting to feel more at ease when Alfred suddenly interjected, "Would you like that lantern?"

This abrupt change of topic caught Malcom by surprise, and before he knew it, he was the proud new owner of an eighteenth-century ship's lantern. It wasn't until Alfred went in search of a box that Malcom realized how late the day had become.

When Alfred returned, Malcom said, "Maybe you can help me with one more thing."

"What's that?" said Alfred. Malcom thought he detected a slight change in the tone of his voice, a wariness perhaps.

"I was hoping to go for a run before heading home. I'm planning on running a race later this fall that's down in this area, and I thought I might be able to check it out."

"What race?"

"The Rockdog Run. It's a trail marathon this November."

As soon as Malcom mentioned the Rockdog, Alfred seemed to perk up. "I've run it before. It's not far from here. I could take you over."

"You don't have to do that."

"It won't be a problem. I need a run, I'll go with you. It's easy to get lost."

"You run?" Malcom blurted out. This revelation shouldn't have surprised him, but it did. At the same time, it explained his impression that Alfred was more fit than he appeared. He quickly added, "Sure. That would be great."

CHAPTER 16

MALCOM FOLLOWED ALFRED'S OLD pickup truck and was surprised when he parked outside a school. There was no sign of the park.

"This is where the race begins. The park is out that way," he said, pointing out behind the school. "The race starts and finishes here. It's two twelve-plus mile loops. How far do you want to go?"

This was way more than Malcom had expected. "I hadn't thought a whole lot about that, maybe eight or nine."

Alfred looked up at the sky. "We'll have enough light for a full loop if you are up to twelve or so."

"Sure, I can do that. Not too fast I hope."

"No. Maybe a ten-minute pace."

"Perfect."

Together they walked toward the back of the school where the afternoon sports practices were in full swing. One of the coaches waved a hello in their direction and Alfred waved back. Malcom couldn't help but notice how awkward Alfred's return greeting seemed.

The pace was easy as they left the school property and headed down what Malcom assumed was a fire road. Without warning, Alfred took a sharp left-hand turn onto a single-track trail. The trail was all rocks and roots, many hidden by the underbrush that encroached on the trail and went relentlessly up. Once at the top, it began a series of descents and rises, punctuated with short, sharp switchbacks, not unlike a roller coaster. He didn't ease the pace as they charged up and down the trail. At one point, as they ran along a ridge above a ravine, Malcom commented on how a trip and fall off the trail could be a serious problem.

"It's easier . . . in the fall . . . when the leaves are off the trees. No matter . . . you do want to pay attention," Alfred said as he continued to lead the way. At one point the trail opened up in a clearing and Alfred slowed to a stop as Malcom caught up. "That's amazing," huffed Malcom. "I run trails . . . at home . . . all the time. We have sixty-five acres . . . out behind the B&B . . . and there are some hills . . . but none like that. Who knew."

"That's about the longest hill, and there are some fairly flat fire roads coming up, but it isn't the last hill either," said Alfred, his breathing already returned to normal.

"Thanks for the heads-up."

"Ready?"

"Let's go."

In spite of the fact that it was late afternoon and the trees provided great shade cover, it was hot and both men were drenched in sweat. Alfred had neglected to tell Malcom about the stretch of road that cut through a low, swampy area that had been flooded from the work of some beavers. It was maybe less than fifty yards in total, but the water was ankle high and there was no way not to get wet. Malcom hesitated before following Alfred across, swearing under his breath. Alfred was waiting for him on the other side and immediately offered an apology. "I thought it would be dry . . . It was two weeks ago . . . I guess the beavers have been busy."

"Not your fault . . . I'm just not a fan of running in wet shoes . . . although, it did feel pretty good."

After the water, Alfred slowed the pace a bit, and as they ran along he became quite chatty. He began asking more about the Inn. Malcom was flattered by Alfred's interest and answered his questions as best he could. He began to seem less strange, and Malcom thought about what a great equalizer running was. Even though abilities might differ, runners ran because they loved it, and out there, whether on roads or trails, they all shared the same experience, which was a large part of what made running unique.

Yet when Malcom began telling Alfred about the quilts, Polly's book, and the letters that inspired it, he sensed another odd change.

Alfred's questions became more pointed, more like an interrogation than casual interest. As he pressed for more details, Malcom began to feel uneasy. He tried to pick up the pace whenever he could, hoping that Alfred's interrogation would cease. This worked initially, but then, as soon as it was possible, Alfred began again. It was as if Alfred was using the lulls to digest what he had just learned, only to return with a new set of questions.

They had been out for nearly an hour and a half and Malcom was feeling the miles in his legs when they came off a particularly challenging section of single track. His heart was pounding and he needed a moment. "Al . . . ." That was all he got out, then he stopped.

Alfred, hearing his name, turned and looked back. He was already about a hundred yards away from Malcom, and all he could see was Malcom walking in small tight circles.

Alfred called out, "You okay?"

He didn't hear Malcom's response, but he did see him give a wave, so he turned and loped back.

As Alfred slowed and walked the last ten yards, Malcom huffed, "Sorry."

"You okay?"

The way he asked the question and the look on his face made Malcom wonder if maybe Alfred was deliberately pushing the pace to test him. He hesitated a moment before answering. "Yeah. That last stretch of single track was tough and I just needed a minute. I'm good to go now."

Alfred didn't say anything else. All he did was turn and begin running again, leaving it up to Malcom to catch up. The pace eased a bit, but it remained deliberately honest.

They spent the remaining thirty minutes running in silence, with Malcom running just behind and off Alfred's right shoulder. Mal could have run next to him, since there were no more single-track trails and the fire roads were plenty wide, but he couldn't shake the feeling of unease that he had felt with Alfred's questions earlier, and then the look and way he had acted when Mal had stopped to catch his breath. Somehow, he felt safer a bit behind. They ran on, their breathing and gravel-crunching footfalls becoming one in a perfectly wordless sync.

It wasn't until they made the turn back onto the school's athletic fields that there was any interaction between them. Alfred slowed, turned his head toward Malcom, and asked how he had enjoyed the run.

"It was good. You were right. I never would have been able to do that without a guide. Thanks."

"No problem." As they walked and cooled down, their conversation stayed on the run and the race. Malcom felt more relaxed, and he was glad that he had been able to get in the run.

The two men said goodbye, and then Malcom started his car. As he was about to pull away he was startled by a knocking on the passenger-side window. He looked up and was surprised to see Alfred staring in. He began to roll the window down, but before it was fully open, Alfred leaned over and in that strange nasally voice, said, "Your wife's book. What was the name of it again?"

Maybe it was the question, or perhaps it was the way that it was asked, but a chill ran down Malcom's spine despite the heat. "*The Captain's Quilt.*"

Without a word, Alfred turned away. After a few steps, he stopped, turned back, and said, "Thanks." There was an almost imperceptible hesitation before he added, "Have a safe ride home." Then, without another word he turned and walked off to his truck, leaving Malcom to shake off the chill.

CHAPTER 17

AFTER HIS RUN WITH MALCOM, Alfred stopped at the only used bookstore in town. To his delight, they had a dog-eared copy of Polly's book.

* * *

As the sun broke the horizon, its rays shining under the heavy clouds, they had the first hint that the storm was finally subsiding. Even though the ocean was still turbulent and the ship's motion had not yet eased, Christine could tell that something had changed. The wind, it was the wind. It no longer howled so in the rigging, and she could hear men moving about on deck. Christine remained huddled in her cabin, in her damp bed under her damp quilt. She heard the ship's bell toll the hour, then she fell asleep, a deep, badly needed sleep.

At first, the knocks seemed a part of her dream. Then, as her mind began to shift from the world of dreams to the present, the knocking continued. She jumped. Part of her now was fully awake, but another was still not sure of where she was. She sat up from under the tangle of covers and looked about. Another loud knock on the door propelled her from the comfort of her damp bed onto the still-pitching floor to the door, and she pulled it open.

The cook, hand raised and ready to knock again, was caught by surprise. "Oh, beggin' your pardon, Miss. The cook fires are lit again and I thought that you might like something hot to eat."

"How kind of you to think of me so." Fear has a way of killing one's appetite and now, at his suggestion of a hot meal, her hunger was overwhelming. "Yes. Yes, that would be very nice. Thank you."

"Ma'am." He turned away to leave, but before his first step, he turned back and said to her, "The Captain sends his regards."

Without giving her time to respond, he retreated hastily.

Food had never tasted so good, and when she had finished eating, she decided to go up onto the deck. She could tell by the motion of the ship—and the familiar sounds of schwooshing water against the hull as the ship cleaved its way through the ever-flattening sea—that the storm was truly over.

She braced herself in the doorway and looked out over the deck to the ocean beyond. The first thing that struck her was the color. The water wasn't the deep blue of home, and it wasn't the colder grey-blue that she had noticed as they had sailed further north. Instead there was a sort of greenish hue to it and it lacked clarity. The muddy quality was particularly fascinating because they hadn't seen land for weeks. Small breaks in the clouds let occasional sunrays illuminate the wave tops, while foam still dotted its surface.

The cry of an unseen seabird drew her gaze upward. The masts were still mostly bare, but the sails that were up were stretched full as they pulled the ship along. A work party was already hard at work washing the deck, and the seaweed and other detritus, which seemed to be everywhere, was slowly being returned to the sea.

She jumped when a hand touched her shoulder, and she spun around to see the Captain standing behind her. "That was quite a blow, but she's a good ship and we survived."

"Captain."

"Yes," he continued. "Yes, it was. I honestly feared we wouldn't survive." It was as if he were talking to himself and she were not there. He brushed past, making his way out onto the deck, shouting commands as he moved.

Christine decided that she would be better off back in her cabin.

CHAPTER 18

ALFRED GLANCED OVER AT THE CLOCK. It was after midnight, but he couldn't put the book down.

* * *

By sunset the ship had been returned to full working order. Because the wind had steadied and the sea had continued to flatten, more sail was added and once again they seemed to be flying across the sea. Christine had returned to the deck to watch as the sun dipped below the horizon amid a wash of pinks and reds.

"That's a good sign." Once again the Captain had silently come up behind her.

"Oh," she said turning. "What's a good sign?"

"The red sky. We'll have good sailing tomorrow."

"How much further? Until we reach Newport."

"Within the week, God willing and providing the wind holds fair."

"Thank you." She wanted to have more of a conversation, but it was obvious that he didn't, so again she returned to her cabin.

Dawn brought clear, blue skies. The wind held steady and when Christine came on deck, something felt different to her. At first she thought it was just the air, or perhaps the motion of the ship, but as she stood by the rail watching, she realized that it wasn't anything physical. The crewmembers on deck had a different air about them. They seemed cheerier, almost excited. "Could we be that much closer to our destination?" she thought to herself.

As she thought about this a cry was heard from the lookout. "Sail Ho!"

Instantly the entire crew was on deck. They were all looking off the port bow in the direction that he was pointing. A murmur went through the crowd as speculations were voiced as to what ship it might be. Christine looked to the horizon with everyone else, but she saw nothing. The cook was standing next to her, so she turned to him and said, "I fear that I do not see anything. How do they see whatever ship is out there?"

"It's a seaman's eye. We are so used to seeing only the sea and the sky that anything, even the tiniest speck on the horizon, becomes visible to us." Before he could say anything else, he suddenly became quiet.

Christine looked at him, wondering why the sudden silence. She was about to say something when the Captain's voice rang out close behind, startling her.

"Lookout. Report."

"Aye Captain. There . . . Off the port bow—a sail."

She turned and watched as the Captain drew the telescope that was in his hand to his eye and scanned the ocean. The crew was silent as they awaited his pronouncement. He lowered the glass, snapped it shut, and said only, "Carry on," before turning and going below.

As soon as he was out of sight, the buzz began as everyone on deck had something to say about the mysterious sails that were seen and the Captain's seemingly odd behavior. Christine continued to stare at the horizon, seeing nothing but the blue sea. Frustrated at not being able to see anything and puzzled by the Captain's sudden departure, she returned below.

At the bottom of the stairs, she paused, glancing toward the Captain's door. It was ajar and she could see that he was pacing, holding a piece of paper. Curious, she began to step toward his door. Suddenly the door flew open and he rushed past. He took the steps two at a time and disappeared on deck. Christine wasn't sure that he had even seen her. Before continuing back to her cabin, she took one more look toward his cabin. Then, compelled by his strange behavior, she returned to the deck.

The Captain stood at the rail, his glass trained on the horizon. Christine focused her eyes in the same direction as the tip of his telescope. For the briefest of moments she thought she saw a flash of white on the horizon. Thus encouraged, she continued to stare until she saw that flash again.

She was not alone in staring at the white speck on the horizon. Over and over the Captain lifted his glass, stared, lowered it, and then started the process again. All the while, that small white speck grew in size. It was still too far off to know for sure whether it was a friend or foe, merchant or warship, pirate or privateer, and she felt the same tension that every member of the crew seemed to be feeling.

All the while the Captain continued to study that ever-growing speck. Suddenly, he lowered his telescope from his eye, and with a loud snap, closed it with such force that for just a moment, all eyes were on him. Then, turning to the first mate, he spoke several commands that produced a flurry of activity. Christine watched as a set of colorful flags were hoisted into the rigging. "What is going on?" she asked as member of the crew rushed past.

"We're to rendezvous," was the fleeting reply.

The tension on deck that she had felt before was now replaced with excitement and the anticipation of meeting this other ship.

CHAPTER 19

Meeting another ship in the middle of the ocean rarely happened and when it did, it usually had a bad outcome. Now the Captain had ordered signals flown and course changed so that the two ships would deliberately come together. For the next several hours time alternately passed both terribly slowly and incredibly quickly as the two ships closed on each other.

Christine remained on deck. She found a place where she could keep that speck of white in her sight, as if that would make all the difference in meeting or not, while remaining out of the way of the crew as they prepared for the meeting. She was fascinated at how it seemed that for the longest time no progress was made, but then, after she looked away for what seemed like only a moment, when she looked back the ship was considerably closer. Several hours passed as that patch of white on the horizon slowly grew in size. Then, for one magical moment, as her ship rose to the top of a large wave, the other also rose to the top of a wave, revealing itself for the first time. And then it was gone, leaving once again only that patch of white sails against the blue sky and the darker ocean.

But now the activity on deck increased, with cries and shouts and much running about. To Christine it seemed nothing more than chaos, but every face reflected a purpose, as did every motion.

The Captain returned to the deck and Christine noticed that in addition to his telescope, a sword now hung from his waist and a pistol had been wedged into his waistband. For the first time, her excitement and wonder were replaced with fear. She made her way from her vantage point where she had been able to observe their progress and the workings of the crew, over toward the Cap-

tain. With glass raised to his eye, he was so intent on watching the other ship, she had to clear her throat in an effort to engage him. "Ahem. Captain. I apologize for disturbing you, but as we near that ship, I can't help but wonder if what we do is not foolish since I now see you with sword and pistol."

Slowly he lowered the glass from his eye and turned toward her. His gaze was intense, but the tone of his reply was actually soothing. "Fear not. We have exchanged signals with that ship. I know of the captain and he sails for your uncle."

"Then why do you wear sword and pistol?"

"'Tis the way of the sea." Then he turned away from her and lifted his glass in the direction of the other ship.

Christine understood that she had been dismissed and that no further conversation would be forthcoming. She retreated back to her corner of the deck still not understanding why he was so armed when his words offered no hint of concern.

As the other ship approached, she could see that its hull was black and the sails that had seemed so white and pure from afar were actually well worn, patched, and even to her unseamanly eye, dirty. The ship had an air of hard use about it that bordered on abuse. The two ships were now less than a quarter of a mile apart, and having hove to, each ship's crew watched the other with curious intensity.

The other ship lowered a boat and Christine watched as a half dozen men, stroke by stroke, drew near. Their arrival was announced by a great commotion, but she could no longer see them since she was not in a position to see over the side. The Captain remained motionless in the center of the deck.

The first man to climb over the rail onto the deck was a stocky, dangerous looking man. His hair and beard were unkempt, and his clothes were as worn and patched as the sails on his ship.

The Captain made no move toward him, nor did he step

toward the Captain. While he waited for the five other men to climb over the rail and join him on the deck, his dark, rat-like eyes nervously darted about, in much the way a wild animal would when placed in a new setting. Christine held her breath, both fascinated and terrified by this man. Then, just as the last man climbed over the rail, his eyes found hers and her heart went cold. His gaze seemed to bore deep into her and she spun away to hide from his sight, gasping for breath as she did so.

"Welcome aboard," she heard the Captain say. She turned back, and saw that she was no longer of interest to him as he was now focused on the Captain. The smile on his face seemed forced and their greeting, while cordial, was not the greeting of two old friends. Words were being spoken, and as they spoke, he withdrew an envelope from his coat and handed it to the Captain. The Captain only glanced at it before putting it in his coat. She could not hear what else was said. However, after a moment, the stranger turned and spoke to his men. Then, turning back to the Captain, he nodded and they headed below.

After an awkward moment of silence, the crews of both ships became one amid much fuss and bother. Their gestures and the sounds of their voices spoke more of a shared common bond, than did the cold cordiality of the two captains. Again, Christine became uneasy when she saw several heads turn in her direction. From the many gestures and laughter that ensued, she knew that she was the object of their attentions. She turned and retreated toward the safety of her cabin below.

Once below, she had to pass the Captain's door, which was ajar, and as she did so, the sounds of serious conversation could be heard. Again her curiosity was piqued, so she paused outside the door. Hardly daring to breathe, she looked in while straining to hear what was being said. The guest had his back to the door and the Captain stood opposite, holding what she presumed to be the

*letter in his hand. She tried to understand the look on his face as
he stared at him. Was it shock? Dismay? Disbelief? She couldn't be
sure. Their words were muffled, but the few she did understand
spoke of unrest and disharmony. She was about to move closer
when the sounds of voices about to descend the stairs gave her a
start and she quickly fled to her cabin lest she be caught.*

*She pressed her door shut and, leaning against it, inhaled
deeply and held her breath lest the sounds of her breathing lead
to her discovery. She could hear footsteps approaching. She prayed
they would pass by. They didn't. There was a knock. She exhaled
and took several breaths, hoping to still her pounding heart before
answering that knock. That unseen hand rapped again, and this
time she heard the cook's voice through the door. "Beggin' your
pardon, Miss. The Captain has requested your presence."*

*The sound of his kindly voice calmed her and she opened the
door. He repeated what he had just said: "Beggin' your pardon,
Miss. The Captain has requested your presence."*

*"Thank you," she said, stepping out of her cabin as he turned
toward the Captain's door. She followed.*

*The cook's knock on the door pushed it open wider. Christine
saw the Captain quickly turn and place on the table behind him
the piece of paper he had been holding. Then, turning back, he
said in a strong voice, "Come."*

*The cook pushed the door fully open and retreated, leaving
her alone in the doorframe. The two men were standing, facing
the door, in front of the Captain's table. This time there was no
hiding as the Captain's guest stared at her. As she had noted before,
his appearance was unkempt, with his clothing in need of replacement for there was little that had not been repaired many times.
He was stout and looked to be a powerful man, one who would
be a formidable adversary in a fight. His beard was flecked with
grey and was in need of trimming, and what skin was exposed*

was rough, ruddy, and pocked. His eyes were close-set, as black as night, and moved about constantly. Only when he stared directly at her did they become still, and she could feel them bore into her with a gaze so intense that she could almost feel him undressing her. She shivered, then crossed her arms in front and held herself as if to prevent her clothes from being removed.

The Captain stood with his hands clasped behind his back, blocking her view of the table. She had the feeling that it was not for her to see whatever was on it. She hesitated, then, he motioned at her to step forward. Tentatively, she moved toward the two men as he said, "Miss Armitage, this is Mr. Josiah Whitbey." Then he added, even though he had already said so to her on deck, "He is an old friend of your uncle's in Newport, Rhode Island."

Alfred stopped. He stared at the page and reread that last sentence: ". . . this is Mr. Josiah Whitbey. He is an old friend of your uncle's in Newport, Rhode Island." He couldn't believe what he was reading. He grabbed some papers covered in scribblings and shuffled through them until he found a particular one. His eyes widened as he read what he had written. His hand began to shake. He looked again at the book, then at his notes, then back at the book again. Countless times his eyes went from one to the other. Each time his heart beat more rapidly and he began to smile. His mind was racing. He had to be the one and the same: the man responsible for his family's misfortunes. Alfred never considered the fact that what he was reading was a novel, fiction. At that moment, in his mind, those made-up characters of Polly's were very real. Any fatigue he may have felt was now long gone. Flush with this new knowledge, he picked up her book and continued.

She was terrified and all she could say was a very faint "Sir," with a slight curtsy.

His voice was as rough as his look as he said, "Miss Armitage, you are as pretty as your uncle said you were."

That statement surprised her, which made her feel even

more uneasy. They made no further attempt at conversation, and after an awkward pause, the Captain dismissed her with a curt, "Thank you, Miss Armitage. You may go."

She understood his meaning and replied, "Sir." Then summoning a stronger voice, she turned her head to face his guest and said, "Mr. Whitbey, it was a pleasure." With that she curtsied again, turned, and walked out. As she pulled the door shut she heard Whitbey say, "She's a lovely girl."

She did not hear the Captain's response because the door clicked shut. Whitbey's words were innocent enough, but something about the way he said them made her uneasy. She returned to her cabin, and it wasn't until she had pulled the door shut tight that those feelings of unease began to release their grip on her.

CHAPTER 20

As she watched the boat pull away, with Mr. Whitbey sitting in the stern, hand on the tiller, there was a flurry of activity as the crew began the ritual of setting sail. They were already underway by the time Mr. Whitbey reached his ship, and as they sailed past, she could see him on the deck. She saw his head turn, his gaze following them, and there was no doubt in her mind that his attention was focused on her. She shivered and turned away.

She did not look again until Mr. Whitbey's ship was far behind them. His sails were up and they were moving rapidly in the opposite direction. It didn't take long for his ship to become a white handkerchief against the dark sea. Moments later it was a mere speck on the horizon. Then it was gone and they were once again alone.

The sun had disappeared over the horizon at nearly the same time that Mr. Whitbey's ship had disappeared. The night air was cool so Christine turned to go below to her cabin. As she turned, the cook approached and inquired if she was hungry. Until that moment, because of all the excitement, she hadn't given food any thought, but now, with its mention, she realized just how hungry she was.

"I am," she replied. He said that he would bring supper to her cabin.

Consequently, she expected that the sudden knock on her cabin door announced that food had arrived, but when she opened it, instead of the cook with her tray, she was face to face with the Captain.

"Miss Armitage, would you join me in my cabin for supper?" His invitation was phrased as a question, but there was no doubt

that she was not being given a choice. Before she could muster a reply, his intent was clarified. "I saw the cook and instructed him that you would be joining me. He is just now arriving."

All she could say was, "Of course. Thank you."

"Good." And with that he turned and strode toward his cabin. She paused a moment, then followed.

Perhaps it was because of her hunger, but the dinner was splendid. The Captain even offered her wine. It wasn't long before the awkward silence that had begun the meal was replaced with polite conversation and laughter.

Perhaps emboldened by the wine, Christine suddenly asked, "Captain, tell me more about Mr. Whitbey."

With that question, she could feel the atmosphere change as a chill descended upon the table, and she knew that she had made a mistake. His smile remained, but now it seemed forced.

"Why do you ask?" Even as he spoke, she could sense that he was trying to mask the tension in his voice.

"I know little about ocean voyages, but it struck me as unusual that we should have run into another ship, a ship whose master was an old friend of my uncle's. Also, he didn't strike me as a very nice man, and I find it hard to believe that he and my uncle know each other, let alone are friends."

"Mr. Whitbey may seem a hard man, but he is a man of great character and a fine seaman."

"Tell me, then, how he knows my uncle."

"As you know, your uncle is a successful merchant in Newport. Mr. Whitbey is one of many shipmasters, like myself, who set sail for your uncle. Simply, he finances the voyage and upon our return, benefits from the profits. Your uncle has been both lucky and shrewd, and as such he is now one of the wealthiest men in Newport."

"I saw Mr. Whitbey hand you a letter. Was it word from my

uncle?"

    If the atmosphere at the table had cooled when she had first asked about Mr. Whitbey, then with this last question it truly froze over. He stiffened and offered no explanation other than a hard look. From his demeanor, she understood that she had pressed too far and that to ask anything further would be a mistake. She said nothing more and simply looked down at her plate. Whatever conviviality had existed before was now gone, and dinner was finished with little more conversation before she returned to her cabin.

CHAPTER 21

Since the start of the voyage many things had changed. Her cabin, which had seemed so much a cell, had now become her sanctuary. The motion of the ship, which once made her wish for death, now felt soothing. The creaks and groans of the working ship, which had terrified her before, now were like music in her ears. Alone in her cabin, with her quilt pulled close, her thoughts turned to home.

That night she had dinner with the Captain, sleep had come easily, but it had not been comforting or restful. At first light, she jerked awake and it took a moment for her to understand where she was. The dream she had been in was fading fast. People and places that only moments before were so real, now were just shapeless phantoms, memories without form or substance. She knew that something was wrong, but what?

The following day, whether on deck or in her cabin, that dream stayed in her thoughts, and it blended with real events until she couldn't separate them. Even though the details had faded, its impressions had remained so vivid that she began to question what was real and what was imagined. Images flashed in and out of her head, but as soon as she tried to summon them for further consideration, they disappeared. It mattered not what she tried—those faces, places, and events remained just out of reach.

The one image that never changed and remained strong was that brief glimpse of the two men as she had walked by the Captain's door. In the Captain's hand was the letter that Whitbey had handed him on deck when he arrived. Whitbey was standing with his back to the door and their movements and muffled words spoke of serious matters. Then later, when she had been summoned to the Captain's cabin to formally meet Mr. Whitbey, the atmosphere was strained and the meeting short. Dream and reality had become as one and she began to question her sanity. She had to know.

As the last rays of the sun dipped below the horizon, Christine looked to the east at the great darkness that was fast approaching. Then, turning to the west, she watched as the final vestiges of light from the now set sun were slowly overtaken by the eastern darkness. The ocean remained calm, as the ship, driven by a steady breeze, continued on toward its final destination. But the serenity of the moment was broken when she heard some voices. She turned to see the Captain, who had just come on deck, gesturing while speaking to the mate on watch. He was clearly agitated and she didn't wish to be witness to his temper, so she returned to her cabin.

Descending the stairs, she could hear his voice as he continued to berate the crew for some unknown offence. As she approached his cabin, she saw that the door was ajar. Curious, she moved toward the door and looked through the narrow opening. Inside, she could see the table, the one that Mr. Whitbey and the Captain had been standing in front of. The image of Mr. Whitbey handing the Captain a letter when he first arrived on board flashed through her head. Then she saw a pile of charts and papers. Irrational thoughts filled her head. She had to know what was in that letter.

Even as every bit of her being cried "No," she put her hand on the door. Taking a deep breath, she considered again what she was about to do. She withdrew her hand and was about to walk away when she turned back. Her hand, as if guided by some unseen force, pushed the door open and she went in.

With her heart pounding, she crossed to the table. It was covered with charts and other papers with strange numbers and markings. She stopped in front of the table, scarcely daring to breathe. Then, tentatively at first, she lifted the corner of a large chart, cautiously peering underneath as if fearful that a serpent lurked underneath. Yet there was no serpent, only more charts and papers. Emboldened and forgetting time, she pawed through the pile. Then, at the very bottom, she saw what she was sure was the letter that Whitbey had handed to the Captain. She slid it out from under the pile and began to read.

"No!" Her thoughts screamed in disbelief as she read the letter. Fighting to keep her hands from shaking she began to read it again. Suddenly she realized that the voices above her had ceased. Hurriedly she pushed the letter back under the pile of charts and fled his cabin. She reached her own just as his first steps landed on the stairs. Her heart was pounding and she was gasping for breath when she fell into her bed and pulled the quilt over her head, as if hiding under it would provide sanctuary and keep her safe.

CHAPTER 22

She closed her eyes, but sleep would not come. The guilt of knowing what she had done and the fear of discovery made sleep impossible. Every creak, every moan of the ship as it sailed through the night, now sent a shiver of fear through her body as she expected that each sound was a precursor to the discovery of what she had done. With each passing hour their journey was that much closer to completion. She thought about the Captain and what he might do if he found out. She had already witnessed his temper, and as she lay there, Christine was convinced that if he found out, she might very well end up overboard with no one the wiser. Whatever tale he offered about her disappearance would be believed because of his stature and standing. No one on board would speak on her behalf, if for no other reason than fear.

No, she had to come up with some way to ensure that if she didn't make it to Newport alive, what she knew would be told. As she huddled under her quilt, an idea began to form in her head. At first it seemed impossible, only a wild fantasy, too risky to even attempt. But, as the night wore on, the idea never left her thoughts. Even when she dozed off, it continued in her dreams. By dawn, she had decided that it could work and she began to set her idea in motion.

First, and most important, she must not allow the Captain to have any suspicions. Things would have to be as they had been throughout the journey, and her first action would be to apologize to him for her impertinence at dinner last evening. Prior to that dinner, they had had little contact other than brief encounters on deck, and that is how it needed to continue. With this settled in her head, her eyes closed, and it wasn't until well past sunrise that she awoke to the sound of knocking on her door. As she untangled herself from the covers a voice came through the door.

"Miss, Miss." She recognized that it was the cook's voice.

"Yes," she replied through the closed door.

"Miss. It is late and you weren't up at first light. I began to worry. I brought you some breakfast. You need to eat."

"Thank you. Just leave it by the door. I'm not yet dressed and I'll get it as soon as I am able."

He did not reply, but she did hear him place the tray on the floor and shuffle away.

As soon as the footsteps were gone, she cautiously pulled the door open a crack, peered out, and saw only the tray of food that had been left. As she ate, her thoughts returned to her plan. It still seemed possible.

When she finally went on deck, the Captain was there. In short order her apologies were accepted and her racing heart began to still. It was some time later in the afternoon that the Captain approached her. He had just returned to the deck and had a look of satisfaction about his person. "Miss Armitage, I have just finished checking my calculations, and if the wind remains fair, we should be in port in time for supper in three days."

"That is wonderful news. I shall pray for continued fair winds when I retire this evening."

Nothing else was said. Then he nodded his head and strode away, leaving Christine alone with her thoughts.

CHAPTER 23

ONLY THE RISING SUN greeted him as he finished the book. When the last page was read and the cover closed, he sat on the edge of his bed, not exactly sure what to do next. He would figure that out soon enough. Slowly, a grin formed across his face. Suddenly he found himself pacing back and forth, that grin, now a smile, frozen on his face, The sounds of his footsteps on the wide pine floors were the only sounds other than his pounding heart and the occasional creaks and moans of the old house. A celebration was in order. He raised his arms as if in victory over a fallen foe in the arena, shouting, "Alfred! Alfred! I figured it out."

Then he did a sort of celebratory jig, halting only when he remembered that he was alone. Alfred, his twin, was long dead. He stopped and sat back on the edge of the bed. The silence returned, and save for the sounds of the celebration that still echoed in his head, it remained his only companion.

Still, his elation held firm. He was dazzled by how much the story meshed with what he knew, thought he knew and made up. In his mind it was the explanation he had looked for his entire life. It was the key and now he knew where he had to go to find the rest of the answers. He wanted to cry out, but he didn't. He just sat on the edge of his bed, continuing to revel in that feeling of triumph and success.

He looked over at the pillows that were still stacked against the headboard, his imprint still fresh. The book was lying on top of the covers, tipping ever so slightly into the dent that remained from his body. Scattered across the bed were sheets of paper—the notes that he had pulled from Polly's fiction, notes that had become, to him, the facts about his family's history, supporting the story that he had created while growing up in the antiques store.

So many years gone by, so much time spent looking for clues, and now, when he least expected it, the answers were just given to him. Luck? Fate? He didn't know or care. The final pieces to the puzzle that had been his life were within his reach and soon, very soon, his family's honor would be restored, wrongs would be righted, and the final vindication would be his as he extracted the justice so long overdue.

For the first time in ages he felt content, and in that moment he realized how tired he was. He lay back across his bed. The papers crinkled as his body crushed them, but it didn't matter. What mattered was what he now knew. Her novel gave shape, form and definition to the dream he had had since childhood.

The dream was always the same. In it, his father's ship was set afire and he watched from shore as it burned. As the fire spread up the masts, the sails looked like so many arms and hands, flailing in agony until they were completely consumed by the flames and all hope was gone. His father was ruined, betrayed by other jealous merchants.

He closed his eyes, the smile still on his face, and fell into a deep sleep.

CHAPTER 24

"HONEY, I'M HOME," Malcom called out as he stepped into the kitchen after coming in through the back door. He always announced his arrival that way, whether she was in sight or not. It was their thing.

Polly was busy working at the sink washing some vegetables. She turned her head slightly and said, "Hi Mal. How was the trip?"

"It was great. I found this really great lantern from a ship that will be perfect for the Captain's suite."

He placed the box on the table while she stopped what she was doing and faced him. She took in his outfit and said, "You're in your running stuff." Even though she phrased it like a statement, it was obviously meant as a question.

"Yeah. I finished early enough to be able to go for a run where that trail race will be held later this fall."

She picked the box up and, giving it a shake, asked, "What trail race?"

"You remember, early November, trail marathon, The Rockdog. I've been planning on this for months now."

Polly nodded her head yes, but her recollection of that was fuzzy at best. She didn't always pay attention to his running. She just didn't get it.

"Anyways, the shop owner where I got this lantern turned out to be a runner. He's a bit odd, . . . no, different, but he offered to go run the course with me. I'm glad he did because I would still be lost in the woods had I gone by myself."

Polly was paying only cursory attention to what he said as she opened the box. All she heard was *run, odd man, lost in woods.* "Oh Mal, it's perfect," she said as she took the lantern out of the box. "Where did you get it?"

"I just told you."

"No, you didn't. You said something about a strange man and getting lost in the woods."

He took a breath. "Pol, I found the lantern, in a store in Essex, Massachusetts."

She looked up at him, questions in her eyes.

"It's right next to Ipswich where the race is." he continued. "There are a lot of antiques stores around there. The shopkeeper was a runner so he went with me, and it's a good thing he did because I would have been lost in the woods."

"That was nice of him."

"It was, but he was definitely a bit odd."

"Mm-hmm." Clearly, she was still more fascinated with the lamp than the details. Turning back to her vegetables she simply said, "This is perfect."

CHAPTER 25

MAX CLOSED THE BOOK.

"Finished?" asked Jack.

"Yes," was her satisfied reply.

He had never seen her so consumed by a book. Secretly he was glad that she had finished, so he wouldn't have to share her with the story anymore.

"I can't wait. Only three weeks," she said.

Jack looked over at her. The puzzled look on his face must have been enough because he didn't have to say a word before she continued. "The Quilt House. Our trip up north, with Patti and Dave."

"Right, yeah, the trip."

"Jack, it was your idea, and it will be fun. Patti and I can shop while you guys run and do guy things all day." Then she added, almost as an afterthought, "Maybe I'll make a quilt."

"You'll what?"

"Make a quilt. This book has inspired me."

"You're k- kidding?" stammered Jack. "You want to make a quilt?"

"What's with the look?"

"Max, you've never done anything like that in your life. You don't even like to sew. What makes you think you can make a quilt?"

"Jack, stop being such a negative Nancy. There's a lot about me you don't know."

"*Probably true, but I do know that you have never sewn anything in your life*," he thought to himself. What he said was, "You're right, I don't know everything about you, and that's what I love, the mystery that is you. If you want to make a quilt, then go for it."

"I will." And with that she picked up a pencil and a piece of paper and began sketching.

He loved Max dearly and he was always the first one to encourage her to do new and interesting things, but right now he wanted some Max-and-Jack time. The past few weeks she had been working a lot at Ben's. The summer staff had returned to their various universities, so she was taking on extra hours. Their time together was limited, and it seemed that all she had wanted to do when she wasn't working was read that book.

"I'm going out for a run," he announced, hoping she'd try to delay him.

"Okay, see you when you get back," was her distracted reply.

As he headed down the road, he thought, "*Well, on the brighter side, I'm getting in some extra mileage and that will make Rockdog easier.*"

His intention was only to run four or five miles, just enough to feel good, but not so much as to temper his desires for Max. He fully intended to seduce her upon his return. He was in the zone when a car horn startled him. It was Max. She slowed to match his pace, and through her open window she shouted that she was on her way over to Patti's and that she'd be back later. All he could do was exhale a "no problem." With that she blew him a kiss and drove off.

As she pulled away, he considered altering his course and increasing the distance. So far he had run nearly three miles. "What the hell," he said to himself. Then he thought, "*She'll be at Patti's for a while; might as well make the most of this since I've gone this far.*"

He was feeling good so he took the next turn, knowing that now his run would be at least ten miles. "*Maybe we'll get home at the same time. I'll need a shower . . .*" He grinned, convincing himself that his idea would work, despite every indication that there wasn't a chance in hell.

* * *

As Jack slowly walked up his drive, he noted that Max wasn't back yet. However, Cat did come out to greet him.

"So, she's not back yet," said Jack as he bent over to scratch Cat's head.

"Mrowh," was her answer. She started purring as she head-butted his leg. Then she quickly backed off as she realized that he was dripping with sweat.

"I know. I know. Come on. Let's go in." He stood and as he walked toward the door, Cat pranced ahead. As soon as they were upstairs she began to nag him for dinner. While she talked and wound herself around his legs, he began stripping off his wet clothes. She skittered away when he dropped his shirt, avoiding it as it landed on the floor. She turned, stared at him, and mrowed loudly, as if to say, "Hey, watch what you're doing—and by the way, where's my food?"

"Okay, okay. I get the message. You want supper," he said to her. She paused in her tirade, looked at him, and said in a much smaller, more coy voice, "Rowh."

"As soon as I take my shower, I'll feed you."

Cat gave him one more look, turned, and walked away mrowing to herself, obviously put out that he wasn't a bit more responsive to her demands.

"Pissy bitch," he said under his breath.

Cat stopped, gave him a look that said, "I heard that," and offered one more, loud mrow before disappearing around the corner. Once again, she had the last word.

After his shower, Jack finally fed Cat. Then he called Dave to ask if he had seen the girls.

"They were here, but they left quite a while ago. I don't think they'll be back anytime soon."

"Let me guess. Max has got Patti all sucked into her quilt project and they are out looking at material."

"That's about it. I think you created a monster with this idea of going to that Quilt House."

"You might be right, but at least we'll be able to get in some good trail running while they do their thing."

"True enough."

There wasn't much else to say so the conversation ended. Jack got a beer from the fridge, returned to the couch, sat down, and immediately had a very happy, satisfied cat in his lap. Max had left the book on the couch so he picked it up and began reading.

He didn't hear the door open or Max coming up the stairs. He had enjoyed the first few pages, but the combination of the ten-mile run and Cat's mojo had put him sound asleep. It wasn't until he felt Max's warm breath on his neck, followed by a soft kiss, that he opened his eyes.

"Hey, sleepy."

"Max. I didn't hear you come in. What time is it?"

"Patti and I had a great time shopping." She didn't answer his question, so he knew that it was late.

"Did you eat?" he asked as he struggled to sit up. Cat, obviously put out that she had to move, jumped off his lap and retreated to find a quieter place.

"We didn't. How 'bout we go get Chinese?"

There was something in her voice that triggered a very private memory involving Mai Tais and Chinese food. He grinned. "Sounds like a great idea. The Wok?"

* * *

"Do you have any idea how special you are to me?" Max whispered in his ear. She was as light as a feather and all he felt was her warmth and the softness of her skin as she lay on top of him.

"No, how? Tell me," he whispered back.

She moved ever so slightly, pressing closer, and breathed in his ear, "No. How about I show you?"

Neither said another word as their bodies did all the talking. Then they fell deeply asleep in each other's arms.

CHAPTER 26

"HEY POLLY, I'M GOING OUT for a run," Malcom shouted. He didn't wait for a response—wasn't even sure she was still indoors—because at breakfast he had already mentioned that this was his plan for the afternoon.

The trails he had gradually cut in over the property's sixty-five acres—just over one square mile—zigged, zagged, and looped around throughout the area, so it was possible to run many miles before starting to repeat sections. At key spots he had also erected signposts pointing back to the Inn, so it was pretty hard to get truly lost, although on several occasions guests found that their hike took longer than they had planned.

Today his run was more about time spent than miles run. He intended to run for at least three hours, and as he went out the door, he took with him a small red backpack that contained several bottles of water, sports drink, and some packets of energy gel. He would leave the backpack at the most crossed intersection in the maze of trails so he could easily get a drink or snack during his run.

As he trotted across the backyard and adjoining field to where the trails began, he smiled in anticipation of a good run. The mid-September heat wave had ended earlier in the week. Now it was about sixty-five degrees and the day would only get cooler, perfect for running. Gone was any hint of humidity, and a light breeze from the northwest was blowing and rustling the changing leaves in the trees. The Inn was almost completely booked for leaf-peeping season so he knew that this might be his last opportunity for such a long run.

At the edge of the field, where the woods began, he turned. Polly was walking toward the garden. He waved and when she saw him, she waved back. She smiled as if she were up to something, but he didn't stop to chat. Even though the lightweight pack on his back was riding comfortably, he was looking forward to taking it off and being truly unfettered for his run.

CHAPTER 27

MALCOM HAD BEGUN TO break a sweat by the time he reached the place where he planned to leave the backpack. The clearing was like the hub of a wheel where several trails all came together. Once, there had been a giant maple tree at this spot, but now all that remained was its stump. The tree had split one winter during an ice storm and had to be taken down. Whenever he was here he remembered how much effort it took to cut that tree up and turn it into firewood, and how that one tree had kept them warm for an entire winter. Now he put the backpack on the stump, had a quick sip of water, checked his watch, and began to run.

The trail he chose to run first was the longest of the loops that circled back to the clearing. The footing was clean, soft, and fast. Over the years, as he cut the trails into the woods, he tried to make sure that each loop had its own personality. One loop had several challenging hills; another was pure single track with few spots where two people could walk, run, or ski next to each other. Another shared part of its way with the fire road that ran from the main road through his property and alongside of the creek.

He planned to divide his run into thirds. The first third would be in the woods, on his trails. This would get him warmed up and into the groove. Then he'd head out onto the town's roads for the next hour before returning to the woods to finish the day.

Almost before the clearing disappeared from sight, a huge grin took over his face. Had anyone else been around to see him run by, they might have thought him deranged, or possibly in intense pain. His stride quickly lengthened, his breath became regular, and his heart rate steadied. He didn't even hear the soft crunchy sound of his feet striking the ground. It was as if he were floating over the trail. A jay called out, warning of his approach, and then a squirrel chirped, repeating the warning as it skittered through the brush to the safety of a nearby tree. It was perfection, and as much as he wished he could share that moment, he was selfishly glad that he had it all to himself.

That first hour passed quickly and it wasn't until he turned out of the woods and onto the road, that things began to change. His stride still felt comfortable, his breathing remained easy, but the intense pleasure he had felt was no longer there. Now, he had to share his run with others; a car would approach and pass by or he'd pass someone out walking or riding a bike. It didn't matter that they might have been experiencing the day much as he was; for him it just wasn't the same.

The thing about running on winding country roads is that you can never completely relax. You can hear birds, but you can't afford to listen for them; you have to listen for cars. Too often, the seeming emptiness of the road—with its rises and dips, zigs and zags—leads drivers to imagine that they are somewhere they are not, and they don't always notice things like runners on the side of the road.

Malcom was reminded of this suddenly when a truck came around a curve and nearly hit him. He was forced to jump off the road, almost falling in the brush. It all happened so fast he didn't even have time to yell at the driver or flip him the bird.

As he climbed out of the brush and back onto the road, he was sputtering a blue streak and had to take several deep breaths to calm down. Instinctively, he started running again, and it took at least a quarter of a mile before his breathing and heart rate had returned to where they should be. It was another quarter of a mile before he began to feel comfortable. He tried to remember the truck: its color, the license plate, anything that in his mind would help him identify it so that he could tell the driver just what he thought if he ever saw him again. Nothing. He only remembered that it was a truck and that he had ended up in the brush.

It wasn't like the movies where every detail is remembered and at some time in the future, retribution meted out. He thought about this phenomenon until he turned off the road and back onto the fire road that would bring him back onto his trails. When he reached the clearing, he checked his watch. Perfect. He had been out for two hours. He squeezed a packet of gel into his mouth, washed it down with some sports drink, watered a tree, checked his watch again, and started his last hour.

This time he ran in the opposite direction. He took the more challenging loops first and left the best for last. The single track trail, and then the hills, reminded him of that run at The Willows with Alfred, whom he had not thought about since that day. "*Good runner,*" he recalled now, "*but odd. Maybe those two qualities aren't totally exclusive to each other.*"

The hard loops finished, he slowed a bit as he began the last loop. He had started his run on this loop, and it was the perfect way to end it. He checked his watch. He would meet his goal of three hours. He felt good, tired but good so he slowed a bit, partly to begin cooling down and partly because he didn't want it to end. Other than his brush with that truck, it had been a perfect run on a perfect day. As he ran those last strides into the clearing, once again he was all smiles.

As he walked back to the Inn, his backpack nestled into the small of his back and pulled him a bit more upright. He squared his shoulders and stretched out of the slight slump he had settled in from running for such a long time. As he neared the Inn, he picked up his pace slightly. He was beginning to feel a bit chilled and he knew that a long, hot shower awaited him.

As the screen door slapped shut behind him, he called out to Polly.

"I'm in here," she called back. He wasn't sure, but he thought there was a bit of a strain to her voice. As he went into the front room, she was standing in front of the window looking out at the road. She didn't turn. "Hey, Pol. What's up?"

"I just had the strangest thing happen."

CHAPTER 28

AS MALCOM SANK INTO A CHAIR, Polly explained what had happened. After he had disappeared into the woods, she had opened the garden gate. Since no guests were staying in the Inn, she had planned a special evening that would start with dinner.

The greens, red leaf lettuce, curly green leaf lettuce, and baby spinach were still producing well and would make a perfect base for the salad she had in mind. As she picked the greens, she planned the rest of the salad. They had several apple trees in the yard, and the day before she had picked the first apples of the fall. She would slice one of them onto the bed of greens, add some chopped walnuts, shave some pecorino romano cheese over the top, and dress it with poppy seed dressing.

Surveying the garden for ideas for the main course, she spied a butternut squash on a vine hiding under one of its leaves. Upon closer inspection she decided that it was ripe enough; this gave her an idea. She looked over her herb patch and picked some parsley, lovage, and chives. With greens, the squash, and herbs filling her arms, she walked back to the house.

Polly nearly dropped the squash as she gingerly pulled the kitchen door open. She managed to get the squash onto the table without dropping it and was putting the greens and herbs in the sink when the front doorbell rang.

Since they weren't expecting any guests, the bell startled her. She walked through the dining room toward the front door. As she passed one of the front windows she looked out and saw an old pickup truck in the drive. A man was walking back toward the truck. She watched as he opened the door and leaned in. He was obviously looking for something. It wasn't long before he extricated himself from the truck and began to walk back toward the inn, this time with a thin valise in hand. The bell rang again.

She went to the door, and through one of the sidelights she got a close look at him. The first thing about him that caught her attention was his glasses. They were thick, giving him an owlish kind of appearance, and the round shape and wire rims only reinforced that look. He was wearing jeans, neatly pressed, and a jacket that was zipped all the way up. One hand held a small briefcase.

"Shit," she thought to herself as she began to pull the door open. Two options flashed through her mind. Either he was a gypsy salesman, peddling generators and power washers, or he was selling salvation. From her experience, both types were usually from Kentucky or Tennessee and neither took no for an answer easily. She wished that Malcom was there. As the door opened he jumped slightly and she had to fight not to giggle.

"Hello. May I help you?" she asked. She held on to the door and did not open it wide.

"Hello. You must be Polly."

That statement stopped her in her tracks. Instinctively she pulled back a bit, placing one foot behind the partially open door just in case he tried to force his way in.

"Who are you?" she asked without answering his question.

"Oh, I'm sorry. My name is Alfred Whitson and I met your husband, Malcom, recently. He bought an antique ship's lantern from me."

She remembered. Malcom had told her about him.

"Oh. Please, won't you come in?" she said as she opened the door and stepped back. "What brings you up here?"

Alfred stepped in, and as he did she took a closer look at him. He was about Malcom's size, and Mal had said he was a pretty good runner. When he looked at her, she was struck by the narrowness of his face and how black and tiny his eyes looked behind those very thick glasses. His voice was slightly deeper than Mal's and had a bit of a nasal tone to it.

"Your book. I read your book and I have some questions for you."

She was not expecting that. "My book?"

"Yes." He opened his case, reached in without looking, and moved his hand around. Suddenly he withdrew his hand, opened the case wider, and looked in. Surprise, agitation, she couldn't tell which, but he suddenly looked up at her and said, "You know, *The Captain's Quilt.*" He slowly withdrew his hand from the case and looked back at her.

She must have been staring at him. "Oh, yes. My book. I'm sorry," she said quite flustered.

"I thought I had my copy with me," he mumbled looking in the case for a second time. Then he suddenly looked up at her and said, "The story. How much of it is true?"

"If nothing else, he's direct," she thought while trying to decide how to answer his question. "Well, it is a novel. Fiction. So I guess I'd have to say that the story is made up, although I did base it on some letters that we found here in the Inn when we bought the place."

"Yes. Yes. The letters. Malcom told me about them. Can I see them?"

Again she was stopped by his directness. "I'm sorry, but we keep them locked away and they're not here. I can show you one of them. We had it framed. It's over here." She turned and pointed at the wall behind her.

He didn't say anything but instead brushed past her to look at the frame. Polly closed the door and watched as he stood in front of the framed letter. She could see his lips moving as he read it. When he was done, he glanced over his shoulder at her, turned back to the letter, and read it again. This time he traced each line with his finger as he read it. Without moving she watched him, fascinated by his intensity.

"In the book, you wrote about a quilt, one that told a story. Could I see it?"

Again, she was surprised by his directness, but this time something about his expression bothered her. He was staring like a dog expecting supper. Not hostile, not threatening, just silently insistent.

She decided to stretch the truth in her answer.

"You mean the Captain's Quilt. I'm sorry, but it doesn't really exist. I made it up."

This wasn't exactly a lie, but it wasn't entirely true either. The idea behind the quilt was very real, but the description in the book was made up and the story behind that description was all fiction.

His expression didn't change.

"I'm sorry."

"I'd like to see it," he said again.

"Really, I made it all up."

"That letter, it talked of a quilt. Your husband told me about the quilts you had found, and how different rooms are named after different quilts. I'd like to see the one you call the Captain's quilt."

She took a deep breath, stalling for time. She could see that he was not going to be dissuaded. Malcom had said he was odd, but also that he was harmless. She decided to show him the quilt. Maybe once he saw it, he would leave.

"Come on." She turned and headed up the stairs.

Halfway up, she paused to make sure he was following. Her heart skipped a beat when she found him to be just inches behind her. "Oh!" she exhaled, "I didn't hear you."

Again he didn't say anything.

As she climbed the last remaining stairs, she began to have second thoughts about her decision to take him upstairs and show him a quilt. Scenarios began to play out in her head: how she would get away if he attacked her, what she could do to defend herself. When they reached the Captain's Room, she opened the door and stepped aside so he could go in first. She did not want to be trapped in there with him.

He didn't hesitate. Without a word, he walked past her, stood in front of the quilt, and stared at it. She watched him from the doorway. His free hand clenched and unclenched, and his lips moved slightly as if he were talking to the quilt. Then, abruptly, he turned and walked back to where she stood in the doorway. Standing uncomfortably close to her, and looking straight into her eyes, he said, "I would like this quilt. And the letter, too."

Polly was dumbstruck, but she knew it was time for him to leave. After a moment, she found her voice and said pleasantly yet forcefully, "I'm sorry, but that's not possible."

"I'm willing to pay. Whatever you want."

"I'm sorry. They're not for sale. No."

This time there was an edge to her voice. He must have gotten the message, because his expression softened and he simply said, "I see. Well, please say 'Hi' to your husband for me. I must be going."

With that he rushed past her, sped down the stairs, and let himself out before she could even catch up.

The front door was still ajar when she reached it, and before she could look out, she heard his truck driving off. Her heart was pounding and her hands shaking as she turned the lock on the door. She knew that it was a futile gesture because he was already gone, but the resounding click as the lock snapped closed made her feel better. She walked over to the window and looked out at the empty drive. The sky was perfectly clear and the sun still bright, even though it was now late afternoon. If she listened carefully, she could hear birds chirping out in the trees as if nothing out of the ordinary had happened.

This is where she had been standing when Malcom walked in after his run.

CHAPTER 29

AS MALCOM ABSORBED THE STORY, his thoughts returned to the afternoon he had spent with Alfred. The man had seemed okay most of the time. Perhaps a bit odd, but not enough to really worry about. Then again, Mal remembered a few times when he had really wondered. Now, as Polly told him about the visit, his sense of unease returned.

"Mal," she continued, "when you told me how odd he was, I didn't really understand what you meant. Now I do."

"You said he wanted to buy the Captain's Quilt."

"Yes."

"Tell me again." Malcom deliberately kept his voice calm, trying not to give away his growing concern.

She turned her gaze back out the window. "Mostly he just stared. He asked me about the letters, too. He wanted to see them. I told him they were locked away, but I showed him the one on the wall. He read it twice, then asked about the quilt, so I took him upstairs to see it. I never heard him following me up the stairs. He was just there. Scared the shit out of me. I opened the room and watched as he went in and stood in front of it for a few minutes. That's when he offered to buy it. I refused and he rushed out when I said it wasn't for sale. That was just before you came in." She paused a moment, then added, "He did say to say 'Hi' to you. 'Hi'."

As she uttered those last words, he stepped toward her and took her in his arms. He felt her sigh. "It's okay. I told you how odd he was. I'm sure that he's harmless and he won't be back." What he didn't tell her was how concerned he really was.

"He really is, uh, different, isn't he," said Polly as she pulled away. She chuckled. He grinned and when her chuckle became a laugh, he found himself laughing too.

"You stink," said Polly. "Go get cleaned up. I have a special dinner planned, for just the two of us."

He didn't miss the look on her face or the inflection in her voice. "Right," said Malcom, and he grinned as he headed for the shower.

* * *

When he returned to the kitchen, he was met with the most wonderful aromas. She was standing in front of the stove stirring something in a large skillet that was bubbling nicely, and he watched as she tasted it, paused, added some secret ingredient, and tasted it again. She looked pleased. Coming up behind her, he wrapped his arms around her and nuzzled her neck.

Polly wriggled and deflected his move by closing off access to her neck with a tip of her head. Under the most ordinary circumstances she didn't like her neck nuzzled, but tonight it was especially sensitive. "Stop," she cooed, "dinner's almost ready, and you're not getting dessert now."

"What can I do to help?" he asked as he peered over her shoulder into the pan of creamy liquid with orange chunks of something in it. A pot of water was boiling away on another burner and he could see pasta cooking in it.

"Pick out a bottle of wine and open it, and leave me alone so I can finish dinner."

The wine rack was in the dining room, and he noticed that the table wasn't set. He picked out a nice Malbec and called out, "Do you want me to set the table?"

"No. It's all set. We're eating outside. Could you light the patio heater and the candles?"

Wine open, matches in hand, he went outside. The temperature was cool, but as soon as he lit the patio heater it was perfect. Whatever breeze had been blowing earlier had stopped, the evening birds were singing their final songs of the day, and the crickets were beginning to chirp. The shadows were growing longer and the sky was beginning to change from the bright blue of the day into shades of pink and purple. Soon it would be dark, and with the clear sky, the stars would be magnificent. All he could do was smile and take it all in.

Polly had thought of everything. She had set the table with their best china, using placemats they had bought from a local weaver. The center of the table held a vase of fresh flowers surrounded by an assortment of candles, each on its own mirror. He poured a little wine into each wine glass so that it would have a few minutes to breathe. Then he began lighting the candles. As he did so, he wondered what the special occasion was.

When Malcom had lit the last candle, he heard the door open. Polly came out carrying two salads. "Would you get the basket of bread?" she asked as she placed one on each placemat.

Mal walked into the kitchen and his stomach growled loudly. The smells coming from the stovetop demanded investigation. He lifted the lid from the skillet that she had been stirring earlier. But before he could do anything more than inhale, he heard her clear her throat behind him.

"Sorry," he said. "I was just checking it out. It smells amazing. What is it?"

"A surprise. Bring the bread so we can eat."

Polly always made interesting salads, and this one was no exception. As he finished the last bite, Malcom said, "My God, Polly, that was incredible. Where did you get that idea for a salad?"

"Nowhere in particular. I just kind of invented it. I'll have to remember it."

They left their salad plates for a moment; it was such a beautiful evening that dinner could wait. But as Malcom sipped his wine, Polly looked at him and asked, "Do you think that there's anything to worry about with Alfred?"

Mal looked at her with concern. The visit had obviously bothered her a lot.

"I don't think so. He may be a bit eccentric, but no, I don't think so."

"I'm not so sure. There was something about the way he asked questions, and when he wanted to buy the quilt . . . Oh, I don't know. He just made me uneasy."

"Pol. Really, I don't think there is anything to worry about."

She took another sip of wine, stood up, and picked up her salad plate. As she reached for his, he pushed back from the table intending to help. But before he could stand, she came around and touched his shoulder. "Stay. I'll take care of these. I'll be right back with dinner."

Malcom couldn't help but notice the softness of her touch, and the seductive tone of her voice. All the right messages were being conveyed, but even as she hinted at as-yet-unspoken delights, he sensed there was something else. He sat back, took a sip of wine, and looked out over the backyard, past the garden, and to the now dark woods. The candles flickered, and his thoughts went to Polly and all the effort she had put into this meal, for no apparent reason.

Then the screech of an owl, telling of his own evening meal, shifted his thoughts. Pol was worried about Alfred, and now, so was he. Why had he come by today? What did he want, besides the quilt, and why that quilt? Malcom remembered some of the uneasiness that he had felt when he first met Alfred. All of a sudden the night seemed much darker.

He twisted around and realized that the light from the kitchen had been turned off. At that same moment, Polly emerged holding a casserole dish in her hands and he got a whiff of those amazing aromas that he had smelled earlier in the kitchen. She used her elbow to push the door shut. Then she walked toward the table, bringing those heavenly aromas with her.

"Dinner is served," she announced as she placed the dish on the table.

"And what is dinner? It smells amazing."

"It's a new recipe I found. Roasted butternut squash from our garden in a cream sauce with pasta. I hope you like it."

"How could I not? You made it."

"You are so full of it. As long as you didn't have to cook it, you'd say that."

"No, really," he protested. "You're cooking is amazing. I don't deserve you."

Polly looked at Malcom. His eyes twinkled in the ever-moving light created by the flickering candles. It was so romantic, and if you believed in magic, clearly a spell had been cast. "You're right. You don't deserve me, but you're stuck with me," she said with a teasing lilt in her voice.

The meal tasted even better than it smelled, and as dinner was finished and the wine bottle emptied their talk became silly, as conversations between lovers often do. The empty wine bottle, the dishes left on the table, and the flickers of the dying candles all held clues to the evening's dessert.

CHAPTER 30

THE RIDE HOME PASSED QUICKLY for Alfred. He kept up a conversation all the way back to Massachusetts. "Damn her," he hit his hand on the steering wheel. Didn't she understand? He didn't need all the letters. He only needed the one. The one he had read on their wall. It was the key. He'd need the quilt as well. In his mind, he'd then be able to prove his theories, and vindication would be his. His family name would be cleared and their honor restored.

By the time he arrived home, he had convinced himself that when they understood why he was doing what he was doing, they would embrace his quest and would even help him. But first, he had something to do. Things had not gone well with Malcom's wife. He would have to fix that.

* * *

Polly was working in one of the front flowerbeds when the delivery man turned into the drive, stepped out, and handed her flowers. She didn't notice the card that was stuck in amongst them, so she assumed that Malcom had sent them. Setting the arrangement on a table in the entry hall, she heard noises in the kitchen. "Mal, is that you?"

"Yeah, what's for lunch?" he said as he scrounged through the refrigerator.

"They're lovely."

He turned and she wrapped her arms around his neck and gave him a kiss.

"Well, thank you," he said, "but what're lovely?"

"The flowers."

"What flowers?"

"The ones you sent. They were just delivered."

"I didn't send any flowers, but with that reaction, I may have to do so."

She pulled away. "You didn't?"

"No."

Malcom followed her out of the kitchen to the hall. "You didn't send these to me?" she asked, pointing at the flowers on the table.

"No, I didn't. Is there a card?"

"I didn't look. I just assumed they were from you."

"Here," he said as he pulled a small pink envelope out from the center of the arrangement.

She slid her finger under the flap of the envelope and pulled it open. Sliding the card out, she looked at it. After reading the card, she looked at Malcom and said, "You're not going to believe this." Then she handed him the card.

Please accept my apologies for
the way I acted when we first met.
—Alfred

"That's too weird," said Polly.

"Agreed. I need to go down that way again before the race, so I'll stop in and see him, make sure things seem okay. In the meantime, at least the flowers are nice."

CHAPTER 31

A WEEK AND A HALF PASSED before Malcom had the chance to go down to visit Alfred. This time he wasn't the only one in the shop. There were at least a half dozen others meandering around. One couple had very distinct French-Canadian accents and were switching between French and English as they leaned over a display case, excitedly pointing and gesturing at something inside. A middle-aged man in a tweed jacket was thumbing through some of the old books that were on display, and a young couple was looking at an old iron bed frame, while trying to hold on to their small child. As his eyes adjusted to the low light in the shop, Malcom looked around for Alfred. With so many customers, surely he must be there, but Malcom didn't see him.

Malcom continued to walk through the shop, eventually pausing in front of a display of lanterns that looked similar to the one he had bought. Suddenly, a strange feeling came over him. He turned, then jumped. Alfred was standing right behind him. "Jesus, you scared the shit out of me."

"Sorry."

But before Malcom could say anything else, Alfred slid off to help the French-Canadian couple, who looked like they had finally made a decision. The young couple, obviously frustrated by their active toddler, hurried out. A moment later, the man in tweed also left.

From his position beside the lanterns, Malcom thought about Alfred's quirky behavior during the run, his visit to the Inn, his interest in the quilt and the letter, his sudden departure, and then the flowers with an apology. None of it made sense. Now, as he watched Alfred's frustration mount as he dealt with the French-Canadian couple, he began to wonder if he had made a mistake in coming down to visit him. Maybe he should have just let things rest.

Not wanting to seem too obvious, Malcom wandered off into another room and picked up an old telescope. He didn't hear the couple leave; nor did he hear Alfred come up behind him once again.

"There's a really interesting story behind that telescope, you know." His voice, so close behind, startled Malcom and he jumped. For the briefest of moments, some very dark thoughts passed through his head. "Is there." Malcom said, more as a statement than a question.

"Yes, but I'm sure that's not why you're here."

"True enough. I wanted to talk to you about your offer for the quilt and the letter and those flowers you sent to Polly."

"I thought so. I only sent the flowers because I couldn't think of any other way to tell her how sorry I was for the way I left on that day when she showed me the quilt and the letter. I had noticed the flower gardens around the Inn, so I guessed that she would appreciate flowers. That's all." He sounded sincere, but something still bothered Malcom.

"You didn't have to do that."

"I know."

"So, Alfred, just to be clear, the quilt and the letter are not for sale. However, I am curious why you are so interested in them."

Alfred hesitated before answering. At first, it seemed like he was still trying to sound contrite, and he apologized again for the way he had behaved. Then he began talking rapidly, and Malcom had a hard time keeping up with the narrative. He talked about his family, their misfortunes, the information that would prove what he now knew, and how Polly had explained it all so clearly in her book.

At that point, Malcom had to interrupt him. "Stop. Alfred, are you telling me that you think Polly's book is the story of your family's misfortunes? And that you need the quilt to prove how they were wronged?"

Alfred stopped. His eyes, distorted by his thick glasses, seemed even blacker and more intense than before as he stared right into Malcom's face and said in a loud whisper, "Yes, that is exactly what I am saying, and I need the quilt and letter to prove it."

Malcom stared back at Alfred. There was definitely something wrong with him. He didn't know what exactly, but his manner and intensity had become unsettling. "Alfred, listen to me. Polly's book, it's a work of fiction. She made it all up. It's a novel."

"So you say," he said firmly.

"Alfred, it is. Whatever you think you are seeing in it is all in your imagination."

"What about the quilt? And the letter," he said sharply.

"It's a quilt that we found in the attic along with the letter. She used them as the basis for her story, but again, she made it all up."

"No! It's true. I need that quilt and letter. I need it to prove . . ." His voice trailed off as if he suddenly realized that he was shouting.

The intensity of Alfred's outburst caught Malcom by surprise. Mustering as much force as he could, Malcom said, "Alfred. I'm going to leave now and I want you to stay away from Polly and the Inn. I repeat. Her book is fiction. The quilt has no secret message in it and neither the quilt or letter are for sale."

He brushed past Alfred and headed for the door. Alfred followed silently and stayed close behind, as if a shadow. Malcom couldn't leave fast enough. The unease that he had felt earlier was now replaced by fear. When he put his hand on the door handle and pushed, it did not move. He shook it, and again it didn't open.

"Here, let me." Alfred's voice was practically in his ear. Malcom spun around just as Alfred reached past him and twisted the lock open. It clicked, the door swung open, and Malcom spilled out onto the porch. He gulped in several lungfuls of fresh air as he stood there staring at Alfred. "I'm serious. Stay away. None of it is what you think it is."

Alfred stared at Malcom from the doorway and said in that slightly nasally voice, "No, it is. I'll see you again."

Malcom didn't respond to Alfred's last statement. As he climbed into his car, his heart was pounding and his palms were sweaty. "*What the fuck is wrong with him?*" he thought to himself as he drove off.

Alfred watched him leave. "I will have them," he said quietly to himself.

CHAPTER 32

BY THE TIME MALCOM drove up the drive to the Inn, his nerves had calmed, but he was stilled bothered by the confrontation with Alfred. The sun was beginning to set. He was hungry and tired. The drive down to Essex had been impulsive, and all the way back he wondered if he had done the right thing.

As he parked his car, he saw several others in the parking lot. He had been so obsessed with Alfred that he had forgotten that they had guests arriving. He walked around to the back door. He wasn't in the mood to meet any new people, and he needed to see Polly. But she wasn't in the kitchen. As he opened the fridge to see what leftovers might be there, he heard some laughter coming from one of the front rooms. A covered casserole dish looked inviting, but he left it on the shelf and let the door close. He knew that if he just helped himself, it would turn out that she had plans for whatever he took. It wasn't worth the aggravation.

Malcom walked into the front room and saw Polly showing an older couple the letter they had framed. She turned as his weight caused a floorboard to creak. "Oh, Malcom. There you are."

"Hi Pol. Sorry I'm late."

The couple turned toward him. She said, "I was just telling Mr. and Mrs. Davidson about how the Inn was named and about the book I wrote."

Malcom stepped forward, and introductions were made.

"Could I borrow my wife for a minute?"

* * *

"Where have you been?" Polly asked as soon as they were in the kitchen.

"I went down to see Alfred."

"You what!"

"I had to see him, to talk to him. I wanted to understand what he wanted."

"Why didn't you tell me?" Her displeasure was obvious.

"I don't know. I guess I didn't want to worry you."

Polly stood there staring at him. Her silence said more than any words. "So?"

"So what?"

"So did you see him?"

"Yes and no."

"Mal, either you saw him, or you didn't. Which was it?"

"I saw him."

"And?"

"We talked."

"What did he have to say?" The tone in her voice conveyed her frustration with his cryptic answers.

"Not a lot. Pol, I don't know what to think."

That statement caused her to pause a moment before she asked, "Other than he's a nut?"

He knew she needed to hear more. "There's that, but there's something else. I can't put my finger on it, but I guess I'd say he was obsessed. He is fixated on the quilt and the letter. He believes that your book is true and that somehow it is the key to some family tragedy."

Polly said nothing for a few moments. Then in a low voice she asked, "So did you get through to him? Do you think he'll leave us alone?"

"I don't know. Still, I don't think he's dangerous, just strange. I'm sure that over time this will all blow over." His face suddenly brightened. "Is there anything to eat?"

CHAPTER 33

"COME ON YOU GUYS. Let's get going," shouted Max to Jack and Dave. She and Patti were already in the car ready to go, and the two guys were standing there talking. They looked over at the car and saw both women give them the "Come on, what's up" shrug. "I suppose we ought to get going before someone has a coronary," said Dave.

"I guess, but look how cute they are."

After one pit stop and two wrong turns, they finally turned up the drive to the Inn. "Two hours, not bad," announced Jack.

Dave agreed, but the women were already out of the car.

"Oh my god! This place is gorgeous," gushed Patti as they both looked around.

"Come on. Let's go check it out," said Max while tugging on Patti's hand.

Patti started to turn back but Max continued to pull her along. "Come on! The guys will get everything. Let's go."

It wasn't until Jack and Dave took the last of the luggage out of the car that they realized that they had been abandoned. They looked toward the Inn and saw Max and Patti disappearing in the front door.

"Hello, and welcome to The Quilt House." Polly was the lone greeter. Earlier in the day, Malcom had received a call from an old friend who needed help with a barn restoration project. The two couples were the only ones booked in the Inn for the next few days, so Polly reluctantly agreed that Malcom could go and help his friend.

"I'm Max and this is Patti," Max said, holding out her hand.

"I'm Polly. Unfortunately, my husband, Malcom, is away."

Before she could say anything else, Jack and Dave arrived with the luggage. Another round of introductions completed the formalities. Then Polly said, "Come. Let me show you to your rooms and give you a quick tour."

Each room was named for a quilt. Patti and Dave's room was called The Patchwork, and Jack and Max were in The Calamanco. The couples spent the next hour unpacking, visiting each other's rooms, and exploring the Inn. Then Polly gave them all a quick tour of the grounds. She gave Jack and Dave each maps of the trails, and they made plans for the next day's run.

CHAPTER 34

IN THE MORNING, THE COFFEE smelled divine as Jack came down into the kitchen. He was the first to arrive. Max would be down shortly, but he didn't know how soon Patti and Dave would show up. Polly greeted him warmly. "Coffee?"

"Please."

"Did you sleep well?" she asked as she poured him a cup.

"I did. Thanks,"

"Cream and sugar is on the sideboard."

While Jack turned to fix his coffee, he said, "This place is beautiful."

He thought she seemed to blush as she replied. "Thank you. It's taken a while. How did you hear about us?"

"Actually, I heard about it on the radio. You were being interviewed on public radio and I caught just enough to be intrigued."

Now he was certain that she blushed. "Oh, yes, my fifteen minutes of fame."

"Well, it worked. We're here. Also, didn't I hear that your husband is a runner?"

"He is. Do you run?"

"Both Dave and I do. That's part of the reason we're here. We're running a trail race later this fall, and the chance to run in the woods while our 'others' shopped was too perfect."

"I wish Malcom was here. He'd love to go run with you. I think he's doing some kind of a race like that later this fall."

"Do you know where?"

"Not really, I'm embarrassed to say, but I think it's down in Massachusetts."

Jack thought a moment, then asked, "The Rockdog?"

"I don't know. Maybe. I really didn't catch the name. Eggs or French toast?"

"French toast. It's a trail marathon. Dave and I are both running it. Maybe we'll see your husband there, if it's the same one."

She cracked some eggs in a bowl. "Sausage or bacon?" she asked as she began to whisk the eggs. Then suddenly she stopped. "I'm sorry. I didn't ask if you wanted to wait for anyone else to join you."

Before he could answer, Dave walked into the room. "Good morning. Is that coffee I smell?"

Polly answered first. "It is. Regular or decaf?"

"Regular. Please."

As she handed him a cup, she said, "I was just about to start breakfast for Jack. He's having French toast. I can do some for you if you like, or would you prefer eggs?"

"French toast sounds great."

She looked at both of them and asked, "Sausage or bacon?"

"Sausage," they answered in unison.

"Okay. Now, while I work on breakfast, why don't you take your coffees out onto the back porch and relax. It'll take me a few minutes to get breakfast cooked. It's really nice out there this morning."

* * *

Polly was right, and even though the porch was still shaded by the surrounding trees, and the crisp night air had not yet warmed, it was beautiful. The sun was just kissing the treetops, and where patches of sunlight touched the dew-covered grass, a thin layer of mist formed. The hairs on Jack's arms stood up. He put his coffee down on the still wet porch railing and rubbed his arms vigorously.

Picking up his coffee, he took a sip. With all of the chit-chat, this was his first real sip. He savored its warmth as it slid down his throat. When the hot liquid reached his empty stomach, he felt its warmth slowly spread.

That moment of serenity was broken by Dave. "Dude, this is great. I can't think of the last time coffee was ready when I got up. And a choice for breakfast! Sausage or bacon!" Then, gesturing toward the woods, he added, "Beautiful."

Jack and Dave had been friends for a long time and while Dave appreciated a good run in the woods or a day fishing out on the ocean, he rarely commented on nature's beauty. This was new.

Jack looked over at him, unable to hide his surprise. "What?"

"It's beautiful," repeated Dave.

"What's beautiful?" Max's voice made him turn his head. The door opened and she and Patti both stepped out onto the porch, cradling cups of tea in their hands to ward off the chill.

"Good morning," said Jack. Max sidled up to him and leaned against him without releasing her two-handed grip on her teacup. He put his arm around her and gave her a kiss on the top of her head. She seemed to purr.

Patti didn't even pause as she left the kitchen. A smile broke out on her face. Silently she walked past the three of them, set her tea on the railing, and walked down the stairs and out into the backyard. Her natural enthusiasm left a trail of footprints in the dew-covered grass as she walked toward a sunny spot. Once in the sun, she stopped, spread her arms wide, closed her eyes, tilted her head back, and slowly turned as if in celebration. After one revolution she stopped and began to run back. "I need my camera, it's so beautiful," she said as she neared the porch. But as she reached the first step, the kitchen door opened and Polly announced that breakfast was ready. The pictures could wait and Max's question remained unanswered.

CHAPTER 35

"I CAN'T BELIEVE IT!" Max cried out, standing in front of the framed letter. "This is really the letter that inspired your book?"

Polly nodded yes. "A copy. The originals are in a safe deposit box."

"I loved your book. I just finished it. So is the quilt real or is it made up?"

Polly blushed. "You know, I get asked that all the time. It's both."

"What do you mean?"

"Well, I used elements of two different quilts to make up the quilt in the story."

"Really. Can we see them?"

"Sure. They're upstairs. Come." As she led the way she continued. "The one quilt is hanging in The Captain's Room. Its panels depict a story, but the other one gave me the idea for hiding the information. It's packed away."

"I'll join you in a minute," Patti said. "I want to grab my camera for those outdoor shots first."

As Patti continued past the placard to the door marked The Captain's Room, Max thought, "*How cool.*"

Polly twisted the knob and pushed the door open. The room was dark. She snapped the light on, walked across to the window, and pulled the drapes open. Max followed. "I keep them closed in all the rooms when they're not in use to try to keep the sun from fading the quilts too much."

The quilt was hanging on the wall. Bright-colored panels depicting the story of a ship's voyage. "It's beautiful," said Max, "but not at all what I expected."

"That's what everyone says."

"Hey Max," Patti's voice broke the silence. Both Polly and Max turned toward her voice, "I'm going down to try and get some pictures out back."

"Patti, wait a sec. Come look at this. It's pretty incredible."

She walked in and joined Max in front of the quilt. Max said, "Isn't this cool?"

"What?"

"The quilt. Have you ever seen anything like it?"

Patti stood and looked at the quilt. It was obvious that she was humoring Max and that she really didn't feel like looking at the quilt. She wanted to get outside. Then, as she looked at the quilt, she raised her camera and began shooting. After the first few clicks of the shutter, Max gave her a quick nudge and whispered, "Don't you think you should ask first?"

She stopped and turned to Polly, "I'm sorry. Do you mind if I take some pictures?"

"Of course not." Polly stepped toward a lamp that was on a small table. "Would you like some more light?"

"No, not really. This is fine." Patti continued snapping away. After several more pictures, Patti lowered her camera and announced, "I'm going down. Maybe I can still get those shots outside I wanted before we go into town."

Max and Polly looked at each other. They shrugged their shoulders in unison as if to say, "*What just happened here?*"

Max helped Polly close the shades as Patti's footsteps disappeared down the stairs.

"Would you still like to see the other one?" asked Polly.

"I would, if it's not too much trouble."

"Come on, it's upstairs."

The stairs were narrow and Max felt like they were walking up a secret passage. The door at the top opened into the attic. A small window at each end of the space let in narrow shafts of light. She could feel the heat from the sun on the shingles of the roof and she could see thin strands of unfinished webs connecting the open rafters together. There were piles of sealed boxes and unused furniture in neat rows.

Near a cluster of chairs and a table was a chest. Polly lifted its scarred lid and inside Max could see several dark-colored sealed plastic bags. Polly took the bags out and placed them on the table. Then, one at a time, she opened each one and looked inside. "Some of these are quilts that I haven't finished." When she opened the third bag, her face lit up. "Here it is. Give me a hand." Max helped her slide out what at first she thought was a large piece of material until she realized that it was actually a quilt. It was made up of three layers—top, back, and something in between—and it was covered with stitching, which made it thicker and heavier than just a single piece of cloth. Carefully they unfolded it. Then Polly said quietly, "Let's take it over by the window so you can see it better."

In the shaft of light, Max could see that it appeared to be quite old. It was stained, and there were some small tears in the fabric. Polly's face took on an almost reverent look as she gazed at the fabric. She explained, "It's called a whole cloth quilt. Look at the stitching. Mostly these were made by women of the upper classes because they were the only ones who had the leisure time to learn the needlepoint skills needed to create the intricate patterns. These kinds of quilts became the precursors to petticoats and other warm undergarments."

"No kidding."

"Look over here," said Polly as she held one section flat for Max to see. "Doesn't this stitching look like writing?"

Max looked closely. The swirls of stitching were tighter than most, and even though there were places where the thread had broken and thus was missing, it did kind of look like writing.

"This is what gave me the idea."

"Why don't you have it on display?"

"It's not in very good condition, and only an experienced quilter would really find it interesting. Over the years I've made several quilts, but I still can't get my stitching this fine."

"And this gave you the idea for the book," said Max.

"It did. Help me fold this back up and put it back in the bag."

As they refolded it, Max said, "Thank you for sharing this with me."

"The pleasure was mine."

They completed the last fold, and together carefully slid it back into its bag.

CHAPTER 36

JACK AND DAVE WALKED INTO the kitchen just as Polly was giving the women directions and tips on where the best shopping was. "You heading out?" asked Jack.

"We are. Anything you want us to pick up?"

"Nah. We're going to go for a run. Those trails look really nice."

"Ciao," was Max's breezy reply.

* * *

The women were gone by the time Jack and Dave were changed and ready to run. Just as Malcom had done, they brought with them a backpack with several bottles of water and sports drinks. They left their pack on the stump, and after one last look at the trail map, they began to run.

Two hours later, they returned to the kitchen.

"That was great!"

"It really was," agreed Jack.

"You know, there's just one thing we didn't think of." Dave frowned.

"What's that?"

"Lunch."

"Shit. And we're stuck here without a car. Any ideas?"

"All I can think is to call the girls and see if they'll come back for us."

"We might have to go shopping," Jack cautioned.

"I know. Flip ya' for who makes the call."

Jack rummaged through the backpack and found a quarter. "Okay, you call it."

"Heads."

The coin clinked onto the floor, spun, and landed tails side up.

"Ha! Tails, you make the call," said Dave triumphantly.

"Phone's upstairs, I'll be right back."

Max answered her phone just as Jack walked back into the kitchen. Dave was sitting at the table with Polly, and they turned together when they heard Jack's voice. "Hey Max. How's it going?" He tried to sound as casual as possible. "What do you mean, what do I want?"

Dave waved and hissed loudly in an attempt to get Jack's attention. "Dave and I just got back from our run. . . . Yeah, it was good . . . Listen, Max, . . ." Finally he noticed Dave's gestures. "Hold on a sec. Dave's trying to tell me something."

As soon as Jack's hand covered the phone, Dave said, "Polly's going out. There's a small store that sells sandwiches not too far down the road and she'll drop us off."

"Hey Max, I'm back. Listen, you have fun. Think about where you want to go for dinner tonight." He listened a moment, then closed his phone. "Thanks, Polly. You have no idea how much grief you just saved us."

"Not a problem. Get cleaned up and we'll go."

* * *

The store was only about three miles down the road. Polly dropped them off and wished them well. Like most country stores, the shelves were jam-packed with groceries, motor oil, snow shovels, stacks of beer, and coolers. Chest freezers held ice cream, sodas, and more beer. Above the cashier, a sign pronounced that fishing and hunting licenses were available, and that this was also a tagging station for deer.

The deli case offered a reasonable selection of meats and cheeses as well as several salads: tuna, egg, potato. Jack ordered a ham and Swiss on rye while Dave ordered an Italian sub. They each grabbed a bag of chips and a Coke. Then they paid the cashier and headed outside to a picnic table, where they sat and ate their sandwiches, watching the cars go by on the road.

"Who knew that this road was so busy?" Dave said as he watched a station wagon pull in at the gas pumps.

'Who woulda' thunk," agreed Jack.

"It's nearly three," said Dave checking his watch.

"I'm done. Guess we ought to start walking back."

"Fine by me. Maybe we'll get lucky and the girls will come by and pick us up."

"I bet they'd honk and keep going, just to mess with us."

"Yeah, you're probably right."

* * *

Twenty minutes later, Dave stopped and swung the case of beer off his shoulder, thrusting it over toward Jack.

"Here, you carry this for a while."

"Gettin' heavy?"

"Yeah. Come on. Trade ya'." He put the case on the ground and reached for the bag of chips that Jack was carrying.

"I told you to just get a six-pack."

"I know, but this is a much better value."

"Okay. But only until you've had a rest."

Dave bent over and pulled open a corner of the case. He took a can out, cracked it open, and said, "Here. I'll lighten your load. Want one?"

"I'll pass, but thanks for your concern." Jack hoisted the case onto his shoulder. Dave took the bag of chips and they continued their trek. Every half mile or so they swapped the case off, and it did get lighter as the distance to the Inn decreased and the number of empties increased. By the third or fourth exchange, they were sharing both efforts equally.

As they paused for another short break, an old pickup truck passed them, followed by a line of cars. Jack noticed that the driver of the truck seemed to really take a good look at them as he went by. "Hey Dave, did you get a look at that guy in the pickup?"

"Couldn't not."

"Gave me the creeps."

It must have been the beer, because Dave then added, "Looked like the evil German camp commander in some awful World War Two movie. 'You vill tell us vat ve vant to know'."

Jack chuckled. "No. Looked more like the evil mad scientist. 'Attach zee electrodes here'," he said in the same bad accent.

The comic relief and lighter load seemed to shorten the remaining distance. Ten minutes later, they were the first to arrive back at the Inn.

CHAPTER 37

"DO YOU THINK POLLY'LL MIND if we put a few beers in the fridge?" asked Dave.

"Probably."

"You're right. I don't think she'll mind." With that, Dave opened the refrigerator door and put the rest of the beers in the fridge.

When the girls got home, they were sitting on the back porch where their day had begun, watching the shadows lengthen.

"Where'd you get the beers?" asked Max.

"What. No 'hello' first?" Jack feigned hurt feelings.

"Oh, poor baby," Max cooed and went over and kissed him on the top of his head.

"How was your day?"

"It was great, but you didn't answer my question. Where'd you get the beers?"

"In the fridge," answered Dave. "Bottom shelf."

"Where's Polly?"

"Don't know. After our run, she was going out. We were hungry and she drove us down to the little store down the road."

"And the beer?"

"Let me get you one," interjected Dave, and he got up and went into the kitchen. Patti followed.

"Dave needed some rehydration after our run. . ." Jack said, throwing his friend under the bus.

"Right," said Max sarcastically.

That was when the kitchen door opened, and Patti and Dave stepped back out onto the porch. Patti was sipping on a beer and Dave had one in each hand. He held one out to Max. She gave him a look of disapproval, but then with a hint of a smile, took the beer.

The sun was pretty well down and Polly still hadn't returned when Dave said, "Is anyone else getting hungry?"

As soon as those words were spoken, everyone suddenly was starving. It didn't take long for them to clean up, leave a note for Polly explaining the beer in her refrigerator, and then pile into the car and head out in search of food. They ended up in Lincoln at an Italian restaurant.

There was no indication that Polly had yet returned when they walked back into the Inn. It had been a long first day, and goodnights were said as they headed for their rooms.

"Oh my God! Those cannolis were amazing," gushed Max as she fell across the bed.

"Your cannolis are amazing," giggled Jack.

"Pig."

"I know, but you love it," he said with a grin as he lay down on the bed next to her. She rolled onto her side facing him, one leg draped over his, and smiled.

"Max . . ." His words were smothered by her kiss as she slid over on top of him. Nothing else was said.

CHAPTER 38

FOR THE SECOND TIME in as many mornings, Jack was the first one up. Polly greeted him in the kitchen with a cup of freshly brewed coffee. "How was your day yesterday?" she asked.

"Great. Thank you for the ride to the store."

"I was going that way anyway. It was no big deal."

"Well, thanks again. Those trails out back are fantastic. I can only imagine how much time and effort went into making them. Your husband should be commended. Will he be back today?"

"Unfortunately not. I talked to him yesterday. The project he's helping with ran into some problems, so he's not sure exactly when he'll be back."

"Not too long, I hope."

"Oh no. Only another day or so."

"Listen, I'd like to apologize for stashing those beers in your refrigerator. I hope that wasn't too presumptuous."

"Since you're the only guests, it's fine. It's only a problem when we have a full house."

Jack started to apologize again, but she cut him off. "I don't mean there's a problem using the fridge," she explained. "It's just that when we're full, there isn't any spare space."

"Oh."

"We've been talking about getting small fridges for each of the rooms. Just haven't yet."

Polly turned her head as Max arrived. "Tea?"

"Oooh. That would be wonderful."

Just as the previous morning, Patti and Dave weren't far behind. As soon as everyone had their coffees and teas, Polly asked about breakfast. "Today I have a treat for you. I made Fruit and Cream. There are also

Danish pastries, eggs are always available, and you can have pancakes if you like."

Max was the first to respond. "What's Fruit and Cream?"

"It's a sweet, sour cream–based custard with layers of blueberries, bananas, kiwi, strawberries, and raspberries."

"That sounds heavenly," said Max. "I'll have one."

Patti and Jack also said yes. Then Jack added scrambled eggs with bacon to his order, while Patti and Max opted for just Danish.

Dave, being the least adventurous eater of the three, stayed with traditional fried eggs, bacon, and toast.

* * *

"Oh, man, Polly. That was so good," said Jack as he placed his fork on his now-clean plate. "Can I get the recipe for that Fruit and Cream? It was incredible."

"Sure . . ." Polly started to reply but Max interrupted.

"And you're going to be making this?" asked Max, looking straight at Jack.

He blushed slightly and looked down at his plate for a second before answering. "Of course."

"Right," said Max with more than a hint of sarcastic skepticism.

"What?" He was immediately cut off by giggles and comments about his culinary prowess.

"Don't worry. It's easy," said Polly, coming to his rescue.

* * *

Once again Jack and Dave took their coffees out to the porch, but this morning the girls decided to stay in the kitchen with Polly.

"You have so inspired me," Max said to Polly as she picked up some dishes from the table.

"I'll get those," said Polly, taking them from Max.

"No, it's okay. Let me give you a hand."

Before things escalated into a tug-of-war over a dirty plate, Patti said that she was going to get her camera and shoot some pictures outside. Considering how many dishes she cleared each day at work, this morning it was a real treat to simply walk away.

After Patti left, Max blurted out, "Polly, would you help me get started making a quilt? Your book really inspired me. I've never done anything like that, but now that I've seen the ones here, I definitely want to give it a try. Patti and I went shopping for fabric at home, but once we got to the store, I wasn't sure what to buy."

Polly stopped and looked at Max. At first, she didn't say anything. Then she continued picking dishes up off the table and walked to the sink. Max grabbed several plates and followed her. As Polly turned the water on, she smiled and said, "Sure. Why not. I have some time today, and I haven't had a girls' day out in a while. Plus, Malcom won't be back until tomorrow. The first step will be to buy a pattern and some fabric."

"Oh, thank you, thank you."

* * *

Again the guys were left behind to run and do manly things while Max and Patti went out shopping. This time though, they went with Polly, so Jack and Dave had a car and wouldn't be stranded.

"I could get used to this," said Dave as they finished another really good run on the trails. "Nothing to worry about, great running trails in the backyard."

"It is pretty sweet," agreed Jack.

"What say we head into North Conway and find some lunch, see what the big deal is."

"Sounds like a plan. Race ya' to the house," said Jack.

Their sprint ended in a dead heat and both men started to laugh. "I think there were a couple beers still in the fridge. Want one?" asked Dave.

"Yeah, why not. We deserve it."

* * *

No more than an hour had passed before Jack and Dave were pulling out of the drive and heading for North Conway. Thirty minutes later they were driving down the stip. "It looks just like Kittery," commented Jack.

"Same stores, same crowds, I don't get it," agreed Dave.

"On your right. There's a parking place."

Jack yanked the wheel and slid into the vacant spot. "Nice job," said Dave. "Hey look, there's Horsefeathers. I read about them in one of the tourist guides. Sounds like a pretty good place to eat."

"Works for me."

As they walked toward the restaurant, a train whistle pierced the afternoon. They turned in the direction of the sound and saw a train station across the street. After another long whistle blast, a steam locomotive pulling several cars began to move.

"That's so cool," said Jack. He watched the train belch black smoke and white clouds of steam.

"C'mon, let's eat." Dave gave him a nudge as the train slowly chuffed away.

CHAPTER 39

FOR THE SECOND DAY in a row, Jack and Dave were the first ones back at the Inn. They were hanging out on the back porch with beers and snacks left over from the previous day when the three women returned home.

"Thank you so much." Max's voice could be heard in the kitchen amid the rustlings of a great number of plastic bags.

"No, thank you. I had a great time."

Patti was the first to come out onto the porch. "There you are."

"Hey, Patti, how was your day?" said Jack.

"It was good. What did you guys do?"

Dave spoke up first. "We went for a run out back and then into town for some lunch. You?"

"Polly took us to a fabric store and . . ." Before she could finish her sentence, Max came through the door with several large bags in hand.

"Look at this cool material I found." Max put the bags on the porch floor next to Jack and began rummaging through one of them. She pulled out a piece of fabric and held it up for everyone to see. "Polly said she'd help me make a quilt. This is going to be the background."

Jack looked at the fabric. It was blue. "Nice blue," he said.

"Jack, you're not looking at it. It's not just blue; there are different shades. And look at the subtle pattern. Doesn't it look like the ocean?"

"Oh, silly me." He smacked himself on the forehead with an open palm. "I see it now." His sarcasm wasn't lost on Max.

"Jack Beale, you're being a jerk. Wait till I finish. I'll show you."

"I'm sorry, Max. I can't wait to see it finished."

She was busy refolding the piece of cloth and wrestling it back into the bag when Polly came out and joined them. "Malcom just called. He won't be back until late tomorrow night." Then looking at Jack and

129

Dave she added, "I told him how much you were enjoying his trails, and I asked him the name of that race he was doing. Does Rockdog sound right?"

"The Rockdog! That's the one Dave and I are training for. Maybe we'll see him there."

"I'm sure he would like that . . . ." Her voice drifted off. Clearly, Polly was as enthusiastic about running as Jack and Dave were about making quilts.

"Patti, come on, help me take this stuff upstairs," said Max.

"I'll join you. I have something else to show you," said Polly.

With another great rustling of plastic bags, the three women went inside, leaving Jack and Dave to their beers and snacks.

Dave looked over at Jack. "She's really going to make a quilt?"

"So she says. Maybe she'll surprise us. That blue was really nice."

"It was."

* * *

Max was already in bed when Jack came out of the bathroom. He snapped the light off and walked toward the bed. The wide pine floor was cold to his feet. "Oh what the hell," he thought to himself and grinned in the dark. He pulled his tee shirt off and dropped his flannel pajama pants onto the floor. Properly naked he climbed into the bed, pulling the covers up to his chin. Then he lay there, on his back, next to her. He listened to her breathing, convinced that she wasn't asleep, and began thinking about the best way to proceed.

He slid one leg over toward her and touched her leg. A tingle and a shiver spread over his body when he felt her bare flesh. He had no expectation that she would be as naked as he was, but in his imagination he was convinced that she was. He rolled onto his side and slid his leg over hers. At the same time he put his arm over her, ready to draw her into a hug. She had a shirt on.

"Max," he whispered.

"Mmmm, what?" her voice was already tinged with sleep.

"I have a naked hug for you."

"That's nice," she mumbled without moving. He slid closer, gradually draping his leg further over hers and pulling himself closer with his arm. He couldn't decide if she was awake, asleep, or ignoring him, although he didn't think that possible since there was no doubt how awake he was.

"Max," he whispered in her ear and then gently kissed her cheek.

She moved slightly and turned her head toward his. Their lips touched softly, tentatively at first, then with more purpose. He could tell that she was now fully awake not only by the way she returned his kiss, but by the sound of her more rapid breathing.

"Jack?" she exhaled.

"What?" he exhaled back as he went to kiss her again.

"You didn't give me an answer."

He stopped mid-kiss, puzzled. "To what?"

"You never said if you like the blue material I bought for the quilt I'm going to make."

He pulled back a bit. His brain screamed, "*What! You want to talk about material at a time like this!*"

What he actually said was, "I like it," hoping those words would be enough so they could get back to where he wanted to be.

"You don't think it's too dark?" she said softly.

"No it's perfect."

"I'm not sure. It may be too light." The way she said it, something was different.

Again he said that he thought it was perfect.

"I'm not so sure; maybe it's too blue to be water. It should be more greenish."

Now he knew. She was messing with him.

He rolled off of her and onto his back. "I don't know. If it's too green it'll look like a field, so I'd keep it bluer." Two could play that game.

"You would?" Now he could hear a hint of frustration in her voice. He grinned.

She must have heard him grin because suddenly she rolled over on top of him and said, "You jerk, shut up," and kissed him.

There was no more discussion of quilts or fabrics or colors. Sleep found them in each other's arms, exhausted and satisfied.

CHAPTER 40

"C'MON, CAR'S LOADED, let's go!" Jack called out.

Max waved at him. He and Dave were waiting by the car, and the sky was getting uglier by the minute. A cold, driving rain had been predicted for the next two days as a storm that had pummeled the midwest now had its sights squarely on New England.

"Ya' know, we really timed this right. Two perfect weather days, great runs, and we didn't have to worry about entertaining Max and Patti all the time. Good thing they like shopping so much, even if I don't get it."

"I know," agreed Dave. "Look. They're finally coming."

As they reached the car, Jack asked Max if they were finally ready to leave.

"We are."

"All right then. Get in and we'll be out of here."

Just as Jack turned the key and started the car, Polly came running toward them with a large, dark green plastic bag. She waved her arm and called, "Max, wait. I have something for you."

Max opened her door and got out. "What? Did I forget something?"

"No. I wanted you to have this."

"What?"

"It's one of my old unfinished quilts. It's kind of crappy. I don't remember why I saved it. It's not really good for anything except as filling for a new one. I had so much fun yesterday, well, I just . . ."

Before she could finish her sentence, Max cut her off. "Polly, you shouldn't have."

"No, I want to," she said pushing the bag into Max's hands. The first raindrops, big and fat, began to fall. "Now, get going." With that she turned and began walking back to the Inn. In an instant those few raindrops became a torrent, and Max jumped into the car while Polly started to run.

"This drive is gonna' suck," said Jack.

* * *

"What is she giving that woman?" Alfred whispered, wondering to himself. For the last two days, he had been watching the Inn, keeping out of sight, all the while formulating a plan. He hadn't seen Malcom at all and the only guests were now leaving. Polly would be alone, and if she went out, he would have his chance.

CHAPTER 41

BY THE TIME POLLY made it to the house, it was pouring buckets and the wind was blowing. The door was nearly torn from her hand as she opened it, but she managed to hold on and pull it shut behind her. The storm had hit with such intensity that it took only those few moments outside to soak through her clothes. Water dripped from the ends of her hair and a puddle was beginning to form on the floor. She shuddered and went in search of a towel.

* * *

While Polly toweled off, found dry clothes, and started some water for tea, the lone occupant of a truck that was parked in the turnoff for the fire road was also toweling off. He too had been caught in the sudden downburst and was soaking wet.

* * *

The two-hour ride to the Inn was nearly doubled on the return. When Jack and Max dropped off Dave and Patti at Patti's place, goodbyes were short, sweet, and wet. The storm had become a full-blown Nor'easter. The wind drove the rain horizontally and it seemed as if the entire world outside was painted in shades of grey. Even at their highest setting, the wipers couldn't keep the windshield clear.

As they approached Ben's, they saw that there were only two cars in the parking lot. One belonged to Courtney. "Jack, pull in."

"What?"

"Pull in. I need to see Court for a minute."

"You can't call her?"

"Just pull in."

He pulled up next to the front door so the building blocked the wind. The rain was still coming down hard, but now, without the wind driving it, the wipers were just able to keep the windshield clear. Even so, Max didn't jump out right away. The flag in front of the restaurant was snapping furiously and Jack twisted around and looked up. Through his window he could see the flagpole bending like a fishing rod with a fish on the line. "You going in?" he asked. His tone implied that she should get going.

She kept looking out the window, with her hand on the door handle, as if trying to time her exit to coincide with some nonexistent lull in the rain. "Yes . . ."

Jack didn't hear the rest of her sentence because she suddenly threw open the door, jumped out, pushed it shut, and ran up the steps.

CHAPTER 42

"ALL SET?" JACK ASKED as Max climbed back into the car.

"Uh huh," was her positive reply. "Cat's still at her house. She'll keep her until tomorrow. I told her that was fine."

It seemed that the rain had let up a bit, but they were still in the wind shadow of Ben's. As soon as they made the turn away from the building toward Jack's, they saw that the let up was illusory. Again, the wipers had a hard time keeping the windshield clear.

Jack backed up the drive and stopped so the trunk was just steps from the door. Great plan—so-so results. They worked quickly to bring their things in, but while they did not get completely soaked, they were more than damp by the time they had everything inside. As they schlepped their stuff up the stairs, they both began to shiver.

The apartment was cool and dark, and the sounds of the wind-driven rain slapping at the windows and skylights made it seem colder than it really was. Moving quickly, Max turned on the lights and Jack turned up the thermostat. The lights made the place feel warmer, and when the furnace clicked on, the change was dramatic. What had felt cold and ominous moments before now became cozy and welcoming.

"Come here," Jack said to Max as he moved toward her.

She stepped into his open arms. For a brief moment, there was an instant chill as the cold, wet fabric pressed between their two warm bodies. But it took only a moment for their body heat to overcome that chill.

"I need to get out of these wet clothes," said Max.

"Need some help?"

"No, I can manage, but thanks for the offer." She pulled away and headed for the bedroom.

"Something to drink?" he called after her.

"Sure, something warm."

"Hot, or cold and warming?"

"You decide."

Jack didn't feel like tea or coffee so cold and warming was it. He opened his liquor cabinet and looked over the bottles. "Oh yeah, perfect," he said to himself as he withdrew a bottle of sipping bourbon. One of his running buddies had given it to him as a present when she moved to Kentucky. He poured two glasses and took a sip. He closed his eyes and savored the warm sensation as it slid down his throat and through his chest.

"This mine?" Max whispered as she reached around him for her glass while running her other hand across his back. He hadn't heard her come back into the room. Turning toward her voice, he found that she had returned wearing an oversized sweatshirt, but her legs were still bare. She took a sip and swallowed slowly. "Mmmm. Perfect," she said.

Jack's heart rate took a jump. Then he said, "I need to get out of these wet things. Be right back."

Jack quickly changed into flannel pajama pants and a long- sleeved cotton shirt that he had won at some long-forgotten race. When he returned to the living room, it took his eyes a moment to adjust to the sudden darkness. Max had turned the lights back off, and only the low, flickering glow of several candles lit the room. Max was curled up on one end of the couch, her legs under a fleece blanket, and she looked delicious. He stopped and looked at her. He could barely hear the storm above the sound of his own heartbeat, pounding in his ears. She looked up and smiled. With great effort he steadied his breathing, picked up his drink, and said, "Room for me?"

Her answer needed no words. He sat at the other end of the couch and faced her, tucking his legs under the same blanket. He watched her over his raised knees. The storm raged, the candles flickered, and they sipped their drinks in silence, each totally focused on the other. Max moved first. Her foot slid under the cuff of his pants and up his leg, causing a warm pressure elsewhere. "Thank you for a wonderful time," she purred.

He straightened his left leg and ran his foot up along her leg, feeling her silky skin. For as long as his leg would stretch, all he felt was ever-warmer skin. Even in the flickering candlelight he was sure that he saw her eyes soften and her neck begin to flush. "You're welcome," he managed to breathe. He swallowed the last of his drink and kept his eyes on Max as he slowly reached back with his right arm, intending to put his glass on the table next to the couch before moving in for more intimate contact.

As he did so, his elbow hit the lamp, which teetered. He had to twist fully to try to grab it with his left arm. This rapid twisting caused his left leg, which had been extended alongside her body, to push her toward the edge of the couch. In an attempt to maintain balance, his right leg swung onto the floor, taking the blanket with it. This pulled Max even closer to the edge of the couch. Yet despite these acrobatic maneuvers, he didn't catch the lamp. Instead, he dropped his glass and ended up sliding off the couch, landing on the floor. Max let out a shriek, and in less than a split second, she too was on the floor. The potential for a most intimate, passionate moment had suddenly become vaudevillian slapstick.

The lamp didn't break; only Jack's pride was hurt. The storm raged on as he and Max sat in stunned silence on the floor in front of the couch. He spoke first. "You okay?" His voice betrayed his embarrassment.

"Yeah," was her quiet reply, followed by a pause.

"Sorry."

"Didn't even spill my drink." A muffled sound escaped from her throat.

Jack, not sure if she was crying or laughing, asked again if she were all right.

"I'm fine." Now he was sure that it was a giggle.

He untangled himself from the blanket and stood. Then he offered his hand to her in an obvious invitation to stand. "So my dear, would you like to try this again?" he said in his best Chief Inspector Clouseau voice.

She didn't say anything. She stood, leaned into him, raised her arms up around his neck, and gave him a kiss.

"Mmmm," he moaned as he pulled her close. As her sweatshirt rose up, the previous moment's clumsiness was quickly replaced with an urgency that needed to be sated.

CHAPTER 43

POLLY HEARD THE DOOR OPENING and knew Malcom was home even before he announced his arrival. She had been waiting up for him, reading, in the kitchen. His late return and the still raging storm had made her anxious, and even though they hadn't lost power, the lights had flickered several times.

"Polly, I'm home," he called out as he pulled the door shut.

"You don't have to shout; I'm right here," she said stepping into the front hall.

He was soaked. "Holy shit, is it raining."

She gave him a look. "Is it now? I hadn't noticed," was her sarcastic reply.

"You know what I mean. Come here." He took her arm and pulled her over to him, intending to give her a hug.

She pushed him away. "No, you're all wet . . ." He didn't hear the rest of what she said because she had already gone around the corner.

A few minutes later she joined him in the kitchen. The microwave was running and he was rummaging through the refrigerator. "Here's a towel. What're you heating?"

"Tea."

"Move." She waved him away. "I saved you some supper. I'll get it."

He did as he was told and was ruffling his head with the towel when the microwave beeped.

Draping the towel over his shoulders, he took his tea out of the microwave and retreated as Polly took a plate out of the fridge, placed it into the microwave, set the timer, and pressed Start.

While the microwave hummed, she went to him, took the cup of tea from his hand, wrapped her arms around him, and said in a soft voice, "I missed you."

"I missed you too." Their kiss was interrupted by the beep announcing that his food was warm.

"So, how was your trip? Did you guys finish whatever you were doing?"

"We did, just as the storm hit. How were things here?"

"Good. Those two couples were here. They were really nice. I even went shopping one day with the two women, and the guys loved your running trails out back. They are planning on running that same race you're running later this fall."

"The Rockdog?"

"Yeah, they said they'd try to find you there. Anyway, they were bummed they didn't get a chance to meet you."

CHAPTER 44

THE SEASON WAS NEARLY OVER, and the motel, because it was one of the oldest in the area and lacked many of the amenities guests seemed to require today, was always the last to fill at the start of the season and one of the first to close at the end. On this stormy night, it would have been completely vacant, and probably closed, except that late in the afternoon a single guest had checked in.

Alfred sat in his motel room alone, with only his thoughts and notes to keep him company. The noise of the rain was so loud that even if he had turned on the television, it would have been hard to hear.

"Tomorrow, the letter will be mine. Tomorrow, I will take the quilt. Tomorrow." He said this over and over as a plan began to form in his head. The Inn had no guests. He had seen them leave. No one new had arrived, and if any were due in, it wouldn't be until late in the day. People always checked in late in the day. In the morning he would return to where he could watch the Inn, and when she went out, he would go in, take what he needed, and leave. He only needed five minutes. He was sure that she would go out and that the Inn would be empty sometime in the morning. He just had to be ready.

* * *

By daybreak, the rain had stopped. The fast-moving storm was past and the sky was beginning to clear. By 9:30 he was sitting in his truck watching the Inn and eating a donut he had picked up at the local donut shop. That's when he saw the second vehicle. "Damn," he said softly to himself. "*He's back*." That would change things a bit, but the result was going to be the same. Nothing was going to stop him now.

It wasn't long before Alfred's first assumption that she would go out in the morning proved itself true. He watched as Malcom walked with her out to her car. They talked, kissed good-bye, and she drove off. *"One gone, one to go,"* thought Alfred as he watched Malcom return to the house.

"Patience. Have patience; it'll all work out." He had to keep reminding himself. When he didn't see any sign that Malcom might be coming out to the other vehicle, Alfred moved to another spot where he could watch the back of the Inn as well. His heart nearly leapt from his chest when he saw Malcom, dressed for a run, walking toward the woods out back. This was it. His chance.

All of a sudden, he was a kid again. His goody-two-shoes brother had run home, not willing to take the dare. But he had stayed. Now he told himself it would be simple. *"Wait, you'll know when it is time. Then run—don't hesitate. Victory will go to the one who dared. It's all about risk and reward. And I will win."*

As soon as Malcom disappeared into the woods, Alfred sprinted toward the back door of the Inn. He passed through the kitchen, dashed upstairs to the room that held his quilt, took it off the wall, folded it, tucked it under his arm, and headed back downstairs. In the room next to the front door he also grabbed the framed letter. Then he looked out the window and, confirming that Polly had not yet returned, left by the front door and ran to the spot where his truck was hidden.

He had done it. He had his letter and his quilt. He began to grin uncontrollably as he stuffed the quilt and framed letter into a black plastic bag and drove away.

CHAPTER 45

TWO DAYS AFTER THE STORM, Malcom was out back mowing the yard around the garden while Polly went to the store. He didn't hear her return. Along with some groceries, she had picked up several new magazines for the front room to replace the ones that were dog-eared. New guests were due in and she wanted everything to be perfect.

As she arranged the magazines on the coffee table, something—or a lack of something—caught her eye. She stood and looked at the wall, then froze. It was gone. The letter was gone. A strange feeling washed over her as she stared at that empty spot. She couldn't move. All she could do was stare while a feeling of panic washed over her. "Malcom!" she screamed.

She knew he couldn't hear her—he was outside mowing—but that scream snapped her out of her growing panic. She ran. She had to get to Malcom.

The door slapped shut behind her. She didn't see him, but she could hear the tractor's engine running. After the gloom of the house, the bright sun was blinding. She shielded her eyes and looked to where she could hear the sound of the tractor. Then she saw him and called out again before running toward him, waving frantically.

When he saw her running toward him like a crazy person, wild thoughts began to run through his head: someone had died; a neighbor's house had burned; there was a dog, dead in the road. He stopped, killed the engine, and jumped off the tractor just as she reached him. Her face was flushed and she was gasping for breath,

"Ma . . ." was all she could get out before he said, "Polly, are you all right?"

"Mal," she gasped. "Did you do anything with the letter we had hanging in the front room?"

He looked at her, wondering where that had come from. "No."

"It's gone."

"What do you mean it's gone?"

"I was just in there, putting some new magazines on the table and opening the shades. Guests are coming. But it's gone."

He hurried toward the house before she could even say anything else.

"What the hell?" he said as he looked at the blank spot on the wall.

"Other than those two couples who just left, no one else has been here. Only us, and then tomorrow we have some new people due in." She paused before continuing. "Those couples. They were too nice. There's no way it could have been them."

"I'm gonna' give 'em a call anyway. Is there anything else missing?"

"Nothing that I know of."

At that moment they both froze and looked at each other. Without a word Malcom walked toward the stairs. Polly must have shared the same feeling because she grabbed hold of the back of his shirt and followed, having no intention of being left behind.

Standing in front of the Captain's room, Malcom put his hand on the doorknob. He hesitated for a heartbeat before twisting the knob. Most of the doors in the Inn were slightly warped due to age, and this one was no exception. There was a distinct sound as pressure was released on the latch and the door relaxed. He held onto the knob, keeping the door loosely closed as they both exhaled and looked at each other. Then, as Malcom pushed the door open, they each inhaled again and held their breaths.

The room was dark. He felt for the switch and snapped it on as they blinked. It was gone. Where the quilt had hung, there was nothing but an empty rod and a blank wall.

Malcom finally exhaled. In a barely audible voice he said, "Son of a bitch."

Polly, still clutching his shirt said, "Do you think . . ." She didn't finish the sentence, as if saying it would make it so.

"I don't know, but I'm going to find out." Malcom's anger was building. He pulled away from Polly's grip.

"Mal. Come on. Call the police and let them handle it."

He stopped and glared at her. "No. We're not going to call the police, at least not yet."

"Why not?"

"Because."

"That's not a reason." She paused and seemed to pull herself together. "Look, I know you think Alfred did this. I do too, but thinking that he did it and accusing him are two very different things. It really is for the police to handle. If you don't want to call them tonight, it can wait until the morning. No point ruining a beautiful evening with no guests."

He knew that she was right. "You're right, Pol. What's for dinner?"

"I picked up a couple of steaks when I was at the store. There are still some greens in the garden."

He was silent as for a moment. "Okay, we'll wait until morning."

"Good. I'll go pick a salad while you finish up outside and put the tractor away. When you finish, open some wine and get a shower. I'll start the grill and we'll have a nice dinner."

* * *

As Malcom lay in bed, all of his hungers sated, sleep wouldn't come. He looked over at Polly, who was already asleep. Despite the shadowy darkness, he could see her clearly, his mind filling in what details the shadows hid, and he smiled, thinking about how lucky he was. Then he closed his eyes and his thoughts drifted back to dinner; the steaks had been rare, the salad crisp, and the wine delightful. There had been no talk about the thefts or Alfred. There had been no need because he had already decided what he was going to do.

CHAPTER 46

OVER BREAKFAST, MALCOM CONVINCED POLLY to let him drive down to see Alfred. If he were unsuccessful, then, when he returned, they would call the police. She didn't like the idea, but she trusted Malcom and so she agreed.

Two and a half hours down and two and a half back, with no more than an hour between. Six hours was all he thought he would need.

* * *

There were no cars parked in front of Whitson's Antiques. Malcom parked, got out, and stretched his legs. Two and a half hours was a long time to be in one position.

Looking at Alfred's store, he couldn't tell if it was open or closed. He walked to the side of the building and peered around the corner. Alfred's truck was parked there. His heart began to beat more rapidly in his chest as he knew that soon they would be face to face.

Malcom took a deep breath, rehearsed in his mind one more time what he was going to say, stepped up onto the porch, and pulled the door open. The bell jingled, announcing his arrival, and he stepped in. It was still cluttered and dim and it took a moment for his eyes to adjust. "Hello," he called out.

There was no reply, so he began to walk around the store, looking for anything that might indicate that Alfred possessed what Malcom knew he had taken. The floor creaked under the weight of his step, and the sound of his work boots as they clacked on the bare wood floors made him wish he had worn a pair of running shoes instead. He remained alone as he toured the store, and the more time passed, the less confident he was in his mission. He thought, *"Maybe Polly was right; we should have just called the police."* Then a voice from behind made him jump.

"Malcom?"

He turned, his heart pounding. Alfred was just as he remembered: shirt buttoned up to the neck, thick, wire-rimmed glasses, and that deep, slightly nasal voice. Taking a deep breath, he said, "Alfred. I think you know why I am here."

Alfred continued to stare at him. "No. Why?" his voice was emotionless.

"I think you do." He tried to sound as intimidating as he could.

"I don't. I really don't. Why don't you tell me." Alfred's voice never wavered, nor did his gaze.

"The quilt. It's gone, and so is the framed letter."

"What quilt? What letter?"

Malcom couldn't believe the balls Alfred had, to stand there and act like he didn't know what he was talking about. "The quilt and letter you stole from us."

"I'm sorry, but I don't know what you're talking about. I don't like being accused of things I didn't do, so maybe you had better just leave before one of us does something that might be regretted later."

"Bullshit. Give them back," Malcom said, his voice beginning to rise.

"Like I said, I don't have them."

"You do," he insisted. This time his voice was a little bit louder and more commanding.

The look on Alfred's face never changed. He continued to stare at Malcom and his voice remained flat. "I don't. I think you should leave."

"I'm not leaving until I have them."

For the first time there was a subtle change in the tone of Alfred's response and a slight shift in his stance. Malcom watched as Alfred's eyes changed. His glasses still refracted them in an unnatural way, but instead of being goofy, they were now hard, cold, and a bit unnerving. "I told you. I don't have them and I think you should leave now." He paused and then added, "and even if I did, what makes you think I'd give them back?"

Malcom didn't move. It was his turn to stare silently. "So you do admit you have them."

"I apologized to your wife. I didn't have to do that. Now, you need to leave."

Malcom remained motionless. "They have nothing to do with your family's troubles two hundred years ago."

That last statement hit a nerve.

"You don't know anything about my family."

"I know what you told me. I know that the letters we found have nothing to do with them. I know. . ."

Alfred leaned in toward Malcom and cut him off as he spoke. "I have spent my life searching for the truth." His voice began to rise as if he were about to lose control. Then he paused, regained control, and in an even, more measured tone, continued, "and now it is within my grasp and I won't let you or anyone else stop me."

Now, with Alfred, only inches from his face, Malcom really began to question his decision to confront him, but it was too late to stop now. "So, you do have them," he repeated.

"I admit nothing. Your words, not mine."

Malcom softened his tone a bit. "Look Alfred, I'm sorry. I didn't mean to give you the impression that I know much about your family. And we haven't reported the thefts yet, because I wanted to give you the opportunity . . ."

"What opportunity?" Alfred continued to stand too close for comfort, and his tone remained defiant. "To what, confess to something I didn't do?"

Malcom tried again. "Just give them back to me and we can forget that this ever happened."

"I can't give what I don't have. And I want you to leave."

"Not without the quilt and the letter."

The speed with which Alfred moved surprised Malcom, who suddenly found himself being propelled toward the front of the store from behind with his arm twisted behind his back. "Hey," cried Malcom.

Alfred's strength was surprising, and he kept pushing him toward the door. But when they were still several steps away from the door, Malcom recovered enough to resist and stop Alfred's forward momentum. He slammed his body back against Alfred while ramming his head back into his face. Alfred cried out, lost his balance, and released his grip at the same time. An elephant leg umbrella stand, filled with umbrellas, fell over, spilling them like so many pick-up sticks in the crowded aisle. As Alfred tried to catch himself he cleared off the nearest display case with his arm, adding to the mess on the floor.

As soon as he was released, Malcom dove for the door, ignoring all the noise behind him. Alfred caught himself on the display case, which stopped his fall, then lunged forward in an attempt to catch Malcom. A sharp pain shot through his ankle when his leg became wedged between several of the umbrellas, and he fell forward over the fallen elephant leg and crumpled to the floor.

Malcom reached the door just as Alfred fell. He turned back as he pushed the door open. Alfred was on the floor in a tangle of umbrellas, lying across an elephant's leg. The whole situation might have been funny if it weren't for what had just happened and all the adrenalin pumping though his veins. He stopped, looked at Alfred, and said, "Have it your way, but this is your only chance to reconsider and return what you took."

As Alfred looked up at him from the tangle of umbrellas, Malcom continued. "Two weeks. I'll be back in two weeks to run the Rockdog, and that's when you will give them back to me."

CHAPTER 47

"HOW'D IT GO?" asked Polly when he walked in the door.

"Okay."

"Did you get them?" She seemed puzzled at his short answer.

"No. I didn't, but I will."

"What happened?" she asked, concern creeping into her voice.

"We talked. When I go down for the race, I expect that I'll get them then." It wasn't entirely true, but it would do.

"Great."

* * *

"Hey Dave."

"Jack."

Dave pulled the car door open, and Jack cranked the heat back to high to overcome the blast of cold air that filled the car as Dave threw his bag and a cooler in the back seat and then climbed in up front.

"Son of a bitch it's cold," he said as he rubbed his hands together. It was in the mid twenties, but sun and low forties were predicted by mid-morning.

"No shit, Sherlock," said Jack.

The moon, having set earlier, left a cloudless sky still bright with stars. The weather channel had promised a perfect fall day. It was just after 4:30 A.M. and the race started at 6:00.

"What did you bring for the aid station?" asked Jack.

"I cooked some new potatoes, cut 'em in half, with a little oil and salt. . . and a bag of M&M's."

"That's all?" said Jack, feigning surprise.

"What do you think?"

Jack said nothing and shifted into gear.

"I do have some adult beverages for after."

Jack smiled. There were some laws of the universe that you could just count on.

"And you?"

"Made a pan of double chocolate brownies."

"Nice."

Not much else was said during the forty-five minute ride to Ipswich.

The highway had almost no traffic so it was a quick forty-five minutes. Arriving at the elementary school where the start was, they were still early enough to get one of the treasured parking places at the school, but there weren't many left. It wouldn't be long before the additional parking would be needed, which meant quite a hike back for those late arrivals.

Despite the security lights around the school, they moved in a world of dark and shadows that was punctuated only by flashes of light from the cars of other arriving competitors, who circled, hoping to find a close-by place to park. As they unloaded Jack's car, their breath swirled about their heads in a way that was made all the more eerie by those circling flashes of light.

In spite of that continuous stream of traffic and the soft muffled voices of other new arrivals, what struck Jack was how quiet it was. Maybe it was the cold. Maybe it was the early hour, or maybe it was just the daunting task ahead, but the usual pre-race noise and excitement was absent, replaced by a more subtle, sober, almost conspiratorial kind of murmur.

As they rounded the corner of the school, things began to change. Ahead was the playground where they would check in, leave their bags, and add their donations to the aid table. Portable floodlights lit the area closest to the school, but you didn't have to go too far away before darkness would swallow you up.

Jack put his bag on the ground and pulled his coat close as he shivered. His fingers were already cold so he blew into his gloves in an attempt to warm his fingers.

Dave dumped his bag on the ground next to Jack's, looked around, and then said, "I'll go check us in. Be right back." Then he walked off.

As Jack watched him leave, he bent and began searching his bag for some warmer gloves. Now was the hard part. He wanted go for a short run to get his blood pumping and warm up, yet he didn't want to waste any more energy than was necessary because there was a very long way to run today. He rubbed his legs, hoping that the friction would suffice.

"Hey." Dave returned, "Here's your bib."

"Thanks. Say, did you happen to see if that guy is running?"

"Who?"

"Malcom. The guy who owns the B&B that we stayed at. His wife said he was planning on running today."

"That's right. No, I didn't even think of it."

"Why don't you stay with our stuff, and I'll go check." Jack hoped that walking around might help ward off the penetrating cold.

When Jack returned, he announced, "He's on the list, but he hasn't checked in yet." As soon as he announced the news, he noticed Paul and Christos, two of his other running buddies. Like everyone else there, they were trying hard to keep warm. Efforts included standing perfectly still in a solo hug while ignoring the cold, shifting from foot to foot as if running in place, blowing into their gloves, or doing what could best be described as small-motion jumping jacks. "Hey guys, I didn't know you were running today."

"We just decided last minute. A couple people couldn't run and we managed to get their bibs," said Christos.

"No shit. That just doesn't happen," said Dave. "Hey, did you know that today is Jack's first?"

"Well, you've got a perfect day for it," said Paul.

"So who were you looking for?" Christos asked Jack.

"A few weeks ago, Dave and I took the girls up north to this B&B,

and the guy who owned it had cut all these running trails in the woods around his property. He wasn't around so we never met him, but the trails were great and we got in some really good miles. His wife said that he was planning to run here today and I hoped to meet him."

"What's his name?" asked Paul.

"Malcom. I don't remember his last name, but I figured that there couldn't be too many Malcoms."

"Never heard of him. Have you Christos?"

Christos shook his head as he glanced at his watch. "It's almost time. I've got to get my headlamp and ditch this coat. I'll see you at the start." He walked off and Paul went with him.

"We won't see much of Paul today, but we can at least start together. Christos is more our speed," said Dave. Then he added, "At least for the first hour. A lot can happen in this kind of race, and it's best not to plan for much more than that. Too easy to get separated."

"Fine with me. I'm just following," said Jack as he dropped his heavy coat onto his bag. Instantly a chill went through him. He adjusted his headlamp and stuffed a heat packet into his glove. "I hate cold hands," he mumbled when he saw Dave looking at him.

"Okay everyone. It's about that time. If you could begin moving out into the field to the starting line, we'll get started in a few minutes," a voice called out.

"Ready?" asked Dave.

"Let's do it," was Jack's answer. Looking up at the still-dark sky, he hoped to see some indication that the sun was about to rise. He thought the sky looked a little brighter to the east, but he couldn't be sure.

Dave knew that Jack was nervous about the run. Having done trails in the dark before, he assured Jack again that it wasn't too bad. "You're gonna' be fine. Just go slow and easy until the sun comes up." Then he clapped Jack on the shoulder. "Let's go."

They joined the crowd of black, alien shapes, each with a headlamp on, out in the field. *How did I ever get talked into this?* thought Jack.

"Hey Jack, have a good run," said Paul before he disappeared into the darkness.

"Thanks."

"Hey guys," it was Christos. "Grilled cheese and tomato sandwiches, bacon optional, at the first aid station. Good luck."

Jack had heard about the aid stations. There were two in the woods and then the main one at the start/halfway/finish. He had added his brownies to the amazing pile of treats and snacks at the start. There really was something for everyone, but when Christos said bacon he had to ask, "Bacon?"

"Oh yeah. The first station is about five miles in and you'll smell it well before you get there. You have no idea how good it'll smell."

"And taste," said Dave.

Before Jack could say anything else, a gun fired and everyone began to move.

CHAPTER 48

THE FIRST FEW HUNDRED YARDS of the run went across the school's athletic fields. The grass was crunchy with frost, and what would have been very flat terrain in the daylight suddenly seemed really uneven and treacherous, even though he was wearing a headlamp. Jack settled into a relaxed and easy pace as he followed Dave and Christos. Well, at least he thought he was following them. In the pitch black he couldn't be sure. They made their way across the field and onto the fire road, the path lit by a series of green glowing light sticks, some on the ground and others hung in trees. It was a strange and scary sensation being able to see only a very small stretch of the trail ahead.

The one time Jack lifted his eyes off the trail, he saw a long dotted line of white spots extending out ahead, each made by a single headlamp. That look only lasted a moment because he immediately felt disoriented, almost dizzy, because of the surrounding darkness. Each step was taken in faith.

As they moved up the fire road, loose rocks and ruts challenged their balance and the strength of their ankles. The sky was beginning to lighten by the time they made the turn off the road and onto a narrow trail. It went up, relentlessly turning and twisting, with switchbacks and very few dips. There were places where trunks of long-fallen trees had to be leapt over or a stone wall crossed. The hill was unforgiving, but as they climbed, so did the sun, ever so slowly.

By the time they had descended the hill and the trail returned them to the fire road, the sky had changed from black to a light grayish blue. Headlamps were removed and their steps became less tenuous and more confident as the path could finally be seen.

Jack picked out Dave ahead, although now there were several other runners between them. He could see that Dave was still running with

Christos.

"Son of a bitch," Jack mumbled under his breath as he rounded a curve and saw ahead that about a hundred feet of the road was under water and runners were splashing through it. It looked to be at least six inches deep and he knew it would be cold. After all, it was November, and the outside temperature was at best still in the thirties.

He watched as Christos and Dave slogged into the water.

The closer he got to the water, the wetter, muddier and slipperier the road became.

"I hate wet feet," a woman's voice said behind him.

He had begun to slow his pace the closer to the water he came. "Me too," said Jack, too intent on his footing to turn and see who had said that.

"I'm on your right," she said as she began to pass him. Reflexively he turned toward the voice to see who it was. His foot slipped, his arms wind-milled, and he cross-stepped as he fought to keep his balance. In that same split second he was trying to keep from falling, she had pulled alongside and, because of his wild gyrations, they nearly collided.

"Ooh!" she cried out as she dodged away from his attempt to dodge away from her. Then it was over. Neither fell, and no real harm was done, but the water was even closer.

"Sorry," said Jack as he finally got a look at her. She had long brown hair that was pulled in a ponytail through the back of her cap. Her ears were cherry red from the cold, as were her cheeks. There was a sparkle to her eyes and she had a big smile on her face. Jack wondered how genuine it was considering their near collision.

"That's okay," she said, waving a red-gloved hand.

As she pulled slightly ahead, he was able to get a better look at her. She looked like she might be a bit younger than Max, nearly his height and thin, not a skinny thin, but a very fit thin. She was wearing the obligatory black tights, but instead of a loose jacket, she was wearing a form-fitting, long-sleeved racing top that had a short turtleneck collar. It too was black, except for some accent panels of royal blue. She could have been a comic book superhero, as her outfit left little to the imagination.

"Come on, don't think about it. If you do, it'll be far worse than it really is," she called out to him as she began prancing through the water.

It was too late to think any more about the water as he followed her lead. He really didn't begin to feel how cold the water was until his last few steps. As Jack emerged from the water, he slowed and stepped to the side of the road and began walking. He was wet only to just above his ankles, but that was enough for him to feel really cold. Other runners continued to finish their trek through the water, some stopping, some walking like he did, while others kept on running. As water squished out of his shoes he looked down the trail for Dave and Christos. They weren't in sight, but she was.

She had stopped and was adjusting one of her shoes. "Thanks," he said as he walked to where she was retying her shoe.

From the look on her face, he guessed that she hadn't seen him approaching. With a last tug on her laces she stood up and faced him. "Oh, you're welcome," she said as recognition washed over her face.

You want to run together for a bit?"

"Sure. Let's go. My feet are getting cold."

He couldn't help but notice how blue her eyes were and how they lit up when she talked.

"My name is Sylvie."

"Jack."

"Nice to meet you Jack. Have you run here before?"

"Nope, first time."

"A virgin." The way she said it was very matter-of-fact, and yet somehow it sounded just a little dirty.

He smiled. "You?"

"My third. I really love running in the woods. So much better than the roads."

Jack had to agree.

Soon they turned off the road again and were back on single track. He was content to let her lead the way. After all, she had run here before. At least, that's what he told himself.

"Do you smell it?" she called back to him.

"What?" he called back.

"The bacon. Do you smell the bacon?"

As she said this, his senses were assaulted by the most heavenly of smells. He smelled the bacon.

They arrived less than five minutes later. An official checked them in by recording their bib numbers. Jack asked about Dave and Christos and was told they had checked in about five to ten minutes ago. He didn't see them so he assumed they were back on the trail.

Other officials directed them to drinks: water, Gatorade, adult beverages. Still others called out from behind the food table, "We have cookies, grilled cheese, bananas." The only thing that needed no mention was the bacon and Jack couldn't resist taking a slice. Sylvia was nibbling on a grilled cheese with tomato sandwich.

"This is amazing," said Jack.

"I know. It's so perfect, and on a morning like this, it just doesn't get any better." She finished her snack and gave Jack the 'you ready' look. He nodded and they were off. The next aid station was about four twisting, torturous miles away over alternating fire roads and single track trails. The treats were welcome, but they lacked the impact that that first station had.

As the miles progressed, occasionally they overtook other runners, and at times they were passed. They alternated the lead and encouraged each other whenever the terrain became extreme. As they returned to the first section of fire road that they had last run in the dark, Jack was amazed to see just how rough it was and how much of an uphill climb it had been. Now, as they ran down, they had to pay close attention

161

to where their feet landed. The surface was covered with loose rocks, many the size of softballs, in ruts where rain had washed out smaller, softer material.

Jack was in the lead when he heard her cry out. He looked back and saw that she was down on the side of the road.

Another runner was standing over her, and by the time Jack got back to her, several others had stopped as well.

"Sylvie, what happened? You all right?" Since he used her name, those who had first stopped to help must have assumed that she was with Jack, because they began, one by one, to stand and resume their races.

Pain and frustration was all over her face, but there were no tears. Her red gloves were covered with dirt, and a hole in her tights revealed a scraped and soon to be bloody right knee. "It's my left ankle."

Jack helped her move into a more comfortable sitting position. "What about your knee?" he asked. She looked down at the reddening scrape and said, "Just a flesh wound. I didn't twist it or anything, but I twisted my ankle good."

Gently he took her ankle in his hands. She grimaced and he could feel her pull back a bit. "Sorry. I don't know if it's broken or just sprained. How does it feel to you?"

"It hurts." She tried moving her foot, and he could tell from the expression on her face that she was fighting the pain.

"Listen, don't move. I'll go get some help. You're in no condition to move." He began to peel off his jacket to give to her.

"No. Help me up. I can make it back." With that she grabbed his arm and began to pull herself up, nearly pulling him down on top of her.

He regained his balance as her grip slipped and she sat down hard. "Sylvie. Wait a minute. This is a bad idea."

"I don't care. Help me up."

He stood looking down at her and could see that she was not giving him a choice.

"Fine, but you know this is a bad idea."

"Shut up."

He shrugged. Then, first standing in front of her, he leaned over her and said, "Okay. You're going to put your arms around my neck so we can get your good leg in a better position for you to stand. I'll help you."

She nodded yes. It must have looked pretty strange to others as they ran by to see this couple entwined like that. He was surprised at how solid she was, and when she pulled up to reposition her good leg, her strength surprised him as she nearly pulled him over again. He had to lean back against her weight and wrap his arms around her, and then with the combination of their efforts and some leverage he was able to pull her up until she was standing.

Her arms remained around his neck and his encircled her waist while their faces stopped inches apart. They each looked directly into the other's eyes for what was probably a split second, but it felt like forever. Her eyes, the most amazing shade of blue he had ever seen, were incredibly sexy, and he was mesmerized.

"Thanks," she said, breaking the spell as she quickly pulled her arms from around him and looked away. He did the same and took a half step back. She was balancing on her good foot but had to steady herself by holding onto his shoulder.

"This is a dumb idea," said Jack.

"No, it's not. If you will help me a little, I'll be able to hop down to the finish area and I'll be fine.

It was slow hopping because of the rocky terrain, but with arms around each other, they finally made it to smoother ground. Once there, their pace increased.

"You know, if this were a three-legged race, I think we'd win," she said, trying hard to make light of the situation. Still, Jack could tell she was in some serious pain.

That was when a pickup truck came up the road toward them. "The cavalry has arrived," said Jack.

By the time the truck had returned them to the start/finish area, both Jack and Sylvie were shivering. Jack stayed with her as an aide ushered them into the warm school, where a waiting EMT promptly looked at her now-swollen ankle. Immobilized and packed in ice, Sylvie braced herself for a trip to the hospital.

"Sorry, Jack," she said.

"For what?"

"For ruining your day. You were having such a good run."

"I'm fine. It's you whose day is ruined. Let me know how things turn out. Maybe we can do this again next year."

"Thanks."

Jack watched as the EMTs began to wheel her out to the waiting ambulance. As the doors closed, he headed out for something to eat before continuing his run. He was going to miss running with her.

"Jack!" When he turned, he saw one of the race organizers walking toward him. "Jack, you're going to go on?"

Swallowing the chocolate chip cookie he was chewing on, he said, "Yes, in a minute."

"Okay. We're going to give you a thirty-minute allowance for what you did in helping her."

This surprised him. "You don't have to do that."

"No, we do." Then before Jack could say anything else, he said, "Have a good run. See you at the finish." And he walked off.

"Cool," said Jack with another mouthful of cookie.

CHAPTER 49

JACK WALKED UP THAT FIRST HILL where the road became trail. He wasn't the only one. There was still a long way to go, the adrenaline rush of dealing with Sylvie was wearing off, and he could feel the trails in his legs. He wondered how far ahead Dave and Christos were. They certainly didn't know about Sylvie.

As he neared the top of the hill, two runners flew past him. He quickly did the math and realized that they had to be running the 50-mile event. They must be on their third loop. "*How the hell do they do that?*" he wondered to himself. All he could do was shake his head and start running again.

Ahead he could see a number of runners strung out single file, but because of all the twists and turns, it was impossible to tell how far ahead they were. At one sharp turn he glanced back and couldn't see anyone. He knew others were behind him, but he still felt very alone and that feeling was a bit creepy.

The day was getting nicer by the hour. Now he could feel the temperature steadily rising. It must be close to forty already. He stuffed his hat in his pocket and unzipped his jacket about halfway as he continued to run along alone. He smiled, and since his goal was only to finish, he did not press the pace. He wanted to enjoy the day and remember every bit of the experience.

Cresting the hill, he remembered that it was a long, tortuous way down before reaching the water. He was not looking forward to splashing through that ice-cold water a second time, but having survived it once, he knew that he could deal with it. Ahead there were some very short, steep rises followed by equally steep drops. He figured that the trail was heading east because of the way that sunbeams knifed through gaps in the trees. At one point, he slowed to take it all in. It reminded him of those tacky paintings you would see on late-night television, where images would flash across the screen while an overly excited voice shouted, "Real Oil Paintings from ONLY $3.99 to $24.99! Credit cards accepted! Call now blah, blah, blah." He almost expected to see a unicorn peek out from behind a tree.

"Come on. Enough of this shit. Get your legs moving," he chided himself. Jack remained alone as he ran, while the trail became increasingly difficult as it followed the ridge of the hill. The quick turns, dips, and rises were exhilarating and made him feel as if he were racing on skis. Each step was more of a hop and leap as his weight shifted right, then left, and his arms flew out to help maintain balance as he careened down the drops before slowing and powering himself up the next rise.

He was on the edge of control as he reached the end of a steep drop, and as the trail flattened out along a ridge, he ran into one of those bright beams of sunlight. For no more than a split second, he lost sight of the trail, but it was enough. He planted his left foot to drive himself to the right, when his foot went out from under him. It might have been a loose rock, wet leaves, or even a patch of dry pine needles that caused his foot to slip. The exact cause didn't matter because in that moment he went from running to tumbling down the side of the hill. All he could do was try to protect himself as he bounced, rolled, and slid over rocks, bushes, sticks, and stones. He felt no pain. That would come later.

The last thing Jack remembered of the fall was seeing a tree he could not avoid. The impact knocked the wind out of him, but he remained conscious. He could see small patches of blue sky above through the trees. As his breath returned, he lay there and slowly began to assess his condition.

He was beginning to feel the effects of the fall. He hurt all over. It was a dull, aching kind of pain. Unable to tell exactly what hurt the most, gingerly he began to move one body part after another. It was a relief that everything worked, but with each movement, the aches and pains became more defined.

Having established that nothing seemed to be broken, he lifted his head. He could feel it throbbing right through his eyeballs as he looked down his body. His tights and jacket were torn, and he could see his feet, all three of them. "Ohh," he moaned and let his head fall back.

As he lay there, still trying to understand what had happened, the throbbing in his head seemed to lessen. He looked up at the sky and realized that he could see perfectly clearly. "*Well, okay then*," he thought to himself, and he lifted his head again. The throbbing returned, but not quite as badly as before. He looked down at his feet again. There were still three of them, and this time he saw that one of the running shoes did not match the other two. He moaned again as he lay back down, trying to understand what was going on. After several deep breaths, the throbbing once again began to subside. Three feet. It made no sense, so he began to sit up again.

Where before he had lifted only his head, this time he pushed himself up using his arms. The throbbing in his head increased and the ground under his right elbow seemed soft. "Mud, I'm in mud," he thought. He turned his head slowly, but instead of mud, a pair of lifeless eyes stared up at him.

Panic overcame pain. "Ahhhh!" he screamed, but no sound came out, only a rush of air as he emptied his lungs and rolled to his left, crabbing away from the body. He cried out a second time, and this time there was sound, loud and primal.

CHAPTER 50

WITH SOME COOKIES and a sports drink in hand, the solitary runner watched the emergency personnel barrel into the school's parking lot. First to arrive was the Ipswich police, followed by an ambulance and a fire truck. The race director greeted them with much gesturing. With grim faces they hustled past the food tables and followed several animated runners.

Moments later, a small pickup truck arrived and drove off after them, eventually picking them up just before they disappeared from sight. The runner walked over to the corner of the school and looked toward the front. The ambulance was parked closest to the school, near the corner, with its lights still flashing. His curiosity satisfied, he walked over to where a group of runners holding red Solo cups were standing and asked, "What's going on?"

"I heard that someone fell down one of the hills and was hurt," a woman said.

Another added, "I overheard that the guy who fell landed on a body."

"Hey, look, it must be really serious," said the first woman, pointing back toward the school.

A contingent of uniformed State Police Troopers, along with another half-dozen men, some with cameras and others with what looked like large toolboxes, were converging on the finish area.

"A body?" he asked.

"That's what I heard," said the second. He was a bit distracted as they watched the race director run over to greet the police. After a moment, with much pointing and gesturing, they too headed out across the fields toward the woods.

"*That was quick.*" He knew that it was inevitable that the body would be found; he just didn't expect it to happen quite so soon.

Aloud he simply said, "That sucks." Then he walked off.

Runners continued to come off the course in a steady stream, some finishing, while others grabbed a snack or a drink and headed back out on to the course. There was a continuous buzz as everyone who arrived heard the news. He watched and listened and was sitting by the playground when the truck returned. In the back were several EMTs and a runner.

He watched as the truck drove past the school toward the waiting ambulance. *"He must have been the one who fell and found the body,"* he thought to himself.

* * *

Jack remembered screaming. Then there were voices calling down to him from the top of the embankment. He scrambled up toward the voices and arms reached out for him as he reached the top. Questions. Answers. Stunned looks. Someone began running back in the direction they had just come from. More people arrived. There was a lot of commotion and confusion. The same pickup truck that had rescued Sylvie brought Jack back to the finish area, as others guided rescue personnel back to the body.

* * *

It was time to go. In all of the confusion, no one noticed as the solitary runner picked up an extra bag and slowly limped toward the parking lot. As he reached the front of the school, he saw the runner who had been brought in by the truck sitting on the back of the ambulance. He was sporting several bandages on his arms and face and looked dazed as he sat staring at the ground. The man kept walking. After all, he had a car to find.

CHAPTER 51

AS DAVE AND CHRISTOS crossed the finish line, they couldn't help but notice that there were several State Troopers as well as local police in the finish area. "What the hell is going on?" Dave asked the timer.

"A body was found in the woods by one of the runners in the race. Word has it, the dead guy was a runner too. They haven't brought the body out yet."

"Holy shit," Dave mumbled. Then, looking at all the police presence, he thought to himself, "*Well, I guess there won't be any beers today.*"

"Hey, there's Paul. Let's go see if he knows anything," said Christos.

"I'll be right with you; I need the head." Dave turned and walked toward the school. As he rounded the corner of the building he could see the flashing red lights of an ambulance and a fire truck, and the blues of several cruisers. When he reached the door to the school he saw Jack, sitting on the back bumper of the ambulance.

"*Son of a bitch,*" Dave thought to himself. Aloud he yelled, "Jack?"

Ironically, it was the same ambulance that had taken Sylvie to the hospital. Jack had a wool blanket over his shoulders and was holding a cup of hot coffee while an EMT bandaged his forehead. Forgetting about nature's call, Dave rushed over.

Jack looked up. "Hey, Dave."

"What the hell happened to you?" he asked, seeing that there were cuts on his hands and knees, and his forehead had been bandaged.

"I fell."

"You fell?"

"Yeah, I fell. I don't know. I was running along. I must have not been watching where I stepped, I slipped, fell down an embankment, and landed on this guy."

"You're the one who found the guy!"

Before Dave could ask any more questions, a police officer walked up to them. "Mr. Beale?"

"Yes."

"I'm Lieutenant Malloy. You okay?"

Jack looked over at him. "I'll live."

"Do you mind if I ask you some questions?"

"No. Uh, sure. Okay." He took a sip of his coffee.

"I'll be right back," said Dave. He really needed to use the head and he had to find Christos and Paul.

Jack repeated his story for the lieutenant, filling in as many details as he could. Dave returned with the guys before Malloy had finished, so they stood by, listening, waiting for him to finish, so they could get the real scoop.

"Thanks," the lieutenant said as he closed his notebook. "I have all your contact information. If there are any further questions, either I or the State Police will be in touch."

A continuous stream of runners walked past the ambulance now, moving to or from their cars, and each one slowed and looked at Jack sitting there. Some asked if he was okay, while others only paused and then hurried by.

That was when a second ambulance arrived. With its back-up signal beeping, it eased up a short distance from the one where Jack was sitting and came to a stop. As soon as it was stopped, they all turned and watched as two men climbed out and hurried off toward the field, their kits slung over their shoulders. That's when the back doors of the ambulance opened and a third EMT climbed out. Dave, Christos, and Paul saw a pair of crutches emerge, but Jack, his view blocked, didn't. Suddenly a woman's voice called out, "Jack?"

He turned his head. "Sylvie?" said Jack. He was surprised to see her again.

Dave, Christos, and Paul all turned their heads at the same time, first toward Jack and then back in the direction the voice came from.

Hobbling toward them on crutches was a very attractive woman wearing a stability boot on her left ankle.

"Guys, this is Sylvie. We were running together but she fell. She twisted her ankle and I helped her back."

"Hi," she said while trying to balance on one leg, hold on to her crutches, and extend her hand out to them all at the same time. She dropped one of the crutches and began to wobble. Christos caught the crutch and then her elbow to steady her.

"Thanks," she said to Christos. She took her crutch and hopped toward Jack, sitting down next to him on the ambulance's bumper. As soon as she was settled, Christos walked off. Then he came back with a blanket and handed it to her.

"Thanks," she said again. She pulled the blanket around her shoulders and turned toward Jack. "So what happened to you?" she asked.

"I fell."

"You too!"

"Come on Jack, tell her the rest of it," said Dave. Then, turning to Sylvie, he added, "You're not going to believe this."

"What?" said Sylvie. Concern filled her voice, and worry showed in her eyes as she turned and looked straight into Jack's.

"I slipped and fell down an embankment and landed on a dead guy."

The color drained from her face. She was about to ask Jack for more details, but before she could say anything else, the third EMT walked up and asked, "You guys okay?"

"Yeah," Jack answered for both of them while she nodded.

Someone shouted, and they all looked back toward the finish area. Coming around the corner of the school, maybe fifty yards away, a full contingent of EMTs, firefighters, and state and local police officers were pushing and pulling a gurney. Lieutenant Malloy was with them. As they got closer, it became clear that strapped to the gurney was a black body bag.

"Gotta' go," said the third EMT, and he rushed back to the ambulance that had delivered Sylvie.

The four guys and Sylvie watched in silence as the gurney was wheeled toward that second ambulance. Malloy halted the entourage before they got to the ambulance and called over to Jack, "Would you mind taking another look, see if you recognize him?"

"Sure." As he stood, his head began spinning and he tipped toward Sylvie.

"Jack!" she cried out as he began to fall onto her. She reached up to steady him as much as to keep him from falling on her.

He paused and the spinning stopped, "Thanks," he said looking down at her. "I'm good."

Gingerly he walked toward the gurney, with Sylvie and his friends following close behind.

Jack's head began to spin again as he reached the gurney. As he reached out to steady himself, Dave came to his side and grabbed his arm. "You okay?"

"I'm fine. Just a little dizzy, but I'm okay."

Malloy unzipped the bag and both he and Dave looked together. Christos, Sylvie, and Paul, also curious, edged closer to get a peek. Jack looked at the lifeless eyes and the pale, bluish skin. He slowly shook his head back and forth, "That's him, but I don't know who he is. Sorry."

"Thanks."

Before Jack turned away he said, "He must have been in the race. Couldn't you just check his bib number?"

"He didn't have one on. We searched the area but didn't find one."

Jack thought a minute, then added. "Once everyone has finished, can't you check the results to see if anyone didn't finish? If he was registered, that should tell you who he is."

"Already thought of that. We're checking everyone off as they come in."

Malloy looked over at Jack's friends. "Any of you recognize him?"

After a few awkward moments, each in turn said no. Malloy was obviously a little frustrated, so before zipping the bag shut, he turned toward the crowd of gawkers that had gathered and made the same offer to them. The result was the same. No one knew him.

Finally Malloy zipped the bag shut. The EMTs loaded the gurney into the ambulance and slammed the doors. Malloy turned toward everyone gathered and said, "Thank you. I know that must have been difficult. If anyone remembers anything else that might be helpful, don't hesitate to give me a call." He handed business cards to everyone as the crowd dispersed. When he was finished, he thanked Jack again and walked off toward the finish area.

"So Jack . . ." Sylvie turned and looked straight into his eyes. Her blue eyes completed the question, while Dave, Christos, and Paul moved in closer.

He repeated his story again.

CHAPTER 52

AS SOON AS THE DOORS slammed shut, the ambulance with the body
drove off. With the body gone, all of the other responders began to
leave. First the fire truck and then the medical examiner and his team,
followed by the State Police Crime Unit. Finally, all that remained was
Lieutenant Malloy. It was now late afternoon and the sun was sinking
as fast as the temperature. The ambulance Jack and Sylvie were sitting
on suddenly roared to life, and one of the EMTs came around to the
back. "Sorry, guys. We have to go to another call."

Jack stood and for a second time was hit with another head rush.
This time he braced himself against the ambulance. "You sure you're
okay?" asked the EMT. "We can pass the call off and take you to the
hospital instead."

"No. I'm fine," he answered. Then he tossed the wool blanket into
the back of the ambulance.

"You sure?" said Dave.

"Yeah, I'm sure."

The EMT climbed in and pulled the ambulance doors shut. It
wasn't until they were closed that Sylvie realized she still had a blanket
wrapped around her shoulders. "Hey wait," she called out, but her cry
was lost as the engine started. "I still have a blanket."

"Here. Let me have it," said Christos. She gave him the blanket at
the same time the red lights began flashing and the ambulance began
to move. Christos banged on the back door, the brake lights came on,
and he disappeared around the vehicle. Almost immediately, the brake
lights went out and the ambulance drove off, leaving the five of them
standing by the school.

The sun was going down and the temperature was dropping
steadily. "I'm cold," said Jack. Then, looking at Sylvie he added, "You

174

must be too."

She nodded yes.

"My stuff's out back in the playground. Yours?"

"Same," and she began hobbling in that direction.

Jack walked beside her, with Christos hovering and the other two following. Little was said on the walk to get their bags. As they passed other runners who were returning to their cars, Jack couldn't help but notice the looks that they were getting. "We must look a sight," he said to Sylvie.

She looked over at him, paused, and then began to giggle. "We must. I think we need a story."

"Isn't the truth good enough?"

"I suppose it is," she said as she continued crutching along.

When they reached the playground, the race director saw them and came right over.

"Hey guys. How're you holding up?"

"Fine, just need to get into some warmer clothes. Any word on who he was?" asked Jack.

"No idea. So far everyone who has finished has been accounted for and the last few dozen out on the course, I know personally."

Lieutenant Malloy joined them. "Jack, Sylvie. You doin' okay?"

They both nodded yes. He added, "I'm going to get going. You have my card, so call me if you think of anything else."

"Sure," said Jack.

The lieutenant turned and walked away.

"So Sylvie, do you need a ride home?" It was Christos.

She looked over at him and smiled. "No, my right foot is fine, so I can drive. I could use a hand getting my stuff to the car though."

"Let me," he said as he reached for her bag.

Turning toward Jack, Sylvie extended her arms while still managing to keep the crutches secure. He stepped into the offered hug, and as they embraced, Sylvie said softly, "Jack, thank you. I hope we never do this again."

All he heard was 'never . . . again.' His heart skipped a beat, and he pulled away as disappointment washed over him before he saw her smile and understood.

She must have seen his reaction because she quickly added, "I mean this," indicating their wounds. "Let's keep in touch." She handed him a piece of paper with a phone number on it.

He blushed a bit as he recovered and stammered, "Yes, let's."

Christos picked up Sylvie's bag. "Ready?"

She nodded and they all headed for the parking lot.

* * *

"Jack! What happened?" cried Max when she saw him.

Dave answered for him. "He had a rough day."

"I can see that. What actually happened?"

Dave started to answer, but Jack cut him short. "I fell."

Max didn't say anything else, but the look on her face demanded a better answer than that. Dave cut in, "He fell on the trail, rolled down a hill and landed on another runner."

"Jack!" she cried again.

"I'm fine."

"You're not."

Dave jumped in again. "No, he's fine, just a few scrapes, bumps, and bruises." Then he added, "and maybe a mild concussion."

"A concussion! Jack Beale, you're getting cleaned up and we're going to the hospital."

"Max, I'm fine. A little rest and I'll be okay. It's nothing, really."

"Yeah, I can see that," Max said sarcastically.

She wasn't buying it, and her look said more than any words could. "And what about the other guy? The one you landed on top of?"

It was Dave's turn, "Oh, he's dead."

An uneasy silence filled the room.

She finally exploded. "Dead! What do you mean he's dead?" Panic had crept into her voice.

It was now Jack's turn. "Max, take it easy. Dave's just messin' with you."

"But he said the guy was dead."

"Oh, he was."

"This isn't funny Jack Beale."

"I know. He was already dead, at the bottom of the hill, and he probably wouldn't have been found if I hadn't tripped and fallen. Landing on him kept me from hitting a tree that probably would have killed me. So we each did the other a favor."

"Oh my God," murmured Max under her breath.

CHAPTER 53

IT WAS MID-AFTERNOON BEFORE Polly realized that she hadn't heard from Malcom, who had gone down to the race the night before. He had woken her up that morning with a phone call at 4:30. In response to her grumpy "Hello?" he had apologized and said that he loved her. Mollified, she had wished him good luck. The last thing he had said before hanging up was that he'd call after the race, just before he started home.

Now she told herself that there were any number of reasons why he hadn't called: maybe there was no cell coverage, maybe he had forgotten, maybe he had lost his phone. She tried calling his cell. It rang, but he didn't answer before it cut to voicemail, so she left a message. Convinced that there was a logical reason why he hadn't picked up, she decided to wait a half hour before trying again. Still, as much as she tried to reassure herself that nothing was wrong, she was worried.

* * *

The race was over for another year. The final fifty-miler finished and it was almost as dark out now as it had been at the start. A final celebratory beer was cracked as the remaining food was divided up, the timing equipment put away, and the results tabulated. Lieutenant Malloy stayed until the very end, but he declined the beer. Everyone was accounted for, even the few who did not finish. The most logical conclusion was that the body they found belonged to someone who had been running as a bandit in the race. It seemed unlikely that he was just some random runner who happened to be out there in the woods that early in the day.

He walked briskly to his car, noting that all the vehicles in front of the school were gone except for the few belonging to the members of the race committee. The remaining dry leaves in the trees surrounding the school rattled as the wind picked up. The temperature was dropping fast; it was already lower than it was when the sun came up and getting colder by the minute. He shivered. As he opened the car door, a gust of wind nearly pulled it out from his hand.

As Malloy waited for the heat to kick in, he reviewed his notes. Even though he had been at the finish line nearly all day, and he had talked with dozens of runners and spectators, he did not have any clues as to the identity of the dead man. As heat began to fill his car, he shifted into gear while thinking to himself, "*Maybe, I'll get lucky and his car will be in the overflow lot down the road.*"

The overflow parking was less than a mile away, but as he circled the lot, he saw no cars. "Damn," he muttered under his breath.

Despite the fact that the inside of his car was getting beyond warm, he was still cold. He stopped and thought about some of what he had learned during the day: Runners were nuts. Why anyone would want to run that far was beyond him; they looked so miserable when they finished and yet acted so thrilled.

* * *

After thirty minutes, Polly placed that second call. Again, there was no answer. By late afternoon, she was calling Malcom's cell every ten minutes, and with each call her panic grew. She called the motel he had stayed at and was assured that he had checked out and had not returned. She found a copy of the race entry and called the information number. There was no answer, but she was able to leave a message. Other calls were placed to Max and Ben's Place, all with no success. She could only hope that someone would call her back.

When darkness fell, Polly moved to the kitchen table. She lit a small candle, just for company. As shadows danced within the room's dark silence she sat cradling a half-finished cup of tea that had grown cold. Sleep finally defeated the dark thoughts that threatened to overwhelm her.

Polly jumped when the sound of the phone reverberated through the room. At the first ring she looked at the clock. For some reason, this seemed an important thing to do. It was nearly 8:00 P.M. Another ring. The sound seemed to explode each nerve in her body. Before the phone rang a third time, she grabbed it with a shaking hand. Her heart felt like it might pound right out of her chest. But the voice on the other end of the line wasn't Malcom's. She took a deep breath before answering. "Yes, this is she."

The conversation lasted less than five minutes, and when the line went dead, she couldn't hang up the phone, as if that single action would suddenly make the words from the call all the more true. All the strength went out of her legs and she collapsed back into her chair. She stared at the phone, still in her hand, as she fought to get a clean breath and regain control.

Before hanging up the phone, she tried to remember exactly what she had been told. A runner had been found dead out on the course, but it wasn't Malcom. The race director was sure of that. Malcom had signed in and finished the race well before noon. There was no mistake. Everyone's number was checked. He was sorry he couldn't help her further. She had his number if she needed to contact him again.

"Malcom, where are you?" she said softly as a tear ran down her cheek. She couldn't put a name to her fear, but she knew it was very real. She looked at the clock. Only three minutes had passed since the call had ended, and yet it felt like an eternity. She took a deep breath and tried to calm herself down. She trusted Malcom. There had to be a logical reason he wasn't home yet. She'd wait a bit longer before calling the police.

CHAPTER 54

THE FIRST RAYS OF SUNLIGHT touched Polly's face and she awoke with a start. She looked around. It had been a dream, hadn't it? Disoriented, her brain did not comprehend at first what her eyes were telling her. She was at her kitchen table, there were scribbles on scraps of paper everywhere, her neck ached, and her mouth was dry. She picked up one piece of paper, looked at it, and put it down. Then she picked up another and did the same. Slowly, the dream faded and reality took hold.

* * *

Several hours south, in Ipswich, Massachusetts, Lieutenant Malloy was already on his way in to the station. He was sipping on his second cup of coffee, ordered from his favorite donut shop. His first cup, at home, merely got him moving and out the door. Today, though, the second cup was more about habit than need; his mind was already puzzling over that runner found dead in the woods.

* * *

Jack had fallen asleep early and quickly, but it wasn't a restful sleep. He tossed and turned as he relived his fall and the discovery of that man at the bottom of the hill. In the dream, he never went back up the hill; he just kept falling, like an endless film loop, and each time he saw something different. Once it was feet, another time, an arm or the man's legs, always a part, never the whole. Every time he fell he was a spectator to his fall, except once. That time he felt every stick as it scratched his skin; he felt every rock as it dug into his muscles; he heard the rustling of leaves and the sounds of his body as it slid and rolled down the embankment. That was the time he saw the dead man's face and he could only stare at it. He wanted to scream, he wanted to get away, but he couldn't move. He couldn't do anything except stare at that lifeless face.

There was something about the expression on his face that both fascinated and bothered Jack. He could see the shock, surprise, and pain that must have been felt, but there was something else. As Jack stared into those lifeless eyes, it came to him. Recognition. The dead man had seen something or someone that he knew, and at that moment Jack knew that his fall hadn't been an accident at all.

That was the moment he jumped and let out a scream—or what felt like a scream. He fell back down onto his pillow and drifted back to sleep. Now Sylvie was there with him.

Either the jump or the scream woke Max, who rolled over and pressed close to him. "Good morning, sleepy head," Max purred into Jack's ear. Hearing Sylvie's voice gave him comfort and he drifted back into his dreams.

* * *

Alfred woke early, but he didn't get out of bed immediately. He lay there, thinking about the previous twenty-four hours.

He had expected that he would be able to explain to Malcom why he took the quilt and letter. He had been certain that this time Malcom would listen, understand, and let him keep them as a gift. That was how it was supposed to be.

He sat up and swung his legs over the edge of the bed. As soon as he did, his ankle began to throb. He looked down and could see that it was swollen. Running a marathon on a not fully recovered ankle was perhaps foolish, but he knew it had been necessary. His eyes drifted to the pile of clothes on the floor, and he saw, still pinned to his singlet, Malcom's number. He smiled at his brilliance.

He'd have to get rid of that. His brother would have been proud. People always thought his brother the smart one, but he had fooled them all once and he would fool them all again.

He replayed every detail in his mind.

Malcom had been so arrogant. All Alfred had done was wish him good luck. Then Malcom had run ahead. He didn't want to talk. He didn't want to hear how grateful Alfred was, how helpful his gift was. He said that as soon as they got back to the start area, he was going to call the police. Alfred couldn't let that happen. He tried to run away but Alfred followed. Suddenly he knew what he had to do. Considering the darkness and the terrain, a slip and fall were inevitable. Alfred made sure of that.

Certain that no one had seen him push Malcom down the embankment, Alfred had followed after him. At the bottom of the slope, he found Malcom's limp body. The headlamp had been ripped off his head and lay on the ground near the body and provided just enough light for Alfred to see that Malcom was unconscious, his face was badly injured, probably from hitting the tree against which he rested, but he was still alive. A short length of broken tree branch finished what the fall hadn't. When he was sure that Malcom wasn't breathing, he removed Malcom's bib, pinned it on his own singlet, and made sure there was no other identification on the body. After smashing Malcom's headlamp and with the stick in hand he returned to the race. Many miles later the stick was discarded and "Malcom" went on to finished his first trail marathon. His ankle was sore and he was limping slightly, but he finished.

Thinking back, he smiled in triumph. Alfred would have been proud. He was always thought of as the better one, but he wasn't. Now he would show them. Years of anxiety and torment over the injustices that his family had suffered were soon to be righted. He had done what he had to do and there would be no stopping him. He had what he needed, the letter and the quilt were his to keep, and now all that remained was for him to put the pieces of the puzzle together and his family name would be restored. He moved his foot. There was pain, but it was a good pain.

After finishing, he watched as rescue people arrived, and he listened to all the rumors and stories. No one had a clue that the terrible accident was anything but. It was so simple to take Malcom's bag, walk to his car, and drive off.

The first thing he did when he arrived back at his store was to drive the car around back, out of sight from the street. It took him less than an hour to clear enough space in the garage below to fit the car in. Before covering it with a tarp and burying it under boxes, he stashed Malcom's bag in the trunk and went through the car one last time. That was when he found the note. It was handwritten, on paper with purple flowers adorning the edges. At the time he shoved it in his pocket without really reading it carefully. There wasn't a lot of time left for him to bicycle back to where he left his truck before the race. Soon the race would be over and he didn't want his truck to be anywhere near there.

Now, sitting on the edge of his bed, he reached over, picked up the note from the nightstand, and read it again.

> Mal,
> Good luck at the race. I miss you. Call me
> before you start home and don't forget to
> stop at Ben's on the way back and pick up
> the quilt from Max. It's important.
> She's expecting you. Don't be late.
> Love you,
> Polly

He was confused. That's when his hand began shaking and a strange feeling washed over him. Had he been deceived? What was this quilt that Malcom was supposed to pick up? Did it have anything to do with his quilt? Could he have taken the wrong one? No. Malcom wanted the one he had back. He had the right one, didn't he? As he sat and mulled this over, his confusion grew. He had to find out. He would have to get that other quilt.

He reread the note again. Ben's? Max? At first the names didn't mean much to him, but then he remembered. He had been in Portsmouth not so long ago, checking out more antiques, and he had stopped at Ben's on the way home. He had sat out on the deck with his lunch, reading Polly's book. "*That must be where I left it,*" he thought. That made sense.

He didn't know who Max was, but he guessed that she probably worked there. He would find out soon enough. He read the note one more time. As he finished, he slowly clenched his hand into a tight fist, crumpling the note in the process. He dropped it on the bed as his mind grappled with this new complication to resolve.

CHAPTER 55

LIEUTENANT MALLOY SAT at his desk, coffee within reach, and began his day by looking over his notes on the John Doe found yesterday at the race. What he didn't know said as much as what he did know, which was little. He didn't know who he was or why he was there. No one recognized him. He had no ID and everyone who had signed up for the race was accounted for. Plus there were no leftover vehicles after the race. How did he get there? If he drove himself, where was his car? If someone dropped him off, why wasn't someone looking for him?

The medical examiner noted that rigor mortis had already set in. Assuming that he had been running, the time for it to set in was probably less than the usual three to four hours. Along with the state of the bruising and the freshness of the cuts on the body, his best guess was that death had come just before dawn.

There was no indication that the victim was anything but the beneficiary of some unbelievably bad luck. He probably tripped, fell, and hit his head on the tree where he was found. Malloy looked up from his notes. Victim. It seemed so straightforward, so why did he think of him as a victim? Maybe it was just too many years on the force that led him there whenever there was no obvious reason for the death, but until the autopsy was complete, he wouldn't know for sure. He was just reaching for the phone to call the coroner's office, when his phone rang.

He answered. "Lieutenant Malloy."

For a moment there was only silence on the line. Then a faint, shaky female voice asked if he were the person to talk to about a missing person.

"Yes, I can help you."

"My name is Polly Christian. I live in Leavitt Town, New Hampshire, and my husband is missing."

"I'm sorry, but why are you calling this department if you are from up in New Hampshire?" He tried to sound as sympathetic as possible, but he had to ask the question.

"He ran a race yesterday, a trail race, and he hasn't come home. I called the race director and he said that his records showed that my husband ran and finished. He didn't. He couldn't have. He didn't come home. I didn't know who else to call."

At the word *race* she had his full attention.

"Mrs. Christian, would you mind telling me a little more about your husband? What he was wearing, height, weight, anything that might help us."

She answered his questions and then finished with one of her own. "Do you know something that you are not telling me?"

Everything she had told him sounded like John Doe, but he wanted to be sure before he either gave her hope or devastating news. He chose not to answer her question. Instead, he thanked her and assured her that he would do everything that he could to find her husband. He didn't like deceiving her that way, but he'd feel better after talking to the coroner.

As soon as he said goodbye to Polly, he made the next call. "Hey Jamieson, can you give me anything yet on that body I sent over yesterday?"

Jamieson Flannigan had been the coroner for longer than Malloy had been on the force. From years of experience, his preliminary assessments were usually spot on. Malloy knew that it could be weeks before all the final reports were prepared, but that wasn't what he needed. Right now he needed an ID and cause of death.

"Mornin' Mark. He's here. I'm about to start on him. What's the rush?"

"I just got a call from a woman up north in New Hampshire who said her husband is missing. He ran the race where we found the body. He was accounted for in the results, but by her description, this guy might be him. Still, I wanted to talk to you first before having her come down."

"I see."

"From what I saw at the scene, it looked to me like he probably slipped and fell down an embankment and hit his head on a tree. When I call her back, I'd just like to be able to tell her that it was an accident and not something else."

"Give me an hour. I'll take a quick look and call you back. Remember, whatever I tell you will be only preliminary, and until I complete a full autopsy I won't really know for sure."

"That's all I want. Thanks."

Almost two hours passed before Jamieson called back. "Hey Mark. It does look like he died from blunt force trauma to the head. The cheek bone under his left eye is broken, and from the cuts, bruising, and pieces of tree in his face, it's pretty certain that his face hit a tree."

"So it was an accident."

"I don't think so."

"You don't?"

Jamieson hesitated before answering. "There's another wound on his head, and in my opinion, it was probably the cause of death. But again, until I finish the autopsy, I won't know for sure."

Now it was Malloy's turn to be silent. Finally he asked, "From the fall?"

"I don't think so, but again, I won't know for sure until . . ."

Malloy cut him off. "In other words, he was killed."

"High probability."

"Thanks Jamieson. Let me know as soon as you have something more concrete. I'm going to call her back and have her come down and look at the body. At least then we might find out who he is. If it is him and it wasn't an accident, we'll at least have a starting point. Thanks."

"Call me when you know what time you'll be coming by."

Malloy sat at his desk, thinking about this new development, picked up his phone, and dialed.

* * *

Polly hadn't expected to hear back from Lieutenant Malloy so quickly. Emotionally drained from a morning spent on the phone with no success, she was just sitting down with a cup of tea. Even though it was lunchtime and she was probably hungry, she couldn't stand the thought of eating anything. When the phone rang, she jumped and nearly spilled her tea. The conversation was short. As soon as she heard his voice, somehow she knew the news wouldn't be good. They agreed to meet at the Ipswich Police Station at 3:30.

CHAPTER 56

SYLVIE REMAINED IN HIS DREAMS, and when Jack finally woke up, he was sweating and his heart was beating rapidly. It took him a few seconds to fully regain his bearings, and when he looked over and saw Max asleep next to him, he took a deep breath, relieved. The dream had been so real it scared him. He had had dreams like that before, but they were always with or about Max.

His whole body hurt, so he lay there looking up through the skylight at the blue sky above. He replayed in his mind his day at the Rockdog. It had lived up to everything that he had been told, and then some. Had things not gone so horribly wrong, he might have had a really good run as well. As it was, what he had was a bruised and sore body, a headache, and a great story to tell.

He had to pee and he was terribly thirsty. He slowly sat up and swung his legs off the bed. He was a bit lightheaded and had to sit for a moment to stop the spinning before he could carefully stand and shuffle off to the bathroom. Cat greeted him at the door and he shushed her to be quiet so she wouldn't wake Max.

After visiting the bathroom, he walked to the kitchen, Cat dancing at his feet and talking all the way. First, he heated a cup of coffee for himself. Then he fed Cat. As soon as he put her dish on the floor, her incessant chatter was replaced by loud purring as she ate her breakfast.

He stood in front of the window, looking out toward the harbor and the ocean beyond as he sipped his coffee. The sky was a flawless blue, and even though the sun was only about two fingers above the horizon, he could already feel its heat on his face. He closed his eyes and his thoughts returned to the race the day before: the predawn start, meeting Sylvie, the sprained ankle, and finally his slip and fall, which led to finding the body. Who was that guy? Why was he out there?

A dark cloud washed through his head and he shuddered as he relived that moment when he realized that he had landed on a body. That split second when reality changed from what he thought had happened to what had really happened hit him like an electrical shock. He understood the emotions, thoughts, and feelings that flashed through his head, but he found it impossible to put them into words. Then, almost as quickly, his thoughts turned to Sylvie. The cloud lifted, and a smile began to form on his face.

He told himself that she was just another runner, but something inside kept telling him that she was not, and that worried him. He hardly knew her. They had run together for less than two hours, and even if he added in the time spent helping her after her fall, it wasn't enough. Or so he told himself. Yet he could not get her out of his thoughts, and this bothered him more than falling on a dead body.

He didn't hear Max come into the room. "Penny for your thoughts," she said as she pressed against his back while wrapping her arms around him.

Startled, his heart began pounding and he hoped Max wouldn't notice. He felt like a child caught with his hand in the cookie jar. Of course, she didn't know, she couldn't, but that didn't ease the guilt he was feeling.

"Mornin'," he answered. "I was just thinking about yesterday."

"You okay?"

Jack paused a moment before answering. "Yeah, I'm fine. A little sore, but okay."

"That's good," Max cooed as her hands began to wander, and now his heart truly was beating rapidly for her.

Max relaxed her arms and he turned to face her, placing his coffee cup on the windowsill. She looked up at him as they pulled each other close. Even through the thick bathrobe she was wearing, he could feel the warmth and softness of her body. He inhaled the scent of her hair. All of his senses were alive, and in that moment, he relived every moment he had ever spent with her and he understood with great clarity how much he loved her.

He ran his hands up and down her back, and he could tell that all she had on was that bathrobe. Jack leaned back slightly and she moved a half step back as well. Their eyes locked. Her green eyes said all that needed saying. He slowly brought his arms from around her back, and ever so slowly untied the sash holding her robe closed. Then, he slid his hands between the folds of the fabric and it fell open.

Her eyes closed and he could hear her breathing becoming shallow as his hands gently cupped her breasts. Slowly, his hands traced a path to her face, his finger tips brushing against her slightly open lips. As he placed one hand on either side of her face, he lifted her face toward his and their lips met.

At the same time that Jack's hands moved up from her breasts to her face, Max's hands moved in the opposite direction. Her hands gently released him from his flannel pajama pants and she felt him suck in his breath at her first touch.

That first tender, gentle kiss lasted but a second before raw physical desire overwhelmed them. They devoured each other. Their kisses were at once both rough and gentle, and their hands touched and explored each other in that exquisite ballet of love as two became one. That choreography flowed from where they first stood to the couch and then back to their bed, and it lasted until they were completely spent. As they lay, unmoving, in each other's arms, Jack exhaled, "Oh my God."

Max blushed and as she looked at him, her expression said the words she was too embarrassed to speak.

CHAPTER 57

"HUNH." MAX SAT UP SUDDENLY.

Jack sat up also, pulled out of sleep by Max's sudden start. He asked, "Max, you okay?"

After their passionate start to the day, they had fallen back asleep in each other's arms. The sun was now high enough in the sky that it streamed in through the skylight above their bed, and he welcomed its warmth.

"Jack, I just remembered something," she continued. She twisted and leaned toward him on one elbow.

"What?" He lay back down and looked at her. After that adrenaline-charged awakening, his sleep-fogged brain was beginning to shut down again and his eyes wanted to close.

"Jack, listen to me."

He could tell that she was not about to fall back asleep and was not about to let him do so either. It took conscious effort on his part to force his mind back awake and to focus on her. "What?"

"Malcom never came by for the quilt."

Not understanding what she was talking about, he asked, "What? Who? What are you talking about?"

"Yesterday, Malcom was supposed to come by and pick up the quilt."

"What quilt? Who's Malcom?" Jack was still not comprehending.

Max sat up straight and turned to face him. He rolled his head to the side, looking at her, but he was distracted by her nakedness. Her breasts had this slight jiggle as she talked and they captured his full attention. He knew she was still talking to him, but he was deaf to her words and he was beginning to feel that wonderful pressure in his groin.

"Jack!" Max gave him a playful slap. "Eyes up here," she said lifting his chin. "Jack, you're not listening to me."

He tried not to grin, but he couldn't help himself.

Max caught that slight grin and her eyes wandered south for the tiniest fraction of a second. Then she understood. Flattered and tempted, but not to be deterred from what she had to say, she playfully slapped him again. "Jack, pay attention."

"Okay. I'm at attention . . . uh . . . listening," he said with a grin. He forced his eyes to meet hers, just as she pulled the sheet up to cover herself.

"Remember, as we left the B&B a few weeks ago, it had just started to rain and Polly had us wait while she ran back in for something. Then she came running out with a plastic bag. She said it was a gift. There wasn't time to talk because that's when the storm hit. She ran back while we drove off. In the bag was a quilt, but I didn't look at it closely until we got home."

As she talked, her level of excitement increased along with the speed of what she was saying, and the sheet began to slip. Jack knew that she was beginning to get wound up, and when she paused for a breath he interrupted her. "Max, slow down. You're losing me."

She pulled the sheet up again and continued. "So Polly had given me this old quilt to use as the filling for the one I'm going to make."

Jack nodded. It was coming back to him.

"Remember, after we were home, Patti and I looked at it and I was sure that she had given me the wrong quilt." He nodded again as he tried to remember the details of what she was telling him. "When she wrote her book, there were two quilts that together became the basis for the one in the story. One, she named the Captain's Quilt because it was colorful, told a story and in good condition and they displayed in the room with the same name. The other, she kept stored away because it was plain and not in very good condition. This second one may actually have more historical relevance and I know was special to her. It was stored away with some old quilts that she had made and by accident, was the one she gave to me when we left the Inn. I offered to bring it back to her, but she said that it would be easier if she just had Malcom stop by on his way back from the Rockdog and pick it up."

Max stopped and looked at Jack with triumph in her eyes, as if she had just solved some great mystery.

"So?" Jack wasn't making whatever connection she was making.

"So! So Malcom never came by yesterday to get the quilt."

"Max, he had just run a marathon. He was tired, it would have been easy for him to forget."

"No," she insisted. "That quilt meant too much to her. He wouldn't have forgotten. Polly wouldn't have let him forget."

Jack wasn't so sure about that. Under the same circumstances, he might easily have forgotten himself. "I suppose, but I'm sure he just forgot."

"Don't you see. He's the dead man you found."

Jack looked at her. She was beginning to get into her conspiracy theory mode, and whenever that happened, she was impossible. "Max. You don't know that," he said trying to defuse her.

"It all makes sense."

"To you it makes sense, but there is no reason for that. Why don't you just call her?"

"Fine, I will," she said with a bit of righteous indignation, and she sat up straight, clutching the sheet to her chest.

"Come here," said Jack, reaching out for her. He had listened, and now he wanted her again.

Max pulled back and began to slide off the bed, "No. I have a call to make."

"Max," he pleaded, but his hand grabbed nothing but sheet.

He didn't let go of the sheet but she did, leaving him to watch her walk away, toward the phone.

* * *

Max made the call, but there was no answer. She didn't give it a lot of thought—after all, it wasn't even noon yet. Polly was probably out on errands. She tried again an hour later, with the same result. A third call also went unanswered.

"Jack, don't you think it's strange that there has been no answer at the Inn each time I've called?" She was beginning to obsess.

"Not really. I'm sure that they're just busy."

"I don't know. I tried a bunch of different times and you'd think that someone would be there. I mean, the Inn is still open, and even if they had no guests, they wouldn't just not be there. Jack, I'm worried." Max hung up the phone for the fourth time.

"Don't."

"I can't help it. Her husband was supposed to stop by and pick up the quilt. I don't think he would have forgotten, considering . . ."

"Max, you're going to make yourself crazy. I'm sure there is some simple explanation . . ."

She cut him off. "Yeah, like he's dead."

"Max, you're being ridiculous."

"I'm not. You fell and landed on a dead body at the race. Malcom hasn't stopped by to pick up the quilt, there hasn't been any answer at the Inn. I'm telling you, it was him."

"Even if it was, why?"

"I don't know. I'm just saying."

"Don't you have to get to work?" said Jack, changing the subject.

Max looked up at the clock. "I'm not due in until four. I still have some time."

"Listen, if you don't have a problem with it, I'm gonna' call Dave and see if he wants to go for a short walk. I need to stretch my legs."

"Go for it. Just be careful."

CHAPTER 58

"SO, HOW'D YOU LIKE YOUR first Rockdog?" asked Dave.

Jack paused a moment before answering. "I liked it, but I could've enjoyed it a whole lot more."

"Yeah. You did have quite the day," Dave said as they completed their first mile.

Dave had just returned from work when Jack called. Even though the sun was nearly set, he too needed to stretch his legs. They planned to walk along one of their usual running routes: a four-mile loop that went south of his place and zigged and zagged through some residential neighborhoods.

"So Jack, what was the deal with that girl? What was her name?"

"Sylvie, and nothing."

"She was hot."

"I didn't notice."

"Liar. . . . Did you see Christos trying to hit on her?"

"Couldn't miss it."

"I think she was interested in you." Dave was obviously trying to get a rise out of Jack, but he wasn't taking the bait.

"We just ended up running together, nothing more," said Jack, but for a second, his dreams from the other night flashed through his head.

"Right," Dave said sarcastically. "What's Max think?"

"She thinks that the guy I found in the woods was Malcom."

"Who?"

"Malcom, the guy from the Inn. We never met him, but he was supposed to run The Rockdog."

"That's not what I was talking about."

"I know."

Dave gave up on Sylvie. "So what's this about?"

"You know how Max can get. She gets an idea in her head and before you know it, she's in full-on conspiracy theory mode."

"Shit," Dave exhaled softly.

"Shit what?"

"Patti's working tonight too. They'll talk."

"Yep. And they'll both go into conspiracy mode."

"Yep," agreed Dave.

They had been walking for nearly an hour and as they returned to Dave's neighborhood, they were hit with the wonderful smells that came from their favorite hangout, the Wok.

"Hey, want to stop for a drink before you head back?" asked Dave.

"Sure. Since Max's working, maybe I'll get her some takeout for later as well."

Dave made the whip-cracking sound and grinned at Jack.

"I know, I know, but if I bring home some for her . . ."

Dave cut him off. "You're right. It works on Patti the same way." He smiled.

It wasn't long before they were seated at the Wok's small bar enjoying Mai Tais and waiting for dinner.

* * *

The bell on Ben's front door clingled as Jack walked in. He noted that there were only a couple of cars left in the parking lot, so he knew that Max wouldn't be too late. As he turned the corner into the bar, Max and Patti looked up from the conversation they were having.

Patti spoke first. "Hi Jack."

"Patti."

Before he could say anything else, Max said, "Long walk? You're kind of late."

"We stopped at the Wok after."

She made a face, but before she could say anything else, he said, "I brought you some."

The face turned to a smile.

Patti, ignoring that short exchange, began to open her mouth to say something when Jack cut her off. "Dave got some for you too."

She nodded, but she clearly had other things on her mind. "So Jack, what's the deal with this chick you met?" Patti wasn't one to beat around the bush.

"What do you mean?"

"What do you mean, what do I mean? You know exactly what I mean. Dave said she was hot and she was flirty."

This was not a conversation he wanted to have, especially in front of Max. "Patti, I wouldn't know. She was just someone I ended up running with. She fell, she sprained her ankle, and I helped her. If you want to talk about flirty or anything else, I suggest you check in with Christos."

"Dave did say he was workin' her pretty good."

"So talk to him." Changing the subject he said to Max, "How was your night?"

"Quiet. I tried calling Polly again and didn't get an answer. I just know something is wrong."

"Max . . ."

Patti cut him off. "You know Jack, I think she's right. That quilt that Max has is really valuable. There's no way that Malcom wouldn't have come by to pick it up. Something's definitely wrong."

Jack gave both of them his best 'You-are-so-blowing-this-all-out-of-proportion' look. He said, "Look, I'm sure that there is a perfectly reasonable explanation. Now, are we going to get out of here? I think I saw the last customers leaving."

* * *

"Jack." Max poked him.

"Unh," he grunted. "Go to sleep Max." The walk with Dave, the Chinese food, and Max's expression of gratitude for her Kung Pao

Chicken had left him exhausted. Now all he wanted to do was sleep.

"No, Jack. Listen."

"What?" he moaned, knowing that until he heard her out, she would keep pestering him.

"I'm working the day tomorrow. If I don't get hold of her tomorrow, we're gonna' have to go up there."

"Fine. Good night."

CHAPTER 59

POLLY ARRIVED IN IPSWICH at 3:30. Lieutenant Malloy was waiting for her at the station. The medical examiners office was about an hour away in Boston, and given traffic he suggested that they go in his car. It was close to five by the time they walked in.

Jamieson was waiting for them. "Mrs. Christian, thank you for coming down today. I know this must be terribly difficult," he began.

Polly took his hand and nodded her head, "Yes, thank you."

Together they walked through what seemed like endless corridors, finally coming to a stop in front of a pair of windowless swinging doors. The two men looked at Polly. "Ready?" asked Lieutenant Malloy. His tone was soft.

She nodded, straightened, squared her shoulders and said in a barely audible voice, "Yes."

Malloy nodded at the coroner, who pushed the doors open and stepped inside the room, still holding one of the doors. Malloy caught the other and held it open for Polly. She stepped into the room. The fluorescent lighting was most unflattering and bright. In the room were several stainless steel autopsy tables. All but one were empty, and that one had a sheet-covered form on it. The room was cool and smelled of disinfectant. Polly paused as the doors were closed. Jamieson Flannigan walked toward the occupied table.

After stepping into the room, Polly stopped. Malloy stood next to her. She was pale, her breathing was shallow, and he could see her swallow several times. Her eyes began to close, so he reached out and gently touched her elbow. If she was going to faint, he wanted to be ready. At his touch, her eyes opened. She took a deep breath, turned her head toward him, and said, "I'm okay."

He gave her his best reassuring smile and applied a little pressure to her elbow, nudging her forward. Together they walked toward the table where Jamieson awaited them.

She looked down at the sheet. The emotional roller coaster that she had been on since Malcom hadn't returned home had completely exhausted her. She felt empty, spent, devoid of any emotions and feelings, a mere shell of a person. Jamieson looked at her and she returned his look with hollow eyes. Then she nodded that she was ready.

His movements were slow and reverent as he first lifted and then gently peeled back the sheet. Time slowed as she stared down at the form on the table. She could feel her heart pounding in her chest and could hear that pounding along with the air rushing in and out of her lungs. She looked, but saw nothing. She wished that he would hurry so that she could get it over with, but he was moving so slowly. She could hear the cloth as it folded back on itself, but she still saw nothing as darkness began to overwhelm her. Then, as all movement stopped and everything became silent, she heard, "Mrs. Christian."

"Mrs. Christian," the words echoed in her brain and in that briefest of moments, the emotional dam burst. The darkness that had been swallowing her up was vanquished. The room's bright lights seared her eyes. All at once, she could hear, she could feel, she could smell. She could see again. And what she saw, staring up at her, was Malcom's face, pale, peaceful, and unmoving.

In that moment, the rush of emotions was overwhelming. All her fears came true. All her previous questions were answered, only to be replaced by a single question: Why? One hand pressed to her mouth as if it could suppress the scream that was welling up from deep inside. Her other hand reached out for the table as her legs began to lose their strength. Inside her head, she heard the scream. It was a deep, guttural scream that built until it emerged as a piercing, primal sound that came from the earliest moments of human history. A sound that could never be mistaken for anything other than what it was: grief, of the deepest kind.

Flannigan pulled the sheet back over Malcom while Malloy put his arm around Polly to steady her. The two men looked at each other, and slowly Lieutenant Malloy guided her out of the room. It was never easy.

"I'm sorry for your loss, Mrs. Christian," Malloy said as he guided her down the hall away from her husband.

She held onto his arm for support as they walked. Then suddenly she stopped and looked at him. "What happened? How did he die?"

"We're not sure exactly what happened, but he was found at the bottom of a hill, in the woods, on the race course. Presumably he fell."

"He was always so careful. I don't understand."

"Come." Malloy guided her further down the hall to a small room where she could sit and they could talk privately, even though the morgue was officially closed and they were the only ones there.

As she sat down at a small table in a sparse room he asked, "Water? Soda? Coffee?"

She shook her head no.

He sat down across from her and held out his hands to her. He knew that this was probably the loneliest moment of her life. No one had come with her, and at moments like this some kind of human contact was essential.

She took his hands and squeezed them. At first he could feel her trembling, but after a moment her hands steadied, as if they received some strength through his.

Lieutenant Mark Malloy hated what he had to do next. He didn't want this to feel like an interrogation, but he would have to ask some hard questions.

Before he could say anything, she asked, "Where are his things?"

Malloy looked at her and then said, "I'm sorry, I don't know. We don't have them. When he was found he was in his running clothes. That's all."

"What do you mean, 'that's all'?"

"There was no identification on him."

"He always wore his Road ID. I gave it to him for Christmas."

"Road ID?"

"It's a small ID tag that a lot of runners attach to their shoes." She paused before adding, "Just in case."

"I'm sorry. He didn't have one. We didn't find anything. Nothing."

"What about his race number?"

"Same. He didn't have one on. All of the runners in the race were accounted for. There were no leftover clothes at the finish and we haven't found his car."

Polly looked at him trying to understand what he was telling her. "Nothing?"

"Nothing. If you hadn't called me, we'd probably still not know his identity."

"How . . ." she began to ask, when he continued. "Mrs. Christian, we don't think that the fall killed him. It appears that he was hit in the back of his head and that was the cause of death. We're not sure yet if that happened before the fall or after, but in any event, it looks like that's what killed him. It wasn't an accident."

At this new revelation, Polly sucked in her breath and stared at him. Her eyes were full of questions and shock. After a few moments of awkward silence, she looked at him and said in a soft but steady voice, "Someone killed him?"

"I believe so."

"That makes no sense. He didn't have any enemies. We ran an Inn, for God's sake. He was a runner."

"I understand. I know it's difficult, but can you think of anyone, for any reason, no matter how farfetched, who might have had a problem with your husband?"

Polly didn't move and Malloy watched as her eyes began to well up with tears. He pushed a box of tissues toward her and she took one and dabbed at the corners of her eyes. Then, in a soft voice she began. "Lately, we've had some trouble. We were always looking for things to use to decorate the Inn. He had such a good eye. He always said it was my taste, but it wasn't. He was the one with the eye. Just after summer ended, he came back from a trip with this brass ship's lantern from the 1700s. It was perfect for the room we call The Captain's Room. I remember that he bought it down here."

"In Ipswich?"

"I think so. No, I'm not sure. I just know it was from somewhere around here."

He wasn't sure what this all meant, but Lieutenant Malloy was patient and would let her tell her story in her own way. "Go on," he coaxed.

Polly sat silent for another moment. Then she said, "The shop-keeper, he was a runner. He took Malcom running in the woods where that race was."

"The Rockdog Run?"

"Yes.

"Do you remember his name?"

"Alfred."

"Alfred?" he said as he scribbled something in his notebook. "Did he have a last name?"

"I don't remember. But several weeks ago, he—uh, Alfred—showed up at the Inn. Malcom was out running and I was alone. He wanted to see the quilt."

"Quilt?"

"Oh I'm sorry. We have a B&B up north that we named The Quilt House." His face remained full of questions. "That was because of all the quilts we found there when we bought the place. Each room is named for a different quilt. He, Alfred, wanted to see the one we called The Captain's Quilt."

"I see. . . . Go on."

"Well, he seemed harmless enough, so I took him upstairs to see the quilt. After studying it he offered to buy it and the letter from us.

Actually it was a copy; but he didn't know that. The real letter we have stored away."

Malloy stopped her again. "Letter?"

"The letter. Oh, yes," her voice dropped and her eyes teared up again."

"Mrs. Christian, are you okay?"

"I'm sorry, I was just remembering that day when we found all those things."

"You were telling me about the letter."

"It was a letter we found in the bottom of one of the chests that had all the quilts. It's what gave me the idea for writing my book."

"You wrote a book?"

"Yes. I wrote a historical novel based on that and some other letters. He seemed really interested in them."

"Alfred?"

"Yes. Anyway, he offered to buy them from us."

"The quilt and the letter."

"Yes."

Her voice had become very small again. Malloy paused to give her a moment and looked down at his notebook. Then gently he asked, "Can you tell me what he looked like?"

Her voice remained flat and distant. "He was odd. He wore these thick glasses that made his eyes look buggy."

"How tall was he? Hair color, anything?"

"He was maybe five foot eight inches, shorter than Malcom. And his hair, even though it was brushed, still looked like he had bed-head."

Before he could say anything else, she looked up, and with a strength that surprised him, asked, "Can I leave now?"

He could tell that she wasn't going to tell him anything else today, and this wasn't an interrogation of a suspect. He couldn't say no and he knew he would talk with her again. "Of course. Is there anyone I can call for you? Are you all right?"

"No. Thank you. I just need to go home. I'll be all right."

He looked at her closely. He knew that she wasn't all right, but at times like this, a kind of survival instinct takes over and he was reasonably sure that she would get home fine. Tomorrow would be much tougher.

They walked out of the morgue and drove back to the station. He opened her car door for her. He asked one more time, "Are you sure I can't call anyone for you?"

"I'm sure. I just need to go home."

"You're sure?"

"Yes."

He couldn't force her to stay. "Someone will be in touch with you about arrangements for your husband. Again, I am so very sorry for your loss."

It was dark and cold, made all the more so by the past few hours. He shivered. He watched her drive away slowly, but he continued to stand there in the cold and the dark, reflecting on what she had just told him. A sharp gust of cold air cut through him. "You son of a bitch. Whoever you are, I'll get you."

CHAPTER 60

FOR POLLY, TIME BECAME A BLUR, an empty, timeless blur that began when she met Lieutenant Malloy at 3:30. She hardly remembered the ride home. She replayed the afternoon over and over in her mind, refusing to believe her new reality.

Over the years, there had been times when she had spent an occasional night alone in the Inn, but she had never felt such overwhelming silence and emptiness. She heard nothing, felt nothing, and saw nothing, not even the flashing light on the answering machine. The night was spent in sleepless denial. as she walked through the empty rooms of the Inn one at a time, remembering. Their dreams, their hopes . . . everything was there and she tried to remember it all. When she closed her eyes, she could still feel his touch. Questions plagued her: did she tell him she loved him before he left for the race? Did she wish him good luck? She didn't remember—no, she couldn't remember. Tears came and went, but most of all she was consumed with an overwhelming emptiness. One moment she would tell herself that he would return soon, but she knew otherwise. He would not return; he would never walk through the door again.

Dawn didn't bring Malcom back to her, but it did bring sleep. Polly had no idea for how long she had been sleeping when she heard the phone ringing. At first, it seemed a part of her dreams, but as she lay there and the fog of sleep began to lift, she started to call out to Malcom to get the phone. Then everything from the previous day came rushing back with a crushing, paralyzing finality. Malcom would never answer the phone again and at that moment neither could she.

* * *

Max had tried calling before she went into work and again just before the doors opened. Neither call was answered, nor could she leave a message on the Inn's answering machine because its recording said it was full.

"Hi there."

Her back was turned toward the entrance to the bar when a deep, slightly nasal voice startled her. She hadn't heard anyone come in. She turned. Facing her, sitting at the bar, was a man with a narrow face. His hair had the look of a failed brushing, dark circles surrounded his eyes which were black and piercing, and his thick glasses made those eyes look buggy, like those on a fancy goldfish. He was wearing a zip-front, hooded sweatshirt that was partially unzipped, revealing a plaid shirt that was buttoned all the way up. He looked like someone who just never quite figured it out as far as fashion was concerned. She had to catch herself from staring.

"Oh, hello. I'm sorry, I didn't hear you come in."

"That's okay."

Max detected a hint of an accent. "*Boston? No, but definitely in the area*," she thought. No matter, she was struck by how the voice just didn't go with the man sitting in front of her.

"What can I get you?"

"How about glass of white zinfandel?" Then he added, "and a menu."

Max handed him a menu and turned away to get the wine just as Patti arrived to pick up some waiting drinks. "These mine, Max?"

Max turned in Patti's direction, holding his glass of wine in her hand. She walked over to where Patti was standing at the end of the bar. They were too busy to notice how the man's head snapped around when Patti spoke Max's name. Nor did they see that he was staring at them.

"*So, you're Max*," he thought to himself.

As Patti left with her drinks, Max turned and walked toward him with his glass of white zinfandel. "I'm sorry," she said as she placed it in front of him.

"That's okay," he said. He continued to stare intently at her.

His expression was making her uncomfortable. "Would you like something to eat?" asked Max, trying to avoid his gaze.

"Yes. I'll have a Caesar salad."

As soon as he said yes, she thought, "*Thank you,*" then she asked, "Would you like that with chicken or grilled salmon?"

"Salmon," he answered.

"Very good. I'll get that going right away," she said and turned to place the order. Since it was now the off-season, the chef would grill the salmon, but she would have to make the salad and that meant she had a reason to go to the kitchen, giving her an excuse to not have to stay at the bar and engage him in conversation.

Max was assembling the salad when Patti came into the kitchen. "What's with that guy at the bar?" she asked in a forced but not too soft whisper.

"I don't know, but he gives me the creeps," said Max. "At least he ordered a salad. I can hide in here for a few minutes."

Max stalled as long as she could, but the salmon wasn't ready so she had to return to the bar without the salad. On the other hand, now she'd get to leave the bar again.

When she walked back into the bar, she was surprised to see the local guys there. Leo, Ralph, and Paulie were nice enough, but only in small doses. Almost anything they heard, from almost any source, was usually treated as fact, and they were nosier than any group of gossips. "*Perfect,*" thought Max, "*can it get any worse?*"

As she walked behind the bar, expecting the worst, the best she could hope for happened. The three of them were trying really hard to engage the odd-looking man in conversation, which meant that she wouldn't have to talk to any of them. She knew what the guys drank, so all she had to do was place beers in front of them and listen to their blather while waiting to go pick up the salad.

"What do you do?" asked Leo.

Ralph chimed in, "So where're you from?"

"I have an antiques shop in Essex, Mass," he said reluctantly, answering both questions at the same time. Inside he was annoyed that he would have to deal with them. It was Max that he wanted to talk to. She had the quilt and he needed to find out more so he could get it.

"That's down by the cape, isn't it?" said Leo.

Paulie smacked him on the shoulder, "You idiot. How long have you lived here?"

"Most've my life."

"Then you should know that it's down on Cape Ann, by Ipswich." Then, turning to Alfred, he added, "Right?"

Alfred looked at him with those goldfish eyes and said, in a kind of disinterested tone, "Yes." He really didn't enjoy these kinds of conversations, especially with 'know-it-all' fools. But, they were obviously regulars and not going away. He thought to himself that perhaps they could prove useful, so he played along. "What do you guys do? You're obviously from around here."

Leo answered first. "I fish, mostly lobsterin'."

"You are so full of bullshit," said Paulie. "He goes out once in a while, only when someone can't find anyone else to help."

"Mor'n you do," he countered, looking embarrassed for a moment.

Alfred looked at Ralph and then Paulie. "What do you do?"

Ralph picked up his beer and took a sip, looking straight ahead, ignoring the question and giving no indication that he was going to answer.

Paulie spoke up. "I do yard clean-ups and odd jobs. Ralph here helps me."

Alfred nodded and looked at Max.

She forced a smile and quickly said, "I'll go check on your lunch. It must be about ready."

As soon as she was out of sight, he turned to Leo, "So what's her story? She's cute, but with kind of an attitude."

"Max?"

"That her name?" He knew that already, but he didn't let on.

"Yea, Max. She's been bartending here for as long as I can remember. She's a good person, gets mixed up in things all the time."

Paulie interrupted what Leo was saying, "Except the last time."

Alfred looked over at him.

Leo corrected his story. "Yeah, last time, she saved Jack's ass."

"*Last time?*" he thought. "Who's Jack? Her boyfriend?"

"I guess that's what you'd call him. They're living together now. He hangs around, does odd jobs here at Ben's, don't know where he gets his money, but he lives in a pretty nice place over across the street."

Before Alfred could ask anything else, Max reappeared with his salad. He turned away from Leo, hoping that it hadn't been too obvious that he had been talking with them. It would be better if she thought him a victim of their attentions. "Thanks, it looks good," he said, avoiding eye contact as she placed it in front of him.

CHAPTER 61

"MAX, WE GOTTA' GET GOING," said Leo. Each of the guys threw some money on the bar. "Nice meetin' ya," he said toward Alfred, who was busy cutting his salad into smaller pieces. Alfred wanted to know more about her, but what he had learned was more than he could have hoped for. Barely turning his head toward them, he nodded goodbye as he watched Max out of the corner of his eye.

As they walked out the bar, Max, obviously annoyed, began picking up the assortment of bills, quarters, dimes, nickels, and pennies that they had left. Miraculously, there was enough to cover the check and give her a small tip.

"Good salad," said Alfred, not looking up from his plate.

"Thanks."

Then he looked up at her and said, "Those guys were interesting."

"I'm sorry you had to go through that. They mean well and they're perfectly harmless."

He returned to his salad. "Your name is Max, I gather," he said, still without looking up.

She shouldn't have been surprised. After all, several times she had been called by name, but she was. And it felt strange. Now it was Max's turn to comment on something overheard.

"I heard you tell the guys you're an antiques dealer."

"Yeah, down in Massachusetts. Got the business from an old couple, after they died years ago."

"Where?"

"In Essex."

"What kind of stuff do you have?"

"A little bit of everything. Nautical stuff, brass mostly, dolls, furniture, lamps, old tools, just about anything old." Then, just to see what she would say, he added, "I even have some old quilts."

Max's response to that last statement surprised him. "Really. Quilts? I'm working on a quilt right now, or at least I'm trying. It's my first."

He tried to not let his interest become too obvious. "How'd you get interested in that? You don't look the type." He knew as soon as those words left his mouth that he had said the wrong thing. The last thing he wanted to do was offend her.

"What type is that?" said Max with more than a bit of indignation.

"I'm sorry, I didn't mean anything by it. I just picture quilts as being made by little old ladies sitting around drinking tea and having lots of cats." For the second time, he regretted what he had said so he quickly added, "Sorry," and went back to his salad.

Max chuckled at his impression of a quilter, and her indignation vanished. Dropping her guard, she began rattling on. "No, that's okay. I thought the same thing until recently. Jack, my . . . uh," she hesitated for a second as if looking for the right word, "significant other, and I went up North with another couple not too long ago. We stayed at this B&B called The Quilt House. It was really cool. The couple who owns it are about the same age as us and when they bought the place, they found a bunch of old quilts in the attic, hence the name. She even wrote a novel about a young woman who makes a quilt and uses it to hide information that's critical to her family's fortunes. She got the idea from the quilts and some letters that they found along with the quilts. As a matter of fact, a while back someone left a copy of her book here in the bar and I read it."

He didn't look up, but inside he was smiling at this nugget. "*I did leave it here.*"

"She even gave me an old quilt to use as filler for the one I'm making."

He looked up with an expression on his face that could either have been surprise or elation. "Really. I didn't know."

She continued, "That's what you do with old quilts, but I'm going to give it back to her."

Alfred couldn't believe his ears. He was talking to Max and she still had the quilt that Malcom was to pick up on his way home. This was his lucky day. "Why?" he asked, trying not to sound innocently curious.

"I think she made a mistake and gave me the wrong one. I think she gave me one that's really valuable. Her husband was supposed to come by and pick it up a few days ago, but he never showed. I've been trying to call her, but no one has answered the phone."

"Why do you think that she gave you the wrong quilt?" Alfred tried to keep his voice calm, almost disinterested, fearful that his building excitement would come through and make her suspicious.

"Well, she showed me all of the quilts that they had found when they first bought the place. The ones in the best condition were displayed in the rooms. The coolest one she called The Captain's Quilt because it depicted a story of a ship's voyage. It was really colorful."

Alfred ate slowly as he listened to Max ramble on, and he had to really work at keeping calm. He knew all about the Captain's Quilt; after all, he had it. But he was anxious to hear more about the quilt Malcom was to have picked up.

Just as Max was about to start a new sentence, the slip printer came to life, chickka-chikka-chunk. Max turned away from Alfred. "Excuse me," she said as she tore off the slip and began making the drinks.

Alfred wanted to shout at her to stop and finish her story, but he knew he couldn't, so he took another bite of his salad and watched her work.

Patti came in to pick up the drinks just as Max finished making the last one. As she began to place them on her tray, she whispered to Max, "That guy is staring at you."

Max started to turn her head, but Patti hissed at her, "Stop. Don't turn around."

"Why?"

"Because he's really creepy and he's still staring."

"Patti, he's harmless. I was just telling him about our trip to The Quilt House."

"Max! Don't. If you have to talk to him, keep it generic, nothing personal. There's something about him that bothers me."

"Patti, now you stop!"

"I'm just saying. When he comes after you . . ."

Max cut her off. "Go. Go deliver your drinks. Get out of here and stop worrying."

Patti snuck one more look at him. He was still staring. She picked up her tray, and as she turned to leave, she said to Max, "Remember what I said."

As Max turned back, Alfred quickly looked back down at his salad, but he wasn't quite quick enough and Max caught his stare. After what Patti had said, it was a bit unsettling.

"So how's the salad?"

"Very good."

"The salmon really makes it," added Max.

Alfred began to get an uneasy feeling that she was not going to talk about quilts anymore, but he needed to know more. "So, what was the title of that book again?"

"*The Captain's Quilt*, same as the quilt she showed me. It was good. If you ever get the chance to read it, you should."

"I will. If I get the chance." From the tone in her voice, he could tell that the conversation about quilts was over. He wondered what the waitress had said to her. In any event, he had found out more than he had expected, so he paid his tab, said goodbye, and walked out of Ben's.

CHAPTER 62

MAX'S SHIFT ENDED AT FOUR, but it was nearly 4:30 before she was finally finished. She was sitting at the bar having a post-shift glass of wine when Jack walked in.

"Hey Max, how was your day?"

She didn't see him come in. As she looked up, she held her phone to her ear, smiled, and signaled both *hello* and *wait*. He sat next to her, asked the night bartender for a beer, and looked at her as she began to speak into the phone.

"Polly? . . . Hi. This is Max. Listen, I've been trying to get hold of you for a couple of days now. Your husband never stopped by to pick up that quilt . . ."

Jack hadn't really been paying much attention to her conversation other than to note that it sounded like she finally got hold of Polly. But he noticed when her voice suddenly dropped to a whisper: "Oh my God."

He looked over and saw the color draining from her face. She slumped and it looked like the life was being sucked out of her. "Max?" he said.

There was no sign from her that she had even heard him; she was so focused on whatever was being said on the other end of the line. "Yes, I see . . . If there is anything I can do . . ." Then she slowly took the phone from her ear and closed it gently, muffling its snap as she looked down at the bar.

Jack was sure that he saw her eyes beginning to well up with tears and he reached over to touch her shoulder. "Max, what . . ."

His question was interrupted by Patti's arrival, "Hey, Jack." Then before she could say anything else, she saw the look on Max's face. She stopped, looking back and forth between them. "Max? Jack? What's going on?"

Before he could respond, Max looked up at him as a tear spilled down her cheek. "He's dead," she croaked in not much more than a whisper.

Jack spoke first as Patti looked on, confused by what she was saying. "Max? Did you just say someone's dead?"

She nodded her head because she couldn't get the words out. Jack got up from his seat, stood next to her, and put his arm around her shoulders. She leaned into him and he gently pulled her close. He felt her shudder as she took a deep breath. Then she pulled away and looked up at him.

Before he could say anything, she wiped her cheeks with her hand and answered his questions. "Malcom, Polly's husband, is dead."

"What? How?" said Jack in stunned disbelief.

"He was the man you fell on."

Now it was Jack's turn to blanch. "What?"

"He never came home from the race. So on Monday, she called the Ipswich Police. They told her that an unidentified man in running clothes had been found in the woods during the race. She went down, and it was him."

"You're shitting me," said Jack. It seemed impossible to comprehend what he had just been told.

CHAPTER 63

ALFRED AND THOMAS WERE IDENTICAL twins, so identical in fact that it was difficult for even their mother to tell them apart. Occasionally, they did twin switches as an innocent prank, and when revealed, those pranks always got a laugh because everyone was fooled. Sometimes, though, a prank went wrong, and when that happened, it was always Thomas who got the blame. No one ever knew how much that hurt him.

When the summer weather was really hot, they would play with their friends down by the river. An old rope hung from a tree at the river's edge, and they'd use it to swing out over the river before dropping off into the cold water. It was during their twelfth summer that it happened. It was terribly hot. A bunch of them were meeting by the river to swim and cool off. Alfred and Thomas were the first ones to arrive, and Alfred beat Thomas to the swing. He swung out over the river, and when he let go of the rope, he tried to do a somersault before hitting the water. He didn't spin fast enough, so he fell into the water backward and upside down. The tide was dropping and the water was shallower than usual. He must have hit his head and broke his neck, because he slowly floated to the surface.

Thomas raced home for help in a panic. When he ran into the house and told his mother what had happened, she panicked. In her confusion, she called him Alfred, assuming that Alfred would never have done such a stupid thing. Thomas never corrected her.

To his surprise, Thomas found that the days that followed were magical. He was fawned over. He was the special one. As he watched his twin being buried, he made the decision to remain Alfred forever.

Now, for the entire drive home from Rye, Alfred felt triumphant. He was going to show them all. Everyone always said his brother was the smarter one, but he was the smart one. He was alive and his brother was not.

* * *

Once home, Alfred checked the paper again for any information about the accident. There was none. The day before, the local paper had run only a single, short article about the discovery of the body in the woods. The body had not been identified and according to the paper it was an unfortunate accident. Alfred smiled to himself.

CHAPTER 64

"JACK, WE'VE GOT TO GO up there," Max announced as soon as they got home.

"Do you really think that's a wise thing to do?" He paused and added, "Hungry?"

"Yes and yes."

They still had Chinese leftovers. While Jack made up two plates, Max disappeared. He was just hitting the Start button on the microwave with thoughts of Max's previous show of gratitude for the Kung Pao Chicken when he heard the rustling of plastic. He turned and saw that Max had returned with the large plastic bag that Polly had given her. He watched her sit on the couch and open the bag. By the time the microwave beeped, signaling that food was ready, Max had pulled out the quilt that Malcom was supposed to have picked up. She sat with it in her lap.

The microwave beeped. He called her. "Food's ready. Something to drink?"

She looked up at Jack. "She just lost her husband; she must be devastated. Picking up this quilt would have been the last thing he did for her. We have to get it back to her."

Max twisted around and put the bag with the quilt aside on the floor next to the couch. Jack brought her plate to her. "It's hot." He repeated, "A drink?"

"Thanks. We'll go up tomorrow. I don't have to be into work until five."

"Something to drink?" he asked again.

"Do we have any beer? If we left mid-morning, we'd be up there by lunch, and I could be back in time for my shift."

"Here," he handed her a glass.

"What's this?" Max asked as she looked at the dark brown liquid.

"There's a new microbrewery in North Hampton, the Throwback Brewery. I checked it out earlier while you were at work. I bought a growlette of Hopstruck IPA. It's pretty good."

She took a sip, and with a slight foam mustache on her upper lip, she agreed with him. "So does that sound good?"

He knew that he had no choice but to agree.

"Okay then. We should be on the road by ten at the latest."

CHAPTER 65

POLLY, STILL IN SHOCK, had spent her Tuesday aimlessly walking around the Inn. She made calls and friends from town came over, but for her, time seemed to have stopped. It was nearly suppertime when Lieutenant Malloy called to say that the body was ready to be released. She asked him again if there was any more information about what had happened to Malcom. He had nothing new to tell her. She said, "Thank you, for all your kindness. Please find who did this."

"I will do everything I can, Mrs. Christian. If you think of anything else, please call me. Anytime." He paused for a moment, hoping that she would have something else to say before hanging up. That moment seemed to last forever. He was just about to put down the phone when her voice came back over the line.

"Lieutenant Malloy."

"Yes."

"There is something. It may not mean anything . . ."

The line went silent again.

"Mrs. Christian?" He waited again, then repeated, "Mrs. Christian? . . . You had something else?" Clearly she was struggling with whatever she wanted to say. Why? Was she embarrassed? From his experience it would probably be totally irrelevant. Most of the time that was the case. But once in a while, that seemingly insignificant nugget would become a case breaker.

"I . . . it's probably nothing, but remember I told you about the antiques dealer who came by and was interested in the quilts."

"Yes." He quickly thumbed through his notes. "Alfred?"

"Yes. After he looked at the one in the Captain's room, he offered to buy it, along with the letter I showed him. I wouldn't sell either to him and he became quite agitated and rushed out."

"Yes, I remember."

"At the time Malcom wasn't around, but later when I told him, I could see that he was upset. He tried to act like it was no big deal, but I could tell. And then the next thing we knew, the quilt and the letter were stolen."

"The one in The Captain's Room?"

"Yes."

"Go on."

"I can't even tell you on what day it was stolen. But one day, sometime after that visit, I noticed that the letter on the wall was missing while I was getting ready for some new guests. Malcom was sure that Alfred had stolen it, and he wanted to confront him immediately. I convinced him that this wasn't a good idea."

"Did you report it stolen?"

"We didn't. Malcom wanted to handle it himself."

"And you're sure he took it?"

"Malcom was convinced. I told him to call the police, but he wanted to handle it himself." She stopped again and this time Malloy could hear her sniffling. Then she began to cry, and between sobs she said, "If only I had insisted, maybe Malcom would still be alive."

"Mrs. Christian, it's not your fault. Your husband probably would have done it anyway."

"No. I should've stopped him."

Malloy knew that there would be no changing her mind. But he needed more information. "When did he do this?"

"The day after we discovered the letter and quilt were missing, about two weeks ago."

"I see."

"Mal drove down the next morning. When he came home, he didn't have the quilt and he was upset."

"Did he tell you why?"

"Not really. He just said that he'd get it back at the race."

The line went silent and he thought he could hear her sobbing. "Mrs. Christian."

"I'm sorry. I'm still here," she said with a quiver in her voice.

"Can you tell me anything else?"

"Not really."

After a few more minutes of meaningless conversation, he hung up the phone. He leaned back in his chair, exhaled, and then sat forward and picked up his notes.

CHAPTER 66

"C'MON JACK. WE'VE GOT TO get going," said Max as she walked down the stairs carrying the quilt.

He was only a few steps behind, but it might have been a mile by the way she was acting. "Bye Cat," he said. He bent over and scratched her head before following Max down the stairs.

It was a beautiful November day. The few brown leaves that were left on the trees stood in stark contrast to the clear blue sky. The ride north was quick and quiet. Since the leaf-peeping season was over and the ski season had not yet begun, traffic was light, which allowed them to make good time. As they neared the point where they would get off Route 16, Jack asked again, "Are you sure you want to do this?"

He didn't look at her when he asked the question. He just stared straight ahead as if concentrating on the road, because he already knew the answer. He could also feel the look she was giving him. They had had this conversation several times already and he knew that her mind was made up. Still, he felt compelled to ask one last time. "Yes. You know I do."

The roads became narrower, with more twists and bumps the closer they got to the Inn. Finally, the sign for the Inn came into view. They saw that someone had tacked on one of those bright-orange stock signs that every hardware store carries: CLOSED.

Jack drove up the driveway slowly as if sneaking up on a doe in the woods. Even so, the soft crunching of gravel under the tires seemed as loud as a barker at a carnival calling out to announce their arrival. He stopped next to the several cars that were parked in front of the Inn and shut off the engine. Neither Jack nor Max made any move to get out of the car. Instead they sat, staring at the Inn, waiting for the other to make the first move.

Max caved in first. As soon as she was out, Jack followed. With the plastic bag under her arm, she walked up to the front door, paused, and then knocked. Unlike their first visit to the Inn, when they were welcomed by an exuberant Polly, this time they were greeted by a woman they had never seen before. Her face was drawn and pale, and her eyes looked like she had recently been crying. She was wearing a pair of ordinary jeans with a burgundy-colored turtleneck shirt under a matching plaid shirt. She held on to the door, opening it just wide enough for her to stand in the opening.

"Hello. May I help you?" she asked softly.

"We're so sorry to bother you. My name is Max, and this is Jack," she said turning toward him. "We stayed here at the Inn not too long ago, and Polly was helping me get started on my first quilt. She gave me this old quilt to use as filler, but I think she made a mistake. I think this one is really valuable, so I am returning it." Max shifted the green plastic bag in her arm so the woman could see it, but she made no move to hand it over.

The woman didn't move or speak for several moments. Then in that same subdued voice she said, "I'm sorry that you drove all the way up here. As you may or may not know, Polly's husband, Malcom, just died. She has closed the Inn and isn't seeing anyone."

"Yes, I know." Max wasn't giving up that easily. "I spoke with her yesterday and she told me. We, uh, I never met Malcom, but from what she said he sounded really special. Jack was the runner who found him in the woods."

Before Max could say anything else, the woman opened the door fully and stepped to the side. "Please, won't you come in?"

They both stepped into the hallway while the woman closed the door behind them. "I'm sorry. My name is Anne. Polly and I have been friends ever since they opened the Inn. Mal . . ." When she started to say his name, she got a hitch in her voice. She stopped, dabbed at the corner of her eye with a wadded up tissue, swallowed, and took a deep breath before starting again. "I'm sorry. Malcom was a very special person to all of us. So full of life. It's hard to accept that he is gone."

Max handed the bag to Jack, stepped toward Anne, and gently gave her a hug. The simple gesture said more than words. The embrace only lasted a moment, but that moment was enough, and as Anne stepped back, she said, "Thank you." Then, with a much firmer voice, she continued, "I'm sure that Polly would have wanted to see you, but she's not here right now. She's only just left, and I'm not sure when she'll be back. You're welcome to wait if you like. I could get you some tea or coffee."

The disappointment was obvious in Max's face as she turned toward Jack and took the bag from him. Offering it to Anne, she said, "Thank you, but we don't want to intrude. If I can leave this with you, we'll get going."

Anne took the bag from Max. "Of course, but are you sure you don't want to stay? I'm sure that Polly would want to see you."

"No, we should get going. Have funeral arrangements been made yet?"

"I think the funeral will be on Saturday. I'm not really sure. If you'll give me your number, I'll let you know."

"That would be so nice of you. Thank you." There was a note pad on the table that had the Inn's guestbook on it. It had little purple flowers on one side, and Max wrote her number on it and handed it to Anne.

Max turned and opened the door. Jack walked out first, followed by Max, then Anne. The sky was brilliant blue and the sun bright and warm on their faces, a stark contrast to the somber, cool darkness inside the Inn. "It was nice meeting you," said Jack to Anne, offering his hand to her. Max gave her another hug goodbye, and Anne promised again to call them about the arrangements. "Our thoughts and prayers to Polly," said Max before she climbed into the car.

"Thank you. She'll be sorry that she missed you."

CHAPTER 67

ALL NIGHT LIEUTENANT MALLOY had been thinking about what Polly had told him about the stolen quilt. As he drove through the predawn darkness, he took another sip of his morning coffee. He hated this time of year. The days were too short, and even on clear, sunny days, the browns and grays of the leafless trees always made the world seem gloomy. The parking lot of the police station was still bathed in the orange glow of streetlights, which gave it an otherworldly atmosphere. He pulled into an empty space but he didn't shut off his car right away. It had finally heated up and for once he was warm. Besides, he still had some coffee left.

He pulled out his notebook and flipped through the pages until he came to the notes he had jotted down when Polly had called him. Murder is never easy to deal with, but when it's so seemingly random and senseless, it is all that much tougher. "What a small world," he thought to himself. "The guy who finds him had been a guest at the Inn less than a month ago. What are the chances?" He'd have to talk to him again.

Then there was Alfred. Who was Alfred? She said he had an antiques store in town. There were many, but his name didn't ring a bell. From her description, his appearance was distinctive, so he shouldn't be too hard to find. Malloy snapped his notebook shut, tucked it into his pocket, took the last sip of his coffee, shut off his car, opened the door, and stepped out into the cold, dark world. He didn't bother zipping his coat shut as he hurried across the lot. Instead, keeping his hands pushed deep into his pockets, he used them to hold his coat closed. He hated the cold.

As the station door slowly shut behind him, he was hit by one last puff of cold air. He shivered. First stop, another cup of coffee.

Sitting at his desk, a fresh cup close at hand, he pulled out his notebook and reread his notes for the second time. He made a check-list of what he wanted to accomplish. At the top of the list was Jack Beale—probably not hard to get hold of. Second was Alfred the antique guy. Malloy always preferred to work his way down to the easiest, so he picked Alfred first.

He started by compiling a list of antiques stores in the area, first those in Ipswich and Essex, and then those a bit further away. He added Hamilton, Gloucester, and Annisquam, each list enlarging the circle of places to look.

By the time he finished making his list, he knew it could be a long day. For as long as he had lived in the area, he had never really thought about just how many antiques stores there were. Each call required an introduction and an explanation. However, after the first few, he began to get the feeling that there was a grapevine at play, because those later calls didn't seem so surprised when he announced his aim.

Eventually, his efforts met with success. "Alfred Whitson, that's who you want," the voice on the phone said.

"You know him?"

"Not well, but we've crossed paths. He's definitely an odd duck. Store's over on one-thirty-three in Essex."

Malloy thanked him for his help and sighed in relief. Now he wouldn't have to sit on the phone all day. He made one more call, to Jack Beale. No one picked up.

* * *

It was just after ten when Lieutenant Malloy found Whitson's store. There were no cars in the lot, but from the sign by the door, the store should be open. However, the door was locked. Malloy cupped his hands around his eyes and pressed his face against the glass. The inside was dark and cluttered, and there was no sign of life. He did the same at each of the windows that flanked the door. Each time, as he peered in, he knocked on the glass, and each time, the result was the same.

Having exhausted the options on the front porch, he penned a note on one of his cards and stuck it in the front door. At first he thought it strange that the store was closed, but as he stepped off the front porch, he decided that since it was off-season maybe it was only open on weekends until the holidays drew near. He made some notes in his notebook and then decided to walk around the building, just in case.

The drive sloped down as it wound around the building, leading to a pair of closed garage doors. There were no cars out back either and the doors were also locked. Again, he cupped his hands around his eyes and tried to see in through the glass panels that were set in the doors. It was even darker inside than it had been upstairs. He tried different positions but the most he could see were some large shadowy shapes. "Damn," he said softly as he walked back up the drive to his car.

Before leaving, he decided to try the front door one more time. His card was still wedged in the frame and the result was the same. He was about to open his car door and climb in when a voice startled him. "He's not around."

He looked up and turned to find himself facing a tall, wiry, older guy on a bike. He had on the full uniform: tight black bicycle shorts over tights with a brand name he didn't recognize emblazoned down the thigh, a tight black jacket with only slightly less advertisement on it than you'd find on a NASCAR entry, black gloves, a colorful helmet with lots of cutouts, and reflective dark glasses that made him look like some kind of an evil bug—a very cold, evil bug.

"Hello. What did you say?"

"You looking for Alfred?"

"Yeah, I am. You know where he is?"

"Nah, but I saw him leaving early this morning. And who are you?"

"Lieutenant Malloy, Ipswich Police." He held out his badge.

"How come you're looking for Al?"

Ignoring the question, Malloy asked, "And you? Who are you?"

"Oh sorry. I live down the road a ways. I've known Al forever. Sometimes we ride together and I see him out running a lot. Name's Charlie Rhodes." He stuck out his hand and leaned toward Malloy.

Malloy shook his hand. "Nice to meet you. You saw him leaving this morning?"

"Yeah, a couple of hours ago."

"Which way?"

He turned and pointed, adding, "West on 133."

"You said he runs?"

"Good runner, but not much of a biker. I'd rather ride, so we don't get together as much as we used to when I ran more." He waved a hand toward his legs, "My knees. Listen, I gotta' go, I'm starting to get cold."

"If you see him, would you ask him to call me?" Malloy handed him a card.

"Sure thing." He tucked the card into his pocket.

"Thanks," said Malloy as he watched him peddle off.

"*You'd never catch me wearing an outfit like that, let alone trekking out in this kind of weather on a bike,*" he thought to himself as he pulled his car door open and climbed in.

He started the engine and waited for the heat to come up, before driving off.

CHAPTER 68

WEDNESDAY MORNING ALFRED was up before dawn. The night before he had decided that today he would return to Ben's. He planned to talk with Max again and explain his interest in the quilt that was in her possession. He imagined that she would understand and give it to him. Even if he had to buy it from her, he was sure she would give him the quilt and he would be another step closer to fulfilling his destiny.

By 8:00 he was on the road heading for Rye Harbor. Rejecting the turn for the interstate, which certainly would have made the ride faster, he decided to take old Route 1, which carried mostly local business traffic as it passed through town after town, each with its own complement of stop signs and traffic lights.

Alfred had been so intent on hitting the road, he hadn't eaten anything. It wasn't long before his stomach told him he needed food.

He considered his choices. Along the way there were many fast-food restaurants, most with drive-thrus. That would give him the option of eating while he drove, or he could stop at any one of the countless donut shops that followed Route 1 north. He made up his mind when the Agawam Diner came into sight. This well-known, historical New England diner was a popular local place and had become a type of pilgrimage for visitors to the area.

As he waited for a gap to develop in the traffic so he could turn in, he watched as an elderly couple exited the diner and got into their car. Carefully they backed out of their parking spot, leaving an empty space. At that same moment, a gap opened up in the traffic flow. As they departed, Alfred turned in and took their place. He smiled as he turned off the truck's engine. It seemed like a sign of good luck. Confidence in his eventual success was growing.

As anxious as he was to get on with his mission, he didn't hurry.

Instead, he took his time, alternately watching the hustle and bustle of the waitresses as they moved the crowd in and out and thinking about his destiny. As he finished eating, he checked his watch. It was nearly 10:00. Almost two hours had passed since he started his adventure, and he was only one town away from his store. It was time to move.

The ride north on Route 1 went better than he had expected. There were no accidents and little construction. He even hit most of the green lights. By the time he reached North Hampton, New Hampshire, he was sure this would be his lucky day. So much was going right. At the intersection of Route 111 he decided to turn right toward the ocean and follow the shore road the rest of the way.

The drive down Route 111 toward the ocean illustrated the economic impact that proximity to the coastline has. The closer he got, the nicer and more expensive the houses became. After he drove past the horse farm and read the billboard that proclaimed its successes breeding racehorses, there was one more short hill before the ocean came into view. As he crested the hill, before him, as far as his eyes could see, was the Atlantic Ocean in full glory. The day was so clear that to the south he could just make out Cape Ann, where he had started his day. Maine was to the north, and the Isles of Shoals stood guard only a short six miles offshore. He turned north onto Route 1-A and immediately pulled off onto the side of the road. He looked down over the edge of the cliff and saw a lone lobsterman just offshore tending his traps.

On a day as calm and clear as this, it was easy to forget that this kind of day was the exception in November rather than the rule. Most lobstermen had begun taking their gear in, and only a very small number were still actively working their traps.

A white fleck on the horizon caught his eye. *"Probably a late-season departure of some sailboat heading for warmer climes,"* he thought to himself. Then, as he stared at that small white fleck, his thoughts drifted and images—mostly imagined but very real to him—flashed through his mind.

First he was on the deck when the Captain's ship met the ship of Josiah Whitbey. Then he was on shore with his family as they eagerly awaited the arrival of Whitbey's ship, filled with enough tea to support them through the long-coming winter. He shared their joy and heady excitement as that ship, so anticipated for such a long time, finally arrived. Then he watched from shore as that last voyage ended in tragedy and ruin. Now he was so close to finally having the proof that would expose the treachery that led to his family's downfall.

With his heart racing he was snapped back to the present by the sounds of sirens fast approaching. He whipped his head around just as an ambulance came up from behind, turned westward onto Route 111, and disappeared from sight. He looked back out over the ocean, and the speck of white on the horizon had disappeared along with his dreams. He had a mission to complete. There were only about three and a half miles to go until he would be at Rye Harbor, where he expected to find Max, the quilt, and success.

CHAPTER 69

THE SIGN SAID THAT BEN'S opened at noon. He was early, which was good. He would be able to talk to her alone. The door was unlocked so he went in. A bell clingled and announced his arrival. As he walked into the bar, he didn't see anyone. Then a cheery voice from behind said, "Hi, may I help you?" It was Patti.

When he turned, he found himself facing the blonde curly haired waitress with the enthusiastic smile.

"Oh, hello. Yes, perhaps you can." But before he could finish, he saw a subtle change take place in her face. Her smile, which at first was open and welcoming, now became forced. It clearly reflected both caution and uncertainty.

"Okay." She drew the word out, and her inflection made it more of a question than a statement.

"I was here the other day, and the woman who was bartending was telling me about her interest in quilts."

Patti's eyes opened a bit wider and she sucked in and held her breath. She hoped he didn't notice how uneasy she felt.

He did, but he continued as if he hadn't. "I own an antique business and I have several quilts that came from an old estate. I thought she might be interested."

Patti began to recover from her initial surprise, but she remained cautious and wary. His story made sense, but when she had first seen him a couple of days ago he had given her the creeps, and that opinion still held and even though Max would be back for her dinner shift.

Patti said, "I'm sorry. She's off today. May I leave a message for her?"

Now it was his turn to be surprised. He had been so focused on his mission that he hadn't considered that possibility that she would not be there. He stared at Patti through those thick glasses and stammered, "Uh, um."

Patti could see his confusion as he frantically tried to stay focused, while at the same time he scrambled to find something to say. Before he found words, his hand, as if it was acting all on its own, began reaching around into his back pocket. That's when his thoughts caught up with his hand. "May I leave one of my cards? Would you ask her to call me?" he said.

"Of course." Patti took the card from him. She looked down at it and then looked up at him. *Whitson's Antiques, Alfred Whitson, Proprietor* was printed on the card with an address and phone number. "I'd be happy to . . ." she looked at the card again. "Mr. Whitson."

"Alfred." Then after a brief pause he added, "Thank you. You must be busy, so I won't take up any more of your time."

Before she could respond, he turned and walked out of Ben's, leaving Patti holding his card and not feeling reassured at all.

* * *

After his failure in finding Max and the quilt, Alfred went straight back to his store. As he unlocked the door, a card that had been pushed into the crack between the door and the frame fluttered to the ground. "What the hell is this?" he said to himself as he bent and picked it up.

He froze and a chill shot through his body when he read the name on the card. Lieutenant Mark Malloy, Ipswich Police Department. On the back was written, *Please give me a call.*

Malloy, that name sounded familiar. He flicked the card back and forth over his hand as he tried to remember why. "Oh shit," he said in a soft but anxious voice.

He couldn't get inside fast enough, and he was already in his office by the time the door slammed itself shut with a loud jingling of the bell. He grabbed the newspaper, rustled through it until he found the article that he was looking for, and reread it frantically until he saw what he had hoped he wouldn't see. "If anyone has any information about this crime, please call Lt. Mark Malloy at the Ipswich Police Department." It went on to list phone numbers, adding that all calls would be kept confidential. The last person he wanted to see was Lieutenant Malloy.

CHAPTER 70

SILENCE FILLED THE CAR for the ride home from the Inn. It wasn't until they were nearly past Dover that the first words were spoken. "Jack, we should go back on Saturday for the funeral."

"Sure."

"Jack, are you all right?"

"Yeah. I was just thinking about finding Malcom and wondering, Why him? Why me? Why us?"

"I know what you mean. But listen, we'll go to the funeral on Saturday. Do you think we should ask Dave and Patti?"

"Probably. I can't imagine Dave wanting to do that, but Patti might."

"I'll call when we get home."

* * *

As soon as they arrived home, Cat greeted them at the door. She had quite a lot to say about having been left outside all day, although she also implied that being fed might earn her forgiveness. Jack went to feed her while Max went to the phone. The light on the answering machine was blinking, but Max ignored it, assuming that it was Patti who had called.

"Hey Patti. . . .We just got back . . . No, I didn't listen to the machine. I must have known that you had called. . . . No, Polly wasn't there. I left off the quilt . . . We're going to the funeral on Saturday. You and Dave want to come? . . . ." There was a long pause. Then her voice changed. When she said, "Stop, say that again," Jack was all ears.

He watched her as she finished the call. Then she slowly walked across the room and hung up the phone.

"Max?"

She looked at him with a kind of faraway look. "Remember, I told you about this really strange guy who came into the bar yesterday? He had an antiques store down in Massachusetts and he was asking about quilts and seemed interested in our trip up to the Inn?"

"Sort of."

"He came back today. Looking for me."

Jack waited for her to continue.

"Patti talked to him, and he gave her his card to give to me. He said he had some quilts he wanted to show me."

"So?"

"So, you don't think that sounds strange?"

Jack shrugged.

Max went on, ignoring him. "She said she got a real weird feeling about him, like he was after something else. All she told him was that I was off for the day and he gave her his card to give to me. How strange is that?"

"Pretty strange."

The light on the machine was still blinking, so without really thinking, Max hit the Play button, intending to erase Patti's message now that she had talked to her.

But the first voice on the machine wasn't Patti's. She lifted her finger and listened.

The message was for Jack. "This is Lieutenant Malloy from the Ipswich Police Department, and I'm looking for Jack Beale." She stopped the message and looked at Jack with her mouth open in silent surprise.

Jack had heard, and he was already on his way across the room. Max stared up at him speechless while he pressed the Play button again. The message continued, "I have a few more questions about the incident the other day at the race. Would you please give me a call back at . . ."

"Jack," Max began, but Jack, staring at the machine, signaled her to stop.

He listened and wrote down the number. Patti's message began to play. Ignoring it, he hit the Rewind button and listened to Malloy's message again, double-checking that he had written down the number correctly. Patti's message followed, and this time they listened to it. There were no other messages, and Jack asked if he could erase Patti's.

"I just talked to her, sure," said Max.

He hit Erase and then saved the message from Malloy.

Max couldn't contain herself any longer. "Jack, what is that all about?"

"No idea."

Max went silent, but he could see that she was full on in conspiracy theory mode.

"Okay, Jack, listen. We went up to the Inn. We never met Polly's husband, but she told us he was a runner and was going to run that race. Then Polly gave me the wrong quilt, and she was going to have him pick it up on his way home. He never showed up. You never saw him at the race—at least you didn't know you had seen him because he turned out to be the dead guy you fell on, but you didn't know that. Now this Alfred guy shows up wanting to talk to me about quilts."

"Max, what's your point?"

"Don't you see? There are too many coincidences. Now Lieutenant Mal . . . whatever his name is . . ."

"Malloy."

"Malloy, wants to talk to you. I bet they are all related."

"Max, you're doing it again. How about we just wait until I call him back."

"I've got to get ready to go to work."

"Good."

CHAPTER 71

MALLOY WAS AT HIS DESK when Jack called. "Yes. Thank you for getting back to me . . ."

After the obligatory pleasantries, Malloy got down to business. He reviewed what had happened at the race, reconfirming the details of Jack's account. Satisfied, he then asked about Alfred.

"No. I don't know anyone named Alfred Whitson," responded Jack.

"He's an antiques dealer from down this way, and apparently he's also a runner. Have you ever met him, or did you maybe see him at the race?"

"Sorry, but no." Jack had a feeling that he was expected to know this Alfred Whitson, but he drew a blank, which made him feel uneasy. "The name doesn't sound familiar. Do you know what he looks like?"

"I haven't met him yet, but the description we have is that he's average height and wears thick glasses. Narrow face. Sound familiar?"

"No. Not really. Why are you so interested in him?"

"Just part of the investigation," he said.

Suddenly, Cat caught Jack's attention as she wound her body against Max's legs. Apparently, Max had just come out of the shower. He forgot all about the phone as her towel shifted while she scratched Cat's head. He smiled and she asked, "Who're you talking to?"

"Lieutenant Malloy," he answered. Then, realizing that he still had the phone in his hand, Jack said to Malloy, "Sorry. Someone just came in."

Jack was still finding it hard to concentrate on what Malloy was saying. "What did you say his name was again?"

"Alfred Whitson."

Jack repeated the name aloud, then added, "I don't know him. Sorry."

Before he could say anything else, Max waved her hand in front of his face. "Jack! That's the guy who came into the bar today. Patti talked to him."

"Hold on a second," Jack said to Malloy and turned toward Max. "What did you say?"

"I said, that's the guy who came into the bar today looking for me."

"Excuse me, hold on again," Jack said into the phone. Then, covering the phone, he looked at Max and said again, "What did you say?"

"Jack, I said he's the guy . . ."

Jack held up his hand to Max and said into the phone, "Lieutenant Malloy, my friend Max wants to talk to you."

Max shook her head "no" vigorously as Jack handed the phone out to her. He repeated the gesture, this time with more insistence.

Max came over to Jack and as she took the phone, her towel began to loosen again. This time she had to catch it with her other hand. Jack grinned as she fought to maintain modesty and concentrate on the call.

Once she was finished, she handed the phone back to Jack and worked on snugging up her towel. Jack, still smiling, listened to Lieutenant Malloy.

"Yes, I understand. We'll be careful. Thank you." Then he hung up the phone.

"I told you so," Max said.

Jack reached out and pulled her close. "Told me what?"

"That the guy in the bar was creepy. He even killed Malcom I bet."

"Max . . ." said Jack through his grin, his mind obviously elsewhere.

"No, it all makes sense." She pulled away from him. He made a feeble attempt to hold on to her, but she twisted out of his grasp. For her, the escape was a success, but he still felt victorious because the towel had loosened even further.

"No. Jack, I'm serious. I have to get to work."

"I'm serious, too."

"Jack, you don't want to talk," she said, stating the obvious.

"I do." Then after a pause he added, "Later."

"You're incorrigible," she giggled, and fled to get dressed.

CHAPTER 72

AS SOON AS MALLOY HUNG UP from his call with Jack, he put on his coat and headed for his car. He and Alfred needed to talk. Moments later, he knocked on the door of Whitson's Antiques. For the second time there was no answer, but he noted that his card was gone. "*Well, Alfred. I know you were here. I am going to find you, and you are going to answer some questions,*" he thought to himself as he knocked again with more force.

"They open?" a voice called up to him. Malloy turned. He hadn't heard the car pull up. A man was standing at the bottom of the porch steps looking up. When Malloy didn't respond, he repeated, "Are they open?"

"No." Malloy walked toward the top of the steps.

"My wife and I," the man continued, nodding toward the car, "had stopped by here a couple of weeks ago and saw some things that we were interested in. Thought we'd pick them up today, before we head home. Will the shop be open later?"

"I'm sorry, I really have no idea."

"Well, we go back to Michigan tomorrow. We've been visiting our son and his wife. We stopped by earlier today and he was closed, but we thought he might be back by now."

Malloy shrugged and was about to walk down the steps when the man asked, "You the police?"

Malloy stopped and looked down at the man. "Why do you ask?"

"I used to be a cop. I can tell. What did he do?"

Malloy was already more than a little annoyed with this tourist from Michigan. The sooner he could get him to leave, the sooner he could get back to finding Alfred Whitson. He walked down the steps and introduced himself. "My name is Mark Malloy, and, yes, I'm a cop.

Lieutenant Mark Malloy from the Ipswich Police Department. And you are?"

The man had a look of triumph on his face. He looked back at the woman waiting patiently in his car. "I knew it. I'm rarely wrong. Names Clive Wilson, detective, retired." He stuck out his hand and they shook.

"Nice to meet you."

"Like I said, I . . . uh, we're from Michigan . . . visiting our kids. We wanted to pick up some things we saw here a couple of weeks ago."

Malloy didn't really want to get pulled into a long conversation with a retired policeman from Michigan. He needed to find Alfred Whitson. Clive must have noticed that he was about to be dismissed, because he said quickly, "You know, when we were here last, a driver nearly hit us as he flew out the lot. When we got inside, the place was a mess. Not in a cluttered, antiques shop way, but more like there had been a fight or something. The guy in the shop was limping around and seemed quite out of sorts."

Malloy stopped and looked at him.

Clive went on, "I asked what had happened, but he really didn't want to talk. He kept muttering to himself as he picked up the umbrellas and stuffed them into an elephant leg."

Clive had won. Malloy was interested.

Malloy looked at him kind of funny. "An elephant leg?"

"Yeah. It was an old umbrella stand, made from an elephant leg. Kind of an old Victorian thing. Anyway, he was picking up all these umbrellas and putting them in the leg."

"Who was he?"

"Oh, I'm sure he was the shop owner."

"Why are you so sure?"

"I could just tell. I guess from the way he acted. He was real upset and was limping around and he really didn't want to talk much."

"What did he look like?"

"Kind of odd, slight build, narrow face, thick glasses, bad hair. Odd."

"Then what?"

"We just walked around the shop and found some things we wanted to buy. But then when we were ready to leave, we couldn't find him anywhere. He was just gone. We called out and waited, but finally we had to leave. We left him a note saying we would be back. And here we are. But he's gone again. What do you want him for?"

Ignoring Clive's last question, Malloy said, "Exactly when were you here last?"

"Let me think. It was midweek, a Wednesday. That's right, it was a Wednesday. Right after that big rainstorm."

Malloy thought back. The only rainstorm that there had been occurred about three weeks ago. He did the math. That was two weeks before the race. A coincidence? "About three weeks ago?" he asked, looking for confirmation.

"That's right." Then, as if he knew the next question, Clive said, "I really don't remember anything about the car, but he was in an awful hurry. I'd ask my wife, but she never notices stuff like that."

"Well . . ." Malloy glanced down at his notes, "Mr. Wilson. Thank you. You've been most helpful."

"You never said why you are looking for him. So what's going on? Is he running drugs? Smuggling?" Then in a hushed tone, "He isn't dead is he?"

"No, I'm sorry. None of the above, I just want to talk to him."

Clive looked at him. Then, in a hushed conspiratorial tone, he said, "Sure, I understand. Here's my card if you need to get hold of me for any reason."

"Thank you," said Malloy. He glanced at the card and then slipped it into his shirt pocket.

Clive Wilson returned to his car and Malloy watched as he spoke with his wife, obviously explaining to her what had just happened, before driving off.

"*That was interesting,*" Malloy thought. Then, out loud he said to himself, "Was he interviewing me or was I interviewing him?" He turned back and looked up at the closed store and again, under his breath, said, "Mr. Whitson, you and I are definitely going to have that long chat."

* * *

Lieutenant Mark Malloy didn't leave Whitson's Antiques immediately. He sat in his car with the engine running and the heat turned up. He took Clive Wilson's card out of his pocket and stared at it, going over what Clive had told him. His story only added to Malloy's curiosity about Alfred Whitson. He jotted down this new information in his notebook and then, as was his habit, thumbed through his notes again.

"*Who are you, Alfred Whitson? And more important, where are you?*" he thought to himself. As he reread his notes, Charlie Rhodes' name jumped out at him. He had said that he had known Alfred "forever," and he had called him Al. Tomorrow he'd talk with Charlie Rhodes again.

CHAPTER 73

HE COULD HEAR THE BELL ringing in the house. Charlie had been out riding when Malloy had called first thing in the morning, so Malloy arranged with Charlie's wife to come over about 10:30. Now a short, thin woman opened the door. Before he could even say hello, she said, "Lieutenant Malloy."

"Yes."

"Come in. Charlie's just getting dressed. His ride took a little longer than I had expected."

"Thank you."

She showed him to the living room. Like most in New England, it appeared little used. There was a fireplace that was spotless, and there was no sign of any firewood, save for three logs carefully placed on andirons. He wondered if it had ever been used. On the mantle were many photographs, mostly family, save one. That one caught his attention.

He picked up the frame and looked closely at it. The black-and-white image had obviously been taken many years ago, maybe in the forties or fifties. In it three boys stood in front of a set of wide steps of a building that looked like it might be a church. That was only a guess because they filled almost the entire frame and there was little else that would allow for closer identification. All three had the manufactured smiles of boys who didn't want to have their picture taken. Two of the boys looked absolutely identical except for what they were wearing. The third seemed familiar, and he guessed that he might be Charlie.

"Officer Malloy, how nice to see you." A voice from behind startled him. It was Charlie.

He turned, still holding the photograph. "Charlie. Hello, I didn't hear you come in." They shook hands.

"That's us when we were twelve, just before the accident." Malloy looked down at the picture and Charlie continued. "That picture was taken in the Spring, probably Easter. We—myself, Alfred, and Thomas—were inseparable. We hung around together all the time. Alfred and Thomas were identical twins as you can see by that picture."

"Twins?"

"Yeah, until the accident. They were so identical that even their mother had a hard time telling them apart. They'd play pranks all the time, one pretending to be the other. It was always a great laugh. I was their best friend and even I couldn't tell them apart most of the time."

"Really. Which one is which?" Malloy asked, first looking at the photo again and then holding it out to Charlie.

Charlie took it and without glancing said, "Thomas is in the middle." Lieutenant Malloy thought he caught a bit of sadness in Charlie's voice. Then he watched as Charlie reverently replaced the picture on the mantle.

"Accident?"

"Yes," said Charlie regaining his composure. "That summer, Alfred and Thomas were down by the river playing. There was this rope swing in a big tree and we played there all the time, especially if it was hot. Well, anyway, this one day, we were going to meet there. I hadn't finished my chores so they went ahead. Before I got there, Alfred came running back. Thomas had swung out and let go of the rope too late. He didn't spin in the air enough. He hit the water on his back and his head hit a rock that was just under the surface."

"He didn't know it was there?"

"Oh, we all knew it was there. That was part of the excitement, the danger, to see who could get the closest without hitting it. Well, on that day the tide was dropping, and it must have been lower than they thought. Thomas hit the rock with his head and was killed."

"I'm sorry."

Charlie looked down, silent. Then he said quietly, "Thank you. Everyone was shocked and yet not shocked at all."

"What do you mean?"

"It just made sense that Thomas was the one to die. As physically identical as they were, he was the wilder one, the more daring one. We used to joke that he was the evil twin, Alfred being the good one. It always seemed that when a prank went wrong or they got in trouble, Thomas always got the blame."

"Really."

"It was rough, especially on their mother. She was never the same, and neither was Alfred. He and Thomas were so close, and to all of a sudden be so alone. It was hard. I don't think he ever fully reconciled the fact that his brother was dead and he wasn't. He kept saying that it should have been him. He felt tremendous guilt knowing that maybe he could have prevented his brother's death. I can't imagine what he went through.

"I know one thing though: there was always something off about him after. We grew apart and there was a stretch when I didn't see him for several years."

"When was that?"

"Oh, I don't know. I guess it would have been when we were in our twenties. It was when I had just gotten married. Come to think of it, he didn't even come to the wedding. Eventually we reconnected, but we were never as close as we had been as kids."

Malloy silently looked at Charlie. He had found out more that he had ever imagined about Alfred and all he had done was let Charlie talk.

CHAPTER 74

AFTER ALFRED FOUND MALLOY'S card in his door, he spent a very long night driving around, thinking. He still didn't have the quilt. He hadn't talked with Max. And now this Lieutenant Malloy was looking for him. A voice in his head told him that whatever Malloy wanted to talk to him about couldn't be good, and that he should be avoided. Alfred had trusted the police once and it had cost him dearly. He wouldn't make that mistake again. By the time the sky had begun to lighten, he had an idea.

He wanted the quilt that Max had, and that meant another trip to Rye Harbor. The rising sun brought with it a feeling of hope as it broke the horizon and shined below the layer of late Fall clouds that had moved in overnight. That bright, early sun infused him with energy and optimism, and he planned a quick stop at his shop for his notes and the quilt. He would need them for his plan to succeed.

He drove in from the back way and parked behind the store to remain invisible from the main road, just in case. He could feel the warmth of the sun on his back as he opened the door and then stepped inside. The windows on the back of the building let in enough light so that he could move about easily, a task that would have been nearly impossible in the dark, even for himself. Ten minutes later, when he returned to his truck, he saw that the sun had hidden behind the clouds, a cold east wind had set in, and the world had turned a somber gray.

With the quilt and his notes on the seat beside him, and his success in avoiding Lieutenant Malloy, his spirits should have remained buoyed. However, as he drove away from his shop, his mood became as colorless, cold, and gray as the day outside. His stomach began to rumble. Hunger and fatigue intensified the weight of his mission and the secrets he was hiding. His body ached, and his eyes wanted to close.

He needed food and coffee. The Agawam beckoned as he drove past, but he needed to keep going, so he opted for the next fast-food place with a drive-thru window that he came to. Fortunately the line was short, and in less than five minutes he had a large coffee tucked between his legs and a breakfast sandwich beside him. This time he headed for the highway, and his mood brightened slightly.

The combination of fatigue and sheer concentration about what he was going to do made him so distracted that he drove right past all the exits that would have taken him to Rye Harbor. He was well into Maine before he realized his mistake. A sign indicated that the next ramp marked the last exit before he would have to pay a toll. A second sign pointed the way to Route 1 and York, Maine.

As he slowed and approached Route 1, he took a right to head south. Not too far down the road, he saw an older motel that looked as if it was well past its prime.

The motel was a long, single-story structure facing the road with a sign proclaiming vacancy: daily, weekly, or by the month. A series of alternating doors and windows defined each of the twenty or so rooms, and the center door had a sign above that said Office. Small signs, with arrows painted on them, lined a drive that disappeared around to the back of the building.

"Perfect," thought Alfred when he saw the motel. Something told him that this would be the perfect place for his intentions.

Alfred turned into the motel's drive as he continued to survey the building. The overcast sky looked as depressed as the motel. There was no doubt that it had been many years since the building had seen a new coat of paint. Across the front was a series of raised garden beds, but few were intact. Most had some part of the brick retaining walls either pushed in, knocked down, or just missing. All of the damage was at a bumper's height. All in all it looked like one of those places that time had passed by and would exist as long as the owners were alive or until its location became too valuable and they would sell out to some real estate developer and move to Florida.

There were cars parked in front of several of the rooms, but by no means was the place fully occupied. He parked in front of the door marked Office and went in. The office was as dated and stale as the outside of the motel. In front of the desk, with backs to the window, were two chairs and a small table with several copies of *Popular Mechanics*, each several years old. On the far wall was a rack with tourist brochures for summertime attractions that were now closed. Next to the rack of brochures was a cigarette machine. Alfred hadn't seen one of those in years. For a moment the collector in him surfaced.

"Hello, may I help you?" The voice startled him.

"Yes. Yes you may. Do you have a room available?"

"How many nights?"

"Two, maybe three, I don't know." Then looking back at the cigarette machine he added, "That machine. You wouldn't want to sell it, would you?"

"Sorry, not for sale. But I do have a room. It's out back if you don't mind. You can stay as long as you like."

"That would be fine," said Alfred. Then he continued to stare at the cigarette machine.

CHAPTER 75

AFTER HIS VISIT WITH CHARLIE, Lieutenant Malloy drove over to the antiques store again. He turned into the front lot, stopped his car, and, leaving the engine running, got out, walked up onto the porch, and tried the door again. It was still locked. He peered in the windows. What little he could see was as he remembered it from the first time he looked in. Leaving the porch, he followed the drive down and around to the back. The cold east wind had begun to kick up, and as he rounded the corner he hunched his shoulders and raised the collar of his coat. It didn't help. He shivered as he checked each of the garage doors, peering in the windows as he had before. Inside, the darkness still hid whatever might be in there. Slowly he walked back to his car, thankful that he had left the car running and the heat on.

He didn't drive off immediately, but rather sat there, staring up at the locked building, wondering where Alfred was, and more important, who he was. The more he learned about Alfred, the less he seemed to know. Charlie told him about the death of Alfred's identical twin, but he needed to know more. Suddenly, he knew right where to go. He shifted his car into gear and left Whitson's Antiques.

Agnes Phillips was the area's unofficial historian. He had met her briefly years ago when he was working another case. He had no idea how old she was, but she was old then, and he hoped she was still alive. He remembered that she lived in one of the oldest houses in the area. It was on a little-used gravel lane that crossed back and forth over the town line between Ipswich and Essex. He wasn't sure exactly which town claimed her as a resident, but the lane began in Ipswich. After several wrong turns, he finally found her road.

The road was still unpaved, narrow, and sparsely housed. As Malloy drove slowly along, every now and again a break would appear in the trees that lined the road, revealing views out over salt marshes or the river and, occasionally, the ocean. He couldn't believe that some developer hadn't yet latched on to this area, but he was glad that no one had.

Rounding a turn in the road, he saw her house. It was as he remembered. The dark-red cape was small and neat. It sat behind a very old stone wall that ran alongside the road. Between the house and the wall there appeared to be flower gardens, though now they were dead and covered in leaves. A small green car was parked in the narrow drive, and there was just room for him to pull in behind it without sticking out into the road. He wondered if it was hers.

CHAPTER 76

THE EAST WIND THAT HAD so chilled him at Whitson's was even more penetrating as he walked to the door on the side of the house. Even though a path led to the front door, he knew that the side door was the entrance that would be used.

Only the smell of wood smoke and its promise of warmth eased the overwhelming gloom of the overcast day. There was no bell, so he knocked and waited. After a second knocking, he heard footsteps. Then the door opened a crack and he faced a young girl, probably of high school age. "Hello, may I help you?" she asked.

"Yes. I'm Lieutenant Malloy of the Ipswich Police Department." He held out his identification and waited patiently while she studied it. She took her time and he appreciated that. When finished, as she handed it back, the look she gave him posed a silent question.

"I'm looking for Agnes Phillips. Is she in?"

"That's my great-grandmother. Yes, she's here. She's not in any kind of trouble is she?"

"No, not at all." Before he could say anything else, he heard a voice from within shout, "Mary, shut the door. Who's there? You're letting all the heat out."

"I'm sorry. Please, won't you come in," she said. She pushed the door open against the cold wind. The wind caught the door and pulled it from her hand. He grabbed it and pulled it closed behind him as he stepped into the mud room. It was filled with coats, boots, stacked firewood, and other stuff—lots of stuff. She led him into the kitchen.

It was tight but neat and functional, and it was obvious that too many years had passed since the last update. The floor was made of wide pine boards. They had once been painted red, he guessed, but years of living had worn most of the paint away save for those corners and edges where a foot wouldn't fit.

The cabinets, which might have been a bright white years ago, now had chipped and dented corners, along with edges that spoke of decades of openings and closings. The countertops were a dark crimson–colored laminate, except in a few spots where age and use had worn through, revealing a lighter-colored center. Bowls, canisters, and crocks filled with utensils seemed to cover all but a ribbon of space nearest the front edge.

The appliances were white, and old enough that replacement would be forgivable, even for an old Yankee. A teakettle sat steaming on the stove, and next to it, on the counter, a teacup sat waiting to be filled. A large soapstone sink was set in front of the only window in the room, and the drain board next to it was filled with recently washed dishes. A large table took up the entire center of the room and, like the counters, it too was cluttered, but with papers, magazines, and some open school books.

"My name is Mary, but I guess you already figured that out," she said, extending her hand to him.

"Mary," the voice called out again. It was strong and clear, and he could easily hear the old Yankee accent.

Looking at Malloy, Mary said, "Lieutenant Malloy, I'm sorry. You'll have to excuse her; her hearing isn't very good. Won't you follow me."

Malloy was struck by Mary's confidence and good manners. As she walked toward the room where the voice came from, he began to rethink his first impression of her age. She seemed way too poised for someone just in high school.

"Thank you," he said, following her into the room.

Once inside, he paused and looked around. The next room felt just like the kitchen: tight, dated and well lived in. The wall on his left contained one small window, which looked out to the road. It was next to the unused front door, which he guessed hadn't been opened in years, if ever. Straight ahead, between two rocking chairs, with a small low table in front sat an old woodstove with wood piled next to it. The wall opposite the front door was dominated by an old upright piano, bookshelves crammed with books, and a closed door that he guessed might be a bedroom. Next to the kitchen another door was open slightly, and he could see that it was the bathroom.

One of the rocking chairs had extra cushions and pillows that made it look like a nest, and tucked into that nest under a crocheted afghan Agnes Phillips sat looking up at him. She was tiny and frail, and yet he could see by the twinkle in her piercing eyes and the way she stared up at him that she was still in full possession of her faculties.

"Grammy, this is Lieutenant Malloy from the police," said Mary. "He's here to see you."

As he stepped toward her, he could feel that wonderful dry heat that you can only get from woodstoves. But before he could say anything, she said in that same strong clear voice that had called out when he arrived, "Malloy? I don't know any Malloys. Are you new in town?" In that instant, he knew where Mary got her poise and confidence from.

Hearing Agnes speak, it was impossible not to know that she was a born and bred New Englander and had lived here her entire life.

"Mrs. Phillips, it's a pleasure to see you again," he said walking toward her while offering his hand.

She continued staring at him, and he could tell that she was trying to remember him. Then, in that heavy New England accent she repeated herself, "You didn't answer my question."

He stopped short. "Well, uh, I moved to Ipswich over twenty years ago. We met once before, when I first joined the force."

"Newcomer," she mumbled in a low voice, confirming her suspicions. "So what do you want with me?"

"Grammy, be nice," interjected Mary. "I think your tea is ready. Lieutenant Malloy, would you like a cup?"

He really didn't, he preferred coffee, but he said yes.

"I'll be right back," she said and disappeared into the kitchen.

"I'm looking for some information."

"What kind of information?"

"Did you ever know the Whitson family? I'm interested in Alfred."

Agnes looked up at him. Her eyes, though bright before, now seemed to light up even more. She sat back in her chair while continuing to stare at him. Then she said, "Sit." She motioned to a chair on the other side of the stove. He sat.

"Whitsons? What's that Alfred done this time?"

Rarely did Malloy allow himself to show surprise, but her question caught him off guard. "This time?" he blurted out.

"Young man, take your coat off," she said.

As he did so, Mary entered the room, carrying a small tray with the tea. "Here you go," she said. She placed the tray on a low table between them.

"I didn't know if you liked milk or lemon, so I brought both, and the sugar is here," she said to Malloy. Then she handed a cup to her great-grandmother. "I have homework to do. I'll be in the other room."

Malloy didn't add anything to his tea. He picked up his cup and said, "As far as I know, he hasn't done anything, but I would like to talk to him and he doesn't seem to be around."

"So why talk to me?"

"Well, like I said, we met once before, when I had just joined the force. I seem to recall that many people consider you to be the unofficial historian of the area, so I thought you might be able to help me." He paused and took a sip of tea.

She wasn't about to let him off the hook, not even for a sip of tea. The look she was giving him demanded more of an explanation.

"I want to find out more about Alfred."

She continued looking deeply at him. Then she began to smile.

The next hour flew by in what seemed like five minutes. Agnes told him more about the history of the area in that hour than he had learned in twenty years on the force.

"Could you tell me a little more about the twins?" he asked when she began talking about the Whitson family.

"Alfred and Thomas. They were a pair, always into some kind of mischief. Thomas was the one always getting caught, while Alfred came across as the good son. Really, though, he was just as bad. They grew up with Trudy, my granddaughter." She paused and then continued. "I remember how she always complained about them."

"Is she still around? I'd like to talk to her."

"No. Moved away quite some time ago. Lives out west somewhere."

"What happened to Thomas?" he asked, gently guiding her back to the twins.

"Terrible accident. I remember that day as clearly as if it were yesterday. I was visiting my daughter when Trudy came running in with the news. The boys had been down by the river. Alfred came running home screaming how Thomas hit his head on a rock and was dead. That much was true, but something never felt right about it. There were rumors."

"Rumors?"

"Not everyone believed that it was Thomas who had been killed."

Malloy put his tea down and leaned over toward Agnes. She had his attention fully. "Couldn't their mother tell?"

"Probably if she was right in the head. Accident really tore her up. Went into shock and clung on to Alfred. She never doubted his word, but she was never right again. After the funeral she never left the house. Alfred pretty much took care of her until she died. That was just a few years later. After her death, he disappeared. No one knew where he went or why. He was just gone. Then one day he was back running that antiques store. No explanation ever given, and I'm not sure that anyone ever asked. He was just there. But he was different."

"That's interesting. What did you think?"

Agnes sat back. She held her teacup in her lap and didn't say anything for a few moments. Then, with what he could only describe as sadness in her voice, she said, "Oh, I don't know. It was such a long time ago. I hadn't thought about any of this until today." Then, looking straight at him she added, "After what he had been through, wouldn't anyone change?"

Mary chose that moment to come back into the room. "Grammy, are you all right?" she said when she saw the sad, tired, faraway look on her great-grandmother's face.

Agnes looked up and smiled at her. "Yes, dear. The lieutenant was just asking me about something that happened a very long time ago."

Mary made a face and looked at him.

"I was asking your great-grandmother about the Whitson's."

Mary didn't say anything, but she continued to look at him from the doorway, her body language saying volumes.

Agnes turned toward Malloy. "She is such a sweet girl and takes good care of me."

"I can see that. You're very lucky." He understood Mary's pose, so he stood and looked at his watch. He said, "Listen, I have to get going." Then he turned toward Agnes and said, "It has been such a pleasure seeing you again. Mary is a delight, and I hope to see you again soon."

Mary followed him into the kitchen, where he received one more surprise. Just before opening the door for him, Mary turned and said, "You've been talking about that strange guy who has the antiques business?"

"Yes."

Mary made a face.

"What do you know about him?" Malloy asked.

"Everyone knows him. In school, the story is legend. No one will swim in the river where his brother died. Everyone thinks his ghost is still there, and at Halloween, someone always dresses as the ghost twin. I know that's not very nice, but he creeps everyone out. As the story goes, he is really Thomas, and Alfred was the one killed. Some people even say that it may not have been an accident." She shrugged as if this were all common knowledge and began to turn the knob on the door.

All that Malloy could think was how little he really knew about this place he had called home for most of twenty years. "Yes, well, thank you Mary. It was a pleasure. Would you mind if I stopped by again if I have any more questions?"

She pulled the door open and a blast of cold air rushed in. "Of course not."

He stepped out into the cold, and as she pulled the door shut she said, "Goodbye."

CHAPTER 77

ALFRED WOKE WITH A START, his heart was pounding as he looked around the room, and it took a few moments for his head to catch up with his eyes. As he shook the grogginess out of his head, he remembered where he was and his heartbeat began to return to normal. He glanced at his watch and saw that it was well after noon. His stomach grumbled. He needed to eat.

Even though there were several fast-food restaurants nearby, none appealed to him, so he kept following Route 1 south. As he drove along, his thoughts returned to the quilts, the one he had stolen and the one that Max had. Which one was the real one? He was so absorbed in his thoughts, he forgot all about food. He drove past the outlet malls in Kittery, and when Route 1 crossed the Piscataqua River, he could see Portsmouth to his left. He followed signs into downtown.

As he passed through a variety of neighborhoods, none quite historic yet, the twisting streets of Portsmouth led him past motels and small strip malls back to the river. The closer he came, the older and more historic the homes and buildings. New luxury hotels, restaurants, shops, and expensive condos now lined the river where once there had been only warehouses, piers, and the more seedy elements common to working waterfronts all over the world. He made one final turn. Straight ahead he spotted a large ship offloading salt in anticipation of the coming winter.

Mesmerized, he parked and sat watching that large ship discharge its cargo. It was probably a combination of hunger, fatigue, and his own demons, but as he closed his eyes he was transported back to a time when his family had been waiting for their ship to arrive and fill their warehouses as well as their coffers. He could feel it, taste it, hear it, and smell it. It didn't matter that his family had lived in another city,

263

in another state, in another century.

The sound of ships' whistles and horns brought him back to the present. Something was happening on the river, but because of the offloading ship, his view of the water was limited to a small gap behind the ship. Amid another chorus of toots and whistles, he finally saw the stack of a tug glide by, followed shortly by another ship heading upriver.

The cloud cover made it feel later than it was, and streetlights began to come on even though there was still some time before the sun was due to set. The cold dampness outside began to creep into his truck and he shivered. He started his truck's engine and continued watching until he felt heat. It was time to go.

Alfred followed the maze of one-way streets until he found himself by a park overlooking the river. A sign proclaimed that he had reached Strawbery Banke, the oldest area in Portsmouth. There was a large common surrounded by carefully restored homes and businesses that re-created Portsmouth as it was two hundred years ago. He could feel that past in every fiber of his being. Across the river from the park he saw the Navy Yard, its lights creating a soft, reflected glow off the low clouds above while they twinkled in the dark ribbon that was the river. He drove slowly through the ever more narrow streets. The houses were so close together that they seemed to be set almost on top of each other.

His stomach grumbled. He still hadn't eaten, but he drove on. At the old cemetery, he turned left. A sign confirmed that he was still heading for Rye Harbor. "Of course," he said to himself, and he smiled. The invisible hand of fate seemed to be guiding him.

As he drove along, he looked left, out over the Atlantic Ocean. Save for the tiny cluster of rocks, barely visible in the gloom, that were the Isles of Shoals, he saw only emptiness. That was the moment when the setting sun dipped below the low clouds and daylight returned to the world. The Isles of Shoals, which only moments before had been dark, lifeless shapes, suddenly lit up as if consumed by flames. Those rays of light reflected red, orange, and silver, off of anything on the islands that they hit.

Alfred wasn't the only one to pull off the road to watch daylight's last gasp before it succumbed to the night. Six other vehicles had also stopped in the overlook. Each parked facing the spectacle. People were getting out of their cars to watch, and Alfred joined them. The cold east wind, which had made the day so raw and bone chilling, hadn't relented. He hunched his shoulders and pulled his coat close as if that could ward off the biting wind. A tear ran down his cheek. Had the bystanders noticed, they would have assumed that it was caused by the cold wind in his face. But Alfred was reliving in his mind once again those events that had destroyed his family. What he saw was their ship, just arrived, burning at anchor.

"Beautiful, isn't it?" a high, raspy voice startled him.

Alfred was jarred out of his trance-like state. "Uh," he said as he looked toward where the voice came from. What he saw was a diminutive, older woman. She was wearing dark green wool pants tucked into leather hiking boots, a navy blue pea coat, and a watch cap pulled down tightly over her head. Bright twinkly eyes peered up at him from her weathered face and even though the strap was around her neck, she was holding onto the largest pair of binoculars he had ever seen.

She motioned toward the now dimming light that had bathed the Isles. "Pretty, isn't it?"

"Yes, yes, it was," said Alfred. He was a bit confused for a moment as he returned to the present.

"I love coming out here when it's stormy. The birds are all swooping and crying. I watch birds."

Alfred was confused and uncomfortable. Who was this woman, and what did she want? Why would anyone just go up to a stranger and start talking to them? "Do I know you?" he said. He was almost certain he didn't, but it seemed like the right thing to say.

"Oh, no. My name is Gladys. I just like to meet new people. I spend most of my time watching birds. It's a pretty lonely thing to do, and since I live alone, whenever I see someone who looks interesting, I go over and say 'Hi' to them. Kinda' like spotting a new bird." She lifted the glasses to her eyes again.

She was making no sense at all to him, and he really didn't feel like talking. "Well, it was nice meeting you," he mumbled. The show was over. The sun was hovering at the western horizon and the world was rapidly becoming black-and-white again. He turned to get into his car. Gladys didn't move; she simply continued to stand there looking out to sea through those enormous binoculars.

Alfred ended up walking in front of her because she wasn't moving and there was no room between her and the front of his truck. She lowered her binoculars and started to say "Goodbye," but he had already climbed into his truck. As she returned the binoculars to her face, he quickly backed out into the road.

CHAPTER 78

"BYE, JACK. I'M HEADING OVER TO BEN'S," shouted Max as she rushed down the stairs.

He was in the shower and didn't hear her call out, but it didn't matter. When he had returned from his run she was already dressed and ready to go to work.

It had taken him most of the day to get out the door for a run. Inside, looking out, one part of his brain had told him that staying inside with a book would be the best option for such an obviously cold, raw, and windy day. However, by mid-afternoon, he was restless. He had lived by the harbor for enough years to know that once he got out the door, he would find that it wasn't as bad out as it looked from inside.

The five miles or so that he ran turned out better than he had expected. Since the wind was from the east, he was able to follow a course that would minimize time spent with a head wind, and by the time he had run a half-mile or so he had begun to break a sweat and it was no longer so cold. Traffic on the roads remained light, and he was on his way back when the sun dipped below the clouds as it set. All of a sudden the world was bathed in an ethereal light, and out over the dark, greenish-gray ocean, the Isles of Shoals had exploded and sparkled in light and color.

Jack slowed his pace and smiled as he became immersed in this moment. He knew that it would only last a very few minutes, and as he reached one of the many small parking areas that dotted the coast, he began walking. There were perhaps a half-dozen vehicles lined up, and most of the occupants were standing outside and looking east at the spectacle. The show was nearly over when he saw a truck start, back up, and leave. He watched it drive off before he walked over to join the remaining spectators. The group had turned and were now facing west to watch the end of the sunset.

"Jack?" It was Gladys, her ever-present, large binoculars slung around her neck, walking toward him.

"Gladys, what are you doing out here?"

"Watching my birds."

"See any good ones?"

"Some. Wasn't that sunset amazing?"

"It was."

"I saw you watching that truck drive off," said Gladys. "Anyone you knew?"

"No. Why?"

"I talked with him a bit. He struck me as odd."

"Gladys, most people are."

"No, he was odd in a different sort of way. I could just feel it. Odd."

He shrugged. "I gotta' get going before it gets too dark. I'll see you soon," he said. He began moving away from her.

"Be safe. Bye," she called as he began running again. Then, while shaking her head she said to herself, "Nice guy, but that one's odd too. Why would anyone want to be out running around like that?"

* * *

Now, as Jack emerged from the bathroom, Cat greeted him with an earful of complaints. Mostly she wanted supper, and as usual she was very good at making her desires known.

"As soon as I'm dressed I'll feed you," he said.

She looked up at him and began to tell him just what she thought of the delay.

Finally, fed and happy, Cat settled down while Jack put on his coat. Now it was his turn. He was hungry and thirsty and Max was working at the bar, so he knew exactly where to head.

CHAPTER 79

AS JACK WALKED INTO THE BAR at Ben's, he paused in the doorway, looking around the half-full room to see if there were any familiar faces. There were none. Several single people were sitting at the bar, each with an empty seat between. The first three seats were empty, so he took the one on the end, nearest the door. This left the other two open so if a couple came in, they would be able to sit together without having to ask someone to move. As he sat, each of the other people at the bar glanced up in his direction and offered a quick nod of acknowledgement. Then they turned back to their drinks. Jack started to give a collective nod back, but he stopped when he noticed the stare of a guy at the end of the bar. As their eyes met, the man quickly looked away.

Max wasn't behind the bar so he guessed that she was out in the kitchen. He glanced up at the television. The news was on, without sound, because Max preferred to listen to music from the radio, usually an oldies station that played tunes from the late fifties to the mid-sixties. They were simple songs, from a simpler time, and he could usually understand the lyrics, not unlike the country he sometimes listened to. As the narrative scrolled across the bottom of the screen and the sounds of Roy Orbison crooning "Pretty Woman" escaped from the radio, Max came in carrying a large salad with a piece of grilled salmon draped over the top. She looked . . . he wasn't sure what she looked, but something wasn't right.

"Beer?" she asked Jack as she walked past him. She returned after placing the salad in front of the guy at the end of the bar.

"Please." Jack's eyes followed her as she disappeared out back to get his beer. Something definitely was not right. He knew Max and he could always tell when she was upset. He noticed that Salad Man was also watching her intently. Jack was used to seeing guys at the bar watch

Max, it came with the job, but this time, something about the way he was watching her caught Jack's attention. It didn't feel right. Jack stopped watching Max and now focused on Salad Man.

Jack didn't like the feeling he was getting. There was something unsettling about the guy. His face was narrow, and he wore really thick glasses. His clothes, though neat, were certainly not trendy, and the way he wore them was seriously nerdy. Even though the bar was warm, he still had his jacket on. It was one of those short jackets that looked like it was from the sixties, made of dark brown corduroy, well worn with gloves hanging out of the pockets. A scarf hung loosely around his neck. Clearly he was someone whose concerns were not with fashion.

When Max returned with Jack's beer, she passed in front of Salad Man without even a glance. It was as if he didn't exist. In contrast, Salad Man slowly turned his head as he followed her every move. Jack had never seen her act this way. "Thanks," he said. "You okay?"

"Yeah." The tone of her voice said otherwise, but it was obvious she wasn't going to offer more.

Jack was staring at her, not sure of exactly what to say, when she asked, "How was your run?"

"Good." Then in an attempt to lighten the mood, he asked if she had seen the Isles light up when the sun dipped below the clouds as it was setting.

"Only for a moment. It was beautiful. Wasn't it, Patti?"

Jack hadn't seen or heard Patti walk in. He turned his head just as she came to a stop next to him.

She said, "Hi Jack." Then to Max, "It was."

Jack turned back toward Max and as he did so, he caught a glimpse of Salad Man quickly turning his head away and taking a bite of his salad. Something was definitely wrong. Normally Patti would be gushing nonstop about the sunset and the photographic opportunity, yet now she barely acknowledged having seen it.

"What's going on?" he asked Max.

"Nothing," she said. Her eyes darted between Jack and Patti.

"Excuse me," Alfred said. "Do you have any fresh ground pepper?"

Max turned toward him and, forcing a smile, said, "Sure." She took several steps toward the kitchen. Then she stopped, turned back toward Jack, and said, "I'll be right back."

"I'll go with you," said Patti. She scurried after Max.

Jack watched them hustle off. Then, turning back, he looked at Salad Man. Sure that he was the reason for the women's behavior, Jack asked him the same question he had asked Max.

"Did you see the sunset?"

"I did. It reminded me of a fire out on the water."

"I hadn't thought about it like that, but you're right, it did," said Jack.

Max returned with pepper mill in hand, brushed past Jack, and handed it to Salad Man, not even offering to grind it for him. Jack noticed and said, "Max, could I see you for a moment?"

She didn't say anything but she walked out of the bar toward the kitchen. Jack followed.

As soon as they were out of sight from the bar, Jack said to her, "What's wrong? You're acting really strange."

"Jack, it's him."

"Who's 'him'?"

"The guy at the bar, with the salad. He's the guy who wanted the quilt. He's the guy who the detective from Ipswich called about. He's the murderer."

Her words came out in a rush while Jack just stared at her. "Max, you're acting crazy."

"No, I'm not. He's the guy."

"Fine. He's the guy who was interested in the quilt. Big deal."

"And the cop from Ipswich is looking for him."

"So give him a call."

"I can't."

"Why not?"

"Because."

"Max, you're acting crazy. If he's the guy, make the call."

"But what if he's the murderer? If I call, I could be next."

"Now you're being silly. Come here." Jack pulled her close, took her in his arms, and whispered, "Max, there is nothing to worry about. I'll stay here and talk to him. Everything will be all right. Go make the call."

Jack returned to his seat while Max ran upstairs to the office.

Across the bar, Jack saw the light on the phone go on, indicating that someone in the building was using the line.

"You from around here?" Jack asked Alfred as he looked at him carefully.

"No, just passing through."

"How's the salad?"

"Good."

It was obvious that Alfred didn't want to talk, but Jack kept at him. "Do I know you? You look familiar."

"I don't think so." Alfred took another bite.

"Name's Jack."

"Nice to meet you. Alfred."

Jack nodded while glancing at the phone. The light was still on. "Max, she's really something isn't she?"

"Who?"

"Max, the bartender."

"Oh. Yeah. She seems nice."

"She's more than nice." Jack paused and glanced at the phone again. Then he looked back at Alfred and added, "She's very special. Especially to me."

Alfred looked a bit antsy, and Jack wasn't sure whether or not he should back off. Alfred looked down at his salad and said, "I was in the other day. I'm an antiques dealer. We got to talking and she told me about her interest in quilts."

"Yeah," said Jack. "She gets going on a kick and there's no stopping her."

"She told me about a quilt she had. I'm interested. Do you think she'd sell?"

Something in the back of Jack's mind told him not to reveal the fact that Max no longer had the quilt. He simply said, "Doubt it. It's not hers."

From the corner of his eye, saw that the light on the phone was still lit. Meanwhile, it was clear that Alfred's anxiety was increasing.

Abruptly Alfred stood and said, "Listen, I've got to get going."

Jack looked at the phone: still lit. There was no way he would be able to keep Alfred there any longer. It seemed the best he could do was try to get a description of Alfred's car.

Nervously, Alfred glanced around for Max. Seeing that she hadn't returned, he pulled some cash out of his pocket, left it on the bar, and rushed out. Jack rose to follow, but as he reached the door, he literally bumped into Leo, Ralph, and Paulie, who were heading in from the cold.

Paulie reached out a hand to steady him. "Hey, there, Jack! What's the rush? No point zipping out to freeze your ass off at this time of year."

Yanking the knob, Jack ignored him. But by the time he reached the parking lot, Alfred had disappeared. Back at the bar, the light on the phone finally went out.

CHAPTER 80

BY THE TIME MAX CAME DOWN from the office, Alfred was already gone, his half empty plate and money on the bar where he had just been sitting. "Where is he?" Max asked Jack, glancing around.

"He's gone. Just left. I tried to follow him, get a description of his car, but he was too quick." He watched the expression on her face change. When she had walked back into the bar, her face registered a kind of excitement, determination, as if she had been given a mission. Now, with the news that he was gone, her face reflected disappointment and maybe even a touch of concern.

"He's gone? Why? How? What did you do, Jack Beale?"

"Nothing. We talked. I told him how special you are to me. He told me he wanted to buy a quilt from you, and I told him it wasn't yours to sell. That's when he got a little weird. Well, he was already weird, but you know what I mean. Then he left."

Max simply stared at Jack.

Jack stared back for a moment, then asked, "So what did Malloy say?"

"Nothing."

"Nothing?" Jack knew that wasn't true, but he also knew Max. Playing the game, he said, "Well, if he didn't say anything, could I get something to eat? I'm starving."

That did it. Max started in.

"He thanked me for calling. He said that he had been looking for Alfred—but we already knew that. He said he wanted to ask Alfred a few questions, but he's had no luck getting hold of him. He asked me if I could keep him at the bar until he could get up here. I said I'd try, but now you let him get away."

"I didn't let him get away. He left. It's not like I could have tied him to a chair. I'm sorry already. So could I get a burger and some fries?"

"Jack Beale, you just let a murderer get away and all you can think about is a burger?"

"You don't know that."

Her look said otherwise.

"C'mon, Max. Malloy said that he only wants to talk to him."

She continued to stare silently at him.

"Look Max, he's gone. Why don't you call the lieutenant back so he doesn't waste a trip up here. I'm sure there's nothing to worry about. Make the phone call, order that burger, and we'll worry about something else."

"Fine. But I know I'm right. You'll see."

CHAPTER 81

EMOTIONS TRUMPED REASON, so as soon as he hung up the phone, Lt. Malloy stood up to leave. He knew that it was unlikely that he could get to Rye Harbor before Alfred left the bar, but he had to try. The more he learned about Alfred—and his twin, the more anxious he became to talk to him. He couldn't help but feel that Alfred had been avoiding him.

Before he even stepped away from his desk, she called back and told him that Alfred was gone, so after reassuring Max that she had nothing to fear, they agreed to meet the next morning.

* * *

Lieutenant Malloy arrived in the parking lot at Ben's a little early. They had arranged to meet at 9:30, but he wanted to have a little time to see the area. The weather hadn't improved. It was still overcast, and the cold east wind continued to blow in from the ocean. Lieutenant Malloy had the engine running and the heat blasting. He was looking at his notes when there was a knock on his car window. He looked up and hit the button to lower his window at the same time.

"Lieutenant Malloy?"

He shivered as the cold air rushed into his car. "You must be Max," he said to the woman standing next to his car.

"I am," she said.

He pulled on his door handle, pushed his door open, and climbed out of his car. "It's so nice to meet you," he said, extending his hand.

Max was all scrunched into a ski parka, with a knit hat pulled down on her head and a scarf wrapped around her neck. She had been hugging herself in an attempt to ward off the cold, but now she reached out a mittened hand and shook his.

"Is there somewhere we could go to talk? If not, we can talk here in my car," he said.

"Let's go inside. I have a key."

The bar was warm, but Max turned the heat up another notch anyway. "Make yourself at home. I'm going to put a pot of coffee on," she said.

Max had just returned with two mugs of steaming coffee when they heard the front door open, followed by a puff of cold air. Then Jack appeared.

"Jack, what are you doing here?" Max asked.

Malloy looked up. "Hi Jack. All recovered?"

Before Jack could reply, his friend Tom entered the bar behind him. Max, surprised to see Tom, looked over at Jack. Before she could say anything, Tom said, "Mornin' Max." He then approached Malloy and held out his hand. "You must be Lieutenant Malloy. Ipswich, right? I'm Tom Scott, Rye Harbor PD. Jack told me about you."

Malloy shook Tom's hand. "Tom. Good to meet you."

"Jack tells me that you are interested in someone who might be hanging around here?"

"I am. Last weekend a man was killed during a race down our way. Jack found the body."

"So I heard."

"We finally identified him and it turns out they," nodding toward Max and Jack, "had met the victim's wife some time before. She had given them, more specifically Max, a quilt. She thought that she had given Max an old worthless quilt, but it turned out she had grabbed the wrong bag. She actually gave Max a more valuable quilt instead. Her husband, the victim, was supposed to pick it up after the race, only he never did. Alfred Whitson, the man I am looking for, was here last night. Max told me it was his second time, and he is interested in that quilt. I'd like to know why."

While Malloy was filling Tom in on his investigation, Max pulled

Jack aside. "What are you doing here, and why did you bring Tom?"

"I'm concerned."

"Concerned? You weren't so 'concerned' last night."

"I was, I . . ."

He began to protest, but she cut him off. "So you're telling me that all of a sudden this morning you had a change of heart and you believe me now."

"I didn't say that. That guy last night was pretty weird and when I got up this morning, well I, uh, decided that maybe it would be good for Tom to know what was going on."

"And you didn't feel that this was, say maybe, important enough to discuss with me first."

Jack was losing. It was only the interruption by the two policemen that saved him.

"Max, could you come repeat for Tom what you told me about this guy?" asked Lieutenant Malloy.

Jack followed her over and listened as she repeated the entire story, from the first time Alfred had stopped by, several days ago, right through last night.

Then turning to Jack, he asked, "While Max was up on the phone with me last night, what happened down here?"

Jack then recounted his own story, apologizing that he wasn't able to offer more.

When he finished, it felt like a very long time went by before anyone said anything, even though the silence lasted only a few seconds.

Malloy was the first to speak. "Max, thank you. You did the right thing calling me last night. I'm more convinced than ever that I need to talk with our friend Alfred. There's probably a good chance that he'll be back in touch with you since it seems that this quilt is really important to him. Tom, any help you can offer would be appreciated, and Jack, listen to her. She has good instincts and I—no, we—don't want anything to happen to her."

CHAPTER 82

The ship burned all night and by morning, it was gone. All that remained were some charred timbers floating in the harbor. A man standing beside him rested a hand on his shoulder. He tried to turn his head to see who it was, but he couldn't move. Then he heard the man speak. "She's gone. Those fools have destroyed everything. We are ruined."

Again he tried to turn toward the voice but couldn't. "Why . . ." Before he could finish his question, a group of men approached and took the man away. He ran after them, but they were always a few steps ahead no matter how hard he ran. He called out. The man tried to turn back, but he was forced forward. Time blurred. Then he was in the courthouse and the magistrate pronounced the sentence. "Guilty." Despite his protestations, the defendant was whisked away.

Alfred sat up, shaking and sweating, the rage and frustration still coursing through his body. The dream was the same one he had experienced so many times before. It took several minutes before his eyes adjusted to the dim light in the dingy motel room, hundreds of years removed from where he had just been, then a few more for him to fully remember where he was and why. He lay back down and thought about what he could, or would, do. She had the quilt. He had to have it. It was the key. As he played through different scenarios in his mind, he gradually drifted back to sleep, and this time there were no more dreams.

The day was still gray and overcast as he pulled the door to the room closed. A strong gust of cold air forced itself through his jacket, pressed under his hat, and threatened to unwrap the scarf that he had wound around his neck. He could feel his truck being rocked by the wind, and he shivered as he started the engine. Even though he knew it would be several miles before there would be heat, he still felt warmer as he drove away from the motel.

Driving east toward the ocean in search of some breakfast, he let his mind wander. The jumble of thoughts in his head made no sense when he focused on them rationally, and yet somehow they made perfect sense when he just let those same thoughts drift. They pulled him, guiding him, and the closer to the ocean he got, the greater his anticipation of that one moment—and there could only be one—when he would first see the water. On this day, when that moment came, all he saw was a field of gray. There was no horizon. The sea and sky had became one. He stopped his truck and stared. Only with great effort could he see that thin line between air and water.

His truck shook as the invisible hand of the relentless wind pushed at it. He thought about the previous night. He mulled over what he had intended to do, what he hadn't done, and what he needed to do. Soon enough, a sense of calm washed over him and he drove back in the direction he had come from. That same invisible force that had drawn him to the ocean now guided him into the pub at the York Harbor Inn.

A feeling of déjà vu washed over him as he stepped into the pub, which had just opened for the day. The décor, though modern, had the feel of an old wooden ship, not unlike the one that burned in his dreams nearly every night. He was the first customer, and the bartender turned as the door closed behind him.

"Good morning! Welcome to the York Harbor Inn," he said. "Make yourself at home. I'll be right with you."

Alfred didn't reply. He stood and looked around the room. Even though he was the only person there, voices and sounds filled his head. He could hear them laughing, he could hear their taunts. He closed his eyes and reopened them, and when he did, the voices stopped and he saw the bartender staring at him. Flustered, Alfred stammered, "Oh, I'm sorry. Thanks," and he moved toward a table by the windows that overlooked the street. He positioned himself so that when he looked out he could see the ocean in the distance. More memories flashed through his head.

"Not a very nice day out, is it?"

Alfred looked up. The bartender put down a placemat and utensils in front of him. Then he took the menu that was tucked under his arm and presented it to Alfred. "My name is Stephen. May I get you something to drink?"

Alfred stared silently at him.

"Coffee? Tea? Something more substantial?" Stephen suggested, still trying to get a response from Alfred.

"Yes, coffee would be good. Thank you."

Stephen turned and headed for the kitchen. When he reached the door he looked back at Alfred, then imperceptibly shook his head. "*Strange, it must be the weather,*" he thought to himself.

Several hours had passed by the time Alfred was ready to leave. The lunch crowd had come and gone. As he looked over the check, he didn't even remember eating what was on the bill, but he knew he must have done so. When Alfred stood to leave, Stephen looked in his direction and for a moment their eyes met. Alfred quickly looked down, dropped some cash on the table, and headed for the door. He never heard Stephen say, "Have a nice day," because of all the other voices in his head.

CHAPTER 83

THE WEATHER HADN'T IMPROVED by the time Malloy was ready to leave, and even though Ben's was open he declined the invitation to stay for lunch. After the conversations with Max and Jack, he was even more convinced of the urgency to find Alfred. Tom offered his help and they agreed to keep in touch.

Sitting in his car, with the engine running, Malloy looked over his notes, then called his office. Jack hadn't been able to catch up with Alfred in the parking lot, but now Malloy verified the plate number and description of Alfred's truck based on its registration and asked his sergeant to issue a B.O.L.O.—Be On the Lookout for. Something about Alfred was gnawing at him. He couldn't put his finger on it, but he was definitely feeling an urgency to find him.

* * *

Unlike Malloy, Tom did accept the invitation to join Max and Jack for lunch. As soon as they had ordered he looked at them and asked, "How the hell do the two of you get into these situations?"

"It's not like we go looking for it," protested Max.

"I know that, but you have to admit, you two seem to get into more than your fair share of trouble."

Max didn't say anything.

Tom looked over at Jack, who said, "Hey, don't look at me."

"Sorry. It's just strange. So would you mind telling me again what happened last weekend?"

Jack finished the story at about the same time they finished eating their lunches.

"That is bizarre," said Tom. "You know, you couldn't write a story like this and have people actually believe it."

"I know."

Max had been relatively quiet during the entire time Jack was telling his story, but now she looked at Tom and asked, "So Tom, what should we do?"

"I'm not sure there's a lot you can do, except keep an eye out for this Alfred and be careful. He definitely sounds a bit unstable to me."

"But what if he shows up again?"

"Call me. Listen, I have to get going. Don't worry Max, I'm sure everything is going to turn out just fine."

He said his goodbyes, leaving Max and Jack alone in the bar. "You're working tonight?" asked Jack.

"Yeah, at five."

"What time should we get going in the morning?"

"Early. The funeral service is at eleven."

"Well, on the bright side, with this shitty weather, you probably won't have a very late night."

"I hope not."

* * *

Even as Alfred drove away from the Inn, he could still hear their voices, telling and retelling the story of the burning of the ship. His head ached from the cruel laughter of those who would profit from his family's misfortune. He knew what he had to do.

Alfred didn't remember anything of the ride back to the motel. As he got out of his truck, the cold wind hit him like a slap in the face. The voices followed him, and as he fumbled with the key, he could feel their presence pressing against him. Finally, as he pushed the door closed, the voices became quieter, but he knew they were still out there. The windows rattled and shook, betraying their presence. He was tired. He collapsed onto the bed, not even bothering to remove his coat, and his eyes closed. "Patience. Have patience," the last remaining whisper kept repeating in his ear as sleep overwhelmed him.

CHAPTER 84

IT DID TURN OUT TO BE an early night at Ben's. The weather hadn't improved, and if anything it seemed colder and windier. Jack drove over to pick Max up, and when he pulled into the lot at Ben's he parked his truck so he could look out over the harbor and check on the boats. He had fallen into this routine when *Irrepressible* was still moored there, and even though she was now gone, the habit remained.

Most of the boats had already been hauled out for the winter and all that remained in the harbor were the few lobster and fishing boats whose captains continued to fish throughout the year. It was a hard life. With his engine running and the headlights shining out over the water, he could see only the *Sea Witch* clearly. The higher than normal tide and the strong east wind created the illusion that she was sitting higher than the parking lot as she tugged and pulled at her mooring.

A wave crashed against the rocks in front of his truck. Its spray, lit by his headlights, sparkled like so many shards of glass before hitting the windshield. As the wind buffeted his truck, he remembered that day when he and Max had barely escaped with their lives as they watched *Irrepressible* sink. The spray from another wave hit the windshield and a tear rolled down his cheek.

The door to the cab suddenly opened and a blast of cold air hit him. He turned. It was Max, and as she climbed into the cab she asked, "Jack, why didn't you come in? What are you doing sitting out here?"

Before he turned to face her he tried to wipe his cheek. He wasn't sure if she had noticed or not. "Oh, I just got here. I was watching the *Sea Witch*." Then, trying to change the subject, he said, "Man, you weren't kidding when you said you were ready."

"You were thinking about *Irrepressible*, weren't you?"

"Yeah, I was," he said softly. Then he added, "On the bright side,

I'm really glad that I don't have to worry about her on a night like this. Look," he said motioning to the way the *Witch* was bucking and swinging.

She didn't turn her head, but rather kept looking at him. "I suppose. Let's go home."

Silently he shifted into reverse.

The relationship between a boat and a sailor can be as personal as that between two people. Life on the sea is unforgiving and if a man takes care of his boat, that boat will, in turn, take care of that man. *Irrepressible* was gone, burned and sunk by a madman who had tried to kill them. Yet they had survived and he hadn't. Jack was so grateful for that. He had loved *Irrepressible*, but he loved Max more.

* * *

As they drove across the road back home, another pair of eyes watched them leave. Alfred had intended to catch Max just before closing, but he was too late. He had to convince her of the importance to him of that quilt. She had to understand. He would see her tomorrow.

CHAPTER 85

POLLY AWAKENED EARLY. She walked down the stairs to the kitchen. Without thinking, she put water on for tea as she had for so many years, then pulled a chair away from the table to sit down and wait for the water to boil. For a moment it all felt so normal. Malcom would be down soon, she'd have her tea, and he would make himself a cup of coffee. They'd talk . . . but that's when it hit her. They wouldn't talk. Today she was going to say goodbye to Malcom for the last time. Then, everyone who knew him would help her celebrate his life in the way he would have wanted.

* * *

While Cat was finishing her breakfast, Jack, coffee in hand, stood in front of the window and gazed out to sea. The storm had passed and to the west there were breaks in the clouds. The early sun was still below the cloud line. Unlike yesterday's sunset, when the Isles had been lit as if by a spotlight, now they were no more than tiny dark specks on an angry sea, and it was the breaking waves that sparkled in backlit splendor.

Cat rubbed at his feet, softly mrowing for attention since her stomach was now full. He bent down, scratched her head, and ran his hand down her back. She began to purr loudly and looked up at him, eyes scrunched shut. Her expression conveyed total contentment. "Cat, you're such a good girl," he said in a voice just louder than a whisper. She knew that. She head-butted his leg and then forced her head under his hand for another ear scratch.

Finally satisfied, Cat sauntered off and Jack returned to looking out at the ocean.

"You're up early," Max whispered in his ear. Startled, he jumped and she giggled. He had been so lost in his own thoughts he didn't hear her get up. He had intended to let Max sleep for a while longer before they would have to get ready for the drive north to the funeral. He turned to face her.

"You're up. I was letting you sleep."

She leaned into him and wrapped her arms around him, her head pressed against his chest. "I know, but Cat had different ideas."

"Figures."

"What're you thinking about?"

"Nothing specific, just looking out at the ocean, watching the sunrise. Looks like it's going to turn into a nice day for a funeral."

CHAPTER 86

TRAFFIC WAS LIGHT AND the farther north they drove, the clearer the sky became. By the time they turned off Route 16, the sky was perfectly blue, much as it had been the first time they visited the Inn. Max checked her notes. The service was scheduled to be held at the Holt-Pierce Funeral Home, followed by a reception at the Inn.

* * *

Alfred awakened with the sun as well, but he didn't have the same dramatic view that Jack had. He lay on the bed in the semi-dark motel room. The curtains on the single window were still drawn, and the only light in the room came from the small lamp next to the bed.

As he stared at the ceiling, he noticed the patterns and shadows cast by the small lamp. Moments later, he slid back into that place somewhere between sleeping and being fully awake.

The voices returned. He could hear shouts and cries. Then he heard a low rumble and felt a shaking and thundering like the pounding of horses' hooves. Fearful that they were coming for him, he slowly, quietly, sat up then moved to the curtained window. As he parted the heavy fabric, sunlight streamed in. He held his hand up to shield his eyes from the bright light that hadn't been seen for several days. There were no horses, only a large truck, its engine rumbling, and several men noisily loading boxes into the back of the truck.

He let go of the curtain and it fell closed again, returning the room to its state of semidarkness. It was time, time to return to Ben's and get what was rightfully his. But first he decided to call, just to make sure that she was there before he made the trip back to Ben's. Last night he had made some assumptions that led to the failure of his mission. Today he would be more efficient.

Moments later, he slammed the phone down and stared at it in disbelief, as if it were the reason for his continued bad luck. He sat down on the edge of the bed. He needed to think. The nice voice on the other end of the line had told him that she would not be in today because she was going to a funeral, adding that Sunday was her day off. Two days. Two whole days before he would be able to see her and convince her how important it was that she give the quilt to him. That was too long. He couldn't wait. His family couldn't wait.

He paced back and forth and as he paced, he listened. Soon it was quiet again outside. He looked out the window. The men and horses were gone. It was time for him to go.

* * *

Lieutenant Malloy took another sip from the extra-large coffee as he drove toward the station. Normally he wouldn't go in on the weekend, but ever since he had begun his search for Alfred Whitson, he hadn't slept well. He knew sleep would be elusive until he found him. Malloy's need for caffeine had also increased proportionally to his frustration.

"Where are you, Alfred Whitson? And who are you?" he said to himself as he pulled into the station. On the way in he had driven by the antiques store on the chance that Alfred would be there. He wasn't, which didn't surprise him. Somehow he knew Alfred wouldn't be there.

Malloy sat at his desk, swallowed the last of his coffee, and reviewed his notes for the umpteenth time. Today was Malcom's funeral. What was he missing? With each passing day, he was more and more convinced that Alfred was the murderer, despite the fact that there was no evidence to confirm that. He just knew it. He had to find him.

He picked up his phone and dialed the number Tom Scott in Rye had given him.

"Hey Tom. Mark Malloy . . . I'm fine . . . The B.O.L.O. is out on Whitson. No sign of him down here and his shop is still closed. Something tells me that he won't be found here and I'm even more convinced that he probably did kill Malcom Christian . . ."

They talked for more than thirty minutes, tossing about ideas, impressions, and theories. By the time their conversation ended, Tom was as convinced as Mark that Alfred was the man they wanted. Now they just had to find him.

* * *

"That was a lovely service. I wish that I had had the opportunity to know Malcom. He was a remarkable man," said Jack as Polly held his hand.

"I know you would have been friends. Thank you for finding him."

Max gave her a long hug and promised that they'd see her later, at the reception at the Inn.

Neither Max nor Jack spoke on the ride over to the Inn. They were among the early arrivals and were greeted by Polly's friend Anne.

"Since we're a little early, would there be any problem if we went for a walk out in the woods?" asked Jack.

"Of course not. Everyone else will be arriving soon. You know where you are going?"

"I do."

Jack and Max walked across the backyard toward the beginning of the trails that Malcom had made through the woods. The ground was still wet and their feet left impressions in the grass. Max pulled her coat close and leaned against Jack for warmth as a cool November breeze began to gently blow through the treetops, rustling the few remaining leaves.

"It's so senseless and unfair. Why do things like this happen to good people?"

Jack had no answer. All he could say was, "Don't know."

They followed the trail, silent, each lost in their own thoughts. Several days of hard rain had soaked and flattened the leaves that covered the trail, leaving a mat of dirty yellows, reds, and browns. It was nature's version of a floor cloth. There was no light crunch of dry leaves underfoot, but rather a more soggy squish. Shafts of sunlight streamed through the denuded trees, revealing what had been hidden from view all summer. It wasn't long before the trail widened, and Jack remembered that it became an old fire road that would take them to the main road. They hadn't realized how close to the end they were until they saw an old pickup truck parked just off the pavement.

"We should get back," said Jack. Then nodding toward the truck he added, "It's probably hunting season and we are not exactly dressed for visibility."

Max gripped his arm more tightly and tugged him toward the road. "Let's walk back along the road," she said in a louder than normal voice.

"Sure."

As they broke out of the woods, Max kept looking about nervously. As they headed toward the Inn, another pair of eyes watched as they walked up the road.

CHAPTER 87

ALFRED LEFT HIS HIDING PLACE shortly after Max and Jack passed him. Glancing back up the road to make sure the coast was clear, he moved quickly in the direction they had come from. It wasn't long before he found a spot where he could watch the Inn while remaining out of sight. "What the hell," he murmured to himself as he watched. First a band set up, then some people brought out grills and lit them, and finally a very large man carried a keg out onto the back porch.

"This is not right," he said to himself. Then a voice in his head said, "*Stop worrying, this may turn out to be a good thing.*" He tried, but it wasn't easy. As more and more people arrived, the band began to play, and he could hear laughter. His confusion grew. It looked like most of the guests had changed out of their dressy, funeral clothes into casual jeans, sweaters, and sweatshirts. He didn't understand. Funerals were supposed to be somber, but this looked more like a party.

He heard her arrival before he saw her. The music quieted and the laughter ceased as Polly, dressed in more proper black, moved about hugging and greeting those who were there. He began to relax. "That's more like it," he said quietly to himself. Her presence had properly restored the festivities to what they were, a funeral.

When Polly disappeared into the house, the laughter returned and the band began to play again. The longer she was gone, the louder the party and the greater his anxiety. Eventually she reappeared, although at first he didn't recognize her because she had changed into jeans and a sweater.

He could smell the food cooking and his stomach growled. Confusion and then anger began to dominate his feelings. As the sounds of people having a good time increased, so did the voices in his head. His family's ship had been burned and these people, the ones who had caused it all, were celebrating. He had to get the quilt. He needed the evidence.

* * *

By the time Max and Jack had walked back to the Inn, so many cars had filled the drive that many were now parked on the road. "I don't remember this many people being at the service. Do you?" asked Max.

"Nope," said Jack and he shrugged. Walking up the drive they began to hear strands of music coming from behind the Inn. As they reached the building, they detected the smell of grilling burgers and chicken. They were about to open the front door when they were met by Anne on her way out.

"Oh, there you are. Polly was just asking about you." She had changed into jeans, a turtleneck, and a fisherman sweater. It was the first time they had ever seen her animated and smiling.

"We came back on the road," said Max before sheepishly asking, "What's happening?"

"Oh, you don't know. Malcom had always said that when he died, he wanted there to be a party. You should always remember the good times and not dwell on the bad. No one remembers funerals, but everyone remembers a great party. Come on in, everyone's out back."

She held the door open and motioned for them to go in. Max and Jack, a bit surprised, looked at each other and then stepped inside. Anne let the door close behind them and headed down the drive.

People were everywhere inside the Inn. Gone were the somber dresses and suits, replaced by everyday clothes. Laughter and the din of a great party dominated every room. The kitchen was the most crowded, with the table covered with casseroles, salads, and desserts.

"I wish I had known," whispered Max to Jack. "I feel overdressed and I would have brought something."

Before Jack could respond, a large man holding a red solo cup came up to them. "Hey, welcome," he said, clapping Jack on the shoulder. "Food's outside, there's a keg on the back porch"—at this he held his cup up—"and the band's out back." Then before Jack could reply he walked off.

"Get you a beer?" he said to Max.

"I guess."

He could see that she was still a bit uncomfortable. "C'mon, let's go find Polly."

As soon as they stepped out onto the back porch, they saw her. She was standing in the yard, next to a large grill, with several people surrounding her. Jack grabbed two cups of beer, handed one to Max, and motioned to her to head down to see Polly.

"Jack, Max. I'm so glad you're here."

They were still a bit overwhelmed and it must have shown. Max gave Polly a hug, and as they pulled apart, Jack could see that Polly's eyes had teared up a bit. He wasn't exactly sure what to say. What came out was, "Great party." Then, before he could embarrass himself any further, Polly gave him a hug as well.

"Thank you so much for being here," she whispered. He was sure that he heard a hitch in her voice, and when she pulled away, he could see that she was fighting off tears. "Get something to eat, I'll see you in a bit," she said and turned away.

The sky remained clear all afternoon and the breeze light. It was chilly, but for a late November day it was quite nice. By mid-afternoon though, the shadows had begun to lengthen and the temperature began to drop noticeably. No one was leaving, but now instead of being spread out, the crowd was gathered in the warm spots: by the grill, dancing, or on the porch for easy access to the kitchen.

CHAPTER 88

ALFRED WATCHED THE REVELERS all afternoon, and as he did, a plan began to form in his head. "Soon," he told himself, "Soon." He shivered. Sunset was rapidly approaching, and after the sun was down, he would have his opportunity.

* * *

Throughout the day, people continued to arrive and depart. Someone tapped a second keg and another lit a fire pit as the temperature began to drop sharply once the sun dipped below the trees. Jack met some of Malcom's running buddies from the area and they began talking about races, runs, and Malcom. That was the last thing Max wanted to talk about—or more correctly, listen to—so she walked off.

Inside the house, walking from room to room, Max remembered those few days they had spent at the Inn. She imagined what life must have been like all those years ago. As she paused in front of the spot where the letter had been, a voice startled her. "It was stolen."

Max turned. "Stolen?"

"I'm sorry, I didn't mean to startle you. The letter. Remember, we used to have a copy of one of the letters that Malcom had found in one of the chests that had all the quilts hanging there. It was the inspiration for my book," said Polly.

"Yes, I remember." Max watched as Polly's eyes took on a faraway look and began to tear up.

"Oh Polly," said Max. She reached over and gave Polly a hug.

After a moment they pulled apart, and Polly sniffled, "I'm sorry," while dabbing at the corners of her eyes.

"Don't be." Max said. Then, looking at the wall, she continued, "Stolen?"

"Yes, that and one of the quilts, the one in the Captain's room."

"How horrible. When? What happened?"

"It's a long story. At the end of the summer, Malcom was down in Massachusetts buying some stuff that we could use to decorate one of the rooms, and he met this odd little man who owned one of the shops. Shortly after, that man showed up here offering to buy the letter and the Captain's quilt. Of course we said no, but then, not too long after you were here, they were stolen. Mal was convinced that the antiques dealer had stolen them. He went back down and confronted the man, but he denied that he had them. Malcom was going to see him one last time on the weekend of the race to try to get them back before calling the police." Her voice trailed off, "He never got them . . ."

As she wiped her eyes again, Polly noticed the strange look on Max's face. "Max, are you all right?"

"Yes, yes I am. You said he was an odd little man."

Polly nodded. "I did."

"That's weird."

"What's weird?"

"Remember you gave me an old quilt."

"Sure."

"You had given me the wrong one."

"Right."

"Well, just the other day, this strange man stopped by the bar asking a lot of questions, and he suggested to Jack that he would like to buy the quilt from me. Of course I didn't sell it to him, I had already brought it back to you, but he didn't know that, and I didn't tell him."

"What was his name?"

"Whitman . . . Whitson, something like that," said Max. Then she blurted out, "I think he killed Malcom."

Polly looked at Max, her face reflecting shock. "What did you just say?"

"Nothing. I don't know why I said . . ."

Polly cut her off. "You said his name was Whitson and you think he killed Malcom."

Now, completely embarrassed, Max fumbled with words, trying to backtrack.

"Sit down," said Polly. "Tell me everything."

They sat and talked until it was well past sunset. Several guests came by to pay respects, but they retreated when they saw the intensity of the women's conversation.

* * *

The sun had finally set and Alfred decided that it was time. He would go to the Inn, walk in, find Max, and convince her that she had to let him have the quilt. She would say yes and he would leave. It was to be as simple as that, except that it wasn't.

Alfred opened the front door to the Inn and stepped inside. He didn't see anyone, but he could hear the sounds of many voices enjoying themselves in a distant room. He looked into the first room next to the entry. It was empty. Then, he looked into the other front room. Polly and Max were sitting there, just the two of them, talking. Standing in the doorway, he watched them for a moment and smiled at his good fortune. *"This is going to be easier than I had imagined,"* he thought to himself.

At that moment Max looked up and saw him standing there in the doorway. She stopped mid-sentence and stared. Polly watched Max freeze and saw the expression on her face change. She turned her head in the direction that Max was looking, about to ask if she was okay, when she saw him, too. Paralyzed, Polly couldn't breathe. All she could do was stare as fear and confusion washed over her.

Alfred saw their reaction. It wasn't what he had expected, and the smile on his face quickly faded. Polly found her voice and screamed. Now it was Alfred's turn to be confused and he began to panic.

Max suddenly stood up. "What the hell are you doing here?" she demanded.

"Shhh. Stop it!" he hissed.

They wouldn't be quiet. As Polly screamed again, Alfred clenched his fists and glared at the two women. He took a step toward them.

At this point, Max was overcome with anger. She moved closer to Alfred and said, "Get out."

For an instant, he paused. Max couldn't tell whether he was about to leave or was preparing to attack. For a moment those terrible moments on *Irrepressible* flashed through her head. As she watched Alfred shift his weight ever so slightly she braced herself, expecting the worst.

Suddenly a voice from behind the women broke the tension. "Polly, you okay?"

Alfred shifted his stare past Max and toward the new voice.

Max didn't take her eyes off Alfred. The voice asked him, "Who are you?"

That was enough. Alfred panicked. "I will have it," he said to Max, catching her eyes one last time before turning and fleeing.

Suddenly the room was full of people. The space became a jumble of noise and confusion, as everyone seemed to be talking at the same time. Anne sat down next to Polly and pulled her close as Polly sobbed.

Max, still standing, suddenly felt weak. She began to shake as the adrenaline rush subsided. Finally she heard the voice she needed to hear. "Max, you okay? What happened?"

Jack reached out for her. At his touch, she fell into him, her body trembling. His shirt muffled her words as he held her close. He asked again, more softly, more gently, "Max, what happened?"

She looked up at Jack. "He was here."

"Who?"

"Alfred. He was here."

It took a second for this to sink in. Then a shiver went through Jack as he understood.

"Come," he said as he guided her out of the room and away from the horde of well-meaning people. He needed to be alone with her.

NO ONE FOLLOWED AS ALFRED ran back to his truck, but he knew he couldn't linger. Still, just before climbing into the cab, he paused to catch his breath. That's when he heard them. The voices. They were back, scolding him, cajoling, mocking. He shook his head and said aloud, "Stop. Leave me alone. I'll get it."

They laughed, but they did stop. Now all he heard was his beating heart and slowing breath.

He cocked his head and listened for any sounds of pursuit. There was only silence except for the soft whispering of the night breeze through the trees. Then he heard it, a single voice, whispering to him. It was softer and kinder, almost forgiving in tone. He strained to understand, but the words were lost in the trees. It didn't matter. He knew what they were, and it was time to go.

The click of the door handle on his truck, followed by the soft snick of the door latching shut, silenced the whispers. Alfred turned the key and the engine fired. It had begun so well. *Why didn't they understand? He had approached the women wanting only to talk, to present his case for the quilt. Why had Polly screamed and summoned the other guests?*

"Shit!" He pounded his hand against the steering wheel. "She didn't have to do that."

* * *

"Max. Tell me again," said Jack.

She did.

"I'm going to call Tom." He pulled out his phone and began to dial.

* * *

The conversation was short and as soon as Tom hung up, he called Mark Malloy in Ipswich.

"We found him. He was just up north at Polly's. He crashed the funeral, found both Max and Polly, and demanded that they give him the quilt."

"Is he still there?"

"No. He bolted when Polly and Max began screaming. He's gone."

"Damn. Listen, there's no point in me driving up there tonight, but how 'bout I meet you at your office in the morning. Maybe we can come up with some way to flush him out. I'd like to talk to Jack and Max as well."

"Sounds good to me. If for some reason he surfaces, I'll call."

"Thanks." Malloy hung up the phone.

* * *

Alfred drove in silence all the way back to the motel in York. He had been lucky tonight, but he knew he couldn't keep taking those kinds of chances.

CHAPTER 90

THEY HAD INTENDED TO DRIVE home that evening, but after Alfred's intrusion, Polly insisted that they stay the night. Max gave Courtney a call, and she agreed to stop by and feed Cat.

Eventually the celebration ended and the guests were gone. While Polly and Anne said goodbyes, Max and Jack slipped out the back to make sure that the fire pit was out. It was after midnight. Max shivered and Jack pulled her close as they stood by the black circle looking up at the stars. "Almost like when we were in Belize," said Max as she pressed herself closer to Jack.

"It could be warmer."

"The stars."

"I know what you meant," he said, and at that moment a shooting star flashed across the sky.

"Quick. Make a wish," said Max.

Jack looked up and then silently pulled her just a little bit closer. "Did you make a wish?" asked Max.

"I did," he said softly.

"Hey, you two. It's freezing out here. Why don't you come inside?" Polly's voice broke the silence.

They hadn't heard her approach, and the sound of her voice made them jump. They separated as if they had been caught doing something they shouldn't have.

"Sorry, we were just looking up at the stars. They're beautiful," said Max.

Polly looked up and with a faraway lilt to her voice she said, "Mal and I used to look up at them all the time, wondering who was out there looking at us." She sniffled. "Now, maybe he's out there."

Max put her arm around her and then gave her a hug.

"Oh Polly. I'm so sorry. Let's go in." With that Max guided her inside to the kitchen, where Anne was just tying up a bag of garbage.

"Anne, let me help you with that," said Max, abandoning Polly.

"This is the last of it."

"At least let me take that out for you," said Jack, wishing he had done more to help clean up.

* * *

"Good morning," said Polly as Jack walked into the kitchen. He hadn't really expected her to be up, but all the years of taking care of guests was a hard habit to break.

"Mornin'. Thank you again for letting us stay. You didn't have to do that."

"No, I did. I can't help but believe that we have been brought together for a reason." She handed him a cup of coffee. It was as good as he remembered from their previous visit to the Inn.

"Thanks." Jack walked over to the door and looked out over the back to the woods. "Will you keep the Inn open?"

"I don't know." She paused before continuing. "For now, I've closed it. I need some time."

He turned and looked at her, "If there's anything that I—uh, we—can do, don't hesitate to call."

"Thanks, Jack." She turned away and he could see her shoulders shaking slightly as she busied herself at the counter.

He hated awkward moments like this. He guessed that she was crying. Deep inside he felt the need to comfort her, but he didn't really know how or what to say so he stood there silently, turned his head, and again looked out toward the woods.

"I don't know why, but I have a feeling that I knew Malcom. I know I had never met him, not really, other than finding him, but I just have that feeling."

Polly turned toward Jack, "I understand. He had that effect on people. I guess that's why managing the Inn was so perfect for him." She paused, "For us."

"I lost someone once, a very long time ago. The pain and loneliness was almost unbearable, but a friend rescued me, and because of him, his friends brought me into their lives and pulled me through. You'll get through and your life will be richer for it." Jack stopped. He looked at Polly and wondered if he had gone too far. He hastily continued, "What I mean is that even though we just met, we'll always be there for you. I mean . . ." He stopped again, now a bit embarrassed, feeling like he was digging a hole that he couldn't get out of.

Polly must have sensed his unease because she stopped him. "Jack, I understand what you are saying. In my head, on one level, I know that eventually everything will work out. But right now . . ." Now it was her turn to fumble for words, and a tear rolled down her cheek.

He stepped toward her and held out his arms. She came to him and leaned against him limply, with her arms at her side. He wrapped his arms around her and held her. She began sobbing uncontrollably. While they stood there, he too began to cry as memories and feelings long dormant surfaced.

"Are you two all right?" Max's voice broke the silence.

Her voice might as well have been a cannon going off in the room from its impact. Polly instantly straightened and Jack released his hold on her. Before turning toward Max's voice, Polly pulled a tissue from her pocket and dabbed at her eyes, and Jack turned slightly away and wiped his cheek with his hand.

Now Polly looked at Max. Her eyes were still red and puffy from crying. She said, "I'm sorry. We were just talking about Malcom and . . ."

Her voice began to crack, but before she could say anything else, Max said, "Polly, it's okay. I understand. Anything you need, just let us know."

Polly sniffled, looked back and forth between Max and Jack, and said in a stronger voice. "Thank you. Now, I'm hungry. How about omelets?"

"Sounds perfect," said Jack.

CHAPTER 91

ALFRED AWOKE WITH THE SUN, his mind racing as he remembered the fiasco of the previous night. As the events replayed in his mind, he resolved that they wouldn't happen again. The voices remained quiet, but he knew that it was just a matter of time before they would begin again, asking, demanding—no, commanding—that he complete his mission. His eyes closed and he slipped back into a deep sleep and another time. This time, he moved into the pages of the book, watching Christine on the ship.

* * *

Christine could sense a change in the crew the closer to port they came. She felt it too, but for different reasons. Some on the crew were looking forward to seeing their families again, but most were in high spirits anticipating drink and women, not necessarily in that order. They had been away for several months and now they would be home. Christine, her anxiety easily disguised as excitement, went out of her way to remain in the Captain's good graces, and she must have been successful judging from his civility toward her. Each night, in the safety of her cabin, she worked on her quilt, using needle and thread to record the contents of that letter in much the same way one would use pen on paper.

* * *

It wasn't until after noon that Alfred reawakened. A shaft of light streamed in from the edge of the window curtain, so he pulled the curtain aside to look out. The sun was just past its peak, but as clear and bright as it was outside, he could tell that it was going to be chilly. With hunger beginning to gnaw at him, he needed to find something to eat.

Outside it was cooler than he had expected. He climbed into his truck, started the motor, and set the heater on full blast. Waiting for the heat to kick in, he shivered and pulled out of the lot.

The fast-food places near his motel did not appeal to him, so he drove east toward the ocean again. The pub had been too unsettling, so when he reached the ocean he turned north and continued his quest. Many of the homes he passed were already boarded up for the winter. Most summer businesses were also closed, and it was nearly an hour before he found a place still open where he could get something to eat.

Ordering his food "to go," he returned to his truck and continued driving. He needed time to think. With the heater full on, his cab was now toasty warm, and he nibbled on the French fries in the bag on the seat beside him as he drove. They were salty, hot, and delicious, and it didn't take too many miles before they were gone. He was groping around in the bag, hoping to find one last fry, when he saw a sign for a closed summer camp, the kind that parents send their kids to for weeks at a time, maybe even the whole summer. It was something that he had never experienced, although he had had friends who had gone away to such places. Had Alfred not died, had he not been sent away after his mother's death, perhaps they might have been able to go to such a camp, but as he had learned, death changes everything. Curious, he turned in.

The camp was made up of a cluster of buildings, and each had a placard nailed above or next to its boarded up door, with a name carved into the wood. Each one was named for some kind of a sea creature. The ones he could read were Periwinkle, Starfish, and Lobster. Only two buildings had other identifying signs: the infirmary and the dining hall. He drove around slowly, studying each building. He wondered what each was for and imagined what it was like to stay there.

Alfred stopped when he reached the furthest building, which was nestled behind some large sand dunes. He shut off his truck's engine and could hear, even feel, the steady rhythm of the ocean as it pounded against the shore on the other side of the dunes. He rolled his window down and as he ate the rest of his food, now barely warm, he listened to the steady thump-shoosh of the breaking waves while the temperature inside his truck went down.

The steady rhythm of the surf soon caused him to drift into another dimension and another time. Memories mixed and swirled, as fact became fiction and fiction, fact.

Had the winds but held, the Captain would have been right and Christine might have been there in time to tell her story. As it were, the winds died and the ship, with Christine aboard, was two days late. When she tried to tell what she knew, no one believed her. The quilt was offered in evidence, but it was seen as the product of an overwrought, hysterical mind brought on by a long and difficult voyage. The Captain, with his stature and reputation, was unassailable and he scoffed at her allegations.

No one believed her. Only he did. He, Alfred, could have helped her then, but he wasn't there. Now, he intended to set the record straight. He had learned his lessons well. He knew how the game was played.

During that dark time after his brother's death, his mother would visit the spot where his brother had died and stand for hours on the river bank staring at the water. Fair weather or foul, he would find her there and on more than one occasion would have to coax her back home. One particular time, during a storm, she slipped out. He searched, but she had vanished. That's when the voices started.

He was alone and the authorities thought they knew what was best for him and sent him away 'to get better'. They were wrong. A smile crept over his face as he remembered how he fooled them. He played his part so well that eventually he was declared cured and released.

That's when he was taken in by that nice couple who had the antiques business. They taught him the business. Everything in the store had a story and he learned them all. If a new item didn't have a story, one was made up and the voices remained muted until he read that book.

Several gulls cried, bringing him back to the present. The cadence of the endless surf never wavered, thump-shoosh, thump-shoosh, and soon instead of the waves breaking on the shore, what he heard were the voices chanting: Get it. Get it. Get it. Time was running out. Soon, others would figure out what he already knew and they would try to stop him. He had to get it.

He shivered from the cold. He didn't know how long he had been sitting there, but all of a sudden he realized that the sun was disappearing and clouds were taking over the blue sky. The voices faded as he rolled up his window and went silent when he started his truck. He swore that tomorrow he would succeed.

CHAPTER 92

"HERE. I WANT YOU TO HAVE THIS."

"No. Polly, I can't."

"Max, I insist. You and Jack have been so wonderful through all of this. Please."

Reluctantly, Max accepted the package as Polly pushed it into her hands. It was the same one she had returned only a few days earlier. "But it's valuable . . ."

Polly shushed and said, "No arguments. I want you to have this."

Surrendering, Max held on to the package with tight reverence. "Fine, but I'm only keeping it for you. When you want it back . . ."

Polly cut her off. "I'm serious Max. It's yours. I want you to have it. There's nothing to discuss."

The quilt was carefully placed in the back seat of the car, hugs were exchanged, promises were made, and even a few tears were shed before Jack and Max drove down the drive and headed back to the coast.

It had been a long two days and they were both physically and emotionally exhausted.

"You okay?" asked Jack.

Max's reply was slow in coming. "Yeah. I guess."

"I don't think I've ever been to a funeral quite like that."

"I know. But you know, I kind of liked it. You could really feel the love everyone had for Malcom and it forced everyone to celebrate his life rather than lament over his passing. I'm not saying that there still won't be a lot of sadness, but I think this was good. I just feel so bad for Polly."

"I know what you mean," agreed Jack.

Max, lost in her own thoughts, watched Jack as he drove. Because of the late hour, it was dark and there was little traffic. In the shadows she could see his face, not clearly, but whenever an oncoming car's headlights flashed over them, for that instant, his face would be lit. Several cars passed before she was sure that he was smiling, and she wanted to know why.

"Jack, what's with the grin?"

"Nothing."

"Bullshit. What's so funny?"

"I'm sorry, but I was just thinking about how I found Malcom."

"That's not funny."

"I'm sure that I'm going to rot in hell for saying this, but I was just remembering how when I first fell and didn't know I was on top of him, I was kind of woozy and I looked down and saw that I had three feet. I remember thinking, '*This can't be right!*' so I looked again and I still had three feet. I was so confused. That's when I discovered I was lying on a body and I freaked out. In a sick and twisted way, it was kind of funny."

"You *are* sick and twisted," said Max with righteous disdain in her voice. She remained silent and then began to giggle.

"What's so funny?"

"You. I was just imagining you lying there, looking down and seeing three feet." Her giggle turned into a laugh. Jack glanced at her and then he laughed too.

Max continued, "I wish I had been there. You must have shit your pants when you realized where that third foot came from." She laughed again.

"It wasn't funny," Jack managed to say, but then he continued to laugh.

For a moment Max paused. "I know," she said in a serious voice. Then she began laughing harder.

They laughed for several miles, until they were laughed out.

"I wish I had known him," said Jack. "He seemed like a really cool person."

"I know. Polly's pretty amazing too."

"I can't believe she gave you that quilt."

"I can't either. We'll have to find some safe place for it. I wouldn't want for it to get damaged. I wonder what's the best way to store something like this?"

"I have no idea." After a moment Jack added, "Do you think that Alfred finally got the message?"

"I hope so. And I hope Tom and Malloy catch up with him soon."

Nothing else was said for the rest of the way home.

CHAPTER 93

"HELLO," JACK SAID IN A LOUD WHISPER. He had been jarred awake by the first ring and had grabbed the phone quickly so as not to wake Max. As he looked over at her he heard Tom's voice on the line. Still whispering, Jack said, "Hold on; let me get into the other room. I don't want to wake Max."

Settled on the couch, he said, "What's up? Did you find Alfred?"

"No, I'm sorry. We haven't. There's a BOLO out for him, but so far, nothing. Still, I did have an interesting conversation with Malloy."

"Yeah?"

"He told me that Alfred had an identical twin brother, Thomas. The two boys often played on a rope swing by the river and as the story goes, one day Thomas swung out over the water, let go, hit his head on a rock that was just below the surface, and was killed."

"So?"

"Well, Alfred was always known as the 'good' twin and Thomas was known as the troublemaker. But Malloy thinks it *wasn't* Thomas who was killed; he thinks it was Alfred. Then, for whatever reason, probably the trauma of seeing his brother die, Thomas assumed Alfred's identity."

"Whoa," murmured Jack. That was a lot to comprehend before his morning coffee. "And does he have any proof?"

"Nothing hard, but it would explain a lot. Malloy has learned that after Alfred's mother's death, before he took over the antiques store, he was institutionalized."

Tom continued, "Malloy has had a hard time finding out the details because Alfred was a juvenile at the time and those records were sealed. But he has talked with people who knew him when he was growing up, and from that information he has been able to piece together a working theory."

Jack said nothing as his mind raced through possible scenarios.

"Jack, you still there?"

"Oh, sorry. I was just thinking."

"Well, listen, you and Max be careful. By all accounts—and certainly from his behavior—he is unpredictable."

Jack interrupted him and said, "Don't you mean *nuts and possibly dangerous?*"

"Your words, not mine. But off the record, probably correct. Hopefully Malloy will get more answers in the next day or so and, who knows, maybe we'll get lucky."

Cat was now awake and had decided that it was breakfast time. She began talking loudly and incessantly, demanding to be fed.

"Is that Cat howling?" asked Tom.

"Yeah, she wants to be fed. She has a way of letting you know what she wants and when."

"I guess! So back to Alfred, we know that (a) he wants that quilt, and (b) he must be getting desperate if he was willing to show up at the Inn last night."

"True."

"And Polly has the quilt. Right? Max returned it, didn't she?"

"Sort of."

"What do you mean *sort of?*"

"Max did give Polly the quilt, but then Polly gave it back to her as we were leaving. It's here."

Tom was silent for a moment. "Alfred wouldn't know any of that. He still thinks that Max has the quilt. You and Max be careful. I'm going to call Malloy and let him know that you still have the quilt." He paused.

"Tom? What are you thinking?" Jack asked. His voice betrayed his suspicion.

"Nothing."

"No. You are thinking something, and I don't like what you're thinking."

"I don't know what you mean."

"Yes, you do. I know you Tom, as well as you know me. You're thinking that if somehow we can get Alfred to come after the quilt, then we can catch him."

Max walked in just as Jack said "catch him."

"Catch who?" she asked.

"Listen, I gotta' go. Max just got up. Talk to you later. Time to feed Cat." As he reached to hang up, he thought he heard Tom beginning to say something, but he couldn't be sure.

Cat jumped into his lap, looked him in the eyes, and "Mrowed" loudly.

"Good morning, Max," Jack said.

"Who was that on the phone?"

"Tom."

"What did he want?"

"He just wanted to make sure that you were okay after the other night."

"I'm sure." The sarcasm in her voice was less than subtle. "He was talking to you about catching Alfred, wasn't he?"

"He was." Jack knew it would be pointless to try to deceive her.

"What's he want to do?"

"I don't know; he didn't say." That wasn't entirely true, but it was close enough for the moment.

"Mrowh," Cat said again.

Jack tried to change the subject. "I need coffee and Cat needs food."

"You're not getting off that easily, Jack Beale." Max followed him and Cat to the kitchen.

* * *

There wasn't much time to discuss the phone call because Jack had offered to help Courtney winterize Ben's. Max was still dressing for her day shift as he headed out the door. Though cold it was a clear day, rare for late November, and he intended to take full advantage of it as he left for Ben's. There was much to do in preparation for winter, but if he was lucky, maybe he would even be able to get in a run before dark.

Jack was putting the last of the deck furniture into his truck to haul to the storage trailer when Tom pulled up.

"Hey, Jack. I thought that was you."

"Tom. Tell me you found him."

"No such luck. But I did talk to Malloy again and he's going to drive up here later this afternoon."

"Why?"

"Didn't say, but it's a safe bet that it has to do with Alfred."

"What the hell is with that guy?"

"Don't know, but until we get him, be careful and keep an eye on Max."

Jack nodded as Tom drove away.

CHAPTER 94

JACK TOSSED THE FINAL CHAIR into his truck and drove around back to the storage trailer. The clouds were beginning to form and the morning's clear skies would soon be a memory. As he pushed shut the steel door of the trailer, he heard Max's voice call out.

"It's freezing out here. You want some coffee?"

He looked over toward the back door of Ben's, waved, and called back, "I'll be in, in a minute."

He didn't really need to warm up—his exertions were taking care of that—but a break would be welcome. He drove around front just as Max was unlocking the door. Officially the restaurant wasn't open until noon, but Max always tried to have the door unlocked thirty minutes early. When he turned the corner into the bar he didn't see her, but he did see the steaming cup of coffee she had left on the bar for him. He smiled and sat down.

"Aren't you frozen?" She came up from behind and startled him. She was carrying a rack of glasses but she paused to smile at him.

"Not really. I was really lugging those chairs around back. Actually, I was pretty hot."

"I know," she said in a teasing way.

He pretended to ignore the innuendo and said, "Tom stopped by. He said that Malloy was coming up later in the day."

She stopped and looked at him. "Did he say why?"

"Didn't. But I'm sure it isn't just social."

Before the conversation could go any further, the bells on the front door clingled and they heard voices in the hallway. Familiar voices. Max looked at Jack and groaned.

"I'm just not ready for this."

"Oh, it'll be fine. They're harmless." He stood to leave.

"So why are you bolting?" she demanded. Before he could answer, Leo, Ralph, and Paulie walked into the bar.

While Jack said a quick hello and goodbye, Max automatically placed three light beers on the bar.

"Hey, Max," said Leo.

"Damn, it's cold out there," added Paulie.

Ralph simply took a big sip of his beer.

They knew the drill. Max was still setting up, so Leo waved at her for the television remote. She passed it to him and he hit the button. First they viewed the weather—at least, until the local forecast was finished. Then one of the sports channels caught their attention until they lost interest, which took even less time. Finally, Leo found one of the nature channels airing a show about how to fish by using your arms as bait.

"Max, you gotta' see this," he said.

She looked up at the screen just in time to see a skinny guy in a torn t-shirt, with few teeth in his smile, burst to the surface of a coffee-colored river, with a large fish that looked like it had swallowed his arm. Leo, Ralph, and Paulie were as excited as the guy being eaten by the fish, and they began cheering.

Max made a face and said, "That's disgusting." Then she turned and walked away.

The day was as quiet as Max had expected it to be. In late November, if the weather was good, you could count on the weekends being busy. The weekdays were another story. Occasionally, if the weather was nice they'd be busy. Yet on other equally nice days, there would be no business whatsoever. This Monday was one of the latter, made even more difficult since the guys were there. Silently she cursed Jack for having made his escape.

By late afternoon she had reached her Leo-Ralph-Paulie saturation point and retreated to the kitchen. She picked up the phone and called Jack.

"They are driving me nuts."

"Come on now, think how bored you'd be without them."

"That's not the point. When are you coming over?"

"I just finished a short time ago and I'm getting changed."

"Really?"

He could tell from the hope in her voice that she assumed he was on his way over to rescue her. He paused before speaking again.

"I'm sorry. I meant, I'm getting changed to go for a run. There's just time before dark."

Now there was a really long pause. Finally, Max responded, "You're going for a run while I'm stuck here with them."

Sheepishly, Jack said, "I'll run fast." Before he could say anything further, the line went dead.

Hanging up the phone, Max growled. To prolong her time in the kitchen, she poured herself a cup of coffee. Out in the hallway, the bell on the front door clingled.

Leo, Ralph, and Paulie heard it, and like Pavlov's dogs, all three turned their heads at the same time. They peered expectantly at Alfred as he turned the corner and looked into the bar.

"*Shit*," he thought to himself. He didn't see Max and he remembered how nosy they had been the first time he met them. Then he squelched his anxiety by reminding himself that they had also provided him with valuable information. He forced a smile and walked in.

Ralph and Paulie turned back to their beers and the fishing show, but Leo continued to look at him.

"Hey," said Leo.

Alfred nodded and without another glance walked through the bar toward the men's room.

Leo's gaze followed him for a moment but then he turned his attention back to the show.

Max came back into the bar before Alfred returned.

"Hey, Max," said Leo as she reached the bar.

"What?" The tone of her voice clearly indicated that she didn't care what he had to say.

"Remember last week, that guy who came in?"

"What guy?"

"That guy who was all interested in antiques and stuff."

It didn't register at first, but then she understood. Her eyes widened and she felt her heartbeat increase while her breath grew short. "Why do you ask?"

"He's in the men's room."

Leo might as well have hit her in the stomach. To his surprise, she quickly turned and walked away.

In the sanctuary of the kitchen, Max picked up the phone and dialed Tom's number. There was no answer, so all she could do was leave a message. Then she tried Jack. Same deal.

Back in the bar, she searched quickly for Alfred. When she was sure he was nowhere in sight, she went straight to Leo.

"Leo, you've got to do me a huge favor."

He looked at her. This was new. She had never asked him or his two friends for anything.

"What?"

"I need you to find Jack."

"Why don't you just call him?"

"I tried. He's out running. I need him here. Right now." Leo just sat and stared at her while his beer-soaked brain processed her request.

"Why?"

The look on her face and the urgency in her voice caught him by surprise.

"Leo. I don't have time for this. Please, just do it."

Max stared at Leo with a look that said, "GO! NOW!"

Then she said, "Your beers are on me."

That never happened, and Leo wasn't about to give her the opportunity to change her mind.

"Hey guys."

Ralph and Paulie turned away from the commercial that had just come on.

"Come on. We've got to go."

"What's the rush?" asked Ralph.

Leo glanced back at Max to make sure she wasn't changing her mind. She wasn't. All she did was mouth, "NOW!" Then she added a shoosh with her hands for emphasis.

"C'mon guys. We've got to go." He grabbed his two friends' arms and gave them a tug toward the door. Grudgingly they responded, and ignoring their moans and groans, he herded them out of the bar. Leo looked back at Max one last time before heading down the hall. As he turned away he heard the latch on the men's room door snap open.

Alfred stepped into the room and saw Max standing behind the bar. He smiled and his heart began to beat faster. She was alone. Things were going to work out. He could feel it.

"Hello," said Alfred. He took a seat at the bar without ever taking his eyes off of her.

Max took a breath and tried to not look too surprised or scared.

"Hi," she said, forcing a smile.

He had chosen a seat at the end, near the wall, where he could easily see her and the door.

"How've you been?" He was trying as hard as he could to sound not threatening.

As Max began to respond, he continued, "I'm sorry about the other night. I only wanted to talk. Maybe it wasn't the best time . . ."

Max cut him off. "It wasn't." Then, in an effort to sound as natural as possible, she said, "What did you want to talk about?"

Before he could begin his answer, she also asked if he would like a drink.

"Thanks. Sure."

"White Zinfandel?"

Surprised, he looked at her and then said, "Yes . . . you remembered."

"A good bartender never forgets what a good customer orders." She forced herself to speak casually even as her heart filled with panic.

Alfred smiled as he watched her pour the glass of wine. He continued to sense success.

"Would you like something to eat?" Max asked as she placed the wine in front of him. "Last time you had a grilled salmon Caesar salad?"

She hoped he would say yes so she would have an excuse to get out of the bar and try calling Tom again.

He was feeling better by the minute. She even remembered what he had eaten. "Yes, that would be great." He didn't want to rush things, so he sat back and took a sip of his wine. Then he began.

"I don't know if you remember, but I deal in antiques. I am really interested in that quilt you have." Alfred was still trying to act as normal and nonthreatening as possible. In his mind he was succeeding.

"I do remember. I still have the quilt. However, I don't think I want to part with it." Max tried to keep her voice light and breezy. "Listen, I'm going to go out to the kitchen to make your salad. We can talk more when I get back."

Alfred smiled and tipped his glass toward her as if to say, "Sure, sounds like a plan." He took another sip as she walked out of the bar.

* * *

Jack had finished the first half of his run in about twenty minutes. Then he saw Leo driving toward him. Even in the gloom of dusk Leo's truck was unmistakable, so Jack deliberately stepped off the pavement. Leo had a long history of driving mishaps, and in this low light, Jack preferred not to take a chance.

As Leo was about to drive past, he slowed, rolled down his window, and shouted, "Hey, Jack! Max needs you at the bar!" Then he kept on going.

Jack stopped running for a moment as he tried to comprehend what Leo had shouted at him. He turned to call him back, but he was already too far down the road. *Why would Max need him at the bar?*

* * *

Before Max assembled the salad, she picked up the kitchen phone and redialed Tom's number. Still no answer. As she waited for the salmon to finish cooking, she hoped he'd get the message very soon.

* * *

Jack began running again. There were a million reasons why she could want him back at the bar. Most were quite innocent, but to send Leo and the boys out to relay a message? It couldn't be good. He noted where he was, glanced at his watch and quickly calculated that he could be back in fifteen minutes or less if he really picked up the pace.

CHAPTER 95

WHILE MAX WAS IN THE KITCHEN making his salad, Alfred sat sipping his wine and looking around the bar. There were quite a few interesting pieces in the room: old wooden lobster buoys, some brass lanterns, a ship's wheel, an oar from a rowing shell. He was always looking to buy or sell something, so he made a note to contact the owner. As he studied an old sign on the wall behind the bar, a red light on the phone caught his eye.

When he came in to Ben's he remembered seeing a sign that said, BAR OPEN – PLEASE BE SEATED. The antiques and the sign behind the bar were promptly forgotten as he considered that red light. If only the bar were open, then only Max and whoever was in the kitchen were working. Who was on the phone? "*It must be her,*" he thought angrily, his paranoia was beginning to surface. He hadn't seen anyone else in the restaurant or bar since his arrival, other than the three guys, and they were gone. "*That bitch,*" he thought to himself. "*She's going to ruin everything.*"

The confidence that he had come in with, the certainty that everything was going to turn out as he had planned, began to drain away. It was replaced with apprehension, and he could feel tension building throughout his body. He watched that little red light and it wasn't going out. He kept staring at it while conversations and scenarios played through his mind. The voices returned. He was feeling warm, almost claustrophobic, when the light finally went out. Picking up a bar napkin, he wiped the sweat off his forehead, took several deep calming breaths, gulped down the last of his wine, and waited for Max.

"Here we go." Max walked back into the bar carrying his salad. She was working hard to relax and not give away her increasing sense of panic. She hoped he didn't hear the quiver in her voice.

As she placed the salad down in front of him, along with a fork, she noticed the empty glass. "Another wine?" she asked.

He said, "Sure, that would be nice." Then, looking at the salad he added, "And a knife, too."

Max thought she detected a slight tremble in his voice. Turning, she said, "Sure." Then, before she poured the wine, she looked him straight in the face. She wasn't sure, but he seemed to be sweating, and despite those thick glasses, his eyes seemed to have hardened somehow.

Alfred watched as she turned away from him to pour his wine. The tension that he had only sensed before was now obvious. It was clear that she was struggling not to spill the wine.

Max felt as if her whole arm was trembling, and as she went to replace the bottle in the cooler, it no longer seemed to fit in the spot from which she had taken it. The noise of glass on glass was amplified by the silence of the room. Finally, she managed to get the bottle nestled back in its place, and she pulled the cover of the cooler toward her to close it, hesitating for a split second before turning back to face him. Forcing herself to remain calm she placed the wine in front of him.

Their eyes met for a moment, as if they were playing a game of who-would-blink-first. Neither flinched.

"Thank you," he said.

"How's your salad?" asked Max as she stepped back. Keeping her eyes on him, she acted as if she had something else to do, hoping that he would not remember the knife.

"A knife," he said. He poked at the salad with the fork and continued to look at her.

"I'm sorry." Max turned and reached over into the basket of silverware that was on the end of the bar. *How dangerous can a dinner knife be?* she thought, trying to convince herself that it was harmless. She handed him the knife and as she did, she glanced down by her sink to make sure he wouldn't be able to reach any of her sharp knives.

"Thank you. It's good."

"Good?" Max was so distracted that she had no idea what he was talking about.

"The salad. It's good."

"I'm glad you like it." She knew she had to keep things neutral. She prayed that either Jack would get there soon or Tom would get her message and arrive. If they didn't arrive soon, at least the chef was out back and she could call out to him for help.

"You know, you have something I need to have." He raised the subject again as he took a bite of salad. He chewed slowly as he looked at her in anticipation of her answer.

"So you have said." Max stole a glance toward the entrance to the bar, every molecule in her body willing those bells on the front door to clingle. Then to stall him she added, "What is so important about this quilt?"

Her question stopped him mid-chew and he looked at her. He seemed to be considering her two statements. He swallowed and took a sip of wine, all the while never taking his eyes off of her. "It's important to my family."

"I don't understand." She tried to sound as sympathetic as possible. "I thought you had no family."

Alfred dropped his fork on the bar. It might as well have been the report of a cannon for how loud it sounded. Then he slapped his hand on the bar. Max jumped.

"I am not alone. My family needs me, and when I have that quilt, I will be able to save them." His voice had risen. It wasn't quite a shout, but it was not conversational.

Max fought to keep her voice as impartial as possible. "How is the quilt going to help?" she asked.

He looked at her in astonishment. He couldn't believe what he was hearing. Everyone knew what it meant. Everyone understood, so how could she not?

"I need that quilt," he repeated with another bite of salad.

"So you have said," Max repeated.

This time, Alfred visibly glared at her. Her tone had made it clear that she was not going to give it to him.

He took a long sip of his wine, nearly draining the glass, and then slowly put the glass on the bar. He was about to open his mouth to say something when the bells on the door clingled. They both looked toward the entrance to the bar.

CHAPTER 96

AS SOON AS JACK rounded the corner and walked into the bar, Max felt a wave of relief wash over her. Leo hadn't let her down.

Still breathing hard from his run back, Jack paused and glanced about, wondering what was up. It was then that he saw Alfred sitting at the end of the bar, staring at him. Jack froze, staring back. Alfred quickly looked away and Jack turned toward Max.

"Hey, Max," he said as he gulped for air.

She didn't say anything as her eyes met his. She didn't need to. Jack understood immediately, and he drew his eyes away from her and looked back at Alfred, whose head was down now as he stared at his salad.

Jack's breathing was rapidly returning to normal so he returned his attention to Max, and asked, "You okay?" He walked over and took a seat at the bar.

"Fine. How was your run? Beer?" She tried to sound as normal as possible.

"Please. And a glass of water."

When Max went out back for his beer, Jack studied Alfred again. To break the silence, he said, "Alfred, right? Antiques?" Then he waited for Alfred's reply.

That took Alfred by surprise. A storm of questions and emotions filled his head. All he wanted was to have a quiet talk with Max. That was his plan. She would understand and give him the quilt. It didn't involve anyone else. Why was this happening? He decided to ignore Jack.

Max returned with Jack's beer and placed it in front of him. As she did so, she glanced over at Alfred and caught him looking at Jack and herself. "Alfred, this is my friend Jack. I think you met the other day."

"We did," said Jack with a smile. He looked back over at Alfred and took a sip of beer.

Alfred's head snapped up and he glared at Max, thinking, "*Bitch! What the hell are you doing?*" The last thing he wanted was for this Jack to stick around any longer than necessary, but now he had to say something. Forcing a smile he asked the obvious. "You a runner?"

"Yeah. Just finished. Wanted to check in on Max before heading home to change."

Alfred nodded. "I run."

"Really?" said Jack. "For fun or do you race?"

"I race occasionally, but most of my running I do on trails." He said this without much enthusiasm, and his tone conveyed the message, "I really don't want to talk to you." Then he turned his head away.

An awkward silence fell over the bar for what seemed like a very long time. Alfred looked back down at his salad and took another bite. Max looked at him and then at Jack, who sipped his beer and discreetly eyed Alfred. All that chewing, sipping, and watching was finally interrupted when the bells on the front door clingled again.

As Max looked toward the door, Jack watched her face. She still seemed anxious, but now it displayed itself in a hopeful sort of way. The relief on her face was palpable when Tom walked in.

Max gave Jack a quick smile and offered to pour another glass of wine for Alfred.

"Hey, Tom," she said. He chose a seat in the center of the bar, two seats away from Alfred and three away from Jack.

"Max. Jack."

Jack thought he saw Alfred jerk his head slightly when she said Tom's name.

Max placed the glass of wine in front of Alfred. He looked up at her and mumbled, "Thanks." Only Jack saw him turn his head just a bit to get a look at the new arrival while Max turned her attention to Tom.

"May I get you something, Tom?"

"Sure. How about a coffee?"

"I'll be right back." She left the bar and Jack noticed a sudden bit of spring in her step.

"Damn, it's cold out!" said Tom, blowing on his hands. "Were you out running?" He looked over at Jack.

"Yeah."

"How far?"

"Only about five today."

"I can't imagine." Before he could say anything else, Max came back in the bar and said, "I'm brewing a new pot. It'll be a couple of minutes."

"That's fine. I'm in no hurry."

"I'll be back as soon as it's ready." With that, Max escaped back to the kitchen.

CHAPTER 97

THIS WAS NOT WHAT ALFRED wanted to hear. He wanted Tom and Jack to leave. They were messing up his plans. He took another sip of wine.

"Tom, this is Alfred Whitson," said Jack, motioning in Alfred's direction. "He's an antiques dealer from down in Massachusetts."

Tom turned toward Alfred. "Nice to meet you. What kind of antiques?"

Jack answered for Alfred. "He's interested in a quilt that Max has."

Tom addressed Alfred directly. "A quilt? I would never think of a quilt as an antique."

Alfred looked up and glared at Tom. "*Hit a nerve with that,*" Tom thought.

Tom didn't let up. "My grandmother had all kinds of quilts. All made of squares of scrap cloth, nothin' fancy. So, could they be valuable?"

Alfred continued to stare at Tom, who went on about his grandmother's quilts.

Jack sat and watched as this mini-drama played out wondering what Tom was doing.

"Most quilts are worthless, as I'm sure your grandmother's are," Alfred finally replied in a dismissive tone.

Tom stopped and looked at him. For a moment, Alfred appeared to be on the verge of losing control. Then he abruptly looked down at his nearly finished salad, pushed the plate away, muttered something to himself, stood and walked to the men's room.

At that point, Max walked back in, carrying a fresh mug of coffee for Tom. The silence stopped her in her tracks, and it was impossible to miss the residual tension that hung in the room. Her eyes moved from one to another with a look that asked, "*What's going on? Did I miss something here?"*

Getting no response, Max walked over to Tom and placed the coffee next to him. "Here you go, freshly brewed."

"Thanks."

As she returned to her spot behind the bar, Tom said, "I talked to Malloy before coming over. He asked me to poke him a bit, see how he reacts, but to not do anything more until he got here."

Before he could explain more, the bathroom door opened.

Jack said loud enough for Alfred to hear, "Alfred was about to explain to us why some quilts are valuable while most are not."

As he took his seat, Alfred slowly turned his head toward Jack and glowered. He did not want to have this conversation. He did not like these people. They were stupid, they'd never understand, and he didn't have the time. Shifting his gaze to Max he said, "Quilts have been in existence for a very long time. Some tell stories, some have hidden meaning in the stitching, and some are purely decorative. It takes an expert to be able to tell the value."

"And I suppose you are an expert?" chimed in Tom. Again he seemed to hit a nerve.

Alfred's look hardened again as he turned toward Tom. "I am," is all he said.

Max surveyed the three men: Tom in the center, Alfred to her left, and Jack nearest the door on the right.

"Well, I think that's fascinating," she said. Looking at Alfred she asked, "So tell me more about how you know if a quilt is valuable. What would I have to look for?"

Jack noticed that Alfred perked up and began focusing on her when she said this, ignoring Jack and Tom.

Alfred started to open his mouth as if to answer Max's question. Instead, he picked up his wine glass and drank what remained in one large gulp.

"Another?" asked Max.

He nodded yes.

"Are you finished with your salad?"

He mumbled 'yes' and pushed his salad plate toward her. She removed it, and then she began to pour his new glass of wine.

Jack and Tom watched her place the new glass of wine in front of him. They were waiting to hear what Alfred had to say about quilts when the front door's bells clingled.

CHAPTER 98

FOUR HEADS TURNED TOGETHER and stared in silence at the entrance to the bar. It felt like forever before Mark Malloy turned the corner and faced those four faces. The first thing he said was "Thomas . . ." The rest of his words were lost when Alfred began coughing and choking, to the extent that he even spewed some of his wine onto the bar. He nearly dropped his glass as he rushed back to the men's room.

Alfred's reaction surprised everyone. Heads turned back and forth as they watched Alfred's retreat.

Tom spoke first, "Mark."

"Hey, Tom. Jack. Max. Sorry for that."

"Don't be," replied Tom.

"That him?"

"Yeah, it is. When you came in he was about to tell us about what makes quilts valuable."

"Good. I don't think he knows me," said Malloy. "Let's keep it that way for the time being." Mark took the seat next to Tom on Alfred's side.

"I thought you wanted to question him?" said Max.

"I do, Max, but I also think that he's unstable enough that perhaps in a less formal setting, I might find out more."

Max wasn't completely sold on the idea, but with Tom, Mark, and Jack in the room, she at least felt somewhat reassured. "Something to drink?" she asked Mark.

He noticed Tom's mug and said, "How 'bout a coffee?"

"Sure," said Max. She walked toward the kitchen.

"What do you think set him off?" asked Tom.

Looking at Tom, Malloy said, "You."

"Me? What the hell are you talking about."

"Your name."

Tom and Jack looked at him with puzzled expressions on their faces.

He went on. "When I came in I saw all of you sitting at the bar. I had an idea. You know I have this theory that Alfred isn't really Alfred, but rather his twin brother, Thomas, who supposedly died, so I decided to call you Thomas to see what would happen."

"Okay, so."

"So, he's pretty unstable. When I said your name, look what happened. I think that's what triggered his reaction."

Neither Tom nor Jack said anything.

"Here you go." Max placed the steaming cup in front of Mark.

"Thanks."

"That's a little thin, don't you think?" said Tom. He stared intently at Mark.

"Maybe, but with what I've learned, it's not so crazy."

Before Mark could explain more, the men's room door opened and Alfred came out. His face was flushed and he was still coughing and blowing his nose. All four heads turned to watch him. As soon as he looked up and saw then watching him, he spun around and disappeared down the hallway. The next sound they heard was the fire door slamming shut.

CHAPTER 99

MAX JUST STARED IN DISBELIEF. Mark ran out the fire door while Tom sprinted toward the front door. Jack simply went to Max. As he wrapped her in his arms he could feel her shaking.

"It'll be okay. They'll get him."

But they didn't.

"What do you mean he's gone?" asked Max when Tom and Mark returned to the bar.

"Gone. Disappeared. There's no truck, nothing. We took a quick look around the building, but found nothing. I called dispatch and the guys on patrol tonight are already out on the roads looking," said Tom.

Mark apologized. "I'm sorry. I should have just grabbed him when I arrived. I took a chance. Listen, I'm going to take off and cruise around. With enough eyes, maybe we'll get lucky."

"What if he comes back?" asked Max.

"I don't think he will," responded Mark. "And besides, Jack, you'll be here, right?"

"Goes without saying. But what if he does come back?"

"He won't. Remember, all we have are some pretty loose theories. So far we have no hard evidence, nothing."

"Mark, you keep saying that, but the reality is, he keeps showing up and asking for that quilt. Max is in his crosshairs."

"You're right. He wants the quilt and he knows Max has it."

Tom, who had been silent through this exchange, now spoke up.

"Jack, we'll drive by your place every hour just in case. If you want us to place a cruiser in your drive, we can do that as well."

"I don't think that'll be necessary," Jack said. "I agree that it's unlikely he'll return tonight."

Max had remained silent through all of these exchanges, but suddenly she spoke up.

"He wants the quilt. Why don't I just give it to him and that'll be the end of it?"

"I wish it were that simple," said Malloy. "I agree—his desire for the quilt seems to be behind everything—but don't forget, this all started with Malcom's death and that needs to be resolved. And besides, we don't know exactly how unstable he is. What if the quilt isn't what he thinks it is? What will he do then? I'm not ready to take that chance."

"But it's a possibility?"

"Anything is possible. That's why we need to catch him. And we will."

"All I'm saying is that these are all just theories. The only thing we know is that he really wants that quilt."

Tom interrupted, "Listen, time's wasting. I'm going to get going. If he's around, I want him caught. You guys, be careful and lock your doors."

Mark looked at Jack and Max. "Tom's right. The sooner we find him, the better. And if I'm right, he really needs help. Take good care."

"We will," said Jack.

Max simply nodded, but her eyes filled with tears.

It didn't take long to close Ben's. As soon as the lock made that final kchuck, Max turned toward Jack and said, "You know he's coming back. They aren't going to find him."

He pulled her close and took her in his arms. He swore to himself that he would keep her safe.

"They'll get him," he whispered. "Let's go home."

CHAPTER 100

ALFRED WASN'T CAUGHT THAT NIGHT, or the next, or the night after that. He had simply vanished. On the second day after his disappearance, Lieutenant Malloy called Tom.

"I've got some news for you about Alfred."

"You've found him?"

"No. But we did search his store, and we found Malcom's car and his stuff. We're still going through the place, but it appears that Malcom may not have been the first. Can't say for certain, but it's a possibility. We've issued a warrant for his arrest."

Tom was silent for a moment. "You're shitting me?"

"I wish I were. At this point, he's considered armed and dangerous. I'm calling Polly next to let her know, but I don't think she'll be in any danger since he knows the quilt is in Rye Harbor."

"You want me to call Jack and Max?"

"Thanks."

"I'll increase the patrols by Jack's and Ben's Place as well."

"Good. We're still going through the store. Who knows what else we'll find. I'll keep you posted."

"Good luck, Mark. Let's hope we get him before he does something rash. I have a bad feeling about him."

"Me too."

* * *

After getting off the phone with Malloy, Tom called Jack and broke the news to him. Jack in turn told Max. True to his word, Tom increased the patrols, and Jack never let Max out of his sight. Several more days passed and there was still no sign of Alfred.

CHAPTER 101

"I HATE THIS TIME OF YEAR," Max said. "It's too cold and gets dark too early."

Jack was sitting at the bar like he did every night, waiting to help Max close up.

"I know, but look on the brighter side. It's getting closer to the holidays," said Jack.

"True, but—" Her thought was cut off when the phone rang.

She picked it up. "Ben's Place, may I help you?"

After a long pause, a voice that was barely louder than a whisper said, "I know you have it. I want to explain everything to you. I know you'll understand."

Jack watched the life drain from her face. She began to tremble as she continued listening.

"Where are you?" she finally asked, trying to keep her voice from cracking.

"Close. I'll be in touch." Then the phone went dead.

Slowly, she hung up the phone, her face ashen and expressionless.

"Max, who was it? You all right?"

"Jack, it was him."

"Who?"

"Alfred."

A chill washed over Jack. Then he asked, "What did he say?"

"It was strange. He said he had to talk to me. He said that when he explains, I'll give the quilt to him."

"That's it. I'm calling Tom."

* * *

"Stay at Ben's. Make sure the doors are locked. Don't leave the building," said Tom. "I'll be right over to escort you home."

Jack wanted to argue, but he didn't.

"What did Tom say?" Max asked when he hung up the phone.

"He'll be right over."

The next thirty minutes felt like an eternity. Finally, they heard knocking on the door.

It was Tom. When Jack let him in, he was blowing furiously on his hands, and his face was red from the cold.

"I didn't mean to take so long, but I tried to call Malloy. He wasn't around, so I went over to your place. I walked around the outside and didn't see anything."

Tom looked at Max. "You're sure it was him?"

"Yes."

"I'll follow you home."

"Nah, that won't be necessary," said Jack. "You said you checked around the place. You've done enough. We'll be fine. I'll call you if I need you."

"Well, if you're sure . . ." Tom said. "I'll take another look and then I'll try to call Mark again." He said goodbye and left Max and Jack alone, once again, in the bar.

* * *

By the time they had closed up for the night, clouds had moved in and it smelled like snow. The heater in Jack's truck hadn't even thought about getting warm by the time they got home. Jack turned off the truck, but neither made any move to get out. They just sat silently in the darkness as the damp coldness crept into the cab.

Jack turned to Max. "Let's—"

Behind him, the door was ripped open. An arm reached in and grabbed his coat, pulling Jack out of the truck and onto the ground. Max's scream and a searing pain in his head filled his last seconds of consciousness.

Shock and fear paralyzed Max as she watched Alfred pull Jack from the cab. She heard a thud and didn't see Jack again. Before she could move, Alfred was at her door, ripping it open.

"I lied. We're not going to talk, but you are going to give me the quilt." With that, Alfred pulled her from the truck and pushed her toward the door.

"Open it," he hissed.

"What did you do to Jack?"

"He's just fine, taking a short nap, that's all. Now, open the door. I really don't want to hurt you."

Max glanced back toward the truck. The driver's door was still open, and the interior light spilled out onto the ground. She tried to see Jack, but couldn't.

"Hurry up," he growled. He gripped her arm a little tighter, causing her to wince. She fumbled for her keys and finally, after several attempts, found the correct key and forced it into the lock.

As soon as the door clicked open, Alfred pushed her inside. "Lights," he said.

Max felt for the switch and flipped it up as soon as she touched it. The bright light blinded her for a moment, but Alfred didn't wait. As soon as it came on, he began pushing her up the stairs. "Move. I want it now."

Max tried to resist, but his grip made that impossible.

"Up," he commanded again.

Once upstairs, all he said was, "Get it." He tightened his grip as a warning.

Cat mrowed as she sauntered out from the bedroom.

"What's that?" he demanded.

"It's just the cat."

"Where's the quilt?" he said, ignoring Cat.

"It's in there," said Max. She pointed toward the door that Cat had just walked through.

His grip didn't loosen as he forced her in that direction. Once in the doorway, he pushed her into the room. "Get it."

Max looked back at him. Anger and fear coursed through her blood. "If I give it to you, will you leave us alone?"

"It's not a case of *if*—it's *when*. *When* you give it to me. And, yes, once I have it, you will never see me again."

Alfred put one hand into a pocket. She couldn't tell if he had a weapon, but she didn't want to find out.

The garbage bag with the quilt inside was under the bed. "It's under there," she said, pointing at the bed.

"Go on!" She thought that his tone had softened a bit, but his one hand remained inside his coat pocket and she wasn't going to test him.

Slowly, she knelt down and awkwardly reached under the bed. As Max groped around for the bag, Cat walked back into the room. She trotted over to Max, curious about what she was doing. Max pushed her away. "Get away, Cat." Cat ignored her and came right back, rubbing up against her.

"Hurry up," Alfred said, hardly even taking notice of the cat.

It took a moment before her fingers finally touched the plastic. When she managed to pull it out, she pushed the bag toward him.

Alfred picked it up, and as soon as it was in his hand, his voice turned cold and menacing again.

"Stay here, don't do anything foolish. I have what I want. I don't want to hurt anyone else, but I will if I have to. Understand?"

Max nodded her assent.

He stared at her, patted his pocket, and then started to leave.

As he turned, Max said softly, "Thomas, I hope you find what you are looking for."

He spun back toward her, his eyes wide and his mouth open as if he were about to say something else. He didn't. He just looked at her and then left the room.

Max didn't see Cat trotting after him. She sat on the floor, frozen, her mind racing as she tried to decide what to do to save Jack. Should she rush outside now? Wait till Alfred was gone?

Then she heard a scream and the sounds of something heavy tumbling down the stairs. Suddenly, all was silent. That's when Cat sauntered back into the room, purring loudly. She stopped, looked at Max, and mrowed.

CHAPTER 102

MAX RUSHED OUT OF THE BEDROOM and to the stairs. At the bottom in a most awkward position lay Alfred, still holding the plastic bag. Her hands shook as she dialed Tom's number, and when he answered, she might as well have been speaking in tongues.

"Max, take a breath, slow down," said Tom. It took a few minutes before he understood what she was saying. "Don't move, I'll be right there."

"But what about Jack?"

"I'm sure he's okay. Stay upstairs, lock yourself in the bathroom. I'm on the way."

The flashing blue lights from Tom's car reflected through the windows, followed closely by the reds of the ambulance.

"Max?" It was Tom.

She walked over to the top of the stairs and looked down. The twisted form of Alfred was still there, now covered in a blanket.

"He's dead," said Tom.

"Jack. What about Jack?" she cried.

"He'll be fine. The EMTs are with him. It looks like he might have a concussion. He took a pretty nasty hit on the head. May need some stitches, too."

Max started to shake. Her legs would no longer support her and her eyes began to tear up. She sat down at the top of the stairs as the tears streamed down her face. Cat bumped her head against Max's elbow and mrowed as if to say, "It's okay."

Max picked Cat up into her lap and Cat, sensing her distress, began purring and settled in.

"Tom, when can I come down?"

"As soon as we get Alfred moved. It shouldn't be too long. Sit tight.

I'll run you over to the hospital once we've wrapped things up here."

Max stood back up and went to the window, Cat still in her arms, and watched as the ambulance loaded Jack in and drove off. The phone rang and she answered it.

It was Patti. "Max, are you okay?"

"I'm fine."

"Listen, the PD just called me to photograph the scene. I'm on my way over now."

"Did you hear about Jack?"

"Yes. Look, Tom says he's going to be okay. I called Dave and he's heading to the hospital to be with Jack. I'll come up and see you as soon as I'm done."

"Thanks Patti. See you soon."

* * *

Max had expected that it would take a lot less time than it did for them to remove Alfred. Eventually, fatigue won out. When they finally took the body away, Patti found her curled up on the couch with Cat, sound asleep.

Max awoke with a start. Still foggy, all she saw was Patti, sitting on the edge of the couch. She sat up.

"Patti, is he gone? Jack? What . . . ?"

"He's gone. They're keeping Jack overnight. The knock on his head was pretty bad and he has a few stitches, but he'll be fine."

"Hey, Max." She heard Tom's voice. She hadn't seen him when she first sat up.

"Tom."

"Hi Max." It was Mark Malloy. As soon as Max had called Tom, he, in turn, had called Malloy.

"It's over," said Tom. "It looks like he fell down the stairs. Can you tell us what happened, Max?"

They talked for several hours. Max carefully answered all of their questions and posed a few of her own as she tried to make sense of what had happened. As the sky began to lighten, Tom closed his notebook. He looked at Mark for a moment and then back at Max. He said, "Max, thank you. I'm so sorry you had to go through this, but I think we can safely say it's over. Get some rest."

The two policemen left, leaving Max, Patti, and Cat to watch the sunrise.

CHAPTER 103

JACK WAS RELEASED FROM the hospital around noon. Other than the thick bandage around his head, he looked none the worse for wear. Dave helped him into Max's car. The sky had cleared, no snow had fallen, and it was turning out to be a pretty nice November day.

"So, I guess you won't be running later today," said Dave.

Patti gave him a playful slap on the back of his head and said, "Dave. What's the matter with you?"

"Just askin'."

Patti walked around to the driver's side of the car to talk to Max.

"I'm beat. I need a nap before work tonight."

"I'll see you at Ben's," Max replied. "I'm scheduled to work at four."

"You should call Courtney and get the night off. You deserve it."

"No, I'm fine."

"Okay then. See you later."

Patti and Dave drove out of the parking lot in front of Max and Jack.

"Did Cat really trip him?"

"Who knows? It seems to be the only explanation."

Jack smiled and chuckled softly to himself. "*Cat*," he thought.

* * *

That night, Jack didn't sleep well. Strange dreams, faces, places, and the events of the last months and even years surfaced, disappeared, swirled, and mixed in his head as he tossed and turned. He wanted to sleep, but he couldn't. He didn't want to disturb Max, and his head hurt, so he left the warmth of their bed and moved to the couch. The stars were visible through the skylight above and the room was cold. He pulled a fleece blanket over himself and with it came Cat. She curled up on him, purred loudly, and began to work her cat-magic. Gradually, as cats seem so able to do, she sucked the turmoil out of his head and he fell into a deep, restful sleep.

As morning approached, he began to dream about Sylvie. Her breath was warm on his cheek as she called his name. He felt her fingers touch him, softly, gently and he could feel his pulse begin to quicken. He could feel her body as she pressed close to him, but as he reached out to pull her closer, she still felt distant. Then her lips softly brushed against his cheek.

"Mrowh." Cat's voice in his ear brought him out of his dream, and when he opened his eyes she was staring at him with a look of triumph on her face that said, "Good, you're awake. Now feed me."

The sun was streaming in through the windows, and he shivered. "Cat, get off me," he said as he pushed her away. As he sat up, his head began to throb, and he had to lie back down again. Cat immediately jumped back onto his chest, talking and pacing as she became more insistent that he needed to pay attention to her needs.

Pushing her off again, he sat up more slowly. Then carefully he stood and stretched. Cat began threading herself around and between his legs, purring loudly and talking to remind him why he was there.

"Fine, I'll feed you, but first I need coffee."

She seemed to accept this. She sat and began grooming herself, all the while watching to make sure that he didn't deviate from the plan.

Jack stood by the window that looked out to the harbor. He sipped his coffee while Cat ate her breakfast.

"You're up early."

"Mornin'," he said, turning. He loved the sound of Max's I-just-woke-up voice. She moved toward him and he put his empty coffee cup down. She wrapped her arms around him and they embraced as closely as possible.

"It's cold," she cooed as they held each other for what seemed like a very long time.

"You're warm. I love the way you feel," he said.

"Mmmm." This was the only sound she made as she shifted her weight, looked into his eyes, and gently guided him back to the bedroom. This time the lips brushing his cheek were not a dream, and the caresses of her fingertips, and the weight of her body as she lay on top of him were very much real. When they had exhausted each other, he slept again.

* * *

"Jack. Jack." Max shook him gently. "I have to get to work; it's nearly noon."

He woke up in time to catch, "Come over whenever you get up."

"I'll be over in a while," he mumbled.

"Good. Gotta' go." She kissed him and disappeared around the corner.

* * *

Max wasn't in the bar when Jack came in.

"Hey, Jack. How's the head?" asked Patti. She searched the bar for her drinks, but Max hadn't made them yet.

Jack had managed to take off the large bandage that seemed to cover half of his head and replace it with something more modest.

"It's okay. A little tender, but I'll live. Where's Max?"

"In the kitchen, I guess. She should be right out. Tell her I'll be back." Then she headed toward the dining rooms.

It was one of those beautiful sunny fall days that was surprisingly very busy. Jack didn't have much to do, so when Max returned from the kitchen he ordered some lunch and a beer and sat back to enjoy the show. Max and Patti seemed to be everywhere all at the same time as they took care of a full bar and the full dining rooms. However, whenever he got up to lend a hand, Max promptly came over and made him sit back down. After all their years together, he knew better than to protest.

As the lunch crowd thinned out and tables emptied, Max and Patti seemed to disappear into the kitchen for increasingly longer periods of time. During one of these gaps, he heard her voice.

"Jack?"

He turned and looked at Sylvie.

She said, "Oh my god, what happened to you?"

It seemed like she had walked right in from his dream. He sucked in his breath and smiled. Memories of their time at the Rockdog flooded his head.

"Sylvie," he stammered. As attractive as he had found her before, now he was nearly speechless. She was wearing tight jeans, high leather boots, a short, form-fitting jacket, and a smile that made him feel like a teenager again. He hoped she couldn't see him blush.

As she approached, he hopped off his bar stool and they hugged hello. He could feel every nerve in his body tingle. He remembered how close they had been as he helped her down the trail after her fall. Now, as brief as this hug was, it seemed to him a little too long and a little too tight to be strictly hello. Then again, maybe his imagination was working overtime.

As they pulled apart, Sylvie gently reached up toward the bandage on his head and looked directly into his eyes. That was how Max found them when she walked back into the bar.

Jack didn't see or hear her come in, but he somehow sensed she was there. Instinctively he pulled back from Sylvie, who dropped her hand. As her eyes questioned his retreat, he turned and faced Max.

"Max . . . I'd like you to meet . . . Sylvie," he stammered. He felt as if his face were on fire. He took a breath to try to calm down. Then he said, just a bit too fast, "She was the runner I met at Rockdog. You know. She hurt her ankle and I helped her out."

With every word he spoke, he felt a wave of guilt wash over him. Even though he hadn't done anything, he felt like a little kid caught with his hand in the cookie jar.

Max stared at them for a moment, her eyes hard. Then with ice in her voice she said, "Sylvie. Yes. I've heard all about you."

To all my fans,
As I've written the Jack Beale Mystery Series, food has come to play an
important role in the lives of my characters, much as it does in our real
lives. Often, I have been asked about those meals, so here are some of those
recipes. I hope you enjoy them as much as Jack, Max and their friends did.
—K.D. Mason

Recipes from the Jack Beale Mystery Series

Fruit & Cream (*Killer Run*, p. 126)

Max was the first to respond. "What's Fruit and Cream?"
"It's a sweet, sour cream–based custard with layers of blueberries,
bananas, kiwi, strawberries, and raspberries."

INGREDIENTS

  1 packet unflavored gelatin
  ½ cup boiling water
  1 cup whipping cream, half and half, or milk (the heavier the cream,
    the richer the custard)
  1 cup sugar
  1 teaspoon vanilla
  1 cup sour cream
  Fresh fruit - Any combination of fresh fruit works. I prefer fruits like
  strawberries, blueberries, bananas, kiwi, and raspberries, but other
  fruits will also work.

In a heat resistant bowl dissolve gelatin in ½ cup boiling water.

Add whipping cream or other dairy product.

Add sugar, vanilla, and sour cream and whisk together.

Cover and chill 4 hours or until set.

After the custard has set — spoon into individual glasses or custard
cups, or a glass bowl, family style, alternating custard and fresh fruit
like a parfait, ending with fruit on top.

Great for brunch or as a dessert. Pretty for special occasions but good
enough to eat anytime.

6–8 SERVINGS

Apple & Greens Salad
(*Killer Run*, p. 92)

"The greens, red leaf lettuce, curly green leaf lettuce, and baby spinach were still producing well and would make a perfect base for the salad she had in mind. As she picked the greens, she planned the rest of the salad. They had several apple trees in the yard, and the day before she had picked the first apples of the fall. She would slice one of them onto the bed of greens, add some chopped walnuts, shave some pecorino romano cheese over the top, and dress it with poppy seed dressing."

Layer in salad bowl

- Place lettuce or greens in a large salad bowl,
- Thinly slice the unpeeled apple - ¼ apple per person seems about right (Cortland, Macintosh, and Granny Smith are all good choices.
- Add nuts (1 tablespoon per serving) chopped walnuts or Pistachios are good.
- Sprinkle cheese over apples and greens (1 tablespoon per serving) Grated or shaved pecorino romano or parmesan cheese are good choices.

Prepared garlic cheese-flavored croutons (optional)
Prepared poppy seed dressing

Toss before serving

This salad is very free form using lettuce or mixed greens, apple, cheese, nuts, croutons and dressing. Amounts depend on how many you are serving and your personal preferences.

Roasted Squash on Pasta
(*Killer Run*, p. 98)

"When he returned to the kitchen, he was met with the most wonderful aromas. She was standing in front of the stove stirring something in a large skillet that was bubbling nicely, and he watched as she tasted it, paused, added some secret ingredient, and tasted it again. She looked pleased."

ROASTED SQUASH

4 cups of winter squash, peeled and cut into ½-inch cubes.
  (Butternut, Hubbard, Red Kuri, etc. are all delicious),
2 tablespoons olive oil
1 teaspoon salt
¼ teaspoon pepper
½ teaspoon dried sage
½ teaspoon dried thyme

CREAM SAUCE

4 tablespoons butter, divided
1 onion, sliced
1–2 garlic clove(s), minced, (optional)
1 teaspoon chicken bouillon dissolved in ¾ cup water
  or ¾ cup chicken broth
4 tablespoons cream or sour cream

Cooked pasta of choice (enough for four)
Chopped fresh herbs for garnish, such as parsley, chives, lovage (optional)
Nuts for garnish, such as pistachios or pine nuts (optional)

Place the cubed winter squash in a single layer in a 9"x13" roasting pan with the olive oil and toss to coat, sprinkle with salt, pepper, sage, and thyme and toss again. Roast at 425°F about 20–30 minutes or until browned and tender. Give a stir after about 10 minutes.

While squash is roasting, cook the pasta and make the cream sauce.

In a large saucepan, over medium heat, melt 2 tablespoons butter. Add onion and cook, stirring, until caramelized. If desired, add 1 or 2 minced garlic clove(s) toward end of caramelization. Add the remaining 2 tablespoons butter and the water/bouillon or broth. Stir and continue to cook until butter is melted. Add cream or sour cream and cook another few minutes to make a cream sauce. Remove from heat, add squash, and stir. Squash may disintegrate, but that is okay. You may serve the sauce on top of the pasta or incorporate the pasta into the sauce. If desired, top with chopped fresh herbs and nuts.

This hearty dish is great in the fall and winter. Easy to prepare, the hardest part being peeling and cubing the squash. Polly served it over spiral pasta (Fusilli Lunghi 58)

SERVES 4

Pressure Cooker Garlic Lime Chicken
(*Changing Tides*, p. 279)
Max followed Nancy into the kitchen, "There was a strange hissing sound coming from the room that accompanied the most wondrous aromas"

INGREDIENTS
- ¼ cup olive oil
- 1 (3½ pound) chicken, cut into serving pieces
- ½ teaspoon salt
- ¼ teaspoon pepper
- 6–8 small potatoes, peeled & halved
- 3–4 large cloves garlic, minced
- ½ cup dry white wine
- ½ cup chicken stock
- Juice & grated zest of 1 lime (green part only)
- 1 teaspoon dried oregano
- Pinch of crushed hot pepper flakes

Heat oil in pressure cooker without top. Add chicken and season with salt and pepper. Cook, turning until well browned (5–7 minutes). Cook in batches if necessary. Remove chicken from cooker. Put bottom rack into cooker. Put browned chicken back in pot with potatoes, garlic, wine, stock, lime juice and zest, oregano, and hot pepper flakes.

Make sure that vent is clear before securing cover. Latch cover and bring to low pressure. Adjust heat to stabilize pressure, cover, and cook with the vent weight rocking slowly for 16–20 minutes. Carefully release pressure. Serve juices over potatoes.

Pressure cookers are not to be feared. They make cooking so quick and easy and the flavors are so much richer.

4-6 SERVINGS

Smilin' Wide
(*Changing Tides*, p. 278)

INGREDIENTS
Four equal parts:
    Amber rum
    Coconut rum
    Orange juice
    Pineapple juice
Optional:
    A slash of cream of coconut

Serve over ice and soon you'll be Smilin' Wide as it transports you to the Islands.

This drink is named after the author's boat, a Fontaine-Pajot Tobago 35 Catamaran named *Smilin' Wide*. When on board you can't help but be Smilin' Wide. As such, the drink is very forgiving. If you have only a single rum available, that's okay; just use two parts of it. If you run out of one of the juices, just use the other. If you run out of juice entirely, well, you will sleep well that night!